ANOTHER HEARTBEAT IN THE HOUSE

Kate Beaufoy

TRANSWORLD IRELAND

TRANSWORLD PUBLISHERS
61–63 Uxbridge Road, London W5 5SA
www.transworldbooks.co.uk

Transworld is part of the Penguin Random House group of companies
whose addresses can be found at global.penguinrandomhouse.com

Penguin
Random House
UK

First published in 2015 by Transworld Ireland
a division of Transworld Publishers

ISBN
9781848271913

Typeset in 10.5/16 pt Giovanni and 12/16 pt Baskerville
by Falcon Oast Graphic Art Ltd
Printed and bound by CPI Group (UK) Ltd, Croydon, Surrey

Penguin Random House is committed to a sustainable
future for our business, our readers and our planet. This book is made from
Forest Stewardship Council® certified paper.

MIX
Paper from
responsible sources
FSC® C018179

1 3 5 7 9 10 8 6 4 2

To Mrs Patterson

*I could not sit seriously down to write a serious Romance
under any other motive than to save my life.*
Jane Austen

1

AMONG THE WORST things that happened to Edie Chadwick during the year that began with the reign of Edward VIII and ended with his abdication were the death of her West Highland Terrier, the duplicity of her friend, Hilly, and the publication of a hugely successful novel, *Jamaica Inn*.

Jamaica Inn should have been a triumph for Edie. Instead, it was a triumph for Hilly. Throughout 1936 Edie watched as her erstwhile best friend rose starrily through the ranks of the Curtis Brown literary agency: Hilly got a mention in *The Bookseller* magazine, Hilly got a salary hike, Hilly got her own author list, and just last month Edie had heard from a mutual friend that Hilly had got engaged to a hotshot American publisher.

And then, two days after Christmas, Edie's little dog, Mac, had died.

A framed snapshot of the terrier sat amongst the para-phernalia on Edie's dressing table. The frame had been a gift from Hilly, but – since it had been purchased at some expense in Asprey – it would have been imprudent to consign it to the bin. It had originally contained a photograph of Edie and Hilly with their arms around each other's shoulders, smiling half at each other, half at the camera; but after Hilly's act of perfidy, Edie had cut out her friend's face with a pair of nail scissors and shut the Kodachrome scrap in a drawer of her bureau. Her initial impulse had been to set it on fire and stamp on the ashes, but someone had told her that if she closed a drawer on a picture of a person and did not open it for a year, some harm would befall the individual before the twelvemonth was up.

Three hundred and sixty-four days had passed since she had turned the key in the lock. In five hours' time she could tick off the three hundred and sixty-fifth. Six months had elapsed since the publication of Miss du Maurier's swashbuckling bestseller, three weeks since the abdication of the king, and a mere four days since Edie had buried her beloved doggie under his favourite tree in Hyde Park.

By-laws forbidding interments meant that the funeral had had to be conducted at dead of night, so Edie had telephoned one of the few friends she knew who owned a car and begged him to help her transport the remains. Because he had been en route to a white tie event, Ian had taken the precaution of protecting his evening garb with a pinafore purloined from his charlady before setting to and digging the grave; and even though he had been running late and had mud plastered all over his patent leather shoes, he had sat by the graveside with Edie for an hour after he'd set down the shovel, sharing nips of remedial brandy from his hip flask.

She hadn't spoken to anybody else about Mac's death. The only person who would understand her awful, raw grief was Hilly, because Hilly had known Mac since he was a puppy, when Edie had found him dumped in a bin outside the Gargoyle club. Edie wished more than anything that she could pick up the telephone now and dial her friend's number. But the last time she'd done that – a year ago to the day – Hilly had given her the news about the du Maurier manuscript. Had that fateful telephone call been scripted, it would have been called THE BETRAYAL, and it would have gone like this:

> *Lights up, left, on an old-fashioned office in Covent Garden. The room is furnished with filing cabinets and shelves crammed with books and manuscripts. Upstage, a large window, the reverse (street) side of which bears the legend* HEINEMANN PUBLISHERS. *On the wall is a calendar: the date reads:* TUESDAY 31 DECEMBER 1935.
>
> *Centre is a desk at which* EDIE, *a pretty girl of twenty-three or twenty-four, sits. She is wearing a French navy dress with white cuffs and a Peter Pan collar. Beside the desk is a dog basket in which a West Highland Terrier,* MAC, *is sleeping.* EDIE *picks up the telephone and dials.*

Lights up on an identical scene, right, minus the dog. Bookshelves, desk, filing cabinets. The reverse of the window bears the legend CURTIS BROWN LITERARY AGENTS. *The telephone bell rings.* HILARY, *also in her mid-twenties, nattily dressed in a tailored suit, picks up the receiver.*

HILARY: Good morning. Curtis Brown Literary Agents.

EDIE: And a gud morrrrning to ye, lassie! I'd like tae send ye ma epic novel of Robert the Brrruce. All ma frriends say it's a stirrring tale of –

HILARY: Hello, Edie. How are you today?

EDIE: Urgh is how I am. I was at the Caribbean Club last night –

HILARY: That explains the hangover humour.

EDIE: – and this morning a manuscript landed on my desk that's easily as long as *Gone with the Wind.* Nine hundred and something foolscap pages, Hilly! If it had arrived a month ago I could have made masses of Christmas decorations.

[HILARY *sighs.*]

EDIE: What's up?

HILARY: I'm busy, Edie. What can I do for you?

EDIE: I hear Miss du Maurier has finished her novel?

HILARY: How do you know?

EDIE: Bush telegraph.

[*There is a long pause.*]

EDIE: Well, what are you waiting for? Send it straight off to me.

HILARY: I can't do that, I'm afraid.

EDIE: You promised I'd get first look!

HILARY: It's been sent to Gollancz.

EDIE: Gollancz? But they publish literary heavyweights!

HILARY: They're branching out.

EDIE: You're kidding. Tell me you're kidding, Hilly! Daphne's home is with Heinemann! We're family; we published her first three novels.

HILARY: She's signed with Gollancz, Edie.

EDIE: You mean you've sent out a contract?

HILARY: Miss du Maurier was emphatic that no one from Heinemann be consulted.

[*There is another long pause.*]

EDIE [*shaken*]: This is pretty bloody unsporting of you, Hilary. You know how hard I've worked on Daphne's behalf.

HILARY: There's nothing sporting about the publishing business, Edie.

EDIE: But you're my friend!

[HILARY *abruptly hangs up the telephone. Fade lights stage right.* EDIE *sits motionless. Then she thumps the receiver back on its cradle, scoops up* MAC *and buries her face in his fur.*]

BLACKOUT
CURTAIN

That was the last time the two had spoken, for that day Edie had gone home after work and locked Hilly's photo in the drawer.

Now New Year's Eve had come around again, and Edie was getting ready to go out. Her reflection in the bathroom mirror told her that the past twelve months had taken their toll on her looks. She had all the attributes of a rejected slush-pile heroine; violet shadows under her eyes, a nascent furrow between her brows, a downcast droop to her mouth. Even the record she'd selected at random matched her mood: Duke Ellington's 'Clarinet Lament' sobbed over the gramophone.

Edie located her clutch bag, checked in the mirror to make sure the seams of her stockings were straight, re-pinned a few stray tendrils of hair and touched up her lipstick. A smidgin of powder, a dab of scent, and she was ready to go. Just as she put the stopper back in her perfume bottle, the doorbell rang. She opened the window to see Ian on the street below, dressed – as he had been the last time she'd seen him – in evening garb.

'May I come up, darling?' he called. 'Or are you on your way out?'

'Nowhere important. Let yourself in.'

Edie located her latchkey, stuffed it into the old mitten she reserved for this purpose, and chucked it out of the window. Then she shifted a pile of books from the sofa to the floor to make room for her guest. Less than half a minute later, Ian was at the door.

'You smell nice,' he remarked as he kissed her cheek.

'Arpège. You gave it to me for my birthday. What brings you here?'

'My date's husband has annexed her for the evening,' said Ian. 'Where are you off to?'

'The Gargoyle.'

Ian's eyes went to the Nubuck wedges she was wearing. She'd teamed them with a dress of maroon crêpe and a woven raffia belt.

'Is that why you're wearing those horrible clothes?'

'It's infra dig to dress up for somewhere like the Gargoyle.'

'Even on New Year's Eve?'

Edie pulled on the beret that matched her shoes. 'I have galoshes, too,' she said, indicating the rubber over-shoes by the door.

'Dear God. Couldn't you at least forgo those?'

'A girl needs them on a night like this, Ian.'

'Not the girls I know. Do you have anything to drink?'

'There's Noilly Prat.' She moved to the tray upon which she had arranged her paltry selection of liquor. 'I pilfered it from the staff Christmas party. And there's Cointreau, and some gin.'

Ian made a face. 'No vodka?'

'No.'

'In that case, I'll have to make a gin martini. Where's your cocktail shaker?'

'I don't have one.'

'What a little barbarian you are. A jam jar?'

'Let me see.' Edie hunkered down and started rummaging in the kitchenette cupboard. 'Marmite, chutney, marmalade . . .' She fished out a jar from the very back

15

of the shelf. 'Will this do? It's got some rather elderly pimiento-stuffed olives in.'

'Excellent. Olives are a bonus.'

Edie watched as Ian took a bowl from the shelf and emptied the olives into it. Then he splashed a hefty measure of gin into the jar, followed by an inch or two of vermouth.

'Any ice?'

'No.'

'It's just as well I have a flair for improvisation.'

He moved to the window and pushed up the sash. Outside, shrieks of laughter rose from the street: New Year's Eve revellers having a snowball fight. Scooping up a handful of snow from the windowsill, he scrunched it into two compact balls and dropped them into the jar. Then he swirled the mixture around, poured it into the glasses Edie had fetched, tossed in a couple of olives, and handed one to her.

'Cheerio, darling,' he said, chinking his glass against hers. 'This is what's known as a "dirty" martini.'

'Why dirty?'

'It has olive brine in it.'

Edie took an experimental sip. 'It's surprisingly good,' she said. 'Cheers.'

'Don't know why I bothered with the ice,' said Ian. 'It's freezing in here.'

'You should know to wear long johns when you come

to visit,' said Edie. She hunkered down and turned up the gas fire, while Ian settled himself on the sofa and stretched out his legs.

'How have you been holding up?' he asked, giving her an appraising look.

Edie shrugged.

'You can always get another dog, sweetheart.'

She shook her head emphatically.

'I know you probably think that's a frightfully insensitive thing to say,' continued Ian, 'but it really could help, and the sooner the better. I know a chap who breeds Jack Russells: they're feisty little buggers; great sense of humour. I could give him a phone call.'

'No. I couldn't keep a Jack Russell in a flat, and it would cause mayhem in the office. They need open spaces, those dogs. Mac was happy just to be near me. I'm sorry. My voice is going all funny because I'm going to . . .'

'Don't cry – please don't cry, Edie.' Ian reached for her hand and pulled her down beside him on the sofa. 'I can't cope when women cry. I find it awfully unsettling.'

'You've never seen me cry.'

'Yes, I have. When your book fell in the sea at Salcombe.'

'I was only eight. Of course I cried. It was *The Railway Children*, and I hadn't even finished it.' She took a hefty gulp of her martini and made a face. 'Do many of the women you know cry?'

'Too many. I've seen them cry over really stupid things.

My last inamorata cried because I killed a mouse. I did her a favour: it had been building a nest under her floorboards, and every time she saw it she had a screaming fit, but when I lifted the floorboard and told her that the nest was full of scraps of ribbon and dried flowers she acted as if I'd murdered Mrs Tiggy-Winkle.'

'Tittlemouse.'

'What?'

'Mrs Tiggy-Winkle was a hedgehog. Mrs Tittlemouse was the mouse.'

'Who was the fox who kidnapped the bunnies?'

'That was Mr Tod, and he didn't kidnap the bunnies. Mr Brock did. He locked them in the oven.'

'I liked that one.'

They sat for a while in silence, Edie trying to remember all the Beatrix Potter stories she had read as a child, to stop herself from thinking about Mac.

'I've had an idea for my book,' said Ian, presently. 'The villain will be a great fat spider-like mastermind who spends most of his time lolling in an armchair sniffing Benzedrine.'

'Sounds promising. Have you started it yet?'

'I don't have time.'

'That's what everyone says, who hasn't written a book. Do you have a cigarette?'

Ian handed her one of his Turkish blend cigarettes, and lit it for her.

'Thanks,' said Edie, blowing out smoke. 'Everyone in London is thinking of writing a novel, and they all think it will be a work of genius. Everywhere I go, once people find out I work at Heinemann they fix me with this intense stare and say: "I have a splendid idea for an adventure story," or "I'm told my memoirs are riveting," or "I could tell some corking yarns about my time spent tiger hunting in Poona."'

'I could tell some corking yarns about my time spent rally driving in Switzerland.'

'I've heard all your corking yarns.'

'That's what you think,' returned Ian, lighting his own cigarette. 'How many manuscripts do you get a week?'

'At least a dozen. Some of them weigh as much as newborn babies, and every single person who submits thinks it'll outsell the Bible.'

'Do you have to read them all?'

'Yes.'

'*Do* you read them all?'

'Yes.'

'Liar.'

Edie made an apologetic face. 'I do try to, honestly I do. I plough through the first chapter, or at least the first couple of thousand words. And if it looks as if it's going to be complete tosh, I always make the effort to write back a polite letter.'

'What do you tell them, in your polite letter?'

'I usually say that their manuscript has the makings of an interesting radio play, and suggest they pass it on to the BBC.'

'So some poor bugger in Portland Place is saddled with it?'

'Yes. Or else it's sent on to some other hapless wretch in Penguin or Macmillan or Dent. What everyone in publishing is looking for is something with enormous commercial appeal, like *Gone with the Wind*. The new Next Big Thing.'

'What's all the fuss about *Gone with the Wind*?' asked Ian.

'Haven't you read it?'

He gave her a disparaging look.

'You're such a snob!'

'Guilty as charged.' Ian inhaled luxuriously and blew out a series of perfect smoke rings. 'What's it about?'

'Love, war, birth, death, hunger, jealousy, hate, greed, joy and loneliness.'

'Sounds a lot like *The Tale of Mr Tod*.'

He'd made her laugh, at last. But Ian *was* a snob. He subscribed to the *London Mercury* and the *Times Literary Supplement*, and stored his collection of first editions in buckram boxes embossed with the Fleming crest, which Edie thought was risibly pretentious. He also had a collection of arcane French pornography, which he displayed to women he invited up to his bachelor pad in Ebury Street in an attempt to seduce or to shock. Edie knew this – not because he had ever tried it on her: she would have laughed in his face if he had – but because Mary Pakenham, the gossip columnist of the *Evening Standard*, had put it about.

Edie had known Ian since she was a little girl. He was the son of the Flemings, friends of her parents who were fearfully posh and glamorous – unlike the Chadwicks, who were quite posh but whose money had all been lost in the financial crash seven years previously. In the old days, before the Chadwicks had gone broke, the families had used to holiday together in Devon, which was fun for Edie because she was an only child and the Fleming boys were high-spirited rowdies. Michael, the youngest, was closest to her in age, but it was Ian she was fondest of, because he had appointed himself her surrogate big brother.

The gas heater was beginning to sputter. Ian gave it a curious look. 'What's happened to your fire, Edie? It's going out.'

'The meter needs feeding.'

'Allow me.'

Ian put a coin in the meter, then reached for the jam jar and sloshed more martini into her glass. The snow had melted and bits of pimiento were floating in the liquid, making it look as dirty as its soubriquet.

'Where were you off to, before your date was scuppered?' Edie asked.

'The Duchess of Wellington is having a soirée.'

'She made a pass at me once,' said Edie. 'And so did her son. *And* her husband.'

'All three at the same time?'

'No. Although it might have been altogether more entertaining if they had.'

'I wouldn't write off the marquess. He's quite a catch.'

'You catch diseases, Ian, not men.'

'How clever. Did you make that up?'

'No,' admitted Edie. 'Dorothy Parker did.'

'You'd end up a duchess if you married him. Just think – I'd have to take you seriously if you had a title.'

'I have a title. It's "Miss".'

Ian gave her a pitying look. 'Aren't your parents worried that you haven't bagged a husband yet, darling? You've been out for what – three years now?'

'They're actually relieved I've bagged a job. They can't afford a wedding – I wouldn't even have been presented if Granny hadn't funded it. Besides, Mister Smug, I don't *want* a husband.'

'You mean you'd rather live in this squalid little flat all by yourself sticking shillings in a meter to keep warm? And sit behind a dusty desk at Heinemann fifty weeks of the year, reading manuscripts you don't even enjoy?'

'I like my job. And my flat is not squalid. It's cosy.'

'If you married the marquess you could host Saturday-to-Mondays in that great pile in Hampshire and have Apsley

House as your pied-à-terre and conduct affairs all over the place.'

'That's my idea of hell, Ian.'

'You'll end up an old maid at this rate. The Mitfords were terribly worried about Nancy. She didn't marry until she was nearly thirty.'

'Which is the age you'll be soon. Why don't you get married?'

'Don't be stupid.'

'Then stop being such a hypocrite, lecturing me about it.'

'It's different for a man.'

'Is it?' Edie countered. 'You're stuck behind a dusty desk too, doing something you don't enjoy, and you're not even good at it. Mary Pakenham told me you're the worst stockbroker in London.'

'Mary should mind her manners. Anyway, I'm not going to stick it for much longer. I've decided I'd be better off doing intelligence work.' Ian blew out another stream of smoke rings and narrowed his eyes. 'I have it on good authority that the Z organization is recruiting top businessmen as secret agents.'

'Well, it's not such a secret, now you've told me.'

Ian ignored her. 'And when I've had enough of espionage, I shall write my novel celebrating the great experiences of life. Love, war, greed, death, hate, and all those other things you mentioned.' Ian drained his ersatz martini.

'God, this stuff really is filthy. I need a proper drink. Maybe I'll drop by Bryan and Elisabeth's do in Buckingham Street. Do you want to come? I'm sure they wouldn't mind. The Gargoyle'll be full of maudlin writers and drunken artists.'

'Lots of talented people go there. Dylan Thomas is reciting his poetry tonight.'

'I rest my case. There'll be lots of eligible chaps at Bryan's.'

'Oh, shut up about eligible chaps, Ian.'

'Is your friend going to the Gargoyle? What's her name – the one with the sweet face and the eyes like chocolate drops.'

'You mean Hilly. I don't know if she'll be there. We fell out.'

'*Again*? You fell out a year ago.'

'We haven't spoken since.'

'Oh, God. Girls and their silly rows. I expect it was over some chap, was it?'

'No, it wasn't.'

'I like Hilly. She's funny and sweet. She reminds me of Betty Boop with brains.'

Girls and their silly rows . . . As she took a thoughtful sip of her drink, Edie felt a wave of nostalgia wash over her, for her old friendship, and what it had meant to her. She remembered the first time she and Hilly had met, at boarding school, when they were both twelve, and the talks they used to have long into the night after lights out; and the first disastrous double date they had gone on together to the Odeon in Leicester Square, and how they had absconded at the intermission, leaving their escorts to enjoy *King Kong* without them; and the joy when they had both landed jobs within a week of each other in the same profession; and suddenly she realized how very much she missed Hilly, and how stupid they'd both been.

Crossing to the bureau, she checked to see if the little drawer was still locked. It was. Hilly's photograph was stuck in there, and she had no idea where the key was.

'Ian, you're clever at this sort of thing,' said Edie. 'Is there any way of opening this drawer without a key? I've lost it.'

Ian strolled over and took a look at the lock. 'I could force it.'

'No – don't do that. I just wanted to test you. If you're contemplating a career in the secret service, you're going to need to hone your burgling skills.'

'Have you a screwdriver?'

'No, don't worry, it can wait.'

But Ian was clearly determined to prove that he was as adroit as Raffles, for he had started prodding about with a paper clip. What on earth would she say if he opened the drawer and found nothing inside but a torn photograph with Hilly's face on it?

'Honestly, it'll do in the morning, Ian. Off you go now,

to Bryan and Elisabeth's. I'll have a good look for the key tomorrow.'

'Are you sure?'

'Of course.'

Of course it would do tomorrow. Tomorrow was the first day of a brand new year, and if Edie set about mending the wounded friendship between herself and Hilly on the very first day of the first month, it would, she decided, augur very well for 1937.

'Do you want to enjoy yourself on the last night of the year, Edie?' asked Ian, lighting another cigarette.

'Of course I do.'

'Then you're coming with me. Go and change out of those rags and put on one of your loveliest cocktail gowns.'

'I only have one cocktail gown.'

'In that case, it had better be lovely.'

'Ian –'

'Go on, darling. There'll be oceans of champagne and as much caviar as you could wish for.'

'I don't like caviar.'

'Devils on horseback, then. You love those. And profiteroles.'

Edie suddenly realized she was starving. She hadn't eaten properly since Mac died. And the food at the Guinnesses' was bound to be cuisine of the *haute* variety, because Bryan and Elisabeth were loaded. And the prospect of listening to Dylan Thomas droning on drunkenly in his

Welsh accent at the Gargoyle seemed suddenly very, very wearisome . . .

'And Stilton.'

'Oh, very well, Ian,' she said.

What a pushover she was!

So off Edie went into the cubbyhole that served as her bedroom to doff her maroon crêpe and shimmy into her lovely little cornflower blue silk while Ian fixed them another drink.

Ten minutes later, she was bowling through Mayfair in the passenger seat of Ian's MG, reapplying her lipstick and humming 'It Don't Mean a Thing', and all thoughts of Hilly had been sent spinning from her head by the effects of that third very dirty martini.

2

AT THE GUINNESSES', guests were milling around being charming to one another. Everyone was nattering about Edward Windsor and the Simpson woman, but the evening was not yet so advanced that vitriol had begun to flow along with the champagne.

As soon as the butler took their coats, Ian was pounced upon by two extremely pretty women, both – Edie could tell by the rings they were sporting – married. They bore him off somewhere, tinkling with merriment, and Edie was left to her own devices.

Her entire flat, complete with its kitchenette and curtained alcove for washing, would have fitted into the grand hallway of the house. Five of them would have fitted. She accepted a glass of champagne from a waiter – it tasted like lemonade after Ian's stiff martinis – and set off on a reconnoitre.

The staircase afforded her a perfect vantage point for the comings and goings of the guests. Waiters were weaving their way across the crowded hallway bearing trays bristling with champagne glasses. Partygoers were strutting and preening, the women showing off slender arms, smooth bare backs and alabaster décolletages, their figures sheathed in bias-cut silk and satin. Hair was kiss-curled and dressed with feathers and artificial flowers, and jewels – rose-cut diamonds, cabochon rubies and pendant sapphires – flashed at every flounce of a wrist or toss of a head.

'Edie! Happy New Year!' A lanky booby she knew lurched into view, careering against her and spilling most of her drink on the floor. 'Oops-a-daisy! Sorry about that!'

'It's not New Year yet,' said Edie, stoically.

The booby brayed with laughter, as if she'd uttered some scintillating wisecrack. 'You *are* a rip! But it *is* nearly midnight.'

Realizing that if she didn't get away she'd be stuck with him when the clocks struck the hour, Edie turned abruptly and stalked into the dining room in search of a fresh glass.

Ian was there, helping himself to oysters.

'You look glum. What's up?' he asked.

'Nothing. Get me a another drink, will you, Ian?'

Ian instantly made eye contact with a flunkey, who appeared genie-like with a tray.

'How do you do that? Waiters always avoid my eye.'

'I have charisma.'

'Oh yes. I'd forgotten.' Edie took an unladylike gulp of champagne.

'Why so glum, little Edie?'

'I'm just feeling rattled, for some reason.'

'You're feeling rattled because it's the New Year.'

'Am I?'

'Yes. Lots of people loathe New Year because it signifies fresh hell.'

'I suppose last year was pretty ghastly. I'd hate to think I was going to have another one of those.'

'Look on it as an opportunity for change. Set forth and find a new direction.'

'You sound like some moth-eaten soothsayer.'

'Sometimes it's good to think in clichés. We're always trying to be so damned original we forget that aphorisms were coined for a very good reason. Why don't you take time off work and go somewhere exciting?'

'Like where?'

'Lahore. Singapore. Shanghai.'

There came the clanging of a gong from the hallway, then a stentorian voice started the countdown to midnight. 'Ten, nine . . .'

'Here we go,' said Edie, with a sigh.

'Six, five . . .'

'You only live once,' said Ian.

'Two, one . . .'

'*Happy New Year!*'

Edie pasted on a big smile as everyone around her started jumping up and down and shrieking and kissing and crying and hooting, and as the band launched into 'Auld Lang Syne' she found herself thinking: I've got to get out of here.

'I hate this song,' she told Ian. 'It makes me want to smash things.'

Making her way towards the French windows, she slipped behind the heavy velvet portières and stepped into the garden.

At moments like this in films, a charismatic stranger would appear out of the shrubbery. Someone with insolent eyes who would make her feel the way Scarlett had in *Gone with the Wind*, when Rhett Butler slid that first dangerous look in her direction. Except Edie had no silk petticoats to swish, no ringlets to toss, no fan to snap open in haughty reproof or pleat sensuously in invitation. What might it have been like to live a century ago, when covert messages were conveyed in the choice of the flower a gentleman sported in his buttonhole, or the way a lady twisted her handkerchief?

'Happy New Year.' A voice came from the shadows.

'Happy New Year,' returned Edie. 'Oh, it's you, Uncle Jack.'

Edie called Jack Frobisher 'Uncle' even though he was more of a second cousin twice removed or something. He was sitting on a stone bench under a lime tree.

'Aren't you cold out here?' she asked.

'I came prepared. Look.' Uncle Jack indicated the heavy woollen rug draped over his knees. 'I have a hot-water bottle, too. Cosy up with me.'

31

He lifted a corner of the rug so that Edie could slide underneath, and transferred the hot-water bottle from his lap to hers. Then he produced a hip flask from his coat pocket, unscrewed the stopper and proffered it. 'Johnnie Walker's finest,' he told her.

'Thanks,' she said, taking a nip.

'What brings you out here? Why aren't you in there swing dancing, or whatever you young things do nowadays?'

'I felt glum.' Glum was a great word, Edie decided. It was the exact word to describe how she was feeling. Sad, disheartened, lugubrious, morose – none of them would do. 'Glum' was the *mot juste*.

Jack nodded sagely. 'Bloody awful things, celebrations. Bally New Years, bally anniversaries, bally birthdays. I hate 'em all.'

'Why did you come?'

'Habit. Habit is what happens to you when you get old. I'm past retirement age, you know.'

'That's not old,' Edie lied.

'It's horrific. I can't do any of the things that used to make life worth living. I can't ride any more. Can't knock a ball about on the tennis court, can't even manage a round of golf.'

Edie cast her mind about for other less physically demanding pursuits.

'Didn't you use to fish?'

'Can't do that any more, either.'

'But I thought fishing was meant to be restful?'

'Not if you've to land a 17-pound salmon it isn't. Caught one once, in the lake by Prospect House. Best fight of my life. Had it stuffed. It's there, still, in a glass case.'

Edie remembered how years ago she and her parents had visited Jack in the house he owned in Ireland. It had been during the summer holidays back in 1924 or '25 and Hilly had come with them to keep Edie from getting bored. Her mother and father had expected baronial halls and deerstalking and clay pigeon shooting and had been so vexed when there had been none of the above that they had gone off to stay in a hotel, leaving Hilly and Edie with Jack and his wife Letty. Because Jack and Letty's children were sophisticated teens who balked at the idea of spending time with a couple of twelve-year-olds, Hilly and Edie had run a little feral that summer.

'What's happened to the place?'

'It's crumbling away like all the other houses in that godforsaken part of the world. We never go there now.'

'Why don't you sell it?'

'We shall, as soon as we can get someone to go over there and shut the place up for us. Letty and I won't make it over there on account of our legs, and the children want nothing to do with it.'

'Why not?'

'They all want villas in the South of France these

days. It would be less hassle altogether if Prospect had been burnt down by Fenian rebels. Hundreds of magnificent houses went up in smoke over there. We live in changing times – I expect insurrection will happen in India too, and the Middle East. The Empire's on its last legs.'

Cripes. Edie knew that if Uncle Jack got going on the subject of Empire she'd be there for the rest of the night. She jumped to her feet. 'I'm starving,' she said. 'I'm going to get something to eat. Can I bring you anything? There are profiteroles.'

'No thanks, duck. I'm fine.' He raised his hip flask. 'Here's to another bally awful year.'

She stooped to kiss him on the cheek, and he looked startled, then pleased. 'First time anyone's kissed me in years,' he said. 'I say, Edie, might you be interested in going to Ireland?'

'What do you mean?'

'To close up Prospect. You could have yourself a bit of a bust, you know. Do you fish?'

'No.'

'You could spend a week hiking or boating. There are bicycles, and there's rather a pretty village just a couple of miles away. You brought a chum with you one summer, didn't you?'

'Yes – a school friend. I'd love to go, Uncle Jack, but I couldn't take the time off work.'

'Oh, I forgot. You work, don't you? Hard luck. But I dare say you'll find yourself a husband soon. You're a pretty gel.'

'Thanks.'

'Who did you come here with tonight?'

'Ian Fleming.'

'Decent chap, Ian. I always thought you and he would end up getting married.'

'What?' Edie's champagne nearly spurted out of her nose. 'We're completely unsuited! We've known each other since we were in rompers.'

'Well, it's about time he settled down. You, too. You're a very bright and presentable young lady, and you've been out for – how many years now?'

'Three.'

'It'll be four before you know it. That's a long time to be on the marriage market.'

'Uncle Jack, I don't mean to be rude, but I'm not *on* the marriage market. I don't want to get married, and certainly not to Ian.'

In the ballroom, the orchestra started to play 'A Fine Romance'.

'You should be in there now,' said Uncle Jack, 'trying to get a husband instead of wasting your time with an old fool like me.'

'You're not an old fool.' Edie tucked the rug under Jack's legs. 'But it's too late in the evening for me to get a husband. I'll get one tomorrow. Goodbye, Uncle Jack. Have a lovely 1937.'

'Oh, God. Is it really going to be 1937? I rather hoped I'd be dead by now.'

Edie moved back through the shrubbery to the French windows. Inside, couples were foxtrotting across the marquetry floor. Sinuating her way past the dancers, she made for the cloakroom.

Ian collared her as she emerged, shrugging into her coat. 'Are you off, little Edie?'

'Yes. I've had enough.'

'I'm sorry. Maybe I shouldn't have put you off going to the Gargoyle.'

'Oh, Ian, it wouldn't have mattered where I was. I wouldn't have had fun tonight if I'd gone to the Ritz.'

'Especially if you'd gone to the Ritz. They're having a costume ball tonight, and everyone has to go as their favourite nursery rhyme character.'

Edie shuddered at the idea of bejewelled toffs dressed up as Bo Peep and Georgie Porgie.

'Phone me tomorrow, darling,' said Ian, dropping a kiss on her cheek. 'By the way, I met someone this evening whose Maltese has just had a litter. She'll be happy to let you have one of the pups when they're ready.'

'A Maltese? Oh, Ian, you are sweet to think of it, but they're *actresses'* dogs.'

She headed out onto the street. It was a clear

evening, though cold, but she wanted to walk to clear her head.

A dog. Even thinking about a dog made her feel disloyal to Mac. But Mac had been good for Edie, and the notion of the year ahead stretching day upon day with no Mac in her life was a dismal one. A Maltese! How silly of Ian to think that she should consider getting a toy dog. She wasn't a toy dog person. She wanted a terrier, a feisty, funny little battling dog. Mac had had the sweetest temperament because he had been a stray with a gammy leg, left to die. That was why she had been able to take him to the office with her: he never moved from her side. She couldn't run the risk of replacing him with a dog that might not have the same saintlike character.

She let herself in through the front door and climbed the stairs. As she unlocked the door to her flat, she saw that a note had been pushed underneath. Picking it up, she looked at the handwriting on the folded paper. *To Edie Chadwick, Flat 6, Onslow Gardens, South Kensington, London SW, Great Britain, Europe, The World, The Universe*. It had been the way Hilly and she had used to address letters to each other when they were schoolgirls.

Dear Edie – she read; the words were in turquoise ink –

It's nearly 1937. We haven't spoken all through 1936, and I can't bear the thought of another year going by without speaking to you. I'm sorry about the whole D du

Maurier thing, really I am, but I can explain everything when we get together again over tea in Valerie's. Please, please say we will! We'll nab our corner table and hog it for a whole afternoon. Tea and macaroons, and then you can fill me in about what's happening in your life and I can fill you in on what's happening in mine – and Edie, I am so, so very sorry about Mac. I just heard today. He was the best dog, and I know that you must be going through such a horrible time.

Anyway, I hope that wherever you are tonight you're having a splendid time, and I hope hope hope that I'll hear from you tomorrow. We have been so stupid. Let's pretend last year never happened.

With all my love,

Your Hillyness.

PS: Am off to the Caribbean Club, but thought I'd drop into the Gargoyle on the way to see if you might be there.

Edie smiled her first genuine smile of the year. How seren-dipitous that they had been having the same thoughts on the same night! How lovely that the horrible year was behind them and they were setting forth into a new era of friendship! Maybe she should take Uncle Jack up on his offer? Maybe she and Hilly could wangle a week or two off work and go back to Ireland on a sentimental journey? She could scarcely remember the place; they seemed to have spent most of their time there out of doors, exploring the woods and swimming in the lake. It would be too cold to swim at this time of the year, but if they left it until Easter . . . ? She would run the idea by Hilly when they had their reunion over tea and cakes in Valerie's.

Edie undressed and washed her face and rubbed in a little Pond's. Then she got into her pyjamas, filled her hot-water bottle and curled up in the dip in the mattress that had been moulded there permanently by Mac's sleeping form. For the first time in a week, she did not cry.

Very early the next morning she was woken by the girl from the ground-floor flat banging on the door to tell her that there was someone on the telephone for her. Edie shrugged into a dressing gown and ran downstairs to take the call. It was from Hilly's sister, to tell her that Hilly had been seriously injured in a car crash, and had been taken to Guy's Hospital.

In Guy's, Edie sat by Hilly's bedside, prattling non-stop. The nurse had said that while she looked impervious to any external goings-on, Hilly could almost certainly hear what was being said, and that it was a good idea to talk trivia.

So Edie told Hilly all about a humourless youth called Toby who had had some poetry published by Heinemann and had been pestering Edie with phone calls ever since to see how sales were going (not very well, but since he was the son of a major shareholder, Edie couldn't be rude to him). She told her about Ian and his ridiculous idea for a novel about the secret service, and how he'd made her a dirty martini from olive brine and snowballs. She told her how miscast Leslie Howard and Norma Shearer were in the new film version of *Romeo and Juliet*, and how beautiful Garbo had looked in *Camille*, and now she was telling her friend all about her plans for their holiday to Ireland.

'Uncle Jack says we can stay as long as we like. We could take the mailboat. Prospect House'd be just the place for you to recuperate, when the weather gets a bit warmer. I always thought that it was such a ravishingly romantic house – like something out of *Le Grand Meaulnes*. There was a carving – do you remember? – in a secret place inside the shutters in the library. It was just a date, surrounded by a wreath of oak leaves and an ace of . . . clubs, was it? No – spades! An ace of spades – but we thought it was some mysterious symbol with all kinds of hidden meanings. Remember the night we stole bridge rolls and ham and lemonade and sneaked down to the lake for a midnight feast, and there were owls in the wood, and when you hooted at them they got really confused and thought that you were an interloper owl? We could do that again, except we could bring a bottle of wine instead of the lemonade. And we could cycle off somewhere, maybe find a quaint little pub with fiddle players, and drink Guinness. There are hills, Hilly, for hillwalking! And maybe we could take a boat out on the lake and catch fish for dinner. You caught a trout once, remember? It would be an awfully big adventure.'

As soon as she uttered the words 'awfully big adventure', Edie wished she could grab them and stuff them back in her mouth, because of course Peter Pan had described death as being an awfully big adventure. What had she said? What had she *said*?

She gabbled through another ten minutes of nonsensical monologue before the nurse came and told her time was up, and as soon as she left the hospital, she cycled home as if pursued by Furies and broke the lock on her bureau and reinstated the torn photograph of Hilly in its silver frame.

But it had been too late.

Hilly died the next day.

3

THE NIGHT BEFORE she was due to go to Ireland, Edie had a rendezvous with Ian. She would have been happy to meet in a pub somewhere, but he insisted on taking her to the Grill Room in the Dorchester. She wore the same cocktail frock that she had worn four months ago – a lifetime ago – on New Year's Eve.

'What on earth made you decide on Ireland?' Ian said, once the waiter had taken their orders. 'You could have taken yourself off somewhere like Capri or Biarritz, and had fun.'

'I should hate to go to either of those places. I thought you knew me better than that, Ian! Besides, I want to go to Ireland as a kind of homage to Hilly.'

Ian looked blank.

'We spent a fortnight there once, when we were kids. It was one of those magical times – you know, when there are no adults to cramp your style. It was the last summer we had fun together before it was time to grow up. The year

42

after, Hilly started taking drama terribly seriously, and I had to learn the oboe.'

'I didn't know you played the oboe.'

'I don't.'

'How long will you spend there?'

'Mr Byard at Heinemann told me to take as long as I like, but I can't afford to take much more than a fortnight. I'll bring some copy-editing work with me. That means I won't have such a huge backlog when I get back.'

Ian lit up a Morland. 'Ireland. My great-grandfather came from County Cork.'

'That's where I'm going.'

'I spent a summer on the north-west coast once. It rains a lot, and there's nothing much to do. I fell in love with a doe-eyed gel named Deidre and got drunk as a long-shoreman on poitín.'

'I'll be kept pretty busy. Uncle Jack wants me to close his house.'

'What will that involve?'

'Packing everything to go to auction and putting the house up for sale.'

'Is it a big house?'

'Not particularly.'

'Georgian?'

'No. Early Victorian, I think.'

'Bloody horrible, Victorian architecture.'

'I liked the house. I remember it as being full of light. Very shabby, but rather lovely.'

'Well, I hope you get some good weather. I'm off to Deauville at Easter, for golf and gambling. I'll send you a postcard to make you jealous.' Ian blew a plume of smoke and squinted at her through it. 'Are you on the telephone there?'

'No.'

'I shall worry about you, you know, stuck in some Irish bog all by yourself.'

'Don't be silly, Ian. I shall be perfectly fine. I'm looking forward to it. I need a change of scenery. I'm fed up with London.'

She said the words lightly. To be 'fed up' was social shorthand for what could better be described as enduring a maelstrom of unspeakable emotions. In Edie's case, these were grief, shock, incredulity and guilt – the worst guilt she had ever felt, the kind of guilt that made her wish that she had been the one who had ended up under the wheels of a car on that hellish New Year's Eve. She had talked about Hilly – of course she had – to friends and colleagues and family; she had spent a long weekend at home in Oxfordshire where she had planned to go through her old diaries and school newsletters – only to find that her mother had thrown them all out in a rare spring-cleaning splurge. Anyway, after four months, she realized that people didn't want to listen any more. It wasn't because they didn't care,

44

it was because they had proffered all the sympathy they could muster, uttered all the words of advice they could dredge up, murmured platitude after well-meaning platitude while Edie cried and cried on shoulders until the time-honoured words: 'There, there,' and 'Hush, hush,' had lost their power to console.

'What *is* your scene these days? Are you still frequenting dives like the Gargoyle?' Ian tapped ash from his cigarette with a manicured fingertip.

'No.'

'I'm glad to hear it. You should come along with me to the Embassy Club some night. I can get you in for nothing. I'm having a fling with one of the Bubble girls there.'

'What's a Bubble girl?'

'She's an actress. Well, a dancer, really. Her name's Storm. They're terribly boring, actresses, you know. They're always thinking about their careers.'

'Would you prefer it if they were always thinking about marriage and babies?'

'Good God, no. Touché.'

Edie took a sip of her posh martini, and decided that she liked Ian's dirty version better.

'Great name, "Storm Fleming",' she said. 'Sounds like the heroine of a romance novel.'

'Very bodice-ripperish. I've been thinking up names for the heroine of my novel, incidentally. What do you think of "Tatiana Romanova"?'

'It's dreadful.'

'Yes, you're right. I'll stick with "Yolanda Pollock".'

'You're incorrigible, Ian. Did you know that Margaret Mitchell's original choice of name for Scarlett was Pansy?'

'Scarlett who?'

'O'Hara, of course. In *Gone with the Wind*.'

'*Gone with the Wind*. It's a really terrible title, when you think of it.'

'Not when it's taken in context.'

'It invites all kinds of jejune jokes. We'd have had great fun in the dorm with a title like that. Have you found yours yet?'

'My what?'

'Your *Gone with the Wind*? You were on a quest for a new bestseller last time we talked books.'

Edie didn't want to talk about her quest for her new bestseller. Since Daphne du Maurier had left Heinemann for Gollancz, since Hilly had died, and since Penguin had taken the publishing world by storm with a new series of pocket-sized titles in paperback, she had felt more and more hopeless. So far this year, no new writing voice had sung to her, no author made her laugh or cry or gasp out loud, not a single manuscript had landed on her slush pile that made her want to sit up all night turning pages. She knew that when Mr Byard, the company director, had suggested to her that she take as much time off as she wanted, it meant that he was worried. Times were tough in the

46

publishing world, and lay-offs commonplace. She knew it was unlikely that the next *Gone with the Wind* was going to come her way, but she had hoped for something rather more gripping than the most recent submission, which was set in a girls' boarding school, and had been written by someone with the unlikely-sounding name of Gropius Greville.

'Actually, now that I think of it, there is a manuscript that you might be interested in having a look at, Ian.'

'What's it called?'

'*Frisky Felicity's Frolics in the Fifth Form.*'

'It sounds like a work of genius. Ah, here come our starters.' Ian stubbed his cigarette out.

'It really is awfully sweet of you to buy me dinner,' Edie said as the waiter set her plate in front of her. 'I could have cooked for us.'

'I can make my own toasted cheese, thanks. Anyway, this may be the last decent meal you'll eat in a while. How are you going to manage in Paddyland? Is there a town nearby where you can stock up on provisions?'

'There's one about five miles away,' said Edie. 'And I have a bicycle.'

Ian guffawed. 'A boycoycle! Shure and begorrah, you could pick your own praties,' he went on, in an execrable Irish accent. 'Isn't that all they do over there? Laze about, eating potatoes and getting stocious on poitín?'

As the waiter unfurled his napkin and draped it over

Ian's lap, Edie noticed that two red patches had appeared on his cheeks, and that a muscle by his mouth was twitching.

'You ought to learn some Irish while you're there, Edie,' Ian continued. '*Pogue mó thóin!* That's a good one! Why are you making those frightful faces at me, darling? Know what it means, do you?'

'I know what it means,' the waiter said, silkily, 'being Irish myself, sir. It means "Kiss my arse."' Then, inclining his head in a courteous bow, he withdrew.

There was a strained silence. Then, 'Why didn't you *tell* me he was Irish?' hissed Ian.

'I tried to get you to shut up, you stupid oaf, but you were having such a lark with your codswalloppy Irish accent that there was no stopping you.'

'I thought he was Scottish.' Ian sprinkled Tabasco on an oyster and slurped it down, then reached for another. 'But begob, don't the Irish have a great sense of humour? I bet you anything you like they're all chuckling away about it in the kitchen now.'

Edie hoped so. But she rather thought that in the kitchen the waiter was reciting 'Peter Piper Picked a Peck of Pickled Pepper' over Ian's beef olives.

4
—

A S THE FINAL passengers boarded the train for Holyhead, Edie saw a man loping along the platform, raincoat all aflap. He was checking the windows of each carriage he passed with some urgency and carrying a bundle in his arms: a baby, by the look of it. As the man drew nearer, Edie realized that it was Ian, and that the bundle he was carrying was not a baby, but a dog.

Excusing herself to her neighbour, she got up from her seat and made her way to the door. Ian was gesturing at her with such animation that the dog's head bobbed up and down like a puppet's.

'Thank goodness!' he said, when she yanked down the window. 'I've caught you just in time!'

'What are you doing here?'

'I've come to give you a goodbye present. Here.' Before she could protest, Ian thrust the dog at her, then slung a Harrod's carrier bag through the window after it. 'His name is Gawain Perkin de Poer. I tried to get a Jack Russell, but they were all gone; there was a run on them, apparently.'

'What are you on about?'

'Gawain Perkin de Poer is a bit of a mouthful, but that's what it says on his pedigree. He's a thoroughbred Maltese – he's part of that litter I told you about back in January.'

'I told you –'

'You might shorten it to Perky. I've been calling him a furry-faced little bastard since I picked him up this morning.'

The guard waved his flag, the whistle blew, and the dog looked up at Edie, its eyes wide, its mouth an 'O' of astonishment.

'All his whatsits are in the bag,' added Ian.

'You can't do this, Ian! I'm not taking a dog with me to Ireland.'

'It's a shame you don't have much choice. Enjoy your trip, darling. I hope you don't get sick on the mailboat – there's a weather warning.' Ian took a step backwards, sent her a breezy smile then strode off down the platform, blowing a kiss over his shoulder.

'Ian!' Edie called, but her voice was drowned by another shrill of the whistle and the grinding of wheels on the track as the train pulled out of the station.

She stood helplessly by the window, watching as Ian's figure receded and the steel girders of Euston station rolled by, then the puppy squirmed in her arms and squeaked at her.

'Stop squeaking,' said Edie.

'I can't,' blinked the puppy. 'I'm only a baby.'

'Well, stay quiet for a minute while I think what to do with you.'

Edie furrowed her brow. The next station was Crewe; could she put the dog out there? She could approach the stationmaster and ask him to have it sent back to Euston on the next train. But how? It couldn't travel loose in the guard's van, and there was no way of letting Ian know that the dog had been Returned to Sender. She was lumbered with the beast until they reached Holyhead, and she'd be hard pressed to find any kind of animal refuge in that godforsaken port. Holyhead was the kind of hellhole where they'd feed Maltese dogs on toast to their Pit Bulls. Damn Ian's eyes! What a tottering crackbrained idiot he was.

'Oh! What an adorable puppy!' A little old lady had stopped to admire Gawain Perkin de Poer. 'What a darling! Hello! Hello there! What's your name, you fluffy little bunnykin?'

'Pansy,' said the dog, blinking his eyes at the doting crone.

'Your name is not Pansy,' said Edie, emphatically. 'It's Milo.'

The old lady looked confused. 'Did you say Pansy?'

'No. Milo.'

'Milo! How sweet. What age are you, Milo?'

Milo looked at Edie, at a loss.

'He's just a few months.'

'Little pupkin! Is this your first time on a choo choo train?'

'Yes.' Edie answered for him.

'Well, enjoy your trip!' said the lady.

'Thank you,' said Edie. Once the lady had gone on her way, she rounded upon Milo. 'What a rotten little fibber you are, to tell her your name was Pansy.'

Milo smiled, pleased with himself.

'If you're not careful, I shall start calling you by your full name.'

Milo looked aghast.

'I'm warning you. You'd better behave yourself. What did Ian put in this bag of yours?'

Inside the carrier bag were a collar of smart red leather and a matching lead, a rubber teething ring, several packets of dog biscuits, a tinfoil package containing minced chicken, a dog bowl, and a knitted kitty with a stitched-on smile and squinty eyes that already showed signs of physical abuse. In an envelope was Milo's certificate of pedigree, with citations from the Kennel Club and details of Sire and Dam, both – according to the paperwork – prizewinners at Crufts. When she got to the bit about his great-grandsire, Supreme Champion Launcelot Lambert de Poer, Milo stuck his tongue out at her.

'There's no need to look so superior just because you've a smart pedigree,' Edie told him, stuffing his accoutrements back into the bag. 'In fact, all that inbreeding means that you're probably even stupider than you look.'

Milo's jaw dropped in dismay as he saw Kitty disappear, and Edie hesitated. 'Very well,' she said, retrieving the toy and giving it to him. 'You may have Kitty to play with on the train. If you're very good, I'll give you a Bonio once we've settled down. But you'll have to wear this.' As Milo tore cotton-wool stuffing from Kitty's forelegs and spat it onto the floor, she fastened the collar around his neck, testing it for snugness, then sat back on her heels to admire the effect. 'Ian is clever. That colour suits you. Just as well he didn't get the tag engraved. Not that there'd be room for your full moniker on it. Come on, then.'

She tucked him under her arm, scooped up the bag and went to resume her seat, registering the exclamations of admiration that came Milo's way as she navigated the aisle.

Twelve or so hours later, after many adventures involving Kitty, the cord on the window blind, her neighbour's knitting and the buttons on Edie's polo coat, they stood together on the starboard deck of the mailboat, watching the lights flare along the Irish coast and the moon ride the clouds. And as the vessel chugged stolidly into Dun Laoghaire harbour, Milo gazed up at Edie with eloquent eyes and told her just how much he loved her.

*

The hackney driver Edie hired at the railway station in the little town of Buttevant tried his best to initiate conversation. He was clearly proud of his automobile – a squat black Ford that smelt of new leather courtesy of Simoniz – but Edie was too shattered after her marathon journey to engage with him. After arriving in Dun Laoghaire, she had had to take a train to Dublin, and then another to Cork, and yet another to Buttevant, in the north of the county. So she pretended to be absorbed in the letter that she had read and reread a dozen times since it had arrived last week at her flat in Onslow Gardens.

It went:

Dear Miss Chadwick,
Mr Frobisher asked me to write to you with some information. I am the keyholder and sometime caretaker of Prospect House.

You will find everything shipshape, I hope. I will leave bread, milk, ect. for you, and will make up a bed, set fires, ect.

Things you need to know: The water is heated by a back boiler, so you will have to light the fire in the library if you want a bath. I will make sure that there is a supply of logs, turf, ect, and candles and oil for lamps.

You will find tea chests for packing things away in the old stable, and I have asked the grocer to let me have any cardboard boxes he can spare. I will leave these in the

54

box room above the kitchen. I will also leave newspapers for wrapping ornaments, ect.

The nearest town is an easy distance on bicycle, and you will find a telephone box at the crossroads. I have left a list of addresses and telephone numbers for doctor, solicitor, police station, ect., and the number also of an auctioneer recomended by Mr Frobisher's solicitor.

I am not on the telephone, but if you need me I am the farm with the red door just beyond the turn-off to Aill na Coill.

Wishing you a good stay.

Yours sincerely,

Catherine Healy (Mrs.)

P.S. I will leave the key under a stone by the boot scraper.

The letter had been written in an immaculate copperplate hand, and aside from the 'ects' Edie's copy-editor's eye had noticed only one misspelling. When it had arrived at her flat a week ago, the stamp on the envelope had brought home to her the fact that she really was off 'somewhere foreign', for Ireland was another country with its own language and customs and laws and currency and, presumably, prejudices.

And lambs! Larking in the fields that flanked the laneways! She had never seen so many! Milo had never seen a lamb in his life; that was plain. He had his front paws up against the rear window of the Ford, like a child at Harrods at Christmastime.

Edie folded the letter and put it back in her handbag. They had been driving for fifteen minutes now; they must be nearly there.

'Excuse me?' Edie asked the driver. 'Where is Aill na Coill?'

'Where did you say, Miss?'

'Aill na Coill. I'm sorry, my pronunciation is probably dreadful. I don't speak Irish.'

'Aill na Coill is across on the other side of the loch, about two miles away by road.' He pronounced it Al na Quill. 'You just follow this road around. They call this the New Road. Before the automobiles came the only way you could get here was by a track through the forest. You'd hardly know it was there now – 'tis barely recognizable as a right of way in places, let alone a thoroughfare.'

The road they had turned onto followed the contours of a lake. The shoreline was of coral-pink shingle that looked as though it had never been disturbed by a human footstep. To the right a steep bank rose into a forest of deciduous trees; to the left, in the distance, she saw a small stone jetty poking into the water, and a tumbledown boathouse.

Edie felt a twist of nostalgia. She remembered sitting on the end of the jetty with Hilly, their legs dangling over the edge as they combed through an illicit copy of

Lady Chatterley's Lover for the dirty bits, sniggering at the woodruff in Constance Chatterley's maiden-hair and crowing with laughter when they stumbled upon a 'wilting penis'.

The house sat on a rise overlooking the lake. To her mind it was still the kind of house one might happen upon in a fairy tale – a low, two-storey dwelling that sat gazing out over the lake with shuttered eyes and an air of Giaconda serenity. A turn to the right took them onto a bumpy avenue that wound uphill between trees and rhododendron bushes to a gateway, through which was a courtyard flanked by outhouses.

The rear of the house seemed less remarkable than it had the first time Edie had been there: the windows appeared smaller, the eaves pulled down lower. The paint on the door was peeling, the drainpipe had come away from the wall, the guttering was sagging in places and weeds sprouted from chimneypots. Some of the windows were cracked – one had been boarded up with a sheet of ply-wood – and a patch that had once been a vegetable garden was overgrown now with giant rhubarb. Nobody had loved this house for a long time.

Edie got out of the car and stood looking around while the driver pulled her luggage out of the boot and Milo skit-tered about, clearly intoxicated by the scent of hedgerow creatures. The fare came to five shillings; Edie handed over five-and-sixpence as she bade the driver farewell, then watched as the car lumbered across the courtyard and back through the gateway. She listened to the receding sound of the engine as it descended the tunnel of trees to the road below.

Then there was silence. It was the kind of perfect silence you can hear. Edie turned to the house, and smiled. It looked back at her with the merest hint of challenge, waiting for her to make the first move. They regarded each other for several moments before Milo returned from his recce.

The front door key was under the stone by the boot scraper as Mrs Healy had said. It was a long iron key with a clover-shaped bow, and it turned easily in the lock. The door swung open, and the house breathed out.

'All right, Milo. Here we go!' said Edie.

The vestibule was as she remembered it: panelled in painted wood, the floor laid with quarry tiles. To the right was a fireplace, disused now and blocked up; above it was mounted a trophy case containing a stuffed fish. The salmon Uncle Jack had told her about, Edie conjectured: when she had last been there it had housed a stuffed pheasant. A recessed window seat upholstered in faded tapestry afforded a view of the courtyard; Edie noticed that tendrils of ivy had pushed their way through the casement. At the foot of the staircase hung a framed watercolour of the lake painted by her aunt, alongside a wall clock that had stopped at ten minutes to ten o'clock. She mentally ticked off the first three items to go on her inventory: trophy case, watercolour, clock. She'd look at them properly another time; right now she wanted to explore.

Milo was curious too. He had given the doormat a thorough sniff, he had scrambled up the staircase and somersaulted down again, he had beamed at her to show her what fun he was having, and now she could hear his clickedy claws skittering down the corridor that led to the heart of the house. She hefted her case inside, shut the front door, then turned into the corridor that ran the length of the building.

The first door opened into the room that she and Hilly had loved because the windows opened straight onto the terrace, like an Italian palazzo. It was a double sitting room with stucco-worked ceilings, a pair of fireplaces, and windows draped with heavy velvet. Under the dust-sheets, the furniture resembled a herd of slumbering beasts. Edie felt loath to disturb them, but did so carefully, as if to avoid a rude awakening. She caught sight of her reflection in a flyblown pier glass as she tugged apprehensively at the edge of a cloth, thinking that she looked like an actor who had stumbled into the wrong period piece.

The first time she had come here, the furniture had looked old-fashioned. She saw now that it was not only old-fashioned, but dilapidated, too. She supposed that since Uncle Jack had grown to realize that none of his children would take the place on, it had been allowed to disintegrate. Brocade upholstery was frayed and worn, with

59

antimacassars draped strategically to camouflage stains. Surfaces that had been French-polished now bore ring marks where no one had bothered with coasters, and were criss-crossed with a patina of scratches. The soft pedal on the piano that Aunt Letty had used to play was missing, and when she lifted the lid a tentative chord told Edie that it was badly out of tune. Armchairs sagged and sofas bulged where springs had gone.

Edie crossed the floor and pulled first the shutters, then the curtains apart, allowing light to filter through a panel of cobwebby lace that lay behind. The garden of the lodge was all hillside, tumbling down to the lake. A limestone terrace lay beyond the French windows, cracked and overgrown and sprouting daisies and groundsel. Some effort had been made to prettify the lawn; a dozen or so shrubs had been randomly stuck in the earth and an attempt made to construct flower beds, but, Edie wondered, who would bother with a formal garden when you had such a gorgeous vista on your doorstep?

'Onward, Milo!' she said, allowing the lace to drop back over the window.

Next on her itinerary were the library and the dining room. Edie drew more curtains, tying them back with frayed silk ropes, and opened windows to dispel the faintly dank smell of disuse. Although it was late afternoon and the sun was low in the sky, light bounced off the lake below and tumbled into the house. The carpets – which Edie was sure were as old as the house itself – had been bleached pussy-willow silver.

Behind the glass doors of the bookcases, a diverse collection had been gathered. Classics rubbed shoulders with more recent publications: Charlotte Brontë stood next to Agatha Christie, Thackeray next to Edgar Rice Burroughs, and Jane Austen next to Dorothy Whipple. The Complete Works of Dickens were bound in morocco leather. A magazine rack contained ancient copies of *Horse & Hound*, *Country Life* and *The Lady*. Jigsaws and board games – the usual ones that were dragged out on rainy days – were stacked in a cupboard. A writing desk was crammed with rubbishy items – old pens, elastic bands, cigarette cards; Edie lit with glee upon a dog whistle.

'Listen to this, Milo! This means you must be a good dog, and come when you're bid.' She blew it, but Milo just stuck his tongue out at her and scarpered into the corridor.

In the dining room, table, sideboard and chairs were shrouded, lending it a spooky resemblance to a funeral parlour. When Edie pulled away the dust-sheets, the air filled with feathers. Some bird must have found its way inside and perished there.

The kitchen was the most modern room in the house, although Edie felt tempted to put inverted commas around the word 'modern'. It was also the warmest. A new stove had been installed since she had last visited, and Mrs Healy had lit it in advance of her arrival. The cupboards were painted buttercup yellow, and had glass panels through which Edie could see mismatched crockery, storage canisters and cookery books. *What Shall we Have for Dinner?*, a *Be-Ro* recipe pamphlet, *Mrs Beeton's Book of Household Management*. The date displayed on a calendar on the windowsill was 9 August 1930: no one had been here for over half a decade. She picked it up to read the motto: *Life is like walking through Paradise with peas in your shoes*.

'Life is like walking through Paradise with peas in your shoes, Milo,' she said, heading back along the corridor to where she had left her luggage. 'So aren't you lucky you don't wear them? Come on. Let's find out where we're sleeping tonight.'

She carried her bags upstairs. Mrs Healy had made up the room that she and Hilly had shared. How strangely comforting to know that there was something of Hilly here, in the room where she would sleep! It was a pretty room, with wallpaper sprigged in apple green. There were two high beds with rose-patterned counterpanes, and there were roses, too, on the accoutrements on the marble-topped washstand: basin, ewer, soap dish and toothbrush-holder.

A patch of damp by the window had caused a strip of wallpaper to come away, revealing a layer of Amaranth purple paper, and beneath that another of Prussian blue. Edie picked at the edge but resisted the temptation to start pulling, because she knew that once she started she would not be able to stop. There was a word for it, she knew – a word for layers upon layers upon layers. Palimp-something. It would come to her later.

Hilly would have known it, for Hilly had been brilliant with words; Edie had badgered her for years to write a novel. She remembered how they had once spent an afternoon concocting a pastiche of a popular bodice-ripper, with a cast of characters that included a heroine with silvery blonde hair, a dashing French aristocrat and a Russian prince. They had all danced to tzigane music at Maxim's and disported themselves on the polo field and on the croquet lawn and in bedrooms in Claridge's, and feasted on Beluga caviar and quails' eggs. Hilly's fabricated blurb described it as a story of dainty sentiment, fishy goings-on and hot kisses, and Edie had laughed so hard that she had fallen off the sofa and onto the fire irons, giving herself a black eye.

Suddenly she felt cold – and she was hungry, too, she realized, and very, very tired. She had had a cheese sandwich on the boat and a bar of chocolate on the Dublin–Cork train, and nothing since.

'Come on, sweetheart,' she said to Milo, who was chewing the fringe on the carpet. 'Let's go get some grub.'

In the kitchen, she set about finding something to eat. Mrs Healy had left milk, butter, eggs, cheese and ham in the cold larder; soda bread, jam, tea and cornflakes in a cupboard. There was a packet of Marietta biscuits, too, and a bowl of apples. She helped herself to bread and cheese and scraped the remnants of yesterday's minced chicken into Milo's bowl, hoping that and a biscuit or two would do him until she could make the journey into town. If he was really hungry, she could give him some ham, or try him on an egg. Mac had loved raw eggs . . .

It was the first time since her arrival that she had allowed herself to think of Mac. Before then he had never strayed far from her thoughts: he and Hilly, though they were dead, were still more real than legions of people in Edie's life. Every day she heard her friend's voice utter the last lines of the letter she had written: *We have been so stupid. Let's pretend last year never happened.* And every day Edie tried her best to pretend because she knew that Hilly would want her to – but it wasn't easy. Every day she thought thoughts like: 'Hilly would love this song!' or 'Hilly would hate this book!' or 'Hilly would know this!'

And then she remembered the word that had eluded her earlier. It was 'palimpsest'. It had been the answer to a crossword puzzle clue, and when she and Hilly consulted the dictionary they had found, among the less prosaic definitions: 'pǎ´lĭmpsĕst, noun: a layering of present experiences over faded pasts'.

For Edie the faded past – the summer holidays, the afternoon teas in Valerie's, the carefree evenings at

64

the Gargoyle – was irredeemably precious. She wished she didn't feel so very guilty for continuing to live in a present that did not have Hilly in it.

The next morning, Edie was astonished to find that she was the recipient of a letter. She had slept well for the first time in months, risen late, washed, and dressed in clothes appropriate for the day's work (an old pair of gaberdine trousers and a flannel shirt). She had just sat down to a bowl of cornflakes when the scrunch of feet on gravel announced the arrival of a visitor. Peering through the kitchen window, she saw that the postman had leaned his bicycle against the wall of one of the old outhouse buildings and was putting something through the letterbox. Turning, she ran across the kitchen floor and started along the corridor, her progress impeded by Milo capering to and fro ahead of her, barking joyously. When she finally reached the front door, the postman had gone – probably unnerved by the ferocious baying of the hound – and there was a letter lying on the doormat. It was emblazoned with the shield, helmet and crest that characterized the Fleming coat of arms.

Dearest Little Edie,

I thought it would be a great wheeze to write, so that you would have a letter delivered to you in Bogland on your first day there.

    I hope you and Perkin de Poer are getting along. I

know you pooh-poohed the idea of a Maltese, saying they were actresses' dogs, but Storm has one (it's called Bimbo), and since I've got to know the little chap, I've discovered that they have a delightful sense of humour. And you, my dear, badly need to be cheered up. So that is why I decided to ambush you with Perkin. I know he won't replace Mac, but would you want him to? That's not why we keep dogs as pets, to have one long succession of companions all with the same traits and temperaments. You will never have another Mac, just as you will never have another Hilly – [here Edie's hand flew to her mouth] *but you have had Mac and Hilly in your life for as long as theirs lasted, and what a privilege that was for you, and, indeed, for them. I'm sorry – I'm not expressing myself very well. I'm awfully bad at this sort of thing, which is why I steered clear of the subject the night we had dinner in the Dorchester. But I can't bear the idea of you beating yourself up over Hilly's death. Nobody is to blame for that – not Hilly, not the driver of the car, and especially not you. Everybody gets drunk on New Year's Eve, and unfortunately some people die, and even more unfortunately for you, one of the people who died that night happened to be your friend.*

Hilly would hate to think of you moping. I know that is why you have gone to Ireland – to mope – and you probably couldn't have chosen a better country to do it, but please don't mope for too long. If Hilly were still around, she would tell you to crack on and stop being such a bloody bore.

Love, Ian.

PS: I won 25 shillings playing backgammon last night. I shall treat you to a night on the town when you have doffed your mourning garb and fancy a bit of fun.

Edie folded Ian's letter and put it back in the envelope. *If Hilly were still around, she would tell you to crack on and stop being such a bloody bore . . .*

It was true. It was time to go to work.

5

WHAT MRS HEALY had called the 'box room' above the kitchen was accessed by a narrow staircase. It was more of a captain's ladder, really, and Edie had to carry Milo up because his legs were too short for the climb. It comprised a long low-ceilinged space that had once been two rooms with windows just under the eaves, and it was crammed to the rafters with junk.

Edie had wrapped herself in a pinafore, piled her hair up under a headscarf and equipped herself with a bag full of dusting rags, as well as a notebook and pencil to make her inventory. She looked as though she meant business, but she kept being distracted by Milo. Nothing was easy with him around; he had decided that everything she did was a game, and everything he happened upon was a toy. He had chewed an old handbag and knocked the head off an ornamental shepherdess and savaged a cushion. Edie found herself cursing him, and cursing Ian too, for being such a bloody fool as to land her with a little dog when she was on a mission, and then Milo would do something to make her laugh and she would find herself blessing Ian instead, for having found her a comrade to accompany her on this enterprise.

But he really was impeding her progress. After ten minutes in the room above the kitchen, her inventory read as follows:

> Item 1: Copper laundry plunger.
> Item 2: Toby jug (ugly).
> Item 3: Lacquered papier mâché tray.

Looking at the three items, Edie decided that she should make the unilateral decision to cross them off the list, dump them in the tea chest marked 'rubbish', and start again. If she were to record every single item stored here, the roll call would be longer than that of Caligula's enemies. Nobody would want a laundry plunger or a hideous Toby jug, and while the tray may have been a work of art once, it would not fetch anything at auction because it was cracked. She'd have to be rigorous.

She sat back on her heels and looked at Milo.

'I think we might have bitten off more than we can chew, darling. Give me that!'

Milo tugged fiercely at the felt slouch hat she was trying to prise from between his jaws.

'This is going to be an enormous undertaking, so we'll

have to approach it rationally. By the look of it, people have climbed this ladder routinely over the years, shoved all the junk to the far end to make room, then dumped more things. Ergo, the oldest stuff will be at the very back. So let's start there, and see if we can make a breakthrough.'

It was with difficulty that Edie proceeded through to the far corner, for there was no clear passage. Milo burrowed through the bric-a-brac, tail a-wag, as Edie clambered over it like Aladdin negotiating his cave. Except she rather thought there would be no treasure to be found here. This was a repository of the unwanted, the superfluous and the forgotten, and to judge by the dates on the newspapers in which some of the items were wrapped, it had been accumulating for decades.

Finally she reached the back wall. Already her clothes and hands were grey with dust; she could feel it gathering in her nose and throat. She would have to light a fire in the library so that she could take a bath tonight.

Here, in this long-abandoned corner, the cobwebs lay thick and undisturbed, as if waiting for Howard Carter and his team of archaeologists. Edie hunkered down, squeezing herself between an ottoman and a wooden chest, while Milo perched on a pouffe and put his head on one side. He looked like a good child anticipating *Children's Hour* on the wireless.

Taking a clean duster from the bag, Edie ran it along the surface of the chest, clearing a swathe that revealed the patina beneath. On either side of the hasp the initials 'E. D.' were carved.

'Look, Milo!' she said. 'Edie! It has my name on it.'

Feeling a little like Pandora, she opened the lid. The uppermost item was a Victorian daguerreotype. It depicted, standing on the terrace outside the French windows of Prospect House, a group of five: three women, a man and a girl whom she took to be somewhere in her teens. They were clad in old-fashioned garb, all gazing unsmilingly at the camera. The legend beneath read, in faded ink, *Summer 18* . . . something. Could it be 1855? Or was it '65?

Edie set the photograph aside, turned a new page in her notebook and wrote, *Item 1: A daguerreotype of a family group.*

Much later, after she had lit the fire in the library and had her bath and scrambled some eggs, Edie leafed through the inventory she had made of the chest's contents, from back to front. They were a disparate lot.

> *Item 91: A toy monkey on a stick.*
> *Item 82: A silver gilt inkstand.*
> *Item 59: A length of Venise lace.*
> *Item 44: An umbrella with a jade handle.*
> *Item 27: A toy Noah's Ark with carved animals.*
> *Item 18: A pair of embroidered Morocco slippers.*
> *Item 12: A mechanical bird in a cage.*

Item 3: Assorted papers, letters & notebooks.
Item 1: A daguerreotype of a family group.

She had listed nearly a hundred items, all from another era – Victorian, she guessed – many of them sartorial. She had unearthed a grey moiré gown with a rose-pink sash, a dark green riding habit, a cashmere robe and a silk damask evening gown. There had been shoes, bonnets and exquisitely embroidered chemises; silk stockings, gloves and dainty reticules. But what interested Edie's editorial eye most was the item she had listed as number 3: the assorted papers, letters and notebooks. These she had sheafed as best she could and stashed in a box file she had found in the library.

'There's an awful lot of reading here, Milo. Newspaper cuttings, *masses* of manuscripts, letters . . . It's going to take for ever to go through it all. No wonder it was dumped.'

Delving randomly into the file, she plucked out a page that had been torn from the *Dublin University Magazine* of June 1843. It featured a review of William Thackeray's *Irish Sketch-Book*, describing it as 'pleasant' and 'amusing' – a volume to 'while away an evening'. In the margin alongside the review someone had written in spiky longhand:

Pleasant and amusing! The country is on the brink of catastrophe.

Another clipping, again taken at random, was from *The Nation*, dated August 1846:

A cry of Famine, wilder and more fearful than ever, is rising from every parish in the land: the sole food on which millions are to be fed is stricken by a deadly blight. Within one month those millions will have nothing to eat. Government will have to bethink themselves how a starving nation is to be fed.

A third dip into the file produced a quire of paper covered in the same spiky handwriting that had penned the marginalia:

E. D.

My story [Edie read] begins in Miss Pinkerton's Academy for the Daughters of Gentlemen in the late summer of the year eighteen hundred and forty. The academy was situated on the Mall in Chiswick – a pretty village on a meander of the Thames an hour by coach from Kensington turnpike. I had endured two years there as an articled pupil, indentured for a handful of guineas per annum to teach the youngest of the gentlemen's daughters French, art and music – without which accomplishments no member of the fair sex can claim to be genteel.

Upon reaching a certain level of finesse, these young ladies proceeded to the marriage market, where they were sorted, valued and labelled by Burke's Peerage, and their mamas deployed in negotiating advantageous matches. Those who were unsuccessful were destined to devote the rest of their lives to the paying and receiving of morning calls, and the embracing of such pastimes as the copying of verses into albums and the reading of mind-improving books. So began the slow descent into apathy and invisibility of a moiety of Miss Pinkerton's pupils, a slippery incline upon which I was determined not to set foot.

On the day I took my leave of the establishment, I paid a visit to the headmistress's study on the ground floor, where a life-sized portrait of my patroness hung behind her high-backed chair. It was a remarkable resemblance – the artist had judged her imperious squint to a nicety, and deftly delineated each of her several chins.

'Good morning, Miss Pinkerton!' said I, in jaunty fashion. 'Is it not a beautiful day?'

Miss Pinkerton did not acknowledge my salutation, nor did she invite me to take a seat. I did so anyway, for I was here to procure a document that she had kindly agreed to supply. I had told her I required a testimonial – a letter of commendation to the O'Dowds of Cork, a family in want of a governess.

'I am come to dictate the letter you promised me,' I told her, with a sunny smile. 'I received my summons yesterday, and I am eager to fly to the arms of my new charges.'

Miss Pinkerton declined to pay me the courtesy of a response. Her hands trembled with ill-concealed rage as she snatched up her pen and her writing paper, and scribbled the address and the date at the top right-hand corner of the page.

I cleared my throat, and contemplated for a moment while I drummed an idle tattoo with my fingertips upon the glossy mahogany of her escritoire.

'"Dear Madam,"' I began. '"I have the honour and happiness of presenting Miss Eliza Drury to her employers as a young lady worthy to occupy a fitting position in any polished and refined circle. After her two years' residence at my Academy, those virtues which characterize the young English gentlewoman will not be found wanting in the . . ." Hmm. Allow me to find the *mot juste* . . . Affable? Good-humoured? What are your thoughts, Miss Pinkerton?'

Miss Pinkerton scowled and remained silent.

'"The *amiable* Miss Drury,"' I continued, '"whose industry and obedience are exemplary, and whose delightful sweetness of temper has charmed both her aged and her youthful companions."'

Miss Pinkerton's fingers exerted so much pressure

on the nib that it gouged the paper as she penned the above paragraph. I uttered a 'tch' of vexation, and resumed my dictation in slightly less amiable tones.

'"In music, in dancing, in drawing and orthography, in every variety of embroidery and needlework, Miss Drury will be found to have realized the highest standards of our establishment. In French her fluency, as befits a birthright speaker, is unparalleled. Regular use of the backboard has contributed in no small measure to the acquisition of that dignified deportment and carriage so requisite –" Miss Pinkerton!' I exclaimed. 'With a little careful penmanship, might you amend that? It is, of course, "requisite", with two "is" – not "requesite" with three "es".'

Miss Pinkerton obliged, dotting the 'i' with another savage jab of her pen.

'"So *requisite* for every young lady of fashion,"' I reiterated, watching Miss Pinkerton's progress over shoulders that were positively hunched with resentment. It struck me that my patroness herself could have benefited from some hours strapped to the contraption that her hapless charges were obliged to endure. '"In leaving my seminary, Miss Drury carries with her the hearts of her companions and the affectionate regards of her mistress, who has the honour to subscribe herself your most humble servant." And now your signature, Miss Pinkerton, if you would be so kind.'

She obliged, but her hand was still trembling as she sprinkled the document with blotting sand and prepared to address it. I stood sentinel until the paper was folded and sealed, and the wax dried upon it.

'Thank you, Miss Pinkerton,' said I, pocketing the letter adroitly. 'Two years in your institution have equipped me with the skill and *savoir faire* necessary to make my way in society. Now I am happy to take my leave of you with a French valediction. *Vous êtes la créature la plus répugnante que j'ai jamais eu le malheur à rencontrer.*'

Despite Miss Pinkerton's academic status, her knowledge of the French language was extremely limited. She had, therefore, not the slightest inkling that I had just told her she was the most hideous being I had ever encountered, and merely folded her hands with a rictus and a bow. Returning the bow, I threw her a sweet smile and sallied forth from the premises into the waiting carriage – the letter of introduction safe in the pocket of my new carnelian wool pelisse – bound for St Katharine Docks and the steamship *Jupiter*.

Edie looked up from the page and turned to Milo.

'Good grief,' she said. 'What have we here? Eighteen hundred and forty, Milo. That's nearly a hundred years ago!'

Reaching into the box file, she extracted another quire of paper. The top right-hand corner of each sheet had been paginated, and here and there the initials E. D. had been jotted alongside the page number. E.D. must stand for Eliza Drury. It seemed to her serendipitous that the author's initials should correspond to her name.

Edie threw another log on the grate and, curling up on the fireside chair with the manuscript on her lap and Milo at her feet, she began to read.

~ *E. D.*

What a damnable voyage *that* was! London to Cork (a city in Ireland, where my future employers awaited me) was a journey of some three days' duration. I had intended to while away the time writing in my journal, reading, and practising whist and piquet. (These games my father had taught me when I was still quite small, having assured me that card games were a more profitable pastime than needlework or drawing.) However, I was distracted from the above-mentioned pursuits by the presence on board of a gentleman, his wife, their two small children – one a girl of four years or so, the other a babe in arms – and their nurse.

The gentleman was tall, well proportioned and not ill-favoured. By contrast, his wife – though pretty – was thin and pallid. I heard her speak but once, when I happened to be passing their cabin. From within came the strains of a melody sung in a passably tuneful, rather plaintive voice. I stopped to listen, then overheard a frightful wail – 'God abandoned, I am! Oh, it is when I am saddest that I sing. Blessings on your tears, William! I would weep too, but my brain is dry and it burns, it burns, it burns!'

'Be comforted, Isabella. Our Janie is in heaven,' came the reply.

'Is she, indeed? And shall we meet again, then? It cannot be too soon!'

I could not place the accent – it had a curious French inflection – but it was followed by a peal of laughter so manic it made me fear for the lady's sanity.

On the first day out, I was sitting upon the deck reading an exceedingly dull and ancient pamphlet that Miss Pinkerton had given me concerning rules of etiquette for children – *'For the Instruction as well as the Amusement of little Masters and Misses'* – when the daughter of the family approached me.

'What are you reading?' she asked.

'It is a book of instruction on how children should deport themselves,' I replied.

'Why?'

'Because I am to be the governess of two small children, and I am keen to know how to make them behave.'

'Why?'

'Because I have no desire to have charge of a pair of savages.'

'Read me something, if you would be so kind.'

Curious to try if the child should make sense of the advice contained therein, I opened the pamphlet at random and read aloud the following: 'Among Superiors, speak not till thou art asked.'

The child looked at me gravely. 'Oh dear,' she said.

'Approach near thy Parents at no time without a Bow,' I continued. 'Jog not the Table or Desk at which another writes. Gnaw not Bones at the Table.'

'Gnaw not bones?'

I fixed her with a look of mock-rebuke. 'Repeat not over again the words of a Superior that asketh thee a question, or talketh to thee. At play, make not thy Hands, Face or Cloaths, dusty or dirty.'

'I hope you heard that, Puss.' The gentleman – who had been passing the time of day with the ship's purser – had drawn abreast of his daughter, and was regarding her with a fond smile.

'Approach near thy Parents at no time without a Bow,' chanted the precocious child. She bobbed him a curtsey, tossed her head, and made to go.

'Wait!' said her father, taking hold of her sleeve and inspecting first her hands, then her face. 'Done and dusted,' he pronounced, releasing her. 'Now, run along with Brodie and take care not to disturb Mama. She's resting.'

'Gnaw not bones,' she replied. 'Gnaw not bones.'

Then she trotted down the timbered deck to where her nurse was waiting for her, chanting the phrase over and over.

'Walk!' her father called after her. 'I keep telling you, Annie, you mustn't run or you may end up in the sea!'

She stopped at once, then turned and gave him a peculiar look. 'I forgot,' she said, before continuing on her way at a more sedate pace.

The gentleman looked down at me and smiled. Behind his spectacles his eyes were both interested and interesting: grey, with a gleam that betrayed humour, and considerable intelligence.

'Permit me to introduce myself,' he said, effecting a polite bow. 'Mr William Thackeray, at your service. The imp is my daughter, Annie.'

'Miss Eliza Drury,' I replied, with a corresponding bow. 'Your daughter is quite charming, Mr Thackeray.'

'That is the first occasion upon which she has ever dropped me a curtsey. I hope she doesn't make a habit of it. It's unsettling.'

'She's very bright. May I ask what age she is?'

'She is not yet four. I hope she was not a nuisance?'

'Not at all.'

I saw him glance at the chapbook in my hand.

'It's *The School of Manners*,' I said.

He raised a sceptical eyebrow. 'I scarcely think you need lessons in manners, Miss Drury.'

'It's intended as a present for the children with whose care I am to be charged.'

'In that case, I sincerely hope your charges won't need it.'

Just then, a movement beyond the side of the ship caught my eye, a strange turbulence in the water. I moved to the rail and looked down to spy a dark shape cutting through the waves. It was followed by another, and another.

'What are they?' I asked a passing deckhand.

'Dolphins, ma'am. They like to ride the bow wave. See there!' He pointed as one of the creatures skimmed the water, leaving a silvery trail of effervescence.

'How many are there?' I asked, but the deckhand had moved on.

'There could be dozens.' Mr Thackeray had joined me. 'Aren't they magnificent! What acrobats!'

We leaned over the rail to watch the spectacle, and presently found ourselves applauding and cheering as the creatures soared and crested in a streamlined water ballet. They accompanied the boat for several minutes, and when they finally sped out of sight, Mr Thackeray and I smiled at each other rather foolishly.

'Would you care to take a turn around the deck?' he said.

To promenade with a gentleman to whom one has just been introduced is generally considered bad form, but I was in holiday mood after being liberated from Miss Pinkerton's academy, and I cared not what charges of impropriety might be brought against me. I simply told myself that the standard rules of social intercourse did not apply on board ship. Besides, the dolphin sighting had forged a peculiar intimacy between Mr Thackeray and me.

'With pleasure,' I replied. 'It would be a most agreeable way of passing twenty minutes, and the weather is improving.'

The sky had been a uniform grey since morning, but now sunbeams were lancing through the cloud and bouncing off the sea.

We set off on a circuit of the deck. I might have dwelt at length on how genial Mr Thackeray was, how witty and amiable; I might have recounted the entertaining stories he told of his childhood in India and his travels in Europe, and his time spent studying art in Paris. Or the sobering tales he told of inheriting a fortune at the age of twenty-one and losing it shortly thereafter through foolish investments. But as we strolled back along the starboard side of the deck for the third or fourth time a strange event occurred that sent all his intriguing anecdotes spinning from my head.

I caught a glimpse of something in the water, some

five hundred yards out. At first I thought the dolphins had returned, but there was no accompanying commotion. The floating object looked like a peculiar raft or the seaborne nest of a large bird – an albatross or sea eagle or some such. I laid a hand on Mr Thackeray's arm to draw attention to the bizarre flotsam but, being short-sighted, he discerned nothing untoward.

''Pon my soul!' I exclaimed, shading my eyes from the dazzling sunlight. 'I could swear it is a lady in the sea.'

'A lady?'

'Yes. Look! Those are her skirts ballooning; they are keeping her buoyant.'

Mr Thackeray's cane clattered to the deck. 'My wife!' he cried. 'It can only be she!' Whirling around clumsily, he set off in a random direction, yelling, 'Help! Help!'

At this, a deckhand put his head over the bridge.

'There's a lady! A lady in the sea!' I shouted, waving vigorously and motioning towards the unfortunate soul bobbing in the waves. Immediately, a whistle started to shrill, and galvanizing calls of 'Man overboard!' went up.

In his panic, I saw Mr Thackeray shrug off his coat, as though preparing to dive into the water. I ran to him and pulled on his shirtsleeve to restrain him.

'Stop, stop! They will get a boat to her – see, they are mobilizing already.'

Seamen were converging on a lifeboat, hauling ropes and winding pulleys with admirable speed and efficiency. Mr Thackeray clutched my forearm; together we watched as the vessel was lowered. The sea had become choppy, and each time a wave reared, his poor wife bobbed like a piece of flotsam. She neither cried out nor struggled, nor did she appear to be in much distress. She just lay on her back, supported by the inflated bell of her corded petticoats, paddling with her hands as the sailors laboured on their oars towards her. When they reached her, they hauled her on board with scant ceremony, laying her on the floor of the boat so that she was hidden from view.

A line of gawkers had formed. Even those who had hitherto been too seasick to navigate the deck had managed to haul themselves to the rail to witness the spectacle. I hazarded a sideways glance at Mr Thackeray, who gave me an agonized look before turning away and bowing his head.

'She's safe,' I told him, laying a hand on his shoulder as he started to sob. 'She's alive, I think, and we must trust that she is well.'

Finally he raised his head. 'It's my fault,' he said. 'I should have known that she might try this. It is a measure of her desperation.'

'Your wife has met with an accident, that's all,' I assured him, 'and luckily has been rescued.'

'It was no accident. She threw herself overboard.'

Before I could respond to this astounding allegation, Annie came hurtling up.

'Papa!' she cried. 'Mama has gone in the sea again!'

'Oh, Puss!' he groaned, hunkering down and embracing the child. Over his shoulder her little face was pale, her brow furrowed in bewilderment.

'Why does she do it? Why does she always have to go into the sea?'

'She fell, Puss. She ventured too near the rail.' He held her at arm's length and smoothed her hair back from her face: I recall the gesture because it was so charged with tenderness. 'That is why I have told you not to run upon the deck.'

'But Mama was not on the deck. She was in the . . .' Annie shot a coy look at me, and leaned forward to whisper into her father's ear.

'How do you know?'

'She left me – she left me with Minnie and Brodie, and then Brodie went away and told us to be good little mice and not move. And I was good and then I got scared and did move. I left the room and went to the – ' she lowered her voice at the word '– privy, and when I knocked on the door there was no answer and I searched for Brodie, I searched and couldn't find her and then I climbed up and I looked over into the sea – '

'You climbed up? Oh, dear God!'

'– I looked over and I saw the men in the boat pulling Mama out of the water.'

'What a cursed fool I am!' Mr Thackeray's tone was one of self-laceration. 'I should not have left her side.'

'Mr Thackeray! Mr Thackeray!' I turned to see the children's nanny staggering towards us, weeping. 'Forgive me! Forgive me! She took her leave of me so calmly I scarcely noticed she was gone from the cabin, for the baby was fretful, you see, and when I got the child to settle and saw that Mrs Thackeray had not returned, I set off to find her and . . .'

Her distraught gaze lit upon Annie, and she fell silent.

'Fetch Minnie from the cabin,' instructed Mr Thackeray. 'Bring her up on deck and keep the children entertained while I tend to Mrs Thackeray. Annie, you must go with Brodie.'

I expected the child to protest, but she simply regarded her father with solemn, intelligent eyes before reaching for Brodie's hand and allowing herself to be led away. It was as though the instruction had become routine to her.

A shout of 'Ahoy!' from below announced the return of the lifeboat. Mr Thackeray turned and looked at me gravely. He had regained control of his emotions, and was clearly steeling himself for what was to come. 'Miss Drury, I am beseeching you with all my heart to show me Christian clemency. Will you help me?' he said.

'I am not a Christian,' I replied. 'But I should be glad to proffer any service I can. What would you like me to do?'

Edie sat for a moment with the quire of paper on her lap. Then she went to the bookcase and pulled out the copy of *Vanity Fair* that she had seen there. She had first read the novel a decade ago, and loved it – even though her English teacher had declared that Thackeray lacked the compassion of Dickens. Edie didn't care. She loved the energy of Thackeray's writing, the casual cynicism, the lack of sentimentality and the sheer joy he took in heaping ridicule upon the establishment. Above all, she loved Becky Sharp, Thackeray's vivacious, unprincipled anti-heroine.

On the title page – *Vanity Fair, A Novel without a Hero* – was a handwritten dedication. It read: *To Eliza, my very dear friend and soulmate, from William.*

Edie turned to Milo, who was sitting on the hearthrug diligently washing his knitted kitty. 'Oh, Milo – what fun!' she said. 'I think we may have found ourselves a mystery to solve!'

6

HAD SHE NOT been set a task akin to Hercules's fifth labour, Edie would have put all her energy into collating the intriguing jumble of papers in the box file. The document that interested her most was the manuscript, which – apart from the first paginated quire or two – did not seem to have been assembled in any particular order. So she decided to spend her days decluttering the house as per her brief, and her evenings reading and sorting through the hundreds of pages of Eliza Drury's handwriting.

Today she had scarcely ventured further abroad than the stable yard, just to allow Milo to do his wees. The weather had been cold and horrible and the best place for both of them, she decided, was by the fire in the library. Besides, Milo got plenty of exercise running to and fro along corridors and up and down stairs all day long, following her as she filled tea chests and boxes with stuff that was destined to be dumped. The more serviceable or uncommon items she carted into the drawing room, where they would remain until they went for auction along with the house.

Toast and Marmite would do her for supper – she could brown the bread on a toasting-fork in front of the fire, the way she and Hilly had used to. It was her second evening in the house, and she thought they were beginning to get on rather well together. She supposed that you would have to get along well with an entity whose nooks and crannies you were probing with barely a by-your-leave. She made a pot of tea, carried a tray through to the library, and started to sift through the papers stowed in the box file.

Finally, she managed to sort another sheaf into some kind of chronology, and this is what she ended up with.

In the cabin it was agreed that I should strip the poor creature of her sodden garments and get her into a nightgown. With difficulty, I managed to unlace her water-logged stays and divest her of her gown and petticoats. The ship's doctor – a florid man with mutton grease on his waistcoat and whiskey on his breath – prescribed rest, and administered a sleeping draught. I piled all the pillows I could find onto the narrow berth and laid the patient against them, and then I removed the pins from her long red hair and set about untangling it.

Mr Thackeray had fetched a cup of hot negus. He sat on the edge of the crib and coaxed his wife to take sips while I brushed her hair dry. She remained inert and uncomplaining while we tended to her, and finally her measured breathing told us she was asleep.

Mr Thackeray set the cup upon the locker, and took the hairbrush from me. 'Thank you,' he said.

'I am glad to help.'

He was drawing strands of his wife's hair from between the bristles of the brush and laying them on his lap. His fingers were long, the nails well cared for – but for the one on the index of his right hand, which had been gnawed to the quick.

There was silence between us for several moments, and then he began to speak in a low voice. 'Isabella is the best of wives, but she believes herself to be a demon of wickedness. I can see what I never did until now, that she has been deranged for several weeks past. I fear she is quite mad.' He did not raise his eyes from his lap, and I made no comment. 'A year and a half ago, we lost a daughter. Her name was Jane. She was sickly, but Isabella would not see it. For two nights the infant reposed a corpse upon her mother's breast, but she would not give her up. In a locket at her throat she keeps a kiss curl, which she took from the child's head as she lay in her coffin.'

I glanced at the locket that lay upon Isabella's

breastbone; I had remarked it as I'd combed out her hair, and had removed a strand of seaweed that had caught in the clasp. Mr Thackeray continued to toy with the filaments he had pulled from the brush.

'A little more than three months ago, another child was born, very like the one that had been lost. I had thought Isabella would take comfort from the arrival of our darling Harriet – we call her Minnie, as a pet name – but after her confinement she remained curiously lethargic. I sought the help of a physician; sea air and sunshine were prescribed. In August we journeyed to Margate; there her strength continued to fail and her spirits became ever more dejected. Sometimes her mind flew away from her – like a balloon, she said, *une femme sans tête*.' He gave me an uncertain look. 'It means, "a witless woman".'

'I know what it means.'

'And then one day at Margate sands she tried to drown herself.' His eyes met mine. 'She tried to drown herself, and to take Annie with her.'

'She tried to drown your daughter?'

'Yes. I am at my wits' end. I am at my wits' end.'

I rose to my feet and moved to the porthole, to allow him time to recover. 'Why are you taking her to Ireland?' I asked.

'Mrs Shawe, her mother, and her sister Jane are there.'

'She is Irish?'

'Her mother is – Isabella was born in Ireland. They have lived for many years in Paris, but her mother has returned to Cork.'

To uproot the young woman from her home and transport her to another country did not seem to me to be the most sensitive solution to the problem, but I refrained from comment. The invalid's dress and under-garments lay pooled in a tin tub at my feet. They would need to be rinsed in fresh water, and put through a mangle, if one could be found. 'We must get these dried somehow,' I said.

'I will ask Brodie to do it.'

'Brodie appears to be a most devoted retainer.'

'She is,' he said. 'We should be lost without her.'

Poor Brodie! She became afflicted with a fever that caused her to be violently sick throughout the remainder of the voyage. So distraught was she at being unable to fulfil her duty of care that I volunteered my services to Mr Thackeray as nursemaid, nanny and auxiliary.

Isabella's condition veered between one of stupefac-tion induced by the quantities of laudanum prescribed by the doctor, and periods of frantic activity during which she made repeated efforts to escape from the cabin and throw herself overboard. Her exhausted spouse dared not drop his guard for a moment, and secured a length of ribbon to her waist to bind her to him at night, lest she sought to steal away while he slept.

On the last night I could not settle. It was not the snoring of the stout matron with whom I was berthed, nor even the promise of a first glimpse of land that induced me to reach for my shawl and slip from the cabin. It was rather an acute disturbance of the mind. They say that one's sensibilities are affected by the phases of the moon. That night it was full and unobscured by cloud, and I felt sure that Isabella's lunatic tendencies would be aggravated by whatever cosmic forces were abroad.

I didn't go looking for her, but all the same I was not surprised when I came upon her crouched beneath the companionway between decks. She was clad only in her nightgown, and was twisting between her fingers the ribbon that Mr Thackeray had tied around her waist. I did not approach her, but remained motionless some two yards distant. For a time she did not seem to register my presence; at length she looked up and fixed me with her huge unblinking eyes. 'They are taking me to the lunatic asylum,' she said.

'No,' I said. 'They are taking you to your mother, to convalesce.'

'Who will care for my babies while I am convalescing?'

'Why, Brodie will.'

'And who will care for Mr Thackeray?'

'Your mother and your sister Jane, of course.'

'Jane! I named my last baby for her. When she was born, William declared I produced children with a remarkable facility. Those were his very words. "A remarkable facility." I suppose three babies in three years is no very great travail. Annie, Jane, and now Harriet. But Jane died. I tried to drown Annie, but she would not stay under the water, so in the end I relented and pulled her out. You must think me dreadfully wicked.'

'I think you are dreadfully unhappy.' Ducking under the companionway, I advanced cautiously, then lowered myself onto the deck beside her.

She shivered, and I put my arm around her and covered her shoulders with my shawl.

'Do you think William writes about me?' she asked.

'Writes about you? Why would he do that?'

'He writes for *Fraser's Magazine* and *The Times*. It does not pay enough, nor is it an occupation for a gentleman, Mama says. He proclaims that one day he will produce a great novel, like *Oliver Twist* or *Nicholas Nickleby*, but he has done nothing but draw some paltry character sketches. William is a clever man and an engaging writer, we all know that, but he cannot tell a story.'

Until then, I had not known Mr Thackeray was a

published writer, but that was hardly surprising since Miss Pinkerton took only the *Morning Post*, and sub-scribed to no periodical other than the *Ladies' Cabinet of Fashion, Music & Romance*.

'He requires a muse. He thought I was she, when he proposed marriage. I, a muse!' Isabella laughed. 'He thought me an affectionate woman, he wanted me to be better than *all* women – a paragon – when I was but a thoughtless girl of eighteen! He pressed his suit too *hard* – I had no option but to marry him!'

Her laugh became shrill, and I was reminded uncomfortably of the time I had heard her laugh in her cabin, when she had called herself 'God abandoned'. She had begun to wind the ribbon around her neck, and I feared that she might become galvanized with that energy I had seen possess her on other occasions when she had screamed and flung herself at her husband and begged to be allowed to take her own life.

'Come, Isabella,' I said, rising to my feet. 'Let us return to your cabin. You will not recover if you do not rest.'

She looked at me strangely, twisting the ends of the ribbon in her hands. 'I will not recover any way,' she said, 'for I am dead already.'

I looked at the moon and the sky above us glittering like smashed black lacquer, and then I resumed my seat on the deck. So fragile and birdlike was Isabella that she reminded me of the tiniest of the pupils at Miss Pinkerton's academy – the ones who used to suck their thumbs and cry themselves to sleep at night. Curling my feet beneath me and drawing her frail form close, I started to tell her a story that began with, 'Once upon a time . . .'

When we disembarked in Cork, I found a handsome barouche waiting for me on the quay, courtesy of my employer, Mr O'Dowd. While the driver took charge of my luggage, Mr Thackeray sought to engage the services of a carman to transport him and his dependants to Grattan Hill, where his mother-in-law was domiciled.

Isabella was sitting on a crate, shoulders hunched, her hands covering her ears against the cries of the herring-women and the din of the coal carts, while Annie gazed open-mouthed at the urchins in their bare feet and ragged clothing careering over the quayside, swarming over gantries and swinging on ropes. I had persuaded Isabella to nurse the baby before we docked, and Minnie was now sated and sleeping in her basket. Brodie, pale and exhausted, was fending off the beggars that were jostling around her, and the driver of the barouche had mounted the box seat and was flicking the tail of his whip over the horses' heads, clearly impatient to be off.

I did not like to leave without bidding Isabella farewell, but when I drew near I saw that she was singing to herself. It would have been unkind to awaken her from the trance-like state that cocooned her from reality, so instead I sent packing a pair of imps who were amusing themselves by mimicking her. I sent packing too the beggars importuning Brodie, and a ragamuffin who was hanging upside down from a scaffold gobbing onto Annie's bonnet. I did not take leave of Mr Thackeray; it was not necessary for, having exchanged addresses the previous day, we knew we would meet again. As I made for the barouche, Annie ran to me and caught me by the cuff of my pelisse.

'Where are you going?' she asked anxiously. 'Why are you not coming with us?'

'I am to join the family who have engaged me as governess,' I told her.

'What family?'

'The little girl and her brother that I have told you about.'

'Are not you to be my governess too?'

'Annie, you are too little yet to have a governess.'

'I am not. Papa says I am cleverer than a monkey and can learn anything.'

'But you are on holiday. Learning is hard work, and nobody works while they are on holiday.'

'Papa works. He works all the time. He worked

when we were on holiday in Margate, and when he is not working he is too busy to teach me anything because he is always worrying after Mama because Mama is mad.'

She said it in quite a matter-of-fact way, as one might say, 'Mama is tired' or 'Mama is cold.'

I looked back at the family group with whom I had become so intimately involved during our arduous three-day voyage. Mr Thackeray was haggling with a carman, Isabella remained locked in her private Bedlam, while Brodie was trying ineffectually to drive off a seagull that had advanced upon Minnie's bassinet. And then I looked down at Annie's worried expression and said, 'I shall visit you. I promise.'

'When?'

'I can't tell. Why not ask those horses? They know everything.'

'Very well.'

Annie approached the pair and stood on tiptoe, looking up at their blinkered faces. I smiled at the driver to acknowledge his forbearance, but he narrowed his eyes and allowed them to roam over my figure in so insolent a fashion that I resolved to punish him by travelling with my back to him.

'The horses say "tomorrow",' Annie reported, having finished conferring with her advisors.

'Hm. They may not mean our tomorrow.

"Tomorrow" in Horse can mean "the day after tomorrow", and sometimes even the day after that. But horses never lie. So you may depend upon a visit from me before the week is out.'

'Huzzah!' said Annie. 'Those horses are wiser than Bucephalus. Goodbye, Miss Eliza.'

She dropped me a curtsey, and as I watched her go it struck me that a child of not yet four who knew who Bucephalus was hardly needed a governess to teach her anything.

7

EDIE STOOD UP and eased herself into a stretch, then meandered through into the kitchen, where Milo's collar and lead were hanging by the door. The only way, she decided, that she could make sense of the thoughts that were crowding through her head like some Joycean stream of consciousness was to babble them out loud to her doggie.

'So,' she said to Milo, 'here they are in Ireland . . . Eliza and Mr Thackeray, and his two daughters and his mad wife. Poor lady! Three babies in as many years – I'm not surprised she was deranged. My mother could barely cope with one. Come on, sweetie-pie. I'd better take you for your evening pee.'

She allowed him to sniff about the courtyard for five minutes, then took him around to the front of the house. The wind was up, the moon riding high above the swaying branches in the woods; below her it threw a lambent path across the lake. On the far shore, a heron cried – a spooky, lonely sound.

Together they walked halfway down the slope, to where a garden bench (wrought iron, patterned with ferns, noted Edie, thinking of her inventory) invited her to sit and admire the moonlight. But it was cold and blustery, and Edie was not inclined to idle. She performed little dance-steps on the spot, hugging herself to keep warm, and turned to look up at the house.

'Would I want to live here, Milo? No. Who would want to buy such a place? Uncle Jack and Aunt Letty enjoyed it while their children were young. But nobody in their right mind would want to spend time travelling all this way from London when they could be sunbathing in Biarritz or skiing in Kitzbühel or gambling in Monte Carlo, like Ian. The house is a white elephant, Milo – lovely and useless, and it will go for a song. Remember what Ian said about Victorian architecture and how ugly he found it? 1841. That's the date carved on the shutter in the drawing room, and Victoria had only been queen for four years. Maybe the Zeitgeist hadn't taken hold by then. Maybe all the buildings were beautiful, still . . .'

But Edie had had a sneak preview of the next page of Eliza's manuscript, and she knew that the house in Cork, where Miss Drury had been engaged as governess, was anything but beautiful. Already, she was looking forward to the following evening when she could divest herself of pinafore and headscarf and allow herself to be invited into that monstrous edifice.

⌒ E. D.

Mr O'Dowd's was an overbearing potentate of a residence. It stood in its own elevated grounds, overlooking the River Lee. A neo-Palladian mansion, it had the appearance of being pieced together from a pattern in *The Architect and Builders' Miscellany*: it was pilastered and pedimented, its imposing entrance flanked with a pair of hideous caryatids and supported by Corinthian columns.

I had expected to be driven past the turning circle to the rear of the house, and was surprised when the conveyance drew to a halt under the porte-cochère. Pether, the driver, who was clearly nettled by my indifference to his charms, unloaded my things, but did not offer to hand me down. I followed him up the steps, surprised that I had been delivered to the front door.

'You are to be treated as one of the family,' he huffed, dumping my luggage by the boot scraper. 'Or so I heard Cook say. Except on company days, when you are to sup with the children – so you may not think yourself so very high and mighty then.'

I gave him a scornful look and told him in French to go to the devil, whereupon he called me *bitseach*, which I think in Irish means a termagant. And so we parted company, like a dog and cat that have crossed paths by chance and presume never to have to do so again.

A maidservant came to the door. She kept her eyes on my face with an effort, for she was clearly aching to see what fashions from London I might be sporting under my pelisse. I was sorry to disappoint her when I handed it over, for I was wearing a plain travelling dress of grey wool, with no ornament other than a mother-of-pearl brooch. 'Please walk this way, Miss,' she said. 'The mistress is in the morning room.'

She led me across a high-ceilinged hallway hung with portraits, one of which depicted a pair of simpering piglets who, I supposed, were the children I had come here to instruct. It had been clumsily executed in the style of George Romney. (My father having been an artist, I knew more than a little about painting.)

In the morning room, a plump, pretty woman of twenty-five or -six was sitting at a Pembroke table. She wore a tea gown of silk jacquard, patterned with roses and oriental lilies; her hair under a dainty cap was ringleted and beribboned.

'Miss Drury! How do you do,' she said, rising to her feet. 'Come, join me for refreshment: Katy, do you go and fetch a cup for Miss Drury, and bread-and-butter and some rout cakes and two or three of those little macaroons – and some Madeira. A glass of Madeira would be most welcome, don't you think, Miss Drury, when you have come so far?'

She resumed her seat, invited me to take the one opposite, and gave me such an open, artless smile that I felt a pang of pity for her. Isolated in this monstrous mansion, she was a young woman clearly in need of a confidante.

'When I said to Mr O'Dowd that I must have a governess for Theodore and Mercy, he proposed placing an advertisement in the *Morning Register*, but I would have a young lady from a London establishment, and I know Miss Pinkerton's to be one of the finest. I was a parlour boarder there myself, a little before your time, Miss Drury, at that illustrious Academy for the Daughters of Gentlemen!' She affected a little trill of laughter. 'My father is a baron, you know, though he has no coronet, being Irish. Now, acquaint me, do, with all the gossip from London. I must have it!'

I was loath to disappoint my employer, so while she busied herself with the tea things and poured Madeira into glasses etched with a dainty grape motif, I entertained her with stories (many of them of my own invention) of the heiresses who had boarded at the academy. After we had prattled on for some time, I ventured to ask the whereabouts of the children who were to be my charges.

'Oh – they will be here presently,' Mrs O'Dowd told me, waving an airy hand. 'There are some kittens arrived, and they must decide which to drown and which to keep. Will you have more Madeira, Miss Drury?' She poured with a liberal hand. 'Are you quite at home? I told Mr O'Dowd that if we were to have a governess we must have someone with whom I could feel quite at ease, and la! here you are, as companionable a creature as I could have hoped for.'

Raising her glass, she squinted at it before putting it to her lips, and I was intrigued, when she set it down, to observe that more than half the contents were gone.

'I find the pale Moscatel helps calm my nerves, you know,' she explained, 'for I suffer from neurasthenia. Now, tell me, do, about dear Miss Georgina Barnes, for I understand she eloped with an Italian diplomat. And is it true that Miss Saltshire has married a fortune?'

On and on she questioned me, and lower and lower went the level of the Madeira in the decanter until – as I was acquainting her with the details of the new *casaques* favoured by fashionable London theatregoers – she said abruptly, 'Oh! Oh, I cannot bear it! I cannot bear to hear more!' and rising, left the room in a flounder of silk, taking the decanter with her.

At a loss, I remained seated, expecting her to return at any minute. However, when I heard the clock chime the hour and there was still no sign of her, I amused myself by embarking upon a tour of the morning room and the drawing room beyond.

It appeared that a great deal of money had been spent on appointing both rooms. And yet, on closer observation, they had an incomplete look. The gilt and lustres glittered, but the wallpaper had been spread thinly, and did not reach the cornices. The furniture was new, and a handsome piano stood by the drawing-room window, but there was no sheet music upon the stand or in the impressive canterbury; there were no flowers in the vases, and no fruit in the epergnes.

Eventually, I found the children in the garden, and saw at once that their portraits flattered them. Brother and sister were staging a trial of kittens on the parterre, in a dock improvised from a trug. They had gone to some trouble, having dressed the unfortunate creatures in dolls' clothes, and bound their paws with manacles fashioned from lengths of embroidery silk. Forcing the corners of my mouth upwards, I introduced myself as the new governess, whereupon the youngsters turned sullen eyes upon me.

'What are you going to learn us?' asked Theodore.

'What would you like to learn?'

'Nothing.'

'I want to learn Indian,' supplied his sister.

'I can teach you Indian geography.'

'I've no use for geography. I want to learn how to speak Indian.'

'I am not conversant in it,' I told her, 'for there are

many varieties of the Indian language. But I can teach you French.'

At this the girl twisted her face into an expression so hideous that I feared she was going to be sick. 'A pox on French!' she exclaimed.

'Yes, a pox on French,' echoed her brother. 'I can speak Chinese. Chin chong ching ching chang chun chin.'

I decided to humour him. 'How clever! What does it mean?'

'It means you are stupider than a donkey.'

One of the kittens mewed, and Mercy turned upon it. 'Silence in court!' she snorted, plucking it from the trug and shaking it until its bonnet fell off. 'You will be punished for – for . . .'

'Insubordination,' I volunteered.

'No! For cheeking me! Jail for you and no supper, and ten thousand Hail Marys.'

As Mercy lugged the kitten off in a small wheeled cart, its siblings set up a clamour of protest, while Theodore set about restoring order to the proceedings.

'Might I be shown to my room?' I said. 'I should like to rest before dinner.'

'You'll find Katy somewhere below.' And young master Theodore turned back to the kittens without paying me the courtesy of a farewell.

When I finally found Katy in the kitchen, she was

gossiping with Cook. They jumped to their feet when I entered, all smiles, and for the world I could not have pictured kindlier-looking servants, nor more efficient. Cook suggested a tray in my room instead of dinner (which offer I declined, being curious to meet the master of the house), while Katy assured me that the room had been aired and the bed warmed. My box had been taken upstairs by Pether, she told me, and she herself had taken the liberty of hanging my dresses and arranging my accoutrements. As we left the kitchen, I heard someone come through the back door.

'I'll wager the precious chit will not last a week,' a voice said, 'for she has such arrant airs –'

But before the loathsome Pether could continue there came a loud 'Shhh!' and an ostentatious banging of pans from Cook.

Katy led me upstairs, prattling in a brogue into which she threw such expressions as 'Lawks!' and 'Sapristi!' which I think were intended to demonstrate how cosmopolitan she was. At the door of my chamber, she bobbed a curtsey and said that if I should like my hair dressed before dinner she would be glad to oblige, for she entertained ambitions to be a lady's maid. I thanked her and declined the offer, recalling the springy ringlets that had comprised Mrs O'Dowd's sheep-like coiffure.

From what Katy had said, I had expected the room

to be furnished with at the very least a hanging wardrobe, a dressing table and a decent bed. The last item was a tester of the antique variety, hung with frowsty damask. A chest, a washstand and a hideous armoire comprised the rest of my furnishings. There was not even a stool to sit upon. However, I was in such desperate need of sleep after the punishing sea voyage that I vowed not to trouble myself over such concerns for the time being: instead I made myself as comfortable as I could upon the quilt and fell at once asleep.

I dreamed that Isabella was sailing out to sea on a raft with a sail made of tattered damask. She was pulling kittens from a sack one after another, examining each one carefully before either returning it to the bag or hurling it into the sea. I was travelling alongside her, propelled by some force of levitation, attempting to make out what she was saying. Her words were snatched sporadically by the wind and blown hither and yon, but one distinct phrase came to me: '*I* can't do it. It is rather a métier for *you*, Miss Drury.' And then she was sailing on down a river that turned into a gurgling torrent and I awoke to find Katy pouring water into the basin on the washstand.

'I brought you some hot water, Miss,' she said. 'And I would be glad to help you change.'

This put me at a disadvantage, for my wardrobe was modest. I was of course in a different category to a domestic servant, but it had not occurred to me that I would be obliged to dress for dinner of an evening.

'I took the liberty of telling Mrs O'Dowd that you had but three dresses,' ran on Katy. 'She's on her way now with some of her own she's picked out for you, that she says you may keep for yourself. They're no longer in the very pink of the mode, but the quality! She must have taken a quare liking to you.'

I was about to retort that I didn't accept charity, then checked myself for my want of sensibility. Were this little maid to be offered cast-offs by her mistress, she would think herself blessed by the Fairy Peribanou.

'Mrs O'Dowd is too generous.'

'Beautiful, lovely Madam!' beamed Katy, swishing the water around the basin with her fingertips. 'Ah sure, she has so many dresses she can spare three or four of her old ones. Now, are you quite certain that you would not like me to fetch the tongs? I'm after re-curling Madam's coiffure.'

'You're very kind, Katy, but I prefer to dress my hair myself.'

'Well for you.' She looked at me critically. 'Might I suggest a touch of bandoline – ah! Here is Madam.' Mrs O'Dowd came into the room, tottering under the weight of an assortment of gowns. 'Madam! You should not be lugging the dresses yourself. Here – give them over to me.'

Katy took the dresses and laid them on the bed, smoothing out the folds with reverent hands. 'The blue taffeta! How lucky you are, Miss Drury! You will look like an angel in that. Now, your water's poured, so will I come back to you after you've washed?'

'There's no need, Katy. I'm used to dressing myself.'

'It would be my privilege, Miss.' Bobbing a curtsey, she retreated.

Mrs O'Dowd had taken a seat upon the bed and was toying with one of her ringlets, winding it round and round a forefinger.

'How fond Katy is of fashion!' I remarked. 'She tells me she would like to become a lady's maid.'

'Yes. She was a housemaid at my father's house; I brought her here to be parlour maid. I brought Grady with me too – he is the butler – and Cook; and as for the rest, they come and go and squabble and steal and gossip as servants generally do.'

'Katy is clearly very devoted,' I remarked.

'She is,' she said, 'and overly familiar too, you might say. But she has been with the family since I was a child, and she is my stalwart. I should be lost without my Katy.'

Mrs O'Dowd's blue eyes misted over, and sensing that an outbreak of sentiment was imminent, I diverted her attention to the mass of stuff upon the bed. 'What a fine collection of gowns!' I said.

'They are for you, if you will have them?'

'I will accept them with pleasure, Mrs O'Dowd, if you are quite certain you can spare them? They are exquisite.'

'Yes, yes – I have outgrown them, you see, and they will fit you to a nicety.' She traced with her fingernail an appliquéd vine that bordered a rose-pink sash. I could tell from that detail and divers others that the needle-work was of top quality, and was glad no hoity-toity impulse had induced me to decline her gift. 'The grey moiré is most becoming, and the green tabinet will go well with your colouring. I should not ever have thought to part with that sweet sprigged mousseline, but it is too small for me now.' She held the dress up by its lace-trimmed sleeves and looked at it with regret. 'I have grown quite plump.'

'Most women fill out, once they have children,' I assured her. Privately I thought macaroons and too much Madeira wine were the more probable cause of her embonpoint.

'Well, there will be no more of *those*!' she said, with some spirit, and for a moment I thought she had read my mind and was referring to the macaroons. 'My second child nearly killed me; the doctor says I will not survive a third.' As she tossed the silk moiré on the bed, a cascade of dust fell from the tester. She looked up at it, as if she had never seen it before. 'This bed was mine, when I was a girl,' she said. 'Oh! How I wish it were mine still!'

And she was gone.

I chose the grey moiré to wear to dinner, but before descending the stairs I embarked upon a private tour of the upper storey, employing the lightness of foot beaten into me by Monsieur Cabriole, my former dancing master. A long passage separated the front and back rooms. The floor was uncarpeted, the wainscot unpainted. Each room I tried at random – tapping gently first upon the door to make sure it was unoccupied – revealed furniture from a bygone era: heavy chests in oak and walnut, worn prayer chairs, and dank-looking court cupboards.

The O'Dowds' residence was all façade, I realized; the affluence on display downstairs did not extend beyond the first-floor landing. Here, hidden away behind closed doors, were the accumulated relics of Mrs O'Dowd's ancestral home. The folderols and fine clothes were for show in her reception rooms, while her private apartments were the repository of all that was ugly and antiquated. It was my guess that Mrs O'Dowd could not afford to finish decorating her house.

The dinner bell rang. I descended to find the mistress below, poking about in her work basket. 'Those

114

wretched kittens have tangled my embroidery silks,' she said. 'You might help me wind them after dinner.'

'With pleasure. Are the children to join us later?'

'No. They are above in the nursery. We shan't see them again today.' I sighed and made a passably regretful moue at the prospect. 'My husband and my father will be dining with us. Grady – some champagne cup for Miss Drury.'

The butler, standing by a sideboard, obliged.

'Champagne cup? Is this a festive occasion?'

She pretended not to hear. 'Tell me more of London, my dear Miss Drury! Have you been to the Beulah Spa? I have heard that the fireworks there are more spectacular than were ever seen at Vauxhall.'

'Oh, they are delightful, Mrs O'Dowd, but Vauxhall boasts by far the finer refreshments.'

I spoke warmly and knowledgeably of the pleasure gardens and the entertainments on offer (I had held the paintbox for my father while he executed *aquarelles* of Beulah Spa, and the tightrope walker who performed at Vauxhall had been a friend of my mother), and Mrs O'Dowd drank a quantity of champagne cup – Grady refilling her glass discreetly on a signal from her pinky finger – until we were joined half an hour later by Mrs O'Dowd's decrepit, taciturn, grey-faced father and her husband.

I am disinclined to furnish you, the reader, with

even a thumbnail description of that man. But if Wordsworth claims that powerful feelings are best recollected in tranquillity, then I must try.

Mr O'Dowd was a man of some thirty-five years; perhaps younger – it was hard to tell. He had been handsome once, I dare say, but now was grown to fat. He had a dissipated expression about the eyes, and a brutal set to his mouth. His forehead was low, made lower by a horizontal sweep of black hair; his nose might have been patrician had it not been realigned by some blow to the face, and his jaw and chin sagged beneath an excess of flesh. He wore a green-striped waistcoat which strained against gilt buttons, and a coat of plum-coloured drap-de-Berry.

At regular intervals he withdrew from his pocket an embossed gold watch-and-chain, from which hung many decorative fobs and seals. This he consulted with much frowning and squinting, as though it were advising him of matters of great import.

We dined, the four of us, on vermicelli soup, roast loin of veal and cabinet pudding. After some preliminary *politesse* for my benefit, Mr O'Dowd discoursed to his father-in-law on the steeplechase and the local stag hunt, then of a disputed case of trespass in petty sessions which led on to a far graver case of criminal conversation in the High Court, which in turn branched out into a heated monologue about political iniquity and the state of the nation in general. During this one-sided debate the hock goblets were taken away and replaced with burgundy glasses, and the burgundy was succeeded by a decanter of port. Mrs O'Dowd treated herself to a 'thimbleful' of cherry brandy to wash down the last crumb of cabinet pudding, then took curaçao with her coffee in the drawing room when we left the gentlemen to their cigars.

As I passed Mr O'Dowd's carver he caught hold of the end of my sash.

'Is not that Maud's gown?' he asked, in a low voice.

'Mrs O'Dowd was kind enough to make me a present of it,' I told him.

He gave the sash a tug. 'I know what devils hide beneath,' he said.

Mrs O'Dowd invited me to play the piano, or at least to join her in a game of *vingt-et-un*: I declined, pleaded tiredness and retired, calling first for Katy to see her mistress to bed.

That was the last time I slept without a knife under my pillow.

I awakened to find a carcass stretched upon me. The bed sheet was over my face but still I got his smell, of Munster cheese and unwashed body linen. He struck me once, upon the mouth, which then he forced open and proceeded to stuff with his neckcloth, pressing all the while upon my throat with his hand.

My mother had warned me it was bound to happen some time – it was one of the penalties of having a pretty figure – and had told me what to expect. From a young age I knew that all a girl could do was protect her face as best she could and not move a muscle, for with resistance comes the risk of injury. 'Practise being dead,' my mother had said.

But for the blow, which caused my teeth to scrape the inside of my cheek, he did not hurt me enough to draw blood; he scarcely moved – just grunted twice and spasmed. Then he slid off me and rolled onto the floor.

I breathed in the smell of him over and over; over and over I inhaled air that he had exhaled. I heard him mutter imprecations against his father-in-law: over and over I heard how he might have married a brewer's daughter with a quarter of a million, how he had been swindled and tricked into marrying his damned wife, how he wished the old man might die so that he could get his hands on the portion of her dowry that was his due. Over and over I heard the incoherent boasts of what he would do to the brewer's buxom daughter if he had her, how he would subject her to the same indignities to which I had been subjected. The salacious words that spewed from his mouth filled me with such revulsion that I drew the quilt over my head and tried not to listen. Finally, after half an hour or so of this disjointed monologue, I heard him stumble to his feet and leave the room.

I waited until first light came through the window. Then I dressed and packed my things. There was room in my old cowskin trunk for all but two of Mrs O'Dowd's dresses; these I bundled into my pelisse, which I hefted onto my hip. Negotiating the stairs was not easy. The box that Pether had thrown so easily over his shoulder on the quayside bumped heavily against the treads, and I had to pause at every other step to catch my breath.

It was on the landing that I happened upon Mr O'Dowd's gold fob watch. It had parted company with its chain, and it had a satisfying heft to it.

Outside on the parterre stood – as I had hoped – the cart that had served Mercy as a tumbrel for her kittens. I loaded it with my baggage, turned my back on the odious O'Dowd domicile, and set off for Grattan Hill.

8

THE GREY MOIRÉ. The rose-pink sash. Unable to wait for evening, Edie had set the alarm clock for seven rather than eight o'clock and read another section of the manuscript over breakfast. She felt her mouth go dry and her heart pitter-pat as she reached for her notebook and ran a finger along the listed items. There!

> 74: *A grey silk moiré evening dress.*
> 67: *A rose-pink sash with appliqué.*

She mentally reviewed the other garments she had found in the trunk – the riding habit, the cashmere robe, the dinner gown – and wondered what had happened to the green tabinet and the sprigged mousseline mentioned by the narrator. Had they even existed? Was the manuscript a work of fiction, or was it a memoir? Had Eliza Drury lived and breathed, and maybe even walked the corridors of this house? And if so, what had brought her here from the O'Dowds' grotesque ménage?

Milo, who had been chewing his teething ring under a kitchen chair, stopped abruptly and pricked his ears. 'Listen!' he said, and Edie heard the scrunch of bicycle tyres outside. The postman! She would not let him get away this time.

'Shut up, Milo!' she commanded, as he started to bark. 'Stay here!'

She slipped through the door, shutting it on Milo's affronted expression, and scooted along the corridor to the front door just in time to see a postcard land on the mat. From the kitchen she could hear Milo wailing in protest at being abandoned.

'Hello!' Edie called, unlocking the door and pulling it open. 'Hello there! Please don't mind the dog – he's only a pup.'

'How are you, Miss?' The postman propped his bicycle against the gatepost and approached cautiously across the courtyard. He nodded at the front door. 'I just left a post-card. From France.'

'Thank you very much,' Edie said, smiling at him brilliantly. 'Oh, it's so nice to talk to someone who isn't a dog with a jejune sense of humour! I've been immured with a Maltese mutt for the past few days,' she explained, on seeing a wary expression creep across the postman's face.

'You're from across the water?'

'I beg your pardon?'

'From England?'

'Yes. I'm here to close the place up for the Frobishers. It's to go to auction.'

'I'd heard that, all right.'

Edie squinted up at the sky, amazed to see that it was cloudless, for a change. 'It's a lovely day! What a surprise!'

'The weather's set to be good for the next day or two.'

Edie's eyes went to the green post office bike.

'May I borrow your pump?' she said.

'What?'

'Your bicycle pump. There's a bicycle here, but I just discovered yesterday that the tyres are flat.'

'Show me,' said the postman, 'and I'll do it for you.'

He detached the pump from the frame of his bicycle and followed Edie into the stable where the bicycles were stored.

'How long are you here for?' he asked, hunkering down to attach the pump to the valve.

'As long as it takes. I thought maybe a week, but there's masses to be done. I keep getting distracted, and thinking about whether or not to put something in the pile that's going to auction, or just chuck it out.'

'You'll never plough a field by turning it over in your mind.' He looked up at her and tipped his cap. 'Am't I after forgetting my manners. Seán the Post.'

'I beg your pardon?'

'That's my name. Seán the Post.'

'Oh. I'm Edie. Edie –'

'Chadwick. Pleased to meet you, Miss Chadwick.'

Edie wondered how he knew her surname, then remembered the postcard that he'd put through her letterbox.

'I'd say there's a lot of junk, all right,' said Seán the Post. 'It's a wonder, what piles up in these old houses over the years. The Grove-Whites sold up their big house in Doneraile in '31. There was stuff belonging to them going back a hundred years or more.'

'Really? How thrilling! I've found trunks full of bits and pieces from Victorian times. When was this house built, do you know? There's a date carved on the shutter in the drawing room, but that could be random.'

'I haven't an idea. It was here during the Great Hunger, far as I know.'

'The Great Hunger?'

'The potato famine that happened back in the last century. Did you never hear tell of it?'

'No.'

'Arra, why should you? 'Twas way before your time. But my grandfather is full of stories of it still.'

Because Edie's history teacher at school had been brain-numbingly boring, her grasp of the subject was flimsy; her acquaintance with Irish history even flimsier. She knew there had been dissension between Britain and Ireland that had led to numerous uprisings and that kind of

123

thing, but any famines referred to in the pages of her history books had happened aeons ago, in places like Egypt and Ethiopia. Then suddenly she remembered the newspaper cutting she had unearthed, which had contained the lamenting proclamation, *A cry of Famine is rising from every parish in the land* . . .

'Did many people die in the famine?' she asked.

Something clogged the air, some taut new dynamic stretched between them. Seán the Post stopped pumping for a moment or two, then began again more vigorously. 'A million,' he said.

Edie said nothing, for her voice had deserted her.

'A million died, and a million emigrated. Ireland lost a quarter of her population to starvation.'

'I'm sorry. I didn't know. I really had no idea . . .' Edie felt herself colour. She wanted to turn and walk out of the stable and be sick from the shame she felt.

'Sure, why would you know? They wouldn't care to remember those times in England. It didn't affect them over there.'

She remembered advertisements she'd seen in the Classified Ads sections of newspapers that stipulated *No Irish Need Apply*, and she felt another wave of shame wash over her. She cast desperately around for a question.

'Was your grandfather alive at that time?' she managed.

'He was just a boy then. But the stories that were

handed down would shock you to the core. There's few living still that survived *an Gorta Mór*.'

'*An Gorta Mór?*'

'When the potato crops failed. *An Gorta Mór* means the Great Hunger.'

'But there must have been other foodstuffs, other crops?'

'They were all exported to England.'

'I'm sorry,' she said, feeling again that rush of mortification. 'How you Irish must hate us.'

Seán's expression was inscrutable. 'It was nearly a hundred years ago,' he said, squeezing the bicycle tyre between fingers and thumb. 'That's good and firm for you now.'

'Thank you.'

Detaching the valve from the front tyre, he set to work on the back one. 'If you want to find out about the house, it's Mrs Callinan you should be talking to. She knows all the history hereabouts. She was the headmistress in the school for years.'

'Mrs Callinan. Where might I find her?'

'I'll write her address down for you.'

'If it's no trouble . . .'

'Sure how would it be trouble? Don't I know the exact whereabouts of everyone in these parts, and in the parish beyond?'

Seán pumped steadily for another minute, then twisted the cap back on the valve. 'There. She'll be right as a trivet for you.'

'I can't thank you enough! I was all set to walk into town today, but it'll be much more fun to cycle, especially since the weather's cleared up. I really need to get some groceries – there's practically nothing in the house to eat.'

Seán took a notepad from his pocket and scribbled something on it with a pencil stub. 'There's Mrs Callinan's address for you,' he said, tearing off a page and handing it to her. 'As for groceries, you'll find everything you need in the general stores or in Tom Sheehan's shop. Earl Grey tea –'

'Oh, good!'

'– and Bath Olivers and Patum Peperium and all.'

'I don't really care for Patum Peperium. Though I am rather partial to Bath Olivers – with Wensleydale cheese. Yum!'

As Seán slung a leg over the crossbar of his bicycle, she thought she saw him smirk. 'Goodbye, Miss Chadwick.'

'Goodbye. Thank you for everything! You're an awfully good sort.'

And off he went.

Edie turned and walked back towards the house, the muscles of her face stretched in a rictus. What a chump she was! What an absolute muggins! She repeated her observations back to herself in a parody of her own voice. *There's practically nothing to eat . . . I don't really care for Patum Peperium . . . I am rather partial to Bath Olivers . . .* This to a man who had just acquainted her with the fact that the population of an entire country had been decimated – more than decimated – by starvation.

He'd been sending her up, of course, with his remarks about Bath Olivers and Patum Peperium and Earl Grey tea. Oh, God. And he was a *post*man! Word would get around to every house in the neighbourhood that there was a bird-brained ninny of a posh girl staying in Prospect House who didn't really care for Patum Peperium, but who *was* rather partial to Wensleydale cheese.

It got worse. When she picked the postcard up from the front door mat, she saw that it was from Deauville.

Fine cuisine! Cocktails by the pool! Baccarat! I'm living la vie en rose! How are you enjoying life among the bogtrotters, darling? Ian. XXX

Edie cycled into the little town of Doneraile that afternoon, since a map of the locality told her that it was closer than Buttevant by a mile or two. After two days stuck indoors it was blissful to be bowling along between hedgerows busy with birdlife, the faint scent of meadowsweet in the air, the sun warm on her face.

Doneraile was a small, pretty town, with plenty of pic-turesque cottages as well as houses of cut stone substantial enough to be dubbed 'residences'. In 'Doneraile Stores' there was a section devoted to animal feed next to the gro-cery counter, and Edie was glad to see Bonios, which were top of her shopping list. There were, of course, no Bath Olivers nor Patum Peperium to be had, but there was decent coffee, Huntley & Palmers Ginger Nuts, and jars of home-made jam as well as all the basics Edie required.

Word had, of course, got out that there was a lady staying in Prospect House. Edie did not even have to introduce herself.

'Are you not afeared to be staying there all by yourself?' asked the shop girl.

Not until now, thanks, Missy, Edie wanted to say, but didn't. Instead she said, 'Not at all! I have a dog for company. And lots to keep me busy.'

'You're very brave. I wouldn't like to be stuck out there on my own,' said the shop girl, shaking her head lugubriously. 'But maybe you don't believe in ghosts.'

I guess it doesn't matter whether I believe in them or not, thought Edie, because you're clearly going to enlighten me.

'My cousin saw a ghost in the woods near there, with her own eyes,' declared the girl. 'She and her sister-in-law and a friend were driving in a gig by the lake when the horse got a stone in its hoof and they got down to walk. Her sister-in-law had gone on in front, and she hadn't got far when my cousin saw a lady in an old-fashioned dress stepping along beside her. But the sister-in-law didn't pay any heed to the lady, and so my cousin and the friend made haste to overtake her. But just when they were catching her up, the lady dashed into the woods by the side of the road and the horse – which up to this had been perfectly quiet – reared up!'

The girl paused for effect.

'Goodness,' said Edie, obligingly.

'It was a bright moonlight night, but the sister-in-law – that the lady had walked beside – had seen nor heard nothing. My cousin described the appearance of the lady to the priest afterwards, and guess what he said? He said, "It is very like a tinker woman who was found dead nearby about six months ago." But my cousin said no, it was a lady.'

Edie thought that this was possibly the most boring ghost story she had ever heard. 'Well I never,' she said, packing her groceries into her string bag. Then, noticing that the shop girl seemed to be disappointed by her blasé response, she added, 'You've sent shivers all along my spine!'

The girl seemed satisfied by this, so Edie made her happier still by asking for a bag of the treacle toffee that lay in a tray on the counter, and two or three postcards – including one of the local Presentation Convent to send to Ian.

'I hope it's a good big fierce dog you have,' said the girl, as Edie left the shop.

She purchased a book of stamps in the post office on the main street, and would have ventured into O'Regan's bar to try a glass of Guinness if a glance through the window hadn't told her that there were no other women in there. As she walked back down the main street to where she had left her bicycle, she passed a grocer's shop boasting a sign that read: TOM SHEEHAN: PURVEYOR OF HIGH CLASS VIANDS. There in the window a hamper was displayed that contained, among other luxury items, Bath Olivers, Earl Grey tea and Patum Peperium.

That evening, sitting at the writing desk in the library, Edie addressed the postcard of the Presentation Convent to Ian in his flat in Ebury Street, and wrote on the back: *Eat your heart out.* On an impulse, to make him feel guilty for having written such a frivolous message on his postcard from sunny Deauville, she added: *PS: This place is haunted.*

Then she turned her attention to the next tranche of Eliza Drury's story.

9

I CALLED UPON THE address that Mr Thackeray had given me, only to find that he and his family were lodged elsewhere. Isabella's sister directed me to a nearby boarding house, a once-grand residence kept by an impoverished widow. On being told of my arrival, Mr Thackeray helped himself to his coat and hat and quit the place at once, leaving Brodie in charge.

As we descended Grattan Hill, making for the river, I told him of the O'Dowds, and of the misery that lay behind the façade of their neo-Palladian mansion. On the opposite bank of the Lee stood the villas, the terraces and parks of the prosperous merchant class of Cork whence I had come, pulling behind me my baggage loaded on a child's wooden truck. A wooden truck! Had I not suffered indignity and degradation enough in that infernal dump? Every time he came to mind I cursed

O'Dowd to hell, and wished on him the worst agonies a sclerotic liver could inflict upon any man. But the experience had taught me that never again would I submit to such abuse by pretending to be dead. That very morning I had purchased in a general store a perfectly serviceable horn-handled hunting knife in a leather sheath.

Our walk had taken us by old Mardyke Avenue, through lush green pastures where contented cattle fed beneath a cloudless sky. How beautiful the scene was, how rich and how happy! Our thoughts, however, in dark contrast to the serene landscape, were fragmented and tumultuous. Both of us were frail-minded and dizzy from want of sleep.

The previous day Mr Thackeray had summoned a doctor for Isabella. Quite demented, she had tried to kill herself again.

'What was his diagnosis?' I asked.

'Melancholy. Mania. Hysteria. The deuce take the man – I could have come to that conclusion myself. Her nerves are raw, her fancy vivid; she suffers dreadful delusions.'

'Such as she endured on the voyage here?'

'Yes. She laughs and laughs uncontrollably, and that frightens poor Annie so. And then she weeps and refuses to be parted from her babes, saying that they will never be returned to her if she lets them out of her sight. And when I try to console her, she maintains that she cares nothing for me, she cares nothing for our children, she cares nothing for herself. The doctor says it is almost certain she will make another attempt on her own life.' He looked quite desolate, a man with little hope for the future.

'What will you do?'

'I have paid a visit to the asylum here – '

'You cannot consign her to a madhouse! That would be unconscionable.'

'It is not what you think!' He hastened to reassure me. 'Everything is conducted with exemplary neatness and cleanliness and kindness. It is so spacious and comfortable that one could only pray to see every citizen in the country as well lodged.'

I gave him a sideways look.

'It is an admirable institution – quite admirable. All the inmates are healthy, well fed and well clad . . .'

My oblique look turned to one of open scorn.

'But still I emerged from the place quite sick,' he confessed.

'I do not doubt it.'

I had heard of women committed to madhouses on what seemed to me the smallest pretexts: domestic troubles, the grief undergone after the death of a loved one, insanity through travail of childbirth. Many of these unfortunates, I suspected, were admitted by their husbands, to teach them obedience. However, I could not believe Mr Thackeray guilty of such subterfuge.

'Perhaps the birth of Minnie so close to the death of your middle child unhinged poor Isabella?' I hazarded.

'Perhaps,' he conceded. 'Perhaps it is my fault.'

'How so?'

'I have had to go about my own concerns so much in recent months that she may feel I neglect her. The truth is that we are in desperate need of money.'

I had deduced as much from what Isabella had told me on board the *Jupiter*.

'The devil is the wear and tear of it!' continued Mr Thackeray. 'I have been in such a ceaseless whirl with writing pieces for *The Times* and *Fraser's* and with the book – '

'What book?'

'My novel, *Catherine*.' He gave a wry smile. 'It was not well received. And then I told her – I should not have told her! – I told Isabella about the hanging.'

'Hanging?'

'I witnessed it at Newgate Prison in July. A valet was hanged for the murder of his master. It was the most wholly sickening, ghastly, wicked scene I have ever had the misfortune to view.'

'Why ever did you attend such an event?'

'I needed material for an article, for *Fraser's*. Dear God – to think that I compromised my integrity for a magazine article!'

'It was a public execution?'

'Yes. It took place before a mob of thousands beneath a burning sun. I had to look away – I could not watch him hanged – but before they put the hood over the man's face he had about him such a helpless, wild, imploring look as I could not endure. I have had his expression continually before my eyes since.'

'And you told your wife of it? Poor Isabella, who had just been delivered of a child! No wonder she is deranged – barely out of confinement and obliged to listen to such horrors!'

Mr Thackeray looked stricken, but I would not let the matter go.

'They had bound him, I presume?'

'Of course.'

'And not two months later you bind your wife to you with ribbon and plot her incarceration?' He had the decency to look shamefaced. 'Your wife is not your puppet, Mr Thackeray, to do with as you please. Look before you! There, there is the free sky and liberty, and sunshine and birdsong and the wind in the trees, and all sorts of life and motion that it is your prerogative to enjoy! How can you deprive Isabella of such things? Are you surprised that you felt sick when you left the asylum? Those places are no better than Newgate!'

He looked at me with enormous self-loathing. 'I cannot – I *cannot* manage her by myself, Miss Drury.'

'You have Brodie.'

'Brodie is kept busy with the children.'

'Then you must ask Isabella's mother and her sister Jane to help.'

He gave a helpless shrug. 'I had hoped initially to leave her in their care while I busied myself with my guidebook.'

'What guidebook?'

'I have been paid an advance by Chapman & Hall – Mr Dickens's publishing house – to write a guidebook to Ireland. But Mrs Shawe flatly refuses to take in her own daughter. That is why we are lodged in that dingy tenement.'

'You must take her home, then, to London.'

'Oh, God.'

'You must. There, you can resume work and earn the means to employ some person to look after Isabella.'

He was about to make some rejoinder, but then changed his mind. Instead, he took out his handkerchief and pretended to blow his nose.

We continued on our promenade, chatting of the river view and the weather and sundry other inconsequential things, when suddenly he turned to me and blurted out, 'Miss Drury – might you consider the position, if I found the means to pay you?'

'Mr Thackeray, I am not a nurse.'

'But Isabella is fond of you! She is calm and

malleable in your presence. And Annie adores you, and I – I have the greatest respect and admiration for you.'

This was not a development that I had anticipated. Happily, two little dogs scuttling across our path provided an opportunity for diversion, during which time I thought strategically. Finally I said, 'Mr Thackeray, will you allow me to be blunt with you?'

'Of course.'

'Consider this. If I were a man, I could make my way in the world in the army or the navy, or by joining some business enterprise. But I am a female without funds or connections, and that is as precarious a state as anyone could wish to abjure. I am fortunate to have had an education, for without that I should be obliged to earn a paltry living by painting porcelain or trimming bonnets or sewing chemisettes for ladies who can afford such fripperies. As it is, I must rely on my wits, which I am glad to say are in plentiful supply.'

I had indeed relied upon my wits until now. As it happened, the situation as governess to the O'Dowd family had been made available to me upon my illuminating Miss Pinkerton on the state of her account books, which had come under my scrutiny one day when she had neglected to lock her bureau. I had expressed such dismay at the discrepancies contained therein, and such concern that the details might reach the fathers who were paying for the privilege of their daughters' education in that lady's establishment, that she had at once volunteered to write any number of eulogies for the edification of my future employers.

Mr Thackeray was regarding me with considerable warmth. 'I have never met a woman as quick-witted and resourceful as you, my dear Miss Drury.'

'Acuity notwithstanding, you will see that I am in need of a husband, or, at the very least, a protector,' I interposed. 'I must put myself in the way of a gentleman with five thousand pounds a year–'

'Five thousand a year?'

'Or more, Mr Thackeray.'

He fell silent.

'Five thousand a year?' he repeated. 'Then I fear I shall have to sharpen my nib.'

I gave him a look, but when I saw how utterly downcast was his demeanour, I refrained from reminding Mr Thackeray that he already had a wife.

How many resplendent town houses in Cork city had been – like the one where I was now lodged – converted to tenement boarding houses? How many elegant abodes degenerated into disreputable slums, their gracious reception rooms divided and subdivided into living quarters that now accommodated the offscourings of society?

The widow Fagan had fallen on hard times since the

death of her husband from crapulence. His portrait hung above the chipped marble chimneypiece in the drawing room, where she and her children now slept. The house was in a sorry state of repair, with few traces of its former genteel character: the stucco work had decayed so that the ceiling roses resembled worm casts, there was no paper to the walls, no locks to the doors, the windows were broken and much of the furniture had been sold or requisitioned for firewood. Now the mistress of the establishment went bare-legged, who had once worn clocked stockings; she mended her clothes herself, who had been attended by a lady's maid.

The house was inhabited by a queer assortment of lodgers. There were whole families confined to a single chamber, while rooms in the upper regions of the house – hardly bigger than cupboards – were home to sundry rascals and draggletails.

Mr Thackeray had taken one of the more salubrious apartments on the first floor. It had separate accommodation for the children and Brodie, who kindly allowed me to share her bed. We slept perforce with Annie – all bony angles and flailing limbs – and were further disturbed by Minnie's plaintive wailing every time she needed to be fed, whereupon Brodie would rouse, lift the babe from the crib and take her next door to her mother.

Mr Thackeray would not hear of my making a

contribution to the lodging-house fees. In return, I volunteered to take care of Isabella while he sought peace to write in the faded grandeur of the public reading room. The manager of a theatre in Covent Garden had commissioned a comedy, and Mr Thackeray laboured to come up with good lively stuff during those harrowing weeks at Grattan Hill.

In the evening, when Isabella finally dropped into an opium-induced slumber, he and I would take supper together, and afterwards a bumper or two of burgundy. Mr Thackeray (William, for we had begun to Christianname each other) regaled me with scandalous tales of London society, while I entertained him with accounts of my unorthodox upbringing.

My mother, an opera dancer and singer, was a native of Paris, where I had been born and lived for some years; my father was an artist. His career as a portraitist came to naught, foundering on the inhospitable shores of Miss Pinkerton's academy (he had painted the likeness of that formidable beldame which hung in her study). He spent the final miserable years of his life as a drawing master in that establishment, then – once my education had been secured – made me an orphan by dying of a fit of *delirium tremens*. By then I excelled at the games of chance learned in his studio in Soho, just as I had mastered the pretty tricks passed on to me by the opera girls in Montmartre.

I like to think I supplied William with material; indeed, I know for certain I did. Sadly, the comic play he finally drafted was never produced in Covent Garden or any other theatre.

Meanwhile, Isabella fluctuated between lucidity and insanity. Her mother bestirred herself to bring the occasional plate of food from her adjacent home, but otherwise did nothing but brag and prate incessantly about her own great merits and sacrifices. As for Isabella's sister, Jane: she came once or twice to read aloud some psalms; that's all.

The widow Fagan who presided over this house of misfits was a pretty, lively woman of five-and-thirty, with three equally pretty, lively daughters. These kind-hearted girls adopted Annie as a sister, taking her with them on expeditions to Tivoli Woods and Netley Abbey, and after some days associating with this trio of colleens the child acquired a fetching brogue. She was joyous and free as a bird, and it perplexed her that her mother showed no inclination to explore these new haunts with her. She would return in the evening, chattering ceaselessly about the adventures she had had, while Isabella lay gazing at the ceiling with vacant eyes, emitting an occasional agonized mewl.

As for me, I pondered what might be my next strategy.

I forged an alliance with the good Mrs Fagan, who

took it upon herself to become my champion. I had showed her the dresses given me by Mrs O'Dowd, whereupon she had gone into an ecstasy of delight, and spoken of effecting an entrée for me into Corkonian society. The *haut monde* of the city and all the baronetcies beyond, she said, would be enraptured by my grace, charm and wit.

We were sitting one day in a shady niche in what had been the garden of her house. It was quite over-grown now with weeds and grass and creeping vines. Ornate urns and empty stone troughs that had held flowers – spouted fountains, even – were crumbling and coated in mildew, but roses grew rampant still, clam-bering over the terrace and through the sashless windows; the parterre was fragrant with their scent.

Mrs Fagan was consulting the newspaper, with a view to having me place an advertisement.

'In the papers, ladies are advertising continually as governesses,' she told me. 'Look here – "Gentlewoman of agreeable manners, and accustomed to the best society is anxious to secure . . ." etcetera, etcetera. And many of them specify that they are "English ladies", for they set great store by all things English here. It is a merit to have dwelt in the city of London; you must turn it to your advantage. I have connections still, you know – I am a woman of property after all, though my income is modest.'

To be sure, Mrs Fagan – when she sallied forth into the public arena – cut a trim figure in her bombazine gown and her straw bonnet with its sober black ribbon. From her outward bearing, no one would have supposed that she pinched and starved at home. She had culled and ripped and snipped every bit of finery she had possessed during her married years to make the most ingenious dresses for her eldest daughter (to whom, it was rumoured, a fortune was to be left by some old aunt), in the hope of attracting a suitor. So Mrs Fagan put forward a good face against fortune, and kept up appearances in the most virtuous manner, though at home in Grattan Hill it was her prerogative to lounge about in a shabby peignoir with her hair in curl papers.

'Aha!' Mrs Fagan lit upon an announcement from the Cork Society. 'There is to be a dinner given for the members of the Irish Agricultural Association, followed by a ball in the Imperial Hotel. You must attend!'

It was plain from my face that I was not a-tingle at the notion of a gathering of farmers, all in breeches and gaiters and with leering red faces, shambling around after a guinea dinner and a feed of poitín.

'Do not disparage it, dear friend,' Mrs Fagan chided me. 'You think of uncouth peasant farmers, but there are landlords aplenty who will be in attendance, many of whose daughters require an education. My own brother-in-law has a demesne not far from here in the village of Doneraile, which is currently the most fashionable place in North Cork. The line of gentlemen's carriages outside the church on Sundays is said to be a mile long.'

That augured well, for I knew that gentlefolk seldom attended church from religious scruple; the service on a Sunday morning was more often an opportunity for each of the ladies to scrutinize the others' attire, and for the bucks to admire them.

'Let us think of practicalities,' continued Mrs Fagan. 'I have no doubt that my sister and brother-in-law will be pleased to escort you: Charlotte will make a splendid chaperone. She is some ten years older than me, and is Viscountess Doneraile.'

'Your sister is a titled lady?'

'I am too. Before I married, you would have dropped me a curtsey and addressed me as Your Ladyship. I – who am now known as plain Mrs Sam Fagan – have a fine pedigree, for I am the fifth daughter of an earl.'

'But surely you retain your rank?'

'Nobody uses my title except in jest.' Assuming a haughty stance, she twinkled and laughed. 'Why bother with it? I might as well be the fifth daughter of a sergeant major, or a clergyman, or an articled clerk, for all the bills my title ever paid. Besides, I loved my husband, though he was a ne'er-do-well.'

I thought of Mrs O'Dowd, whose father had been a baron, and of the girls at Miss Pinkerton's academy whose education would count for nothing once they were married, and of all those impoverished Russian princesses whose names appeared in *Galignani's Messenger*, and now, looking at the widow Fagan, I thought of all the daughters of peers who must take second, third, fourth or twentieth place to their younger brothers, and who must – if they were to survive – dream of marrying only for money, and never for love.

'Now,' Mrs Fagan resumed briskly. 'The kingfisher blue taffeta is the most becoming of your gowns. Have you jewels to wear?'

I laughed. 'Not even paste.'

'No matter. I have an heirloom or two still in my jewel case. I can lend you some pretty pieces – I have a necklace and ear bobs set with turquoises and pearls that would go charmingly with the blue. I must ask you for a deposit; for form's sake, you understand.'

'I understand, dear Mrs Fagan – '

'Maria, please! It is time we Christian-named each other.'

'—my dear *Maria*: but I have no money.'

And then I remembered the watch that Mr O'Dowd had consulted so ostentatiously at the dinner table on my first and only night spent under his roof. I felt neither contrition not compunction for having taken it; my sole regret was that I had not augmented my spoils with the snuffboxes and other gewgaws strewn around that man's drawing room, for he owed me more than a gold time-piece. 'Wait here,' I told Maria.

I tripped upstairs to fetch it, pausing briefly at Isabella's door when I heard her moan in pain. I was mistaken – it was Jane, her sister, singing a doleful hymn.

I had sewn the watch into the wadding of my bonnet. As I unpicked the stitching to retrieve it, I heard Annie's voice float up from the street below. I looked down to see her and Louisa – Maria's youngest – absorbed in scolding a pair of dollies that they had made out of pegs and shreds of gingham. 'We'll put the childher to bed with no supper,' said Louisa, 'and then we'll sit down together and have a bumper of wine.'

I smiled at this scene of tender domesticity, then made my way back to Maria in the garden. She was shooing off a tomcat who had come calling on her pretty tabby.

'Here,' I said, offering her the watch. 'Will this do as collateral?'

She took it and looked at it curiously, then held it closer, the better to inspect it. 'Do you know what you have here?' she asked. 'It is a Breguet. See here, on either side of the numeral XII, in minute characters, is his signature. You are in luck, my dear, for Breguet is the finest watchmaker in Europe.'

'Is it worth a deal of money?'

'It is worth a *great* deal of money. If you take it to the pawnbroker's it should fetch at least £150. How did you come by it?'

'A gentleman gave it to me.'

Mrs Fagan held my gaze. The imperturbability with which she regarded me moved me to amend my story.

'I took it from a savage who committed a heinous trespass against my person.'

She leaned forward and took my hand. 'Then I am more inclined than ever to help you,' she said, with a smile.

10

D ONERAILE! EDIE WAS intrigued to know that the town she had visited today – which was scarcely more than a village – had once been esteemed the most fashionable place in North Cork. She wished she had swotted up on it before she had left London. Perhaps there was a travel guide or suchlike in the bookcase that could tell her more about the history of the place?

There wasn't; although the copy of William Thackeray's *Irish Sketch-Book*, published by Messrs Chapman & Hall in 1843, told her that his travels had taken him to Cork city and nearby Lismore. There was, however, no mention of Doneraile in the index. Perhaps she would find more in Eliza's records?

A glance at her wristwatch – a girl's Timex that she had had since she was at school – told her it was past ten o'clock. Edie was dog-tired after her long cycle into town and back, and a day spent lugging furniture around. But she was awfully anxious to know, among other things, if Eliza *had* gone to the ball . . .

Just one more chapter, she promised herself, and then she'd go to bed.

Mr O'Dowd's watch – which was engraved with the motto *Nunc vino pellite curas* ('Now Drive Away Your Cares with Wine') – fetched more than ten times what poor Brodie might earn in a year.

Amongst the flashy French and plated goods shops that lined the Mall, I found a *Magasin des Modes*, in which establishment I purchased a beaded reticule, a pair of kid gloves, a fringed cashmere shawl, a fan of dyed satinette feathers and a dainty pair of shoes of the same colour with Louis heels.

Mrs Fagan – Maria – helped me dress. The blue taffeta fitted perfectly, demonstrating how tiny Mrs O'Dowd's waist had been before the birth of her two lumpish children, and the pearl-and-turquoise jewels that hung from my ears and coiled serpent-like about my throat enhanced the aquamarine gleam in my eyes. I wore my hair in glossy bandeaux, coiled to show off the pearl clasp at the nape of my neck, and applied the merest touch of lip salve to my mouth.

Before I left the house, I called upon Isabella in her apartment. She shrieked when she saw me, and asked if

I was a fairy. I assured her that I was no fairy, but rather her friend, upon which she threw her arms around me and implored me with copious tears not to leave her, for if I did she surely never would see me again. I distracted her with a china doll that I had bought for Annie that morning – a beauty, with a painted face, a dress of sprigged muslin and button boots – then made my escape. As I slipped from the room, I caught William's eyes upon me. I cast him a look over my shoulder which plainly said *Noli me tangere*. I had become inordinately fond of William, but I could not allow any sentimental attachment to him or his family to impede my progress.

The ballroom of the Imperial Hotel was a strange, merry, mongrel place. Maria's brother-in-law and her sister, the Viscount and Viscountess Doneraile, were among the more venerable of the guests attending the gala. The Viscountess, Lady Charlotte, had condescended to accommodate me in her brougham. She questioned me about my provenance as we trundled thither, and seemed satisfied when I told her that my father had been the favourite portrait painter of Lord Bingham (of whom he had once made a satirical sketch) and that my mother was descended from the noble family of Pirouette-Entrechats in Gascony.

'So you speak French?' the grande dame asked.

'Yes, very well, Your Ladyship.' I cast my eyes modestly down to the floor of the brougham, where Lady Charlotte's pug squatted. 'I taught French for two years in a most illustrious establishment – Miss Pinkerton's academy in Chiswick. When my parents died I was fortunate enough to be offered a place there, and that is how I have earned my living since.'

'How very refreshing,' Lady Charlotte remarked, clearly won over by my humility, 'to encounter candour when one is constantly beset by parvenus, bragging and clamouring for notice. What position do you currently hold?'

'Alas, I am unengaged, Your Ladyship,' I told her. 'The anticipated post of governess that brought me to Ireland is no longer vacant.'

'How so?'

'It is a rather tragic story.'

'Oh?' Lady Charlotte leaned forward in the carriage with such eagerness that she almost crushed her pug. 'Pray, tell me.'

I adopted a low, confidential tone, even though there was no one to hear us but His Lordship, who was snoring in the corner of the brougham. 'The gentleman who engaged me passed away, and his wife and children are emigrated to Australia.'

'Indeed! Who were they? Should I know them?'

'They were the Reckitts of Castlereckingham.'

'I can't say I've heard of them. How did this Reckitt pass away? It must have been sudden?'

'It was, madam. It was sudden, and agonizing.' I invested my voice with intense chagrin. 'It was a consequence of the same delicate ailment that afflicted Louis XIV of France.'

'Ah,' said Lady Charlotte: and that is all she needed to say, for it was known in all the best circles that Louis XIV nearly expired of an anal fistula.

'I must enquire who among my acquaintance may be in need of a governess,' she continued. 'It is to your certain advantage that you speak French, for everyone wants a French governess. It has – it has . . . What is the word I am looking for? It's a French word.'

'*Cachet*,' I supplied.

'That'll do,' said Lady Charlotte. 'In the meantime, tell me some of the goings-on in London,' she commanded. 'Especially the more tragic ones.'

And as the brougham lumbered on its way along the Mall, I reeled off the same stories of life among the fashionable elite of London that I had fabricated for the enlightenment of Mrs O'Dowd two weeks earlier.

The table in the supper room of the Imperial Hotel resembled a still life by some second-rate Dutch painter. It was a triumph of content over style, comprised as it was of massive trenchers of sliced beef, ham and tongue, all garnished with crudely carved vegetable flowers. There were platters of poached salmon, prawns in mayonnaise and oyster patties; there were dishes of custard, fruited jelly and vanilla cream, trays of fancy pastries and tartlets, and salvers of shortbread biscuits and bonbons. The beverages included a selection of champagnes, wines and liqueurs, and although the bottles in the ice-well clinked and tinkled enticingly, I permitted myself to drink only soda water.

While the gentlemen poured more wine and raised their glasses in a series of roistering post-prandial toasts, the ladies retired to an antechamber to rearrange their dress. A cheval glass had been strategically positioned to facilitate them in their appraisal of each other's reflections, which ritual they performed with swift, rapier glances.

The room was aflutter with skirts in organdie and tulle, gauzy sashes of tarleton and tiffany and mousseline, gossamer lace fichus, coiffures crowned with confections of ribbon and silk, and fans, feathers and ruffles of every hue. Sharp eyes assessed the yardage of taffeta that comprised my gown and the quantity of flounces sewn into its skirts, and calculated the weight of the gems I wore. I manifested my indifference by turning my back to the glass.

The supper table having been cleared away, the real business of the night – which, to feminine minds, was the quest for potential suitors – began. There was an undignified melée amongst the younger ladies as they surged from the antechamber, but I held myself back. When I finally issued forth it was with the demeanour of one whose coiffure, jewels and costume had not required a moment of attention, as if my panoply of gleaming armour had been simply shrugged on – *Voilà!* The silence that fell when I made my entrance was superseded at once by the nervous staccato of my rivals, seeking vainly to distract their beaux.

The assorted elderly gentry had kept themselves a little apart from the squireens and squiresses in an unassailable clique. I joined Lady Charlotte, who was holding forth to her fellow dowagers by the chimneypiece, and listened – not to her imperious monologue, but to the first strains of the violins summoning the dancers to the floor. I watched the young ladies float and swish past me in the arms of their escorts, and wished that I could show off some of the lively new dance steps I had learned from Monsieur Cabriole: the Polka, the Schottische, the Mazurka . . .

One of the old gentlemen of the company, perceiving the agitation of my satin-clad toes beneath the hem of my gown, took pity upon me and asked me to dance. I sent Lady Charlotte a look of enquiry as though asking permission, rather hoping that she would refuse and send me to fetch her an ice. But she gave a gracious nod, and so I took a turn with the pantaloon before returning him to his seat under the pretext that his dancing was too nimble for me; in truth, I was fearful that he might fall victim to a fit of apoplexy.

Shortly thereafter a gawky youth – whose pock-marked face might have benefited from a lavish application of Rowland's Kalydor – importuned me to partner him in the quadrille; then I was intercepted by a mustachioed cavalry officer of whom I asked questions that I proceeded to answer in a roundabout way myself, so that he appeared very clever without having to say a word. My fourth partner was a small, stout gentleman upon whose shining pate, fringed with a wisp of ginger hair, I gazed as I danced. His undershot jaw caused his two front teeth to protrude so alarmingly that I was put in mind of the vampires of Eastern Europe. He hummed as he danced, but spoke not a word. I was now so bored that I was mentally rehearsing the dialogue for my next encounter with Lady Charlotte, when I hoped to inter-rogate her on the marital status of the better-looking agriculturalists present.

I was making my way back to her when I caught the eye of a gentleman who, if he were horseflesh, I could only describe as thoroughbred: a racehorse, a bay hunter. His appearance was sleek – debonair, even – yet he had about him an untamed air. His eyes were knowing, his mouth sensual; the symmetry of the bones beneath the wind-burnt face recalled to me a painting my father had made of the Greek hero Achilles. He moved with an easy grace, that fluid articulation of the limbs peculiar to men who have practised those arts essential to true manliness – boxing, riding and dancing.

I raised my chin and adopted an insouciant attitude, toying idly with the tassel on my fan, but his saunter was so indolent, his smile so impertinent, his demeanour so cavalier, that as he approached I felt as though he had just taken hold of my ear bob and tweaked it.

With the merest suggestion of a bow, without even asking my consent, the stranger extended an arm to encircle my waist, and drew me onto the dance floor. He smelt of leather and Marseille soap.

The musicians struck up a waltz. *One-two-three, one-two-three, dip-two-three, change-two-three* . . .

Hallelujah! For the first time that evening I was partnered by a man who knew what he was doing. Monsieur Cabriole, whose star pupil I had been, was an expert dancer and a proficient teacher, but dancing with him had been like dancing with a pixie. The men who cavorted with me when I lived at my father's house in Soho were usually too inebriated to remain upright, and I had but a vague memory of those beaux of my mother's who had twirled me around her apartment in Montmartre.

This man was designed to be danced with. His supporting arm was firm, his palm against the skin of my shoulder cool, his movements were assured, stylish and accomplished, and I matched him glissade for glissade. The ennui to which I had been subjected while being shunted around by a succession of tongue-tied imbeciles vanished, and I felt charged with renewed vigour.

For several bars of waltz-time we danced without speaking, and I began to wonder if he was as tongue-tied as the other dolts. Then he smiled down at me and said, not quite under his breath: '*Quelle jolie minette.*'

I raised an eyebrow in reprimand. 'Sir, it is ungentlemanly of you to compare me to a pussy-cat, be she ne'er so pretty.'

'You understand French?'

'*Je parle parfaitement la langue.*'

'Pray accept my apologies. It was meant as a compliment, Mademoiselle.'

'Not a euphemism, then.'

'A euphemism . . . ?'

'Surely you know what a euphemism is?'

'You might be so kind as to give me an example.'

'A euphemism is what an agriculturalist is, who might once have been called a farmer. Or a gentleman who is no better than a cad.'

'So it's a namby-pamby way of not calling a spade a spade.'

'You're an able pupil.'

He looked at me narrowly as we sidestepped and dipped. 'I can't say I was expecting word-play to be on the agenda this evening,' he remarked. 'I see I should have donned my considering cap.'

'What were you expecting on the agenda?'

'At a *ceilí*?' He gave me a mildly supercilious look. 'What do you think?'

'I don't know what a *ceilí* is.'

'Now I have the advantage. *Labhairt liom Gaeilge líofa.*'

'Bravo!' I tilted my chin up at him. 'What a pair of linguists we make.'

The second violinist took up his bow and the music surged. *Change-two-three, left-two-three, sidestep-and-dip* . . .

'Tell me, mademoiselle, where did you learn to speak French?'

'At my mother's knee. I was born in Paris. Where did you learn to speak Irish, monsieur?'

'My ghillie has the gift of the gab.' *Whisk-beat-change, left-two-three* . . . 'So you are a genuine Parisienne?'

'I am descended from – '

'The Pirouette-Entrechats of Gascony. I had my spies make enquiries. Any relation to the Arabesques-Fouettés?'

I tucked the corners of my mouth into a smile. 'They are very near cousins.'

'Do you mean kissing cousins?'

158

'If your spies were competent, you ought to know that already – just as you ought to have known, when you took the liberty of calling me "minette", that I understood French.'

'My . . . sister has a little cat called Minette,' he said. 'You remind me of her. She is a very pretty cat.'

I dare say he was expecting me to conjure some riposte about cats and their nine lives, or cats looking at kings, or some such flirtatious flimflam. Instead I said, 'Never antagonize a cat. They were worshipped by the ancient Egyptians.' *Dip-two-three, change-two-three.* 'You may have heard tell of their revered cat goddess.'

He shook his head.

'Her name was Bastet. She was the goddess of pleasure, women and secrets. And though she was but little, she was fierce.'

'Bastet. If I get to know you better, I shall call you that. I rather fancy the notion of worshipping a cat goddess.'

His impudence was catching. 'I confess that when I saw you, I too was put in mind of a beast.'

'Which one?'

'The steed that belonged to Alexander of Macedon.'

'The best Thessalian strain,' he said. 'You're alluding to Bucephalus.'

As the final notes of the waltz sounded, my smile was still hovering between lips and eyes. Around us the filmy sea of organdie and chiffon subsided as the dancers came to a susurrous standstill.

My partner made another bow. 'Jameson St Leger, at your service.'

I dipped a curtsey, regarding him from under my eyelashes. 'Miss Eliza Drury,' I said, unwinding the silk tassel of my fan from my wrist.

The orchestra leader raised his baton. Another waltz began, but as Mr St Leger claimed my hand, I snaked away from him, giving him that look I had given William earlier, the one that had warned him to pull back: *Noli me tangere*. Then, with my most winsome smile, I snapped my fan open. As I moved across the dance floor, sashaying a little in time to Schubert's *Caprice*, I rested its feather-tipped ribs upon my bare shoulder.

Rejoining Lady Charlotte and her companions, I wondered whether my dance partner was familiar with the language of fans. He was clearly an educated man. I had been impressed that my small friend Annie Thackeray knew who Bucephalus was, but I was even more impressed that a roué at a provincial shindy should do. However, the discourse of fans was a nuanced one, in which not all gentlemen were versed. Had I twisted the tassel in my left hand, it would have indicated indifference; had I wound it around my left forefinger, it would have signified that I was affianced. But by resting the blade of my fan upon my shoulder I had effectively told Mr St Leger, *Farewell – until we meet again.*

I rather hoped we would.

'Sir Silas Sillery was very much taken with you,' Lady Charlotte pronounced, as we drove back to Grattan Hill in her brougham. Through the window I could see crowds of rowdies trooping onto the street from some hostelry less salubrious than the one we had just vacated. Shabby dandies they were, in ragged frock coats and steeple hats, staggering arm in arm across the street, and yelling songs in chorus.

Lady Charlotte was fondling her pug, oblivious to the uproar beyond the snug confines of her sedan. She was feeding the animal shortbread, which she had purloined from the supper table and stowed in her sizeable reticule. Lord Doneraile was asleep again in the corner of the carriage.

'You may expect a letter from Sir Silas tomorrow – he has you in mind for a governess,' Lady Charlotte told me. 'His wife, Lady Sybil, has eight children under the age of ten who are in need of schooling.'

I had danced with Sir Silas, who had practically salivated over my décolleté. He had spoken in a choked voice of his love of poetry – especially that of Catullus and Rochester (poets whose works I was familiar with and knew to be obscene). He was especially fond, he told me, of certain of their verses which he would be pleased to have me translate into French and declaim aloud for his delectation, in the seclusion of his study.

'Sir Silas seems to be a most learned man,' I remarked.

'Yes, and a cultured one. He is forever tearing up to town to see the opera. He has travelled a great deal, and has imported some noble pictures and statuary from Greece to beautify his house.'

'It is quite the fashion to collect antiquities. I understand Lord Elgin has purl – has accumulated quite a hoard from the Parthenon.'

'Good for Lord Elgin, I say! It's perfectly acceptable to help ourselves to their antiquities, since ancient Greece is an idolatrous country.'

I wasn't sure how to answer this, for I believe Lady Doneraile thought ancient Greece to be some separate geographical entity entirely to the new Republic. Thankfully, she continued without waiting for my answer, glancing at her husband and lowering her voice. 'I hear Sir Silas has a private chamber in his house painted in frescoes that he has had copied from the walls of Pompeii.'

I nodded cordially and refrained from pointing out that Pompeii was in Italy, not Greece.

'Did you benefit from a classical education, Miss Drury?'

'I did, Your Ladyship.'

'I, alas, had few opportunities to peruse the writings of Homer and his antique ilk.'

The carriage swung suddenly to the right as the coachman swerved to avoid a hobbledehoy cutting capers on the cobblestones. Lord Doneraile jerked awake momentarily, snorted, then lolled back against the upholstery with his mouth open.

'In my husband's family the only book they study is the Racing Calendar,' remarked Lady Charlotte, with a sigh. 'His great-uncle established the flat race at Doncaster, you know.'

'The sport of kings,' I murmured, politely.

'Indeed. It has become a much celebrated thousand guinea championship, the St Leger.'

I stiffened. 'I beg your pardon, Your Ladyship. Did you say St Leger?'

'Yes,' supplied my companion. 'Lord Doneraile is a St Leger. The title was created for his family by King George III – the second title, that is. The first was created in 1703. And here we are at last, at Grattan Hill.'

11

E DIE WOULD HAVE stayed up to read more of Eliza's story were it not for the sputtering sound that told her the Aladdin lamp was running low on oil. In the kitchen she lit the storm lantern, shrugged into her polo coat and ventured abroad with Milo.

'Remember the satin shoes we found, Milo – with the Louis heels? I wonder were they the ones she wore that night, with the blue taffeta, and the turquoises? I'd so love to know what she looked like! We shall never find out, of course, because there were no photographs then. Oh, don't do it there, darling – I'm bound to tread on it if you do it there. Come this way a little, over here – good boy! Maybe there's a portrait somewhere? A little one, hidden, that we haven't found yet – a miniature. And him! St Leger. Do you know who he reminds me of? Sergeant Troy, in *Far from the Madding Crowd*. Dashing and handsome and heroic, and yet a cad! Do you think he's a cad, Milo? I'd say she could whistle for him! Have

164

you finished yet? Oh, do hurry up, it's freezing out here.'

It was colder than previous nights; the sky was clear, with that crystalline quality that presages frost. Beyond the roofs of the stable yard Edie could see the tops of trees surrounding them on three sides. The fourth side was, of course, all lake and hills.

The house would have been virtually inaccessible before the new road was built, she conjectured. One would have had to approach it through the forest, via the track that ran at a tangent to the avenue. It was an unlikely location for a dwelling, so far removed from the town. But Edie supposed the situation outweighed mere geographical inconvenience. Imagine waking up to that view in the morning!

Breathing in the cold air, she savoured the aroma of woodsmoke. 'I do love an open fire, Milo! I know it would make more sense to just live in the kitchen here, but there's something so indulgent about sitting by a blazing library fire. If I had lots of money, I'd have a library. How grand! Imagine, on the telephone: "I'm working from home today, correcting galley proofs in the library." La-di-da! Are you all done now? Let's go.'

She started to stroll back towards the house. But Milo didn't come scampering to overtake her as he usually did. When she turned round to chivvy him on, she saw that he was standing rigid, staring out past the stable to where the trees were fenced off from the yard. Behind the fence, all was forest.

'Milo? Come on!'

Edie took a couple of paces towards him but the dog remained in the aggressive, stiff-legged stance that even the smallest dogs adopt when there's something up. It convinced her to stop and listen, and for a while she could hear nothing but the gentle soughing of the trees. Then she became aware of a sound she had never heard before. Milo was growling.

Edie had slept well since coming to Prospect House – a blessing she attributed to a combination of bracing country air and hard physical work. But on that clear cold evening after she had dragged Milo back into the house, locked and bolted both doors, pulled the shutters over the French windows, crawled into bed, extinguished her bedside lamp and curled up with Milo at her feet, fatigue hadn't been enough to tumble her into the arms of Morpheus. She had lain there clutching at hazy rags of sleep as they drifted past her, before starting awake again.

She remembered the ghost story that the girl in Doneraile Stores had told her earlier that day, of the lady in the old-fashioned dress who had walked the lakeshore road alongside her cousin. Edie didn't believe in ghosts. Nor did she believe that Friday the 13th, black cats or walking beneath a stepladder brought bad luck. She had read too many rubbishy manuscripts sent in to Heinemann about curses and hauntings and black magic to give credence to such superstitious tommyrot. But in that case, why had she locked Hilly's photograph in the drawer of her bureau?

Edie slid out of bed, wrapped herself in her dressing gown and went to the window. Outside it was pitch black, and the sound of the wind infiltrating the cracks between sash and window frame was tuneless as a gap-toothed whistler. How dark and wintry and steeped in misery the months had been, after Hilly's death. She had woken each morning to the same thought – 'What is wrong? Something is wrong' – before remembering that of course her friend was dead and that it was her fault.

'It wasn't your fault,' said Milo.

He was sitting on the bedspread watching her.

'Are you eavesdropping on my thoughts?' she asked.

'Yes. It wasn't your fault,' Milo said again. 'You did it because you felt Hilly had betrayed you. And when a friend betrays you, a big lump of anger starts to build up inside you. So you did the only thing you could. You cut away the anger and shut it up in a drawer.'

'And then she died!'

'If you really believed she was going to die, you would never have done it.'

'But I did do it!' wailed Edie.

'And it didn't kill Hilly. A car killed her, silly. Come back to bed, Edie. Come and cuddle me.'

She slid back between the sheets and took the dog's warm little body in her arms.

167

'Please don't cry on me. I hate having soggy fur,' said Milo.

Edie wiped her nose on her pyjama cuff. Together they lay, each listening to the other's breathing until it was synchronized. 'What made you growl, on the edge of the wood?' Edie asked sleepily.

'I was practising being a guard dog.'

'How brave you are.'

'My great-grandsire saved the life of his mistress by leaping at the face of an intruder and ripping his beard off.'

'He actually ripped his beard off?'

'Yes. He was a great big fat man all dressed in red with a fur-trimmed hat, and my great-grandsire tore his beard to shreds.'

'Oh, Milo, I do love you.'

'I love you too, Edie.'

The following morning she awoke realizing that although Milo's queer behaviour on the edge of the forest had unsettled her, if she scraped away the layers – like a palimpsest – she could trace a creeping sense of unease back to yesterday, when Seán the Post had told her about an apocalyptic event that had killed a million people.

In the kitchen she riddled the stove, put a kettle on for coffee and poured herself a bowl of cornflakes. Then she went into the library and took from the box file the folder that she had earmarked for old newspaper cuttings, so that she could go through them while she ate her breakfast.

The first cutting was from the *Cork Chronicle and Munster Advertiser*, and it was dated May 1846:

> Ireland must behold her best flour, her wheat, her bacon, her butter, her live cattle, all going to England day after day. She dare not ask the cause of this fatal discrepancy – the existence of famine in a country, whose staple commodity is food – food – food of the best – and of the most exquisite quality.

The next was from the the *Cork Examiner*, and it was dated December of the same year:

> There is disease and death in every quarter – the once hardy population worn away to emaciated skeletons – fever, dropsy, diarrhoea, and famine in every filthy hovel, and sweeping away whole families . . . seventy-five tenants ejected here, and a whole village in the last stage of destitution there . . . dead bodies of children flung into holes hastily scratched in the earth without shroud or coffin . . . every field becoming a grave, and the land a wilderness.

But it was the editorial that had been cut from the London *Times* of September 1846 that made Edie put down her spoon and push away her bowl.

There are ingredients in the Irish character which must be corrected before either individuals or Government can hope to raise the general condition of the people. It is absurd to prescribe political innovations for the remedy of their suffering or the alleviation of their wants. Extended suffrage and municipal reform for a peasantry who have for six centuries consented to alternate between starvation on a potato and the doles of national charity! You might as well give them bonbons.

Edie couldn't bear to read more. She dumped her breakfast dishes in the sink, shrugged into her pinafore, swathed her hair in a scarf and worked and worked until the sun sank into the lake and it was time to light the fire in the library.

E. D.

The next day I received a letter from Sir Silas, by messenger.

It came as I was sitting with Maria in her apartment. The former drawing room, which had been divided with flimsy lath and plaster partitions into two or three smaller rooms, still bore traces of its former grandeur: gilt cornices that had not been dusted for a decade, faded yellow satin hangings, a magnificent soup tureen which now served as a coal scuttle, and the aforementioned portrait of the deceased Mr Fagan in his rococo frame. A bust on a pedestal bore the likeness of the Earl of Bandon, Maria's father. Because the coat of arms engraved on the base was a constant reminder of her lost status as scion of a noble family, Maria snubbed the heirloom by making it a convenient repository for her bonnet.

We had been speaking of the ball (which had been reported in the morning newspaper thus: 'After the grand dinner came a grand ball, which was indeed one of the gayest and prettiest sights ever seen; the ladies of the city mixing with the ladies from the country, and vying with them in grace and beauty'), and now we were assessing the fortunes of the gentlemen I had met there.

The graceless, pockmarked youth was a strong matrimonial candidate, according to Maria, for he was a viscount and first in line not only for his father's title (which was of little import to me) but also for a substantial inheritance (which was). I was on the point of quizzing her on her connection to the St Leger family, when Eilish, the housemaid, flung into the room and thrust Sir Silas's letter at me. I scanned it, laughed, then began to read it aloud to Maria:

'My dear Miss Drury,
Did you by any chance last evening form an idea of the
extent of my intrepidity? If you did, I have a notion that I
shall now exceed whatever might have been your estimate.'

'His . . . intrepidity?' said Maria, raising an eyebrow.

'What a bumptious, conceited clown the fellow is!
He would not appear out of place in Astley's circus.
Look – here is his version of the Allemand, which I was
obliged to dance with him last night.'

I rose from my chair and performed a creeping,
hopping movement on my toes, my hands groping the
air like the paws of a palsied cat. Maria started to laugh,
and the harder she laughed, the more exaggerated my
impersonation became, until we were both helpless with
merriment. Finally I subsided into my chair, and reached
for my handkerchief to wipe the traces of hilarity from
my cheeks.

'I danced with many square-toed bores last night,
Maria, but believe me, Sir Silas was the most lethal of
them. The military ought to requisition him as a weapon
of torture.'

'Tell me the rest of the letter,' urged Maria.

I composed myself, and continued reading.

'I am about to ask you – to ask you plunging without preface
or apology – to go to work for me, and to give me *only,*

because I *have the intrepidity'* – that word again! – *'to ask for what every body would wish to have from you, and nobody who had any pretence to modesty would venture to think of asking for.*

    Most truly your Affectionate friend,
    Sir Silas Sillery (Bart).'

Maria and I regarded each other in disbelief. Then, screwing the *billet doux* into a ball, I aimed it at the Staffordshire coal scuttle.

'He wants you to be his whore,' Maria said.

'So do most men,' I replied with a shrug, 'but he was right about his intrepidity. He has sufficient of *that* to ask me outright, which the majority of his rank would hesitate to do. One would be tempted to admire such candour in another gentleman, were he well-favoured and agreeable enough.'

My thoughts, I confess, had turned to Jameson St Leger. Some nuance in my expression alerted Maria to a possible imbroglio, for she said at once, 'What man was there last night, who has turned your head?'

'No one,' I protested, scrutinizing the lace hem of my handkerchief.

'You fib, Eliza. You're thinking of someone in particular. Allow me to guess at Mr St Leger, who I know attended.'

I gave up any pretence of examining the lace, and

raised my eyes to hers. 'I cannot deny, dear Maria, that I did feel a strong affinity with that gentleman.'

'You are not the only female to have felt an "affinity" with him,' she declared. 'He is a great flirt. Half – nay, *all* – of the eligible ladies in the county pursued him before he married.'

'Oh!' I tossed my head in vexation. 'He is *married*!'

'To a milk-and-water countess, the only daughter of the Earl of Roesworth in Buckinghamshire.'

'Are there brothers?'

'No.'

I leaned my elbows on the table and fixed Maria with a purposeful look. 'So is she heiress presumptive, or apparent?'

'Apparent. The succession was contested by some pinchbeck baronet, but the House decided in her favour.'

'Then she is in line for a substantial inheritance.'

'The estate is entailed in the absence of a son.'

'Has she children?'

'No. A daughter was stillborn; the travail nearly killed her, as it did her mother before her. She is a delicate creature, narrow in the hips. Women like her should never bear children.'

'Who stands to inherit if no son is forthcoming?'

'Her cousin. Sir Silas Sillery.'

At this I laughed heartily. 'It is a Flemish knot! I tell

you, Maria, I'd rather be Sir Silas's whore than his governess, for he has eight children.'

'Eight! No gentlewoman should be obliged to have charge of eight pupils. They should all be packed off to school, by law.'

I looked at the broken seal on the letter, which bore a double 'S' over a coat of arms. 'The laws of primogeniture are quite egregiously baffling,' I declared.

'Quite. Redress the balance, allow women to inherit, and all might go well with the world.'

Just then, Eilish put her head around the door and announced the arrival of Lady Charlotte.

'My sister!' said Maria. 'She must have stayed the night in town. Bid her come in, Eilish. And bring us tea.'

'Still in your morning gown, Maria!' remarked Lady Charlotte, as she swished into the room with her pug under her arm.

'Why should I change out of it, dear Charlotte,' retorted Maria, 'when I have nowhere to go, nor any inclination to gallivant? I am perfectly snug and well set up here in my own house.'

'As long as you have tenants to pay the rent.'

'I have plenty of tenants.'

'You'll find they'll renege,' said Lady Charlotte, 'if you allow the place to sink like a dilapidated ship. Have you done no repairs lately? The front door knocker came off in my hand, and I saw what I took to be a broom handle propping up the sash of the upper salon.' She turned to me with a compassionate smile. 'No wonder, my dear Miss Drury, you are anxious to find a situation. Did you receive a letter from Sir Silas?'

'Yes, this morning by messenger. Thank you, Your Ladyship, for your advocacy.'

'Pooh. Forget about Sir Silas and his brats. I have a better proposition for you.' She took a seat upon one of the spindle-backed chairs that flanked the table, and set the pug on the floor. 'I understand that all the fashionable ladies in London are engaging companions nowadays. None of your dowdy spinster-cousin charity cases, neither, but accomplished young ladies.'

I saw my opportunity, and grasped it at once. 'Oh, it is quite the done thing, Your Ladyship! A companion is as vital a necessity to a lady of fashion as is her reticule, or her lapdog! You will not see *any* modish gentlewoman in a public place without a smart companion in attendance.' I remembered what Maria had said the previous day, about the carriages lined up outside the church in Doneraile. 'Especially at church on Sundays.'

'In that case, I propose to take you on. Since my son left Doneraile Court for London I no longer have access to the intellectual stimulation his tutor used to afford me. We delighted in our tettatets, Mr Chummy and I, and I confess that I miss our lively games of piquet and backgammon.'

'I play both.'

'Do you play well?'

'Well enough, I hope, to match Your Ladyship,' I said. I had learned all manner of tricks from my father and his friends, but I did not wish to jeopardize any opportunity of advancement by revealing just how proficient I was.

'Then perhaps you will pay me the compliment of coming to live at Doneraile Court?'

'Where the hems of St Leger garments have been kissed for centuries,' snipped Maria.

'Oh, you!' snapped back Charlotte. 'Are you bitter, Mrs Sourpuss, because you cannot afford to engage a companion?'

'I am at liberty, Charlotte, to choose my friends and send them packing when they cease to amuse me. I have no need to purchase company.'

'And I wouldn't waste *my* money on the company you keep.'

Although the words were barbed, neither seemed to take much offence. I suppose that is the nature of sisterhood; I have had no experience of it.

Lady Charlotte turned back to me. 'I am to take tiffin with my friend Lady Fitzpatrick.' She consulted a silver-gilt watch. 'I shall come back and pick you up at three o'clock.'

'Will you not stay a while?' asked Maria. 'Eilish is bringing tea.'

'No. I promised Caroline all the news from last evening, and she talks so much I will barely have an opportunity to relay it if I don't get to her on time.' She rose from her chair and made for the door. 'I see *this* handle is in good repair. Perhaps you are not so deficient in housekeeping skills as I thought,' was her Parthian shot.

Maria resumed her seat. 'I noticed she didn't pay you the compliment of waiting for an answer to her charming request for company. If you accept her offer I hope you will teach her some manners; my sister takes for granted that everyone will do her bidding. I wish you could have told her to make herself scarce.'

'I am in no position to turn down employment,' I told her, 'and I'd rather be companion to your sister than governess to Sir Silas's litter of eight.'

'It will be nine soon, for I hear that Lady Sybil is *enceinte* again. It is because she *will* send her infants to a wet-nurse. If she nursed them herself, she should not conceive so quickly. It is a sure preventive, you know.'

At this, Eilish arrived with the tea. 'Mr Thackeray is without,' she announced, as she set the tray on the table, 'and wanting to speak with you.'

'Bid him come in,' said Maria.

William looked morose as Eilish showed him into the room. His neckcloth was dégagé, and he was unshaven. He had clearly spent another sleepless night watching over Isabella.

'Sit down, Mr Thackeray,' said Maria, 'and join us in a cup of tea. Or would you prefer beer?'

'Beer, if you please.'

'Bring us some beer, Eilish. We all three will have some, I think.'

The housemaid said, 'tch', and sloped off to fetch it. A glass of beer was a most welcome notion, following my abstemiousness of the previous evening when I had not allowed so much as a sip of champagne to pass my lips.

As William joined us at the table, a yelp rose from beneath it.

'What the deuce is that?' asked William.

'Oh, it is Charlotte's new pet,' said Maria, scooping the pug up from the floor. 'It will vex her that she has forgotten it, for I am sure she wanted to show it off to Lady Fitzpatrick.' In imitation of her sister, she assumed an autocratic voice. 'It is all the fashion, you know, to be seen in society with a lapdog.'

She sat the dog on her lap, where it assumed the stance of a constipated gargoyle. 'It will be one of your duties, I dare say, Eliza, to take the creature out twice a day to make sure it moves its little bowels.'

'One of your duties? What's this?' William turned a look of enquiry on me.

179

'I have been offered a situation as companion to Lady Charlotte.'

'Who is Lady Charlotte?'

'She is the wife of Hayes St Leger, Viscount Doneraile,' Maria told him, 'and I have the misfortune of being her sister.'

'And she lives here, in Cork?'

'She lives at Doneraile, a neighbourhood crowded with seats of the gentry, of which my brother-in-law's is the most conspicuous. It's a fine, handsome residence, Eliza. You will be very comfortable there.'

'Isabella's grandparents are from Doneraile. It's a market town, is it not?'

'It is a gentleman's village,' Maria told him, 'and the pleasantest place in Cork. Eliza could not have hoped for a better situation.'

'You are staying on in Ireland?' William asked me.

The way he looked at me reminded me of a moony messenger boy in Chiswick who had used to run errands for naught but the pleasure of being of service to me.

'Yes.'

Maria suddenly made a face, and sniffed at the dog on her lap.

'Pooh! It must want to do its business. Bad, smelly creature.' Holding the animal at arm's length, she rose to her feet and hastened from the room.

A silence descended between William and me. It

endured for a minute or more, until he said, 'How will I manage without you, Eliza?'

'You shall manage very well. You have done until now.'

'I never knew you until now. Until now, I didn't know that a woman could be my equal, my confidante.'

'Well, now you do,' I replied brusquely, keen to change the subject. 'How is Isabella?'

He shrugged, wearily. 'There has been no change. I must give up any notion of leaving her here in Cork, and get her to Paris somehow.'

'Why Paris?'

'There is a highly regarded *Maison de Santé* in Ivry, not far from the capital. It's not cheap.'

'What about the guidebook you came here to write?'

'I shall be obliged to put it on the long finger, as the Irish say. Isabella's health takes precedence over everything.'

'When do you go?'

'Tomorrow. You?'

'Lady Charlotte returns for me at three o'clock this afternoon.'

'So we shall not see each other again. This is . . . abrupt.'

'Yes.'

'I think there is no hour in the day has passed since I met you that I have not thought of you.'

'You stupid man!' I exclaimed. 'Stop this talk at once, for if you don't, I will never see you again. Never. And I *want* to be able to see you again, when you return to write your book.'

'That's not likely to happen, burdened as I am with responsibilities.'

'You must earn the advance the publishers paid you.'

He slumped back in his chair. 'It was a paltry sum,' he said, running a hand over his hair, 'and it is spent already.'

I had no idea of how much a writer might earn, and was curious to know. 'May I ask how much?'

'A hundred and twenty pounds.'

That was less than Mr O'Dowd's gold watch had fetched.

'How much might it earn for you when it is published?'

'I stand to make around four hundred pounds.'

'How many copies would you need to sell?'

'Over a thousand.'

I did some calculations. It struck me that four hundred pounds was unlikely to cover Isabella's medical expenses for a year. 'Your publishers distribute Mr Dickens's books?'

'They do.'

'How much does he earn?'

'I dare not speculate, for it would make me mad with envy. In one month he sold twenty thousand copies of *The Pickwick Papers*.'

'*Twenty thousand!* So literature has become a lucrative profession?'

'For those who succeed at it.'

'What does it take to succeed?'

'A commission for a serialized novel, to start off with. Readers are avid for them.'

A serialized novel . . . I thought of the journal I had kept intermittently over the years, its pages packed with tidbits of gossip. At Miss Pinkerton's my hand had been as pretty and fashionable as ever was found in the best finishing schools, but when I wrote in my journals, my thoughts ran so fast that my pen could scarcely keep up with them. There were notes and footnotes and scribbled marginalia on every quarter-inch of paper, scandalous goings-on recounted in detail, and the names on the memorandum page were catalogued in a code that only I could decipher, for they were those of the illustrious rogues who had frequented Soho to carouse with my father and his cronies, happy to pay for the privilege of drinking wine, smoking on narghiles and ogling beautiful models in artistic surroundings.

'You narrow your eyes,' observed William. 'What are you thinking?'

'I am thinking that I could become a writer. Miss Austen made a name for herself. Why shouldn't I?'

'Miss Austen did not have to keep herself.'

'No. But I would rather make my own way in the world than be dependent on the charity of my family, as she was. I could be a good woman if I had a thousand pounds a year.'

William laughed. 'A thousand pounds would set most people up very well for life. How much do you expect to earn in Lord Doneraile's establishment?'

I knew that poor Brodie was paid fourteen pounds a year to manage Isabella and her two children. Her board and lodging were *compris* of course, but as companion to Lady Charlotte I might earn two to three times that.

'A good deal less than His Lordship spends on his horses. I wonder what it is to be a country gentleman's wife?'

'I don't imagine you would find that to your taste, any more than you would living *en famille* as a spinster aunt.'

'I could dawdle about in the greenhouse, and count the apricots on the wall.'

'You could pick off dead leaves from the geraniums.'

'I could ask old women about their rheumatisms, and order half a crown's worth of soup for the poor. I could go to church and sleep behind my veil.'

We looked at each other and smiled.

'We would do well together, you and I,' said William.

Still we looked.

'Will you write to me, Eliza?'

'Yes.'

He leaned towards me, and just then Maria came hurtling back into the room.

'Help!' she cried. 'Charlotte's dog is after being scrawbed by the cat!'

The pug's eyes were so protuberant they looked as though they might pop out of its head, and beads of ruby blood were plopping onto the floor.

So we daubed its scratches with lint soaked in rose water, and rubbed brandy on its lips to calm it down, and then Eilish came with the beer and I gave another presentation of 'Sir Silas Sillery, Bart., Dancing the Allemand' for William's delectation.

12

WHEN EDIE WENT to take Milo for his constitutional that evening, she remembered Eliza's counsel to Lady Charlotte: *A companion is as vital a necessity to a lady of fashion as is her reticule, or her lapdog . . .*

'A lapdog, Milo! Is that what you are? You're small enough to be one, but I'm not sure you have the temperament. I've been thinking, you know,' she continued, as she watched him pootle around the stable yard, 'that sometimes, when I read Eliza's . . . *what* is it, Milo? It's not a journal, and "chronicle" doesn't sound right. And I can scarcely call it a memoir since I don't know for certain that it's a record of events that really happened. But then, I don't know if it's fiction, either. Isn't it funny? Sometimes I feel as if I've heard her voice before, or seen something in a book that sounds as though she might have said it. I could swear I've read about counting apricots on the wall and going to sleep behind a veil in church – I used to envy my grandmother because she was able to do just that.'

Milo snuffled off to investigate a patch of dandelions, and Edie followed him.

'Listen to me, rattling on! What would I do, if I didn't have you to talk to, little doggie? I should have to talk to myself, and then I'd be afraid that I might be going mad. But then, I guess I am a little spooked. I know I don't believe in ghosts and I know it's silly to even think of them, and I know that if Hilly were a ghost she'd be an awfully benign one. I mean, she'd never try to frighten me or anything. And the story that the girl in Doneraile Stores told was just stupid and pointless. But what if people really did die here? They must have done.'

Edie looked up at the moon. It was a little leaner than it had been on her first night at Prospect House, but the stars compensated for the attenuation, glittering up there in their millions.

'A million stars,' she said, 'a million dead, and a million gone overseas . . . Those poor people. How bloody, bloody wretched. It's just horrible to think that all that happened less than a hundred years ago. Just utterly horrible.'

Milo was looking at her winningly, ready to go back inside. She was glad they hadn't gone near the perimeter of the woods tonight. She knew that if they had, her eyes would have sought out shapes in the bosky shadows, and that most of them would have looked like the picture she had seen that morning in the cutting from the *Illustrated*

London News of 1847, of a mother and her children, haggard and clad in rags.

'Edie?' said Milo.

'What's up?'

'If you had to choose between kissing a gorilla and kissing a camel, which would you do?'

'What kind of a question's that?'

'I'm only trying to distract you,' said Milo. 'If you *had* to choose . . .'

But instead of allowing Milo to distract her with absurd hypotheses, Edie distracted herself by taking a hot-water bottle, a mug of cocoa and another chunk of the manuscript to bed with her.

⌣ E. D.

The elegant chimneys poking up above copses of oak, beech and sycamore alerted me to the profusion of stately homes around the pretty town of Doneraile. Maria had been right: this was a rich person's haunt, and Lord Doneraile owned most of it.

Her Ladyship had been most instructive throughout our journey. She had commented on every landmark we passed (had William been with us she would have made an invaluable consultant for his guidebook), and as we rumbled through the massive gates that opened onto the estate she told me – nodding her head graciously at the ancient who staggered out of the gate-lodge to kowtow to her – that this was the 'triumphal archway' built in 1820 to commemorate the coronation of George IV.

'Splendid hunting in these parts, you won't be surprised to know,' guffed Lord Doneraile.

We were bowling along an avenue flanked by parkland where sheep and cattle ruminated, and deer paused to gaze at us with startled eyes before springing away to take cover in the woods.

'See over there?' His Lordship indicated with the silver knob of his cane a stone wall surmounted by a hedge, with a deep ditch on the far side. 'Fellow cleared that last month, but came off two strides later and broke his neck.'

Because he looked as if this heroic failure deserved some kind of endorsement, I gave a bright smile to show how impressed I was.

A contingent of flunkeys awaited us on the steps of the perron. They looked as if they had been put in place by a giant hand, ranged against the imposing backdrop of Doneraile Court like painted characters in a pasteboard theatre. The great house comprised three storeys over a sunken basement, the entrance flanked by Ionic columns. The façade was elegantly proportioned and genuinely gracious – unlike that of the O'Dowds' parody of a Palladian mansion – with the St Leger coat of arms carved in Portland stone above the entrance.

'I think you will be quite comfortable here, Miss Drury,' pronounced Her Ladyship as a footman divested us of our travelling accoutrements. 'A maid will unpack for you. Dinner is at seven. Until then you are at liberty to roam wherever you please. You will find books aplenty in the library – we try to keep up with all the new novels – and there is a fine pianoforte in the music room. Do you play?'

'Yes.'

'You may entertain us after dinner.'

'Thank you. It is delightful to be at Doneraile Court. I could not have hoped for a more felicitous situation than here as companion to Your Ladyship.'

Lady Charlotte bestowed a gracious smile upon me.

'I shall be glad of your company, Miss Drury, especially in the winter, when the evenings are so long. Lord Doneraile spends all his time in London then, for he sits in the House.'

A bird – a thrush, I suppose, or a blackbird; I was not an expert on birdsong – was perched on the manicured tip of a box tree, trilling away.

'As it is such a beautiful evening,' I remarked, 'I think I shall take a stroll in the garden.'

'Do. The flower beds are not at their best at this time of the year, but our gardeners do what they can, and there is much to admire. Take Sooty with you. She needs exercise after being cooped up in the brougham.' Lady Charlotte thrust her pug at me and sailed off.

Sooty still smelt of the rose water Maria had daubed on her bloody nose. Together we stood for some minutes at the top of the steps, looking over the thousands of acres of parkland that belonged, by accident of ancestry, to one person. All this! Every blade of grass that grew on every sod of turf that comprised every hectare of countryside that had been tamed and prettified and planted with rare shrubs by generations of St Legers, or turned into arable or pastureland for their fat cattle to graze on: it all belonged to the spindle-shanked old man with whom I had driven here today. Every drop of water in the rivers and the fountains and the picturesquely cascading waterfalls and the man-made canals and the fish ponds that, Lady Charlotte had told me, were teeming with pike and trout, were his. Every stone that had been hewn to build gate-lodge and stables and outhouses and ornamental bridges and pavilions and gazebos and pleasure gardens, and the great Palladian mansion itself; every neighbouring townland through which the carriage had transported us – Ballyellis, Ballyandrew, Castlepook, Kilbrack, Carkerbeg, Ardgillibert, Ardadam, Carrigine – all, all belonged to Hayes St Leger, Viscount Doneraile.

How could this be right?

That evening after dinner I played and sang some new Schumann *lieder* for Lady Charlotte in the drawing room. She thought the songs were by Schubert, who had been dead for over ten years, but I did not presume to enlighten her. We talked a little of music and art and literature. Her favourite composer was Haydn ('because his music is so gladsome' – as good a reason as any, I suppose, to like a composer), her favourite artist was Sir Joshua Reynolds (he had done a portrait of some old ancestor of hers), and Sir Walter Scott (whose work I despised) was her favourite writer. She was, she told me, delighted at last to have a kindred spirit with whom to talk of culture and fashion and novels, and when I told her that my mother had composed for the opera, she declared that she would take pleasure in introducing me to her friends tomorrow at church.

I did not tell her that my mother's most famous composition had been a song entitled 'When Venus Roams by Eventide', which she had sung to popular acclaim at the *Théâtre des Variétés* in Montmartre, nor did I tell her that I had not been to church since I had been christened. Miss Pinkerton had required me to write weekly reports every Sunday for the students (insisting that those who came from the most well-to-do families were awarded 'O' for 'Optimus'), and because these works of fiction took the best part of the day to compose, I had remained behind at the academy while the other young ladies attended the service at St Nicholas's.

On the morrow, I would simply have to observe how my fellow churchgoers behaved, and do my best to emulate them.

The next morning, the small church of St Mary's, which had been built by the St Legers two hundred years previously, was crowded with gentlefolk clad in their Sunday finery: the blades in fancy waistcoats of silk and velvet; the young ladies in pretty dresses, beribboned and trinketed, like figures that had just stepped from the pages of a book of fashion.

I knew that the eyes of the congregation were upon me as I walked down the nave in the wake of Lady Charlotte. I knew, as I sat demurely in the great family pew of the St Legers, that the gentlemen assembled under that vaulted roof were inspecting me the way they had done since I was twelve years old: some in a knowing way, with narrowed eyes, some in a slippery way, as if afraid to be caught looking, and some agog, because they simply couldn't stop themselves. The expressions I saw when I raised my eyes after murmuring a devout 'Amen' made me want to laugh out loud, but because I knew that would be a scandalous thing to do in the house of God, I diverted myself by conjugating the Latin verbs I had used to scan of a Sunday in my previous life.

After the service the parishioners congregated outside the church: the ladies to exchange gossip and admire each other's dresses and parasols, the gentlemen to recount hunting anecdotes and talk politics. It was now the turn of the fairer sex to examine my figure. While at prayer under the watchful eye of the minister they had maintained a front of piety, but now they could look with impunity.

'May I present – ' began Lady Charlotte, and in the time it took for me to assume my most amiable expression, I was surrounded by a circle of rustling skirts and bobbing bonnets.

Somehow the story of my arrival in Ireland had become the stuff of local legend. It had percolated, I imagine, through the substrata of the servants' quarters last evening to the breakfast rooms of the gentry this morning, for I had taken care to let Lady Charlotte's housekeeper know that I was descended from a noble Gascony family, and that I had found myself in Ireland, an orphan all alone without a protector.

Dear Lady Charlotte! How charitable she was to take me in as her companion! What a pleasure it had been last night to sit together at the pianoforte and sing *lieder*! And why, yes, I had read Mr Dickens's *Nicholas Nickleby* – did they know that Queen Victoria had stayed awake until after midnight to finish it? – and I had devoured every instalment to date of *The Old Curiosity Shop*, but no! I would not reveal what became of little Nell and her unfortunate grandfather, no matter how they might plead! Yes – I *was* a tease!

The post-church ritual of simpering and preening for the delectation of the young bucks went on for some time. While keeping the full beam of my attention fixed on each sweet, silly face that importuned me for scandal from London, I had, like a raptor, kept my peripheral vision honed. There was Sir Silas, holding forth on some arcane subject to the clergyman who had bored us earlier, there was the stout, bald gentleman with the protruding teeth who had partnered me at the agricultural ball, there was Lord Doneraile honking about horses. I could, however, discern no sign of the only gentleman who had piqued my interest since arriving in Ireland.

What had led me to expect that he might be there? I suppose the fact that the church had been built by St Legers. I suppose because I thought his residence might be one of the many studded throughout this prosperous parish. I suppose because he was a cousin of my employer. I suppose, in the end, I had believed he might be there simply because I so wanted him to be.

Gradually the company dispersed: the young married ladies were driven off in smart phaetons by their husbands, the debutantes dutifully followed their mammas into the family landau. Lady Charlotte was engaged in earnest discussion with another dowager. As I approached them I overheard the word 'climacteric' and at once sought some pretext to make myself scarce.

'Lady Charlotte,' I ventured, 'I thought I might walk down to the shop on the main street to purchase some peppermint oil. May I bring you anything?'

'Oh, you are a thoughtful young person, Miss Drury! Some lavender oil, now that I think of it. I am having trouble sleeping at night.'

At this, Lady Charlotte's companion nodded sagely. I left them confabbing about night flushes, and set off towards the main thoroughfare of the pretty little town.

The maid who had brought me my hot water that morning had told me that Mr Shinnors's shop was the rendezvous for the neighbouring gentry at post time in the afternoon. It was also, she said, a favourite destination for officers garrisoned at nearby Buttevant, who liked to ride over in the hope of a romantic dalliance with a house- or dairymaid in the lower orchard. As it was Sunday, the shop would close at midday, and since I would have no call to visit it next week at post or any other time, I thought it worth my while to reconnoitre while I had the chance.

The shop stocked a miscellany of items: gloves, wine, spirits, soap, essences, tobacco, pocket handkerchiefs, good-quality beeswax candles. The interior was dim: a gentleman was there before me, his back to me. He had not heard me come in. He asked for snuff – the best they had. I listened to him banter with the shop girl, I watched the way he watched her when she turned to slide open a drawer, I saw his hand stray towards his privates, I inhaled a scent I remembered from the night I had lain on a bed, gagged by his neckcloth, with his hand on my throat . . . I made for the door, pressing my handkerchief to my mouth.

Before I could reach it, another gentleman entered the shop. His tall frame in the doorway made escape from the confined space impossible.

'Why, Miss Drury!' said Jameson St Leger. 'Whatever is the matter? Are you not well?'

At the counter, Mr O'Dowd turned to see what was happening.

It was an instance of *pis aller*. I had never before played the card which so many ladies keep concealed under the lace edgings of their sleeves, but it was finally time to resort to that threadbare feminine trick. I fainted.

Mr St Leger took charge at once. 'Prop the door open,' I heard him say. 'Quickly! The window, too. Clear a space – remove yourself, sir, if you would be so kind.'

I heard the rap of a cane against the floorboards, felt them shift beneath me at his heavy egress. From between my eyelashes I saw the shadowy bulk of my rapist leave the premises.

'Have you salts?' St Leger asked the shop girl.

'Yes, Your Honour,' she said, 'I'll fetch a bottle right away, Your Honour.'

I continued to lie there, waiting for the bile that had risen in my gorge to subside, and for my thoughts to order themselves. Had Mr O'Dowd recognized me? I had taken care to keep my face averted, but he had heard my name called, glimpsed the silk moiré that his wife had used to wear. He had undoubtedly missed the watch: it would have been easy for him to apprehend me just now, and have me arraigned for larceny. But perhaps he had chosen not to know me? Perhaps he was fearful that I would bring a charge against him? Unlikely, as such a charge would never stick. What hope had I, his erstwhile servant, against a man of his standing in a court of law?

Whether he had recognized me or not was a matter of indifference to me, I realized. I was glad not to have to look him in the face again, glad to be beyond reach of his loathsome touch. I heard the jingle of harness outside and a ribald laugh as he exchanged some jest with his coachman, and hated him anew. The odious Pether shouted *Gee-up!* and as the vehicle took off, I hoped passionately that it would end up in a ditch between here and the city.

I felt a hand on my brow; a finger smoothed a tendril of hair away from my cheek, brushing the edge of my ear as it did. I felt St Leger's breath on my skin as he brought his face closer to mine, smelt the subtle scent of leather and soap, heard his low voice enquire if I could hear him.

I was uncertain how long I should maintain this masquerade. How long might a swoon endure? Two minutes? Three? However, once the phial was held to my nose I had no choice but to revive, for the vile and pungent odour of *sal volatile* was an assault.

I opened my eyes, fluttered my lashes briefly, and made a vain attempt to bat the bottle away; but St Leger took hold of my wrist and kept the phial in place until I sneezed, rather indelicately.

'I'm quite well,' I told him, trying to reclaim my hand.

His grip was unyielding. 'You must keep still,' he said. 'Any sudden agitation could bring a rush of blood to the head.'

He took my handkerchief from me and wiped my nose.

'Leave me alone!' I cried in affront. 'I'm perfectly well, now that I can breathe again.'

It *was* a relief to breathe without the stench of that beast O'Dowd clogging my throat. I would have preferred to inhale *sal volatile* for the rest of my life than be obliged to share the atmosphere with that man.

The shop girl had hunkered down beside me and was starting to pull at the bodice of my dress.

'What are you *doing*?' I snapped.

'I'm loosening your clothing, ma'am.'

'An excellent notion,' observed St Leger. 'You are perspicacity personified, young Florrie.'

'Thank you for your concern,' I said, brushing dust from my skirt, 'but there is no need to go to such lengths. I came here for peppermint oil: that will clear my head.'

The shop girl bustled back to her place behind the counter, and consulted the labels on a row of small bottles. 'Peppermint oil is just the thing, ma'am,' she agreed. 'It will see you rightly if you dab it on your handkerchief.'

'And lavender oil too, for Viscountess Doneraile,' I said, extending my hand to St Leger so that he could help me to my feet.

'You are here with my cousin's wife?' he asked in some surprise.

'I am,' I told him, raising my chin. 'I am living at Doneraile Court, as her companion.'

I looked at him levelly, my hand still in his. And even as Florrie set the packages on the counter and stood meekly waiting for payment, he seemed reluctant to let it go.

*

For several weeks thereafter Jameson St Leger made a habit of visiting Doneraile Court on the slightest pretext, to stalk me as I imagine a hunter stalks . . . I would have said a fox, but that analogy is not quite right. I fancied myself a rather more elusive quarry, mercurial as one of Diana's dryads.

I was dallying in the lime tree walk one evening when he 'happened' upon me, as he often did at this hour. Together we strolled towards the summerhouse, a jewel box of a folly that Lady Charlotte had had copied from a book of Persian gardens and in which it was her fond fantasy to lounge upon a sofa taking tea as the memsahibs did in India.

Unfortunately, the vagaries of the Irish weather had not allowed her to indulge in this ritual on a routine basis. Cook had told me that after completion of the structure, tea had been served there but once, by footmen who had stood apart under umbrellas while Her Ladyship had sat beneath the fluted roof with rain pelting tinnily down. When a fork of lightning had struck perilously close to the ornamental cupola, Her Ladyship had retreated unceremoniously to her boudoir to take tea there instead. The little summerhouse had languished like a child's derelict playhouse ever since.

As I preceded St Leger through the Byzantine archway, I noticed that the ribbon on my shoe had come loose. I made a little moue and 'Alas,' I said, raising the hem of my gown a bare inch, and arching my foot prettily in the way Monsieur Cabriole had taught me as a prelude to a *pas de bourée*.

'Allow me,' St Leger said, effecting a low bow.

But instead of retying the ribbon, he slid my shoe off and trailed a finger along my instep.

Smiling, I raised the hem of my gown another inch, wondering whether I should draw it above the ankle to allow him a glimpse of my well-turned calf.

That was not necessary. An inch was all it took.

13

THE FOLLOWING MORNING after breakfast Edie poured herself a fresh cup of tea, shambled through to the library in her slippers, and opened the shutters to allow in the morning light. The picture postcards she had bought yesterday were lying on the window seat; one was of Doneraile Court. It was a big, imposing block of a mansion, with seven bays, numerous windows and a great roof beneath which there was ample attic space to accommodate a battalion of servants. The blurb on the back read, 'Seat of the St Leger family; built *c.*1725 by the second Viscount Doneraile.' So Eliza had lived in the Big House just five miles down the road! How had her belongings ended up here, at Prospect House?

Sitting down at the writing desk between the two windows, Edie reached for the pile of legal documents that she had been trying to put into some semblance of order, so that Uncle Jack could go through them. She ran her eyes over a survey for Prospect House commissioned in 1885.

Except it hadn't been called Prospect House then. It had been called by an Irish name – Lissaguirra. That's when the place had been bought by a member of the Frobisher family, some antecedent of Uncle Jack's, and the name changed: there was the certification dated, stamped and registered to a P. Frobisher, Esq.

The land immediately surrounding the house was estimated to comprise '2 acres, 3 roods, 6 perch, or thereabouts', plus fishing rights. In a column headed 'Observations' on a yellowing document from the Valuation Office, the following legend had been written in a clerk's careful hand: 'Value reduced one half for extreme remoteness of situation: dwelling is approached by a bridle path 1/2 mile away from a very bad road.' It made the house sound like an end-of-sale bargain, or something left over from a jumble sale. Edie trusted it would fetch a decent price for Uncle Jack, now that the new road had been built and the place was more accessible.

There were no records dating back earlier than the 1885 survey. But the house had been built more than forty years before that; there was the date to prove it, carved into the shutter of the library window with its wreath of oak leaves surmounted by an ace of spades: 1841.

Edie stood up from the desk, stretched, pulled her hair into a scrappy ponytail and secured it with an elastic band. She hadn't washed it since she'd come here, because the plumbing was too primitive. The bathroom was in an annexe partitioned off from the master bedroom, and the bath was a great antiquated beast on clawed feet that had probably been put in by the first Frobisher. It took hours to fill so – apart from one piddling lukewarm bath an inch deep – Edie had limited her washing to a swipe or two with a flannel in cold water at the washstand in her bedroom. She would adore to soak in a really luxurious bath, with bubbles and a book and a box of chocolates. In a hotel, perhaps, with a lover waiting for her on a balcony, over-looking the sea somewhere with hot blue skies. Maybe Ian had the right idea, dallying in a deluxe hotel in Deauville.

But could a sea view beat this one? The sun was dancing diamantine on the lake, and a pair of swans had drifted in from their nest in a reed bed. They were residents: Edie had seen them earlier in the week when she had strolled down there with Milo. He had eyed them suspiciously and made the occasional feinting lunge at them, but the swans had just given him a disdainful look and sailed on.

'Listen!' Milo said now, pricking up his ears and frowning. 'There's someone in the house.'

Edie froze. Milo was right: someone had come in through the kitchen door. She could hear the scraping noise it made against the tiled floor.

'Hello!' called the person. 'Is anyone in?'

It was a man's voice.

Milo immediately jumped down from the footstool he had been sitting on, and trotted out of the room going

'Grrrr'. Edie wrapped her dressing gown tighter around her, secured the knot, and followed her intrepid hound on rather more cautious feet.

The man in the kitchen was big, bluff and florid, nattily got up in a double-breasted suit and a paisley-patterned bow tie. He doffed his hat as Edie stepped into the room and said, 'Good morning! Miss Chadwick, I presume? I'm pleased to meet you. Francis Quilligan of Quilligan & Quilligan Auctioneers and Valuers.'

'How do you do?' said Edie, taking his proffered hand.

'I'm sorry to arrive unheralded like this, but there was no way of letting you know I was coming. *Aire Puist agus Telegrafa* haven't got this far yet.'

'I beg your pardon?'

'Posts and Telegraphs.'

'Oh, don't worry, I'm perfectly happy without a telephone. There's one at the crossroads if I need to make a call.'

Edie was aware how disreputable she must look in contrast to Mr Quilligan, in her slippers and candlewick robe that had paw prints all over it and a jam stain on the lapel.

'Will you have a cup of tea, Mr Quilligan?' she asked, trying to appear as gracious as if she were decked out in a hostess gown.

'If it's no trouble.'

'No trouble at all. Please take a seat. I'd ask you into the drawing room, but everything's such a mess in there with

206

the packing cases and everything, and it's warmer here in the kitchen.'

'The heart of the home!'

Pinning on a smile, Edie set about putting fresh water on to boil and transferring milk from the bottle she had left by the sink into a jug. Her mother would have been appalled to think she had been pouring milk into her tea straight from the bottle!

'Ginger nut!' she said, reaching for the packet, then felt a rush of discomfiture because Mr Quilligan had such quantities of tufty carroty hair. 'I mean, would you like a Ginger Nut biscuit?' she amended.

'My favourites!'

'Mine too!'

Once the tea things were organized and she and Mr Quilligan had exchanged pleasantries about biscuits and the weather, Edie sat down opposite him at the kitchen table.

'I just dropped by to tell you that I have an interested party coming to have a look around,' he said.

'So soon! Goodness! The place is in an awful state.'

'Don't worry. Whoever buys it isn't going to be concerned about dust on the picture frames. Have you seen the advertisement?'

'No.'

'I'll put one in the post to you. Anyways, you seem to be doing a great job here, more power to you. I saw a pile of junk in the stable on my way in – I'll organize someone to take it to the dump for you.'

'Thank you. I've sorted the sheep from the goats, as it were, and stored anything that might be worth a few bob in the drawing room – apart from the heavier items of furniture, of course.'

'Find anything interesting?'

'Yes – masses! There are some ripping clothes that must be at least a century old, and some press cuttings and journals and things.'

Mr Quilligan looked unimpressed. 'Any accredited documents?'

'A few official-looking things. I should probably let you have a look at those. Old Land Registry maps and records from the Valuation Office and suchlike. I suppose Uncle Jack – Mr Frobisher – has all the important stuff.'

'He'll have copies, anyway. The originals were all destroyed in the War of Independence.'

Edie's bemused expression must have betrayed her lamentable ignorance of political history, because Mr Quilligan went on to explain:

'The National Archives were housed in the Four Courts in Dublin during the rising. Record books dating back centuries were used in the barricades and blown up – Lissaguirra's among them.'

'Goodness.' She humbly proffered another Ginger Nut. 'You call the house by its old name?'

'Out of habit. But Prospect View is the name on the advertisement.'

'Who lived here originally, back in the 1840s?'

'One of the St Legers was said to have built it.'

'I'd love to know more. There's . . . an atmosphere.'

'So you've seen the ghost?'

'What ghost?'

'A little joke!' said Mr Quilligan with an unconvincing laugh. 'Everyone has a story about the place. Little girls in nightdresses and old ladies in evening gowns and phantom horsemen: sure the woods are coming down with them, if you were to credit half the tales that are told.'

Edie did not want to hear about more spooky shenanigans. 'Will you have another cup of tea?' she asked.

'No, thank you kindly, Miss Chadwick. I'd best be off. I just dropped in to warn you, so I did, about the gentleman that will be calling to view the property.'

'Thank you. I'll do what I can to smarten the place up.'

'As I said, there's no need. The same gentleman'll not want to be holding garden parties here.' Mr Quilligan rose to his feet.

'Grrr,' said Milo.

'Arra why would you be worrying about ghosts?' he said with a laugh. 'Isn't that a grand little guard dog you have there? Good day to you, Miss Chadwick.'

'Good day, Mr Quilligan.'

Edie watched as he crossed the stable yard and got into

a shiny green Austin. He tooted his horn as he started the ignition, and then he was gone, leaving Edie alone with Milo and Eliza Drury.

⌒ E. D.

As I had often observed to William when he was in a funk, good humour may be said to be one of the very best articles of dress one can wear in society. In the months that followed my arrival at Doneraile Court I sang, I played, I laughed, I conjured gaiety from the simplest things, and Lady Charlotte and her pug, Sooty, soon learned to love me. I organized *conversazioni*; I devised theatricals and parlour games; I marshalled wassailers at Christmas time, and staged a masque for St Valentine's Day. I enticed everybody from society to the house, and I made Her Ladyship believe that it was her graciousness and wit that gathered the beau monde of North Cork about her.

At dinners, ancient, doughty warriors exhausted me with tales of battles and victories at Waterloo, self-described wags made my face ache and learned lords fascinated me with soliloquies from Shakespeare; at dances, cavaliers abducted me, and dashed me around the floor like winged Mercuries; at musical evenings I might listen to a lament honked on the national bagpipe, or an Irish folk melody scratched upon a fiddle. Sometimes I was obliged to accompany divertimenti from *William Tell* or *The Barber of Seville* while milady played the harp, and on one occasion I was quite unable to hold back the tears as a debutante sang an aria from last season by one of the most *en vogue* London composers.

St Leger came often, sometimes riding alone on his gallant chestnut hunter, sometimes with his wife in the phaeton, or the landau when it rained. Her name was Sophia; she was frail-looking, with dun-coloured hair and pale eyelashes. She spoke seldom, and declined all invitations to join in games. It seemed to me that she did not like to laugh. Maria had told me that she resented having been plucked from her father's mansion in Buckinghamshire and set down to live among the barbarous Irish beyond the Pale. She had met St Leger while on a visit to the County Cork estate of her cousin, Sir Silas Sillery, but had not expected that her spouse would have chosen to spend more time on his Irish demesne – where he could ride from dawn until dusk – than at their London town house.

Sequestered with her one day when her husband had come to speak to Lord Doneraile on some equestrian matter, I asked what pastimes gave her most pleasure. She enjoyed needlework, she told me, showing me the exquisite piece of embroidery in her hands. In

211

lustrous silks, and with tiny, couched stitches, she had worked a tree upon which flowers in jewel-like colours bloomed, and strange fruits glowed. A motto, half finished, read *Fais ce que* . . .

'It is beautiful,' I told her.

'Thank you. It depicts the tree of knowledge. It is for a fire screen.'

'How will the motto read, when it is finished?' I asked, expecting her answer to be some housewifely homily or facile epigram.

'*Fais ce que tu voudras*,' she told me.

'Do as you please?'

'Yes. It was a motto coined by one of St Leger's ancestors. A member of the Hell-Fire Club.'

I saw now, half concealed by the foliage of the tree, a serpent within its branches, its eyes worked in silver thread.

'It is remarkably fine,' I said, as I returned it to her.

'It gives me great pleasure.'

What other talents had she? I enquired.

'I have none of your accomplishments, Miss Drury,' she replied. 'The tranquil *andante* of our country life seems to have transformed itself since your arrival into an *allegro vivace*.'

I plucked at the musical reference.

Did she sing? No. Play? Yes – the piano, a little. She started to work the downward stroke of the '*t*' in '*tu*'. Did she ride to hounds? Oh, no! Did she draw? No. Did she read? No. Did she not like to read with her husband after dinner? Reaching for another skein of silk, she gave a little shrug. After dinner, she generally left her husband to his cigars and brandy and retired to the drawing room where she was content to be alone with her embroidery. Although, she added, executing a series of precise stitches, sometimes she wished that she had a little companion to sit by her in the evening.

'A dog?' I asked.

The look she gave me with her silver eyes made me amend my conjecture.

'A child,' I said.

We sat in silence for a while, then: Did she hope for a son? I ventured to enquire.

Yes, but she had been told it was not God's will to grant her any children.

She dug the needle into the canvas as she said this, and bit down on her lip. Then she said an astonishing thing.

'I would swear to abandon Him, if there was a way for me to present my husband with a son.' The emphasis she put on the pronoun made me deduce that she meant God, and not St Leger.

From the pavement beyond the Venetian window, I heard Lady Charlotte calling me. I rose to fetch Sooty for her walk, and glanced down at Sophia's head bowed over the embroidery frame. I would have felt sorry for her, had I not been conducting an intimate intrigue with her husband.

Suddenly Sophia looked at me from under her sparse lashes. Without breaking eye contact, she reached for a little cloisonné thimble. Then she held it at arm's length, opened her fingers and cast it upon the floor. It skidded across the marquetry and ended up under a console table. 'How clumsy of me,' she said, regarding me pointedly.

I rose, and as I went to pick it up I thought very fast and very hard. St Leger and I had been circumspect. For us there was no groping or fumbling against a tree trunk in the lower orchard, or rolling in the hay in Nugent's field. Instead, I had found a way of admitting him to my apartment at the dressing hour for a *rendez-vous galant*. I knew that my way to St Leger's heart lay in civilized seduction – the type he may have encountered among the *poules de luxe* in Paris or London, but to that I added a little humour, a little comradeship, a little repartee. We were well matched.

But I had not factored Sophia St Leger into the equation. I had never dreamed that she would prove to be more than just a cumber-ground. I had made that most elementary mistake: I had underestimated my opponent.

'Attend.'

Sophia's voice stayed me as I was on my knees, fishing for the thimble under the table. It was authoritative; a command rather than a plea. Steeling myself against invective, I turned. She had set aside her needle-work and was sitting very upright and composed, her hands folded in her lap.

'I have a proposal for you,' she said.

14

My dear Eliza,

I have something stupid and ridiculous to impart. Foolish as ever, I am writing to you instead of telling you this, which I should have done the last time I saw you, in Mrs Fagan's house in Cork.

I am in love with you. I thought I would cure myself by seeing you quite simply as a friend, and then I thought my feelings would abate when we said our farewells. I know, Eliza, that you will say, 'Oh! Another fellow who has become a nuisance' (for I am sure I am not the first to have fallen in love with you). But I beg of you, if you intend to say you doubt the truth of what I am writing, then I had rather you did not answer me at all. I dare say I have nothing to hope for in imparting this. But I know that you are kind, and I put my trust in you, not as a mistress, but as a frank and loyal comrade.

William Thackeray

My dear William,
I am replying to your letter, not because I doubt the truth of what you write, but because I know all too well how you feel, and I must – <u>must</u> – tell you that you cannot express such sentiments again, because I do not want to lose a friend.

Please write a more cogent letter. I should like to hear news of you and Isabella and Brodie, and Annie, of course. Tell her that a horse very like Bucephalus comes galloping by here every now and then.

Eliza Drury

PS: Please send news from Paris of what the fashionables are wearing. <u>This is very important as I need to keep the ladies here informed and up to date</u>. Also, tidbits from Galignani's Messenger, *and a list of all the new novels.*

~

My dear & ever-valued friend,
You are right. If ever I write such sentimental balderdash to you again, please take no notice. I am heartily sick of myself. I want simply your friendship and respect more than anything else in the world. From now on, I shall write only with news, and with some sketches diligently copied from the latest book of fashion. Tell your North Corkoniennes

that it is de rigueur in Paris to wear pineapples on the head, to carry little piglets instead of pugs, and to wear very high pattens indoors.

I am living with my parents on the Avenue Sainte Marie. Isabella is now installed in the Maison de Santé of which I spoke. She has become more docile; less silly, talkative and excitable and less prone to the hysteria that makes her mad. I visit her often, and I did begin to think we were at last to have her well, but I was discouraged latterly when I saw some fierce wild women rambling in the gardens there. I do not want her to associate with mad women. I am planning to take her to a sanatorium in Germany for hydrosud therapy, which might prove to be the great remedy for which we have been searching. I confess that I feel old, very old, and sad.

The fees at Ivry are twenty pounds a month. I embarked on this journey with just that sum to my name, and am now at a loss as to how I will manage. I can no longer scrape by on bits and pieces of newspaper work – I am writing for my life. If I could find time to start on my great novel, I tell myself that all would be well! Perhaps I will find inspiration in Ireland. I am determined to go back there, not just to fulfil my financial obligation to Messrs Chapman & Hall, but to see you, my dear _friend_.

Your own wretched W.T.

My dear William,

A lady of my acquaintance in the county Cork travelled to a convent in Marienbad to undergo the therapy you mention, for it is very much in vogue. This is how it went for her: she was roused at five in the morning and rolled in blankets like Cleopatra in her rug. Once unrolled, she had gallons of icy water flung over her. Then she was rolled up again, then sluiced with more water, & so forth & so forth. If you think that journeying all the way to the Rhine to see a quack who will subject your poor wife to such treatment is an act of altruism, then 'Good luck to your honour'.

When are you coming to Ireland? If you are decided on a spree, I should love to accompany you.

Your friend,

Eliza Drury

15

Of the many diversions and festivities I organized for Lady Charlotte in the first months of that year eighteen hundred and forty-one, the most ambitious was a treasure hunt, to celebrate her birthday. Some two dozen local gentry were invited. Having engineered the event I was, of course, ineligible to compete, and had to sit the hunt out. And because St Leger had sustained an unfortunate sprain to his ankle, he elected to keep me company.

Together we observed the goings-on from one of the ornamental gazebos that studded the grounds of Doneraile Park. From our vantage point on a hillock we could see the gentlefolk scampering towards the lime tree walk where the first clue was hidden, and hear their distant squawks: from their perspective below we must have looked like a pair of birds in a latticework cage, sitting side by side on a filigree'd perch.

I knew the treasure hunt would take two hours or

more to complete, for I had laid the trail over several acres of parkland, and contrived to make it fiendishly difficult, culminating as it did in a boxwood maze. Until the victor returned, St Leger and I had plenty of time to ourselves. I had packed a basket with fruit, lemonade, quails' eggs, some bread and cheese, and my sketch-book, to make a pictorial record of the pastorale.

'Where do you stay, when you go off hunting for days at a time?' I asked St Leger, as I shaded in the bole of an oak tree with my pencil. 'Sophia tells me that you keep the location secret from her.'

He looked surprised. 'You and my wife are Christian-naming each other?'

'We have become quite good friends.' That was a lie. Sophia and I would never be friends, but between us we had come to an arrangement that promised to be to our mutual benefit. I dimpled up at him. 'Where is this place? Is it an inn?'

'No. It is a bothy. It lies some half-dozen miles from here, on the shores of Loch Liath.'

'Whatever is a bothy?'

'A bothy is a . . . type of dwelling. I built it myself with the help of my ghillie and some stout men.'

'What's a ghillie?'

'Oh, you are too sophisticated, Eliza! A ghillie is a guide for hunting or fishing. A local man who's skilled in tracking and other country lore.'

'What made you decide to build this bothy?'

'We were on a hunt one day – '

'What were you hunting?'

'Wolves.'

'Liar. There have been no wolves in the British Isles for a hundred years.'

'They were roaming wild here in Ireland more recently than that. You'll find that the skin of a great grey is more efficient than a quilt at night for keeping the cold at bay.'

'You have a wolfskin on your bed?'

'I do.' He gave a smile that made me want to pull his hair and kiss him, but because we were in view of all at large, I resisted. 'I like to picture you as Diana, goddess of the hunt,' he continued, 'supine across my bed on a spread of fur. Perhaps I should commission an artist to paint you like that.'

He took a grape between thumb and forefinger, and slid it into my mouth. It ruptured against my tongue in a burst of sweetness.

'Back to the bothy,' I said. 'I want to know more about it.'

'What has you so intrigued?'

'Everything about you intrigues me, St Leger.'

'It is an interesting story,' he said, adopting the authoritative stance so beloved by men when they have a tale to tell: arms folded, one foot set forward. 'Because the roads between here and the lake are impassable in bad weather, we decided to build a shelter where we might lay our heads for a night or two, rather than make the journey there and back in a single day. A place where we could roast a rabbit and down a few flagons of wine after a day spent fishing. We scoured the country-side for weeks to find the best location, and when we couldn't fix on one, we agreed to build where the first hare got up.'

'And you did?'

'We did. "Build," said O'Looney – he is the ghillie, and quite a character – "Build," he said, "where the first hare stands."'

'It was that arbitrary?'

'It was. And I was in luck. Lord Abingdon, who owns the land thereabouts, was amenable to selling me a parcel of forest for next to nothing.'

'What did you build?' I pictured a pavilion, or a cot-tage in the style of Marie Antoinette's Petit Trianon.

'A cabin, with a fine thatch to protect us from the rain.'

'A thatch?'

'A thatch is – ' he began, patiently.

'Oh, I know what a thatch is!' I said, trying not to sound disgusted.

Below, the Grove-Whites emerged from the lime tree walk, and waved up at us. Mrs Grove-White had a scroll in her hand: the first clue in the treasure hunt. There were twelve clues in all: I still had plenty of time. I turned a page of my sketchbook and began a new drawing.

'We have added more rooms since,' continued St Leger. 'It is a fine edifice now, with a flagged floor and stone and mortar walls. There is a spring nearby; we plan to dig a well.'

'How many rooms?'

'Four good-sized ones. And there is a lean-to kitchen, and splendid views over Loch Liath. We felled two dozen trees to make the lakeshore accessible.'

'Is there land attached?' I asked idly, pencilling in a little figure of Mrs Grove-White in her poke bonnet.

'Two acres.'

Two acres, with access to hunting and fishing with a fine view and potable water . . . It was time to reveal my hand.

'Would it do for my accouchement?'

His back was to me. From between my eyelashes, I saw his shoulders tense.

'Accouchement?'

'It's a French word. It means "lying in".'

'I know what it means!' He turned to me with a hard face. 'You're with child?'

'Yes.'

'How long have you known?'

'Long enough to be sure that I am carrying a boy.'

Anticipating pause for thought, I set down my sketchbook, rose to my feet and eased myself into a lazy stretch.

'A boy? How can you be sure?'

'Wise women can foretell such things. An *accoucheuse* in Soho showed me how to predict the sex of an unborn child.'

'I don't believe old wives' tales,' he said.

'Believe what you like, St Leger,' I said, giving him a Giaconda smile as I moved to the table. 'You believe an eccentric old ghillie who tells you to build a house where the first hare stands.'

He looked away from me, and fixed his gaze on a herd of deer grazing in the parkland.

'What did you do to – what makes you think it is a boy?'

'I took a hair from the head of a woman heavy with child and suspended from it a blown duck egg. Then I held it perpendicular to my belly. It swung to the left. Had it swung the other way, I would not be telling you this, for that signifies a girl.' Breaking a bread roll, I discarded the doughy interior and bit into the crust. 'See? For the past two months I have eaten only the crust of the loaf. Another sure sign that I am carrying a boy.'

I had learned nothing from any wise old *accoucheuse*, but I had learned many lessons from the models who had used to sit for my father. Among the most useful was that, when it came to matters concerning the bearing of children, you could bamboozle a man with any old flim-flam. I had no better idea than St Leger of the gender of the child I was carrying, but until it was born I would allow him to believe I did. I was playing a game of chance for very high stakes.

St Leger was watching me with a kind of bemused fascination. 'Sophia ate only the soft white portion of her bread rolls.'

'And she produced a dead daughter. Worthless to an estate that is, in default of a son, entailed to a dissolute cousin.' I bit the crust again, for emphasis. 'This boy is yours, St Leger. He is yours and Sophia's to take and rear as your own.'

'What are you saying?'

'I am carrying your heir – if you want him.' Resuming my seat on the wrought-iron bench, I picked up my sketchbook and pencil. 'It's not unheard of, when a wife has trouble conceiving, for another woman to bear a child for her. It's been done covertly countless times. We are the resourceful sex.'

'You are insane, Eliza.'

I gave him an arch look. 'Then so are any number of women. Even queens have been known to feign pregnancy, and at least one prince has been born by proxy. Everyone knows that the Jacobite king was smuggled into the royal birth chamber in a warming pan.'

He shook his head in bewilderment. 'This is madness. Sophia would never agree to it.'

'She already has.' I almost laughed at the expression on his face. 'Sophia and I had a long discourse. Women can be allies, you know, if it is to their mutual advantage.'

To buy time, St Leger moved away and made a show of perusing the picnic basket. He helped himself to a quail's egg, peeled it and dipped it in celery salt.

'I've heard that Irish women get up to all kinds of tricks with newborns,' I continued smoothly. 'Changeling children! That's clever – to blame it on the faeries.'

Abruptly, he turned back to me. 'What is the benefit to you, Eliza?' he asked.

I had been expecting this question, and knew that the best way of parrying it would be to dispense with prevarication. 'It's perfectly uncomplicated,' I said. 'I shall expect you to provide me with a home and an income.'

'Don't be stupid.'

This, too, I had anticipated. I made a little moue. '*Dommage*. Sophia will be disappointed. I'm sorry, St Leger. I had thought this proposal would meet with a more exuberant response.'

I held up my pencil to measure perspective. I

suppose he had expected me to weep or plead or sulk, and when instead I went back to my drawing he looked so baffled I almost felt sorry for him. 'What will you do now?' he asked.

'Now? Oh, I will abort.'

He flinched. 'How?'

'Mushrooms, wormwood, saffron, hyssop, tansy – any manner of herbs, so long as they're prepared by a woman who knows what she's doing.' With a few deft strokes, I captured a wood pigeon in flight. Then: 'Oops – I forgot,' I added with mock contrition. 'You set no store by old wives' tales.'

'Where . . . where will you find such a woman?'

'Alas, I must return to London. If the miscarriage does not come on, there is always the Foundling Hospital in Bloomsbury.'

That shook him, as I had known it would.

'Don't, Eliza,' he said.

'Don't what? Abort? Or consign the child to the poorhouse?'

'Do neither.'

'Then what do you suggest?'

'Rear him yourself. I will furnish you with an allowance – '

'I don't want him. But you do. You want an heir, St Leger, and with a little connivance and cooperation, I shall be happy to give you one. If we keep it between us

228

three – you, me and Sophia – no one will ever know that the child is not legitimate.'

Down by the lake, Mrs Grove-White was leaning into the reeds, manfully pulling another scroll from the swan's nest where I had concealed it. A pair of the outraged birds were speeding towards her, like galleons in full sail, hissing vociferously.

'A home. Is that what you said?'

'And an income,' I reminded him.

'A home, and an income.'

'Yes,' I said, putting an 'O' for Mrs Grove-White's mouth as her bonnet went scooting across the lake.

I heard him sigh. 'So that is why you quizzed me about the bothy. I thought it strange.'

'I don't want a *bothy*, St Leger.' I invested the word with scorn. 'I want the present structure turned into a house, with stairs. I want an upper storey, and four more rooms, and I want a porch, and a pavemented terrace.'

'Be reasonable, Eliza. It's perfectly adequate as it is – sturdy and weatherproof.'

He made it sound like a pair of clogs.

'Oh, joy! I can keep hens, and pigs in the parlour and invite the neighbours in from time to time to swig poitín and dance a few jigs. That sounds mighty bucolic, Mr St Leger, but it is no place for a lady.'

He gave me a challenging look. I gave it right back.

'For that is what I am,' I said, 'and I want a lady's

residence, properly appointed. Don't tell me you can't afford it.'

He allowed his eyes to travel over my form. They came to rest on my belly.

'What if the child is a girl?'

I gave a baroque shrug. '*Les jeux sont faits*, St Leger. I would stake my life on it being a boy, but there's no knowing what your meddlesome Irish faeries might do. Either way, *rien ne va plus*.' A shriek from below diverted my attention once again to the treasure hunt. Mrs Grove-White's bonnet was being carried aloft by a triumphant cob. I waved brightly at her, then went to the table, picked up the grape scissors and helped myself to a cluster of the fruit. 'If you are agreeable, I'd like to inspect the property and engage an architect before your lawyers draw up the conveyance. Once the deeds have been signed over to me, we have a contract.'

I saw the muscles clench along the line of his jaw.

'Beggars can't be choosers,' he said, without conviction.

'I am not a beggar, St Leger.' I tossed a grape at him and smiled sweetly. 'And unless you want your wife's fortune to pass to her cousin, you are in no position to choose.'

16

THE FOLLOWING DAY, a letter arrived in the post for Edie bearing a fancy logotype:

Quilligan & Quilligan
Auctioneers and Valuers, Est. 1898.

Dear Miss Chadwick,
Unfortunately I have been unable to arrange a definite date with our client, Mr O'Brien, to view the property. I hope it will not inconvenience you if he arrives unannounced.
Please find enclosed our advertisement, as promised.
Thanking you,
Yours sincerely,
Francis Quilligan, Esq.

What exquisite handwriting Mr Quilligan had! It was old-fashioned copperplate, not unlike that of Mrs Healy, the caretaker who had written to Edie in London.

Turning her attention to the advertisement, Edie saw that both sides of the leaflet were given over to Prospect House: on one side a floor plan with measurements accompanied a fuzzy photograph, and, on the other, a detailed blurb outlined its charms.

PROSPECT HOUSE

LOCATION
This property is situated on the southern shore of Loch Liath approximately 5 miles north of the picturesque village of Doneraile. The countryside around Doneraile is very scenic and has a wealth of historical associations. The village is also a haven for anglers and acts as a convenient base for exploring this beautiful part of the world.

DESCRIPTION
The subject property comprises a prominent six bay two storey dwelling constructed *c.*1840 with its most recent use as a fishing lodge.

The attractive period property is of traditional masonry construction with wet dash concrete rendering and is set back from the local road on its own private mature grounds overlooking Loch Liath.

The property is in reasonable condition throughout and retains all of its period features but requires extensive modernization and refurbishment.

ACCOMMODATION
Hall, double drawing room, dining room, study, kitchen, and all the usual offices on the ground floor with stairs leading to three/four bedrooms and bathroom on the first floor. Box room over kitchen accessed via captain's stair.

TITLE
We understand the property is held freehold.

SERVICES
We understand that drainage is via an on-site septic tank, water is provided via an on-site well.

POTENTIAL
This represents a rare opportunity to acquire a unique property with potential for refurbishment and renovation for a variety of uses including guest house, bed and breakfast etc.

PRICE
On application.

VIEWING
Strictly by prior appointment with sole selling agents, Quilligan & Quilligan.

Edie had slaved away the previous day, getting the place into shape for the viewing. She had armed herself from a cupboard in the pantry with a long-hair broom, a staircase broom, a scrubbing brush, a dusting brush and a cornice brush. Although Mr Quilligan had said that there would be no need to clean the house, Edie was anxious to show off its loveliness, and determined that it should be as pristine as she could make it.

She wished she had some furniture polish; she would love the smell of beeswax to welcome the prospective buyer. And what a pity that daffodils were no longer in season; it would have been a nice touch to fill three or four vases with blooms. However, since the house would never be a candidate for *Ideal Home*, the least she could do would be to offer tea and biscuits and furnish prospective buyers with a little local, anecdotal history. After she'd cleaned the windows and pulled up the weeds that proliferated on the terrace she would cosy up in the library and learn a little more of the history of Doneraile and its environs courtesy of Eliza's manuscript.

Lord and Lady Doneraile had been invited to Dublin, to a grand dinner in the viceregal lodge in the Phoenix Park. I was to accompany them, and had had the foresight to suggest a spree that would take in not just the dinner, but an excursion to the Zoological Gardens, an exhibition viewing at the Academy, shopping on

Sackville Mall and a visit to the Theatre Royal, thus prolonging our stay by an extra day. We were to put up for two nights at the Shelbourne Hotel.

But alas! On the morning we were to make the journey, I fell ill with a malady that no number of James's Powders would alleviate and that a journey to Dublin in the brougham would most certainly exacerbate. I bade my mistress farewell with a sorrowful countenance, urging her to make the most of her time in the capital and assuring her that there was nothing so seriously wrong with me that a little bed rest would not cure. When she asked what she could bring me back, I importuned her for pattern books and catalogues of the latest furnishings, for Lady Charlotte was, with my help, to redecorate her parlour.

I told Cook that I would keep to my room, and that the dry toast I had consumed at breakfast was all the sustenance I would require for the next twenty-four hours. Then I took myself off to my apartment at the top of the house and changed into the clothes I had worn on my voyage to Cork, and a pair of stout boots.

St Leger was waiting for me by the 'triumphal' arch at the bottom of the avenue, where his carriage dog was sniffing around the piers. He leaned across the driving seat and stretched out a hand; I took it and, using the hub of the wheel for purchase, sprang up beside him. Leaning in towards my lover, I kissed him warmly before doffing my bonnet and unpinning my hair, allowing it to fall loose around my shoulders in the style adopted by so many Irish girls. As the phaeton bowled away from Doneraile Court I felt free, and inordinately happy.

The hedgerows were oozing honeysuckle and boisterous with birdsong, the breeze was a zephyr, the air redolent of wild garlic. The road seemed to unwind like a ribbon before us; the sky was a canopy of heliotrope, with traces of cloud insubstantial as bog cotton. I felt as though I could compose verses worthy of inclusion in an anthology of Romantic poetry; verses that might surpass even those of William Wordsworth.

St Leger lilted some Irish lay as we jaunted along:

> *A h- uiscí chroidhe na n-anamann,*
> *Leagan tú ar lár mé*
> *Bim gan chéill, gan aithne,*
> *'Sé an t-eachrann do b'fhearr liom!*

He sang it over and over, urging me to join in, laughing at my lamentable accent, and making me repeat the words after him, the way I had used to make my pupils repeat 'Au Clair de la Lune', or some other French ditty. This was no rhyme I could teach a schoolgirl; it was an ode to whiskey, and I am pleased to say that by the time we reached our destination I could carry it off in a rollicking brogue.

The final stage of the journey took us down a gradient flanked by woodland, along a road little more than a track. Beneath the leafy canopy, dense thickets of holly and rowan grew, cross-hatched with thoroughfares where badgers and foxes conducted their business. The carriage dog was in paradise, his tail in perpetual motion. He raced ahead, lagged behind, snuffled around bushes and disappeared on excursions into the undergrowth. St Leger told me that wolves had once colonized caves in the heart of the forest, and that I ought not to wear my carnelian pelisse when I ventured forth, lest I was mistaken for Red Riding Hood.

The track emerged into a clearing where the house stood on a slight eminence. Long and low, wrapped around on three sides by ancient sessile oaks, it fronted a slate blue lake. On the far side of the water a range of heather-clad hills sprawled like a sleeping dragon.

St Leger watched as I slid down from my seat in the phaeton. I did not wait for him. I made my way along a path that skirted a small storm porch and rounded a corner, emerging onto a grassy ridge that ran parallel to the south-facing façade. A sward of green fell away towards the water, upon which a single rowing-boat was moored. The shores were of shell pink shingle, the lake so still that the hills mirrored on its surface appeared to be tumbled in its depths. I leaned against the wall of the house, feeling its sun-warmed stonework on my back, and gazed and gazed.

And that is how St Leger found me, with a smile upon my face.

'What do you think?' he asked.

I wanted to say that I thought it perfect – that house, view and situation surpassed anything I had hoped for; but that would have meant revealing my hand, and I did not want to spoil my chances of gaining further prizes.

'The view is magnificent,' I conceded. 'Your ghillie was right when he told you to build here. But I should like to see inside now.'

'There is very little furniture.'

'No matter. I shall want to choose my own.'

'It is rather rudimentary still,' he said, stepping aside so that I could precede him along the path that led back to the porch. I was glad to see that he looked uneasy: he was clearly keen that my new home should comply with the high standards I had stipulated. 'But be assured, Eliza, that my architect will resolve any concerns you may have.'

Taking a key from the pocket of his greatcoat, he unlocked the door and held it open. I did not dare pass through, lest he see the jubilant expression on my face as I stepped across the threshold.

'Be kind enough to fetch my sketchbook, St Leger,'

I told him. 'I shall want to make drawings, and some notes.'

He retreated, and I took my first step into the harbourage of my own house. It was dark inside. I did not care: once a staircase was built, a window on the return would throw light into the entrance hall. Beyond the porch, a corridor ran the length of the building, with doors off to the left. I scarcely dared to breathe as I entered the first room.

The windows were hung with makeshift curtains of burlap. I pulled them aside; dust motes were sent spinning into the sunlight, so that my first impression of the interior was through a golden haze. The room was spacious, high-ceilinged, with a doorway to an adjoining chamber. There were four window apertures in all, and two fireplaces.

In my mind's eye, I saw a double salon. I could have the stone and mortar walls plastered, and decorated with cornices and gesso panels, or with wallpaper; nothing overly ornate. I could consult a catalogue for furniture and have it delivered from Cork or Dublin. I could be comfortable here in winter, and in the summer – once the windows were refashioned in the French style – I could step out onto my terrace beyond.

The next room was equally well proportioned. This would be my library and study, boasting a view to inspire. Further along, my dining room was situated across the passageway from the kitchen, with windows on two sides. The kitchen was little more than a lean-to: it would have to be pulled down and a proper cuisine constructed, with a larder and a scullery.

At the far end of the corridor I found a half-door, bolted on the inside. I opened it and descended a short flight of steps to a stone platform abutting a waterfall. The water cascaded to a shallow pool, where it swirled and eddied, surging over a shelf of granite to the lake below. Taking off my boots and stockings, I sat at the edge of the slab, dangling my feet in the cool water. This was a belvedere to rival any of Lady Charlotte's!

I looked up to the branch of a silver birch where a blackbird was singing. Once the upper storey was built, I would reserve this south-eastern corner for my private apartments: I could fall asleep to the rushing sound of the stream and wake to the dawn chorus. I could lounge upon a window seat and look down on an expanse of water the colour of pewter in winter, lapis lazuli in summer. I could stock my library with books and retreat there to write and to muse. I could receive guests when I chose, and bid them farewell as I chose. I could wander lonely as a cloud beneath the trees and by the lake, like Wordsworth. If the mood took me I could sortie abroad, and be in society for a day or two a month. This would be my own domain, where I would live under obligation to no one, solitary and proud.

And then, when it suited me to return to civilization, I could sell the house and the fishing rights and become a lady of independent means.

St Leger was back with my sketchbook. I took it from him and began at once to make notes.

'Your builders will need to get started directly, if the work is to be complete in time.'

'They'll want sweeteners.'

'The cost doesn't concern me.'

'It concerns *me*. What if –'

'No "what ifs", St Leger. I warned you.'

He fell silent. He knew – we both did – that this scheme had the potential to go calamitously wrong if I miscarried or produced a child that was malformed or – despite my assurances to the contrary – a girl. But we both knew the risks we were taking, and I had been a gambler since the age of seven, when I had bested my papa's ace of hearts with one of spades.

'What will you do, when you live here?' he asked, hunkering down beside me.

'I'll write my book, of course.'

He looked perplexed. 'What book?'

'I have an idea,' I said, 'for a picaresque novel.'

'How can you write something picturesque?'

'You dear dolt! It's "picaresque". Picaresque is a story in which the principal character is obliged to make his – or her – way in the world by living on his wits.'

'Like you?'

'Just like me.'

I handed him my sketchbook and pencil, then rose to my feet and started to undo the tiny buttons that ran down the front of my dress.

'What are you doing?'

'I want to feel the breeze on my skin.'

He watched as I shrugged out of my bodice and divested myself of my heavy skirts. The material pooled at my bare feet. I kicked it away and, gathering my petticoats up about my thighs, leapt off the stone slab where we had been sunning ourselves, and ran down the grassy slope towards the lake.

St Leger drew level with me just as I reached the shore. 'Don't go in the water!' he said, catching my wrist.

'Why not?'

'It might do the baby harm.'

'He's perfectly snug and safe and buoyed up in here.' I smiled up at him, took his hand and laid it over my belly. 'He's moving with me, feeling with me, hearing with me. He came here today with the sound of hooves in his teeny tiny ears, and now he's likely dreaming about chasing after foxes on horseback. Didn't you say you were practically born in the saddle?'

'You're right. He's a St Leger.' He ran his hand over the thin cambric of my chemise. 'When will I feel him move?'

'Not for months yet! He's hardly bigger than my thumb.' I kissed the pad of my thumb and pressed it to his nose. 'Your nose is so noble! I do hope he inherits it.'

'In that case, I am very glad you're not carrying a girl. My nose would not sit well on a girlish face.'

I looked down at my thumbnail and pretended to examine it. 'What are you going to call him?'

'He'll be Jameson too, I suppose. Or Frederick, after my father.'

'Frederick of Roesworth. Whoever would have imagined I'd beget a duke!'

I turned and danced after the dog, which had come careering down the hill after us, his tongue flapping from his mouth like a slice of glistening ham. He barked joyously as I picked up a stick, called out 'Fetch!' and tossed it into the water. As he doggy-paddled in pursuit of his quarry I watched ripples spread outwards across the placid surface of the lake. I could hear the crunch of St Leger's boots on the shingle; I sent him a smile that made my dimples play before resuming my contemplation of the water.

Last night an idle curiosity had compelled me to try the trick I had told St Leger about, the one that was believed to foretell the gender of an unborn child. I had performed it, not with a duck egg and a hair taken from the head of a pregnant woman, but with a needle

243

suspended from a thread, the way the dancers at the *Variétés* had used to when they were *enceintes*.

It had swung to the right.

Before my mistress returned from Dublin, I spent much of my time sequestered in my apartment at Doneraile Court with my sketchbook. In it, I drew up plans for my house, adding a kitchen, lobby and stairs to the ground floor, and designating the rooms already there as double salon, library and dining room. A bay with superimposed windows to the left of the stairwell extended to the first floor. Beyond the pencilled wall of the upper corridor I outlined four rooms. My apartment – sitting room, bedchamber and dressing room – would take up two of the first floor rooms; the remaining two would serve as guest chambers.

My house was far enough off the beaten track to discourage casual visitors: this suited me admirably, for I did not want people arriving uninvited. If, however, I chose to entertain, I could offer my guests comfortable accommodation. This afforded me the best of both worlds; I could have my cake and eat it too.

I incorporated window seats into all the corner rooms, added an external privy, and a pantry alongside the kitchen, and, upstairs, I made sure to pencil in a window overlooking the stream. I went about the drawings in a steady and concentrated way, enjoying the work because I was utterly certain of its purpose. As an afterthought, I sketched in a discretionary extra storey above the kitchen, for I would need staff.

After I had submitted my drawings to St Leger's architect, I mulled over the pattern books that Lady Charlotte had brought back from Dublin, and made a list of the furniture I required: I did not want furniture for show or prestige – as had been the case in Mr O'Dowd's flashy mansion and Lady Charlotte's country seat – but for comfort. I wanted bookcases and a writing table for my library; a cheval glass, wardrobe and *table de toilette* for my dressing room; a games table and drawing-room suite for my salon; chairs, table and a sideboard for the dining room. Sundry chaises longues, sofas and beds (I specified a half tester with drapes for my own use); screens, lamps, carpets and clocks.

For the first time ever, I wished I had a doll's house. I would have taken untold delight in arranging and re-arranging tiny movables in a facsimile of my home. Instead, I pictured myself walking along the corridors, upstairs and down, passing through doorways leading to other doorways, and through French windows to the terrace where . . . there ought to be a sundial!

Maria had a sundial in her garden. It was an ornate affair wrought in marble and brass, the final extravagance of her late bankrupt husband. It was the last thing of any value that she owned, apart from her jewels. She had kept it because it made her laugh every time she passed it: Mr Fagan had had it inscribed with the motto *Memento vivere* (Remember to live) a week before his untimely death.

I added 'sundial' to the list, along with 'stone jardinières'. On the page opposite was a record of invoices received for carpentry work, plastering, slating and glazing.

Running an eye over my inventory, I wondered if St Leger would balk at the expense. But when I handed him a statement of monies due, he did not cavil.

'What will you call your house?' he asked.

'Call it? I had never thought of calling it anything.'

'You must give it a name. It's your palace.'

I contemplated. 'What is that in Irish? Palace?'

He narrowed his eyes and smiled. '*Lios*. It rhymes with "kiss".'

'*Lios*. I like it. And what is the Irish word for "hare"?'

'"Hare"?'

'You said you had built your bothy where the first hare stood.'

'It's *giorria*.'

'Say it again.'

'*Giorria*. Guer – ri – a.'

I tried it out on my tongue. It sounded rich, and faintly pagan.

'So if you put them together, to make "the palace of the hare" you would get "Lissaguirra"?' I asked.

'Yes.'

I turned to him with a smile. 'That's it. That is what I shall call my house. Lissaguirra.'

Edie was entranced. Prospect House was Lissaguirra! It had been built to the specifications of her beloved Eliza – for Edie now felt such close rapport with the writer of the manuscript that she felt entitled to claim her as a beloved. She located the advertisement that Mr Quilligan had sent her and, following the floor plans, walked the corridors and the rooms upstairs and down, taking the same route as Eliza had done in her imagination, descrying the objects with which she had furnished her dream house: the bookcases and the writing table in the library; the drawing room suite with its threadbare silken upholstery; the elegant chairs, table and sideboard in the dining room. She looked with a new eye at the chaises longues and sofas, and at the screens, lamps and carpets that were now piled higgledy-piggledy in what had once been Eliza's beautiful double salon, and at the rococo gilt-framed looking glasses waiting to go under the auctioneer's hammer.

She felt anxious now, about the people who were due to come tomorrow. Would they look at the furnishings and curl their lips? Would they open the lids of the trunks full of old clothes and shut them again with distaste? Would they sneer at the quarry tiles on the kitchen floor and talk about ripping out the chimneypieces?

Edie felt a great surge of love for the house. She wanted to protect it, to cocoon it, to magically grow a forest of briar roses around it as the fairies had done in the story of the sleeping princess, shielding it from the outside world and preventing anyone from trespassing.

She wished that Hilly was there, so that together they could sift through Eliza's manuscripts and put all the pieces in place like a jigsaw puzzle. She remembered how, the summer they had holidayed here, it had poured with rain for two consecutive days and they had spent hours at the dining-room table doing a huge jigsaw puzzle of Notre-Dame. It was the most tedious subject imaginable, but they had persisted until the final stone curlicue on the final flying buttress had been slotted in. The ironic upshot of this was that Uncle Jack had presented Edie with boring jigsaws on her birthday for years afterwards: Westminster Abbey, Edinburgh Castle, the Giant's Causeway – jigsaws of such awesome, tedious complexity that they had become a running joke between Edie and Hilly. Now Edie had a perfectly extraordinary puzzle to put together, and no one to share it with.

For the second night in a row she took a chunk of the manuscript to bed and carried on reading, hoping that if she fell asleep with the pages on her pillow, perhaps Eliza would come to her in a dream and show her where the pieces ought to go.

⁓ E. D

The invoices piled higher. I had not dreamed that so much expense could be accrued in the building of a house, but St Leger was extremely generous. It was as though, now that he had been confronted with the corporeality of his unborn child (albeit in the form of speculation about the size of its nose), he was determined to ensure the comfort and well-being of its mother.

I had few opportunities to visit my future home, but on three occasions I tucked Lady Charlotte up in bed with Sooty and made her tea from valerian root (the best cure for her sick headaches and a reliable soporific), before surreptitiously changing into my old grey travelling gown and driving out with St Leger to see how the building work was progressing.

The first time I visited, the scaffolding was in place and I had to climb a ladder to inspect the work; the second time our horse lost a shoe and we had to go back; on the third occasion I did what I had until then only dreamed of – I walked the corridors, upstairs and down;

I passed through doorways leading to other doorways, and stepped onto a terrace that had been paved with slabs of local white limestone.

For several months I had managed to conceal my condition with the help of corsets and shawls, and by making a great show of consuming sweetmeats to explain away my embonpoint, but when it became necessary to lace my stays more tightly and reef my petticoats higher to hide my thickening figure, I knew that it would soon be time to withdraw from the world.

I wrote to Maria, requesting a meeting. I guessed that she would not care to visit Doneraile Park (for Her Ladyship was longing to show off her newly decorated parlour), so when my mistress mentioned that she was fearful to entrust a pair of Venetian glass vases she had ordered to a clumsy Corkonian carter, I offered to fetch them myself.

In her house on Grattan Hill, Maria seemed blithe as ever when the maid showed me in. She was kneeling on the floor peering into a wooden crate in which the house cat was giving birth.

'Will these kittens never cease!' she lamented. 'Here comes another one. She has had four already.'

I crouched down to inspect the mother. She was sprawled comfortably in a nest of wood shavings like an odalisque, and she was purring loudly.

'She seems to be enjoying it,' I remarked.

'Yes,' said Maria, in a perplexed tone. 'She enjoyed her last labour too, the contrary thing. I swore after my first that I would never do it again, but then I produced four more, just like Madam Tabitha here.'

I looked at the kitten sliding into the shavings, all bloody and damp and covered with what looked like curds. 'Was it so very dreadful?'

Why did I ask? I knew it was dreadful – dreadful beyond description: I had heard the opera girls' stories of the agonies they had endured, the terror of imminent death, the fear that they might expel a mutant (in some instances they had – the deformed infants being spirited away at once by the midwife). But I asked Maria all the same, because, I supposed, I hoped for some words of reassurance or comfort from her.

'Oh, yes, it *was* dreadful! It was like being kicked from inside by a mountain goat, or pulled apart by demons. It was as if red-hot claws . . .'

I tried to stop listening. Someone had once told me that women swap childbirth stories the way men do tales of derring-do. My mother had warned me not to heed the vaunting boasts of the pain borne and the torment suffered by her cronies, because one day I would have to undergo it myself. Here I was with a child on the way, watching a cat deliver kittens and listening to Maria describe how one of her babies had been delivered by forceps. The cat started to paw and sniff at what looked like a morsel of raw liver.

'Tabby! You're disgusting,' scolded Maria.

'What's she doing?'

'She's eating the afterbirth.' Gently, Maria picked up one of the minuscule babies and placed it next to the cat's belly so that it could find a teat. 'Still, it must be good for her, if she wants to eat it.'

I eased myself from my kneeling position on the floor up onto the couch and pressed my hands over my mouth.

'They say the placenta's full of nutrition. They made me drink raw eggs beaten with milk when I . . . Oh. What's the matter, Eliza?' Maria looked at me with apprehension. 'Are you going to be sick?'

I shook my head, my hands still clamped over my mouth.

'Do you need a basin?'

I shook my head again. I felt as I would do when dance music stops abruptly while romping through a quadrille: disoriented and dismayed.

Maria opened her mouth as if to say something, then shut it. She folded her hands neatly in her lap, looked down at them, then tried again. 'You're not . . . you're not pregnant, are you?'

I nodded.

'Oh.' Maria stood up and made a show of brushing

her skirts. Then she sat down beside me, trying to look unruffled. 'I was exaggerating, you know, about the pain. It's not so bad, really. Some women pop their babies out. Why, they say that one of Louis XIV's mistresses gave birth while she was dancing, and just kicked the newborn out from under her skirts.'

'What?' My hands dropped to my lap.

She nodded vigorously. 'It's true. She couldn't let anyone know that she was *enceinte*, so when it came during a saraband or some such she just sent it scooting across the floor with her foot. So they say.'

'What happened to it?'

'I don't know.'

On another occasion I might have laughed. 'I don't think it will be that simple for me,' I said.

'Who's the father?'

'Jameson St Leger.'

'Oh, the deuce!' Maria seized my hand. 'Tell me.'

I told her. I told her of the circumstances surrounding the conception and the intended outcome, and of the benefits it would bring to all parties.

'It will certainly *not* be simple,' she said, when I'd finished. 'Where do you propose to deliver the child? In your new house?'

'Yes.'

'Who will help?'

'I don't know.'

Maria looked at me as if I were a simpleton. 'You won't find a licensed midwife in those parts, Eliza, and a local woman will spit on the child to baptize it the minute your back is turned.'

'That's Jamey's concern, not mine.' I shrugged and smoothed my hair. 'Anyway, I'm young and healthy and I'm sure I can manage on my own – '

'And I'm sure you can't. Besides, it's abnormal to have no one attend a mother at the birth of her child. It makes you an outcast.'

'I'm casting myself out, you ninny.'

'You could bleed to death. I heard a story of a woman who had a massive haemorrhage and lost – '

'Perhaps I should seek out a medical man?'

'No! Men are far too rough. They hurry you on, and pull at the placenta instead of waiting for it to come. Why, I even heard of a physician who simply lopped off the baby's limbs when it got stuck and – '

Here I put my hands over my ears and started to cry.

'Eliza!' Gently, Maria drew away my hands and held them between hers. 'Eliza – shh. Shh.'

'I can't do it!' I sobbed. 'What made me think I could?'

'Can you send for your mother?'

'She's dead.'

'A sister, or an aunt?'

I shook my head. I had no relatives living except for an obscure uncle in France, and he, too, was more than likely dead by now, of drink or of the pox.

Maria rose from the couch and fetched two glasses. She uncorked a bottle on the sideboard and poured a measure of gin into each. In the crate at my feet, Tabby was washing one of her slug-like kittens. Maria sat down beside me, and handed me a glass.

'Here.'

I took the glass and drank from it, which was strange, because even the smell of gin usually made me nauseous.

'I don't generally tolerate gin,' I told Maria.

'You will find yourself tolerating all sorts of things you would not normally countenance.'

'I never cry, either.'

'All women cry when they are with child, just as all babies cry when they are born.'

I set down the glass, and looked at her helplessly. 'What am I to do?' I asked. 'Who can I ask for help?'

Snug in their nest, the kittens were suckling at their mother, who was purring louder than ever. Maria picked out some shreds of bloodied wood shavings and cast them onto the fire. Then she picked up her glass and took a deep breath before throwing back the contents.

'I will help you,' she said.

Instead of giving Lady Charlotte my notice directly, I wrote her a letter. In it, I advised her of three faux pas that irked me, and that I had longed to correct since I had first come to live with her:

1: The Schubert song she loved so much was by Schumann.

2: She must stop dabbing at her mouth with her handkerchief (in coded language it was an invitation to flirt: I had seen many a young man snigger at her behind his hand).

3: The painting attributed to Velázquez that hung on the first-floor gallery was a copy, and not a very good one.

Unfortunately, she happened upon me at first light, as I was dragging my trunk across the hall to the front door. Whatever she was doing out of bed at such an hour (not even the housemaid rose that early) I shall never know. She was in déshabille with her hair in papers, but did not seem out of countenance when she spied me standing fully dressed in bonnet and pelisse with my carpet bag in one hand and my reticule in the other. I was put in mind of how I had once found Miss Pinkerton's sister sitting on the stairs of the academy in the middle of the night wearing her nightgown, with the biscuit barrel on her lap. I suppose ladies in their middle years are allowed their eccentricities.

'You've packed your box!' she exclaimed. 'Are you leaving us, Eliza?'

'Alas,' I replied, economically.

'You can't go! 'Twould be disloyal. You are my companion.'

I wanted to tell her that loyalty had nothing to do with it, that she was mistaking companionship for friendship and that friendship could not be paid for, but I knew that Lady Charlotte was of the opinion that everything could be bought.

'But why are you going? *Where* are you going?'

I wasn't inclined to give her an answer. She would find out soon enough that I was ensconced in Lissaguirra as mistress to Jameson St Leger.

'You can't go!' she said plaintively. 'You haven't finished reading me *The Old Curiosity Shop*. I must find out what happens to Little Nell.'

'She dies,' I said, hazarding a guess.

'Oh! Why did you *tell* me?'

'You wouldn't have found out otherwise. I'm sorry to leave you without giving notice, Your Ladyship, but unforeseen circumstances oblige me to make myself scarce.'

She stamped her foot.

'Unforeseen circumstances! So you're with child. I have had three of my staff leave in the past year, citing "unforeseen circumstances". I should have known, when I saw Sir Silas mooning around you.'

257

'Sir Silas?'

'I dare say Lady Sybil has had enough, and barred the door of her bedchamber. She should have done it years ago.'

I heard the sound of a coach pulling up on the gravel sweep outside.

'Who's that?' demanded Her Ladyship.

'It is the carter, come to take me to town.'

'Well, good luck to you, Miss Drury,' said Lady Charlotte sniffily. 'Do I owe you wages?'

'No.'

I was, in fact, due money – I had had none since the last quarter: but I no longer needed Lady Charlotte's. More particularly, I didn't *want* her money. I had my own house and an allowance from St Leger, and I had plans to pursue a profession as a writer. I was as independent as a woman could be, and no longer required a servant's risible salary.

The chiming clock on the chimneypiece in the drawing room struck five.

'I must go,' I said. 'The Sisters of Charity are expecting me.'

Lady Charlotte nodded. 'Sir Silas will provide for the child, I have no doubt. Perhaps you will have the good fortune to miscarry. I will keep you in my prayers.'

'I am much obliged.'

'Farewell, Miss Drury. I suppose I must wish you Godspeed.'

She retreated, and through the cotton of her nightgown I could make out the shape of her unlovely haunches, her spindle shanks and her incipient dowager's hump. Poor lady. She had been destined from marriage to sit out the dances, instead plotting in a cabal in a corner of the ballroom with the other matrons, and jockeying perpetually for position. I'd rather the life of her sister, frayed around the edges from child-bearing but merry still, though she was a widow and poor.

Reaching for the strap on my trunk, I yanked it the remaining few yards to the door. I did not care that no footman had been summoned to help me, for I had acquitted myself with dignity.

Outside, the sun was coming up. A glance through a window would have told Lady Charlotte that there was no cart waiting there to convey me to some unsavoury lying-in establishment. It was St Leger's carriage that had drawn up outside, emblazoned with his coat of arms and drawn by a pair of horses.

I dumped my trunk on the perron, and waited for the coachman to come and take charge of it. Once it was strapped to the roof, he would hand me in to the sedan and I would settle back against the upholstery and daydream until we arrived at my new home by the lake. I would spend the hour between here and Lissaguirra making notes in my sketchbook of the narrative that was beginning to take shape in my head. I had given my heroine a countenance that pleased me, and I had outlined her beginnings in an artist's studio in Soho, where she had been brought, after her French mother's untimely death, by that poor lady's twin brother.

And so, with my head full of stories, I took my leave of Doneraile Court.

17

Dear William,

Here I am, quite set-up and comfortable in my own house. It is a good-sized hunting lodge, with a library and French windows on the ground floor overlooking a resplendent view. I have staff, and a pony and trap for transport, and a lake to gaze upon and a wood to go walking in.

You will ask how my fortunes have changed that I have a house and accoutrements, but I shall not tell you here, for I must save my ink for writing my novel.

What I must tell you is this: since leaving Doneraile Court I have seen a different aspect of this forsaken country. It seems the rich live the high life and the common people must starve for it. Yesterday I went to the other side of the lake, to a village of mud cabins. You will recall the beggars we saw in Cork who had not an intact coat nor an intact shirt nor an intact pair of trousers? You would think them dandies by comparison with these wretches. They are wrapped in rags – rags made of rags, with whole parts of their bodies left bare. Everything about them hangs loose; bits of cloth flap around, before and after them. They wear no shoes; they are unshorn, unshaven and unwashed. Never have I seen such poverty: Mr Dickens himself could not describe it. I came away feeling ashamed.

But I do not intend to stay here long – I could not bear it. A year or two will suffice for me to finish my novel. Then I can sell this place and return to London, having made my fortune, and with a song in my heart – tra la la.

If you come to Ireland you will find me a most munificent hostess.

Eliza.

~

My dear Eliza,
A library! A view! I envy you, for I am writing to you in a cubbyhole (which the concierge of the establishment has the nerve to call a chambre meublée) at a rickety table that scarcely allows space for paper, inkstand and . . . There! My elbow has just knocked my cigar box to the floor.

Isabella is a little improved. Champagne is the panacea, but alas, until I can find some way of bringing in the thousand pounds a year that you & I deem requisite to being good people, funds do not permit a bottle a day. I am working on a plan to bring the family to London, but the move is determined by money.

I am curious to know how your good fortune came about. Perhaps it is the luck of the Irish. I must try if some of it will rub off on me when I visit that country as indeed I must, for Messrs Chapman & Hall want their guide-book.

I have found a character for a story that I am sure will be amusing.

My God, how I wish I had you to be with.

Yours,

William

~

Dear Eliza,
When will it be convenient for me to present myself to you at Lissaguirra?

Jameson St Leger

~

Dear Jameson,
I am now quite set-up and comfortable in my house.

Thank you for the pony and jingle, in which I trot decorously up and down hills and through dales, and for the view, which changes every day.

I shall expect you on Thursday.

Eliza Drury

18

THE NEXT MORNING Edie was on her hands and knees scrubbing the kitchen floor when a knock came to the front door. Milo at her heels, she hurried along the corridor, untying her pinafore as she went. Before she answered the knock, she divested herself of her headscarf, and smoothed her hair with an automatic hand.

The man at the door was tall, dark and Greek-god handsome, which Edie had most certainly not been expecting. She rather wished she had spent more time on her own appearance than that of the house, and that she had had a bath instead of her usual cursory wash.

'Good morning,' she said. 'You must be Mr O'Brien.'

'Good morning.'

'I didn't hear an automobile – you took me rather by surprise.'

'I left it below at the jetty,' he said, 'and went for a walk along the lakeside.'

Edie dimpled a little. 'It's beautiful, don't you think?'

'I suppose it is. I was keen to assess the potential.'

'You're a fisherman, then?'

'In a manner of speaking.'

'That fish up there,' she said, indicating the stuffed salmon in its glass case, 'was caught by my uncle.'

He narrowed his eyes, as if doing mental calculations. 'A seventeen-pounder, I'd say.'

'Yes – I think that's what he said it weighed.'

'I'd like to think there were plenty more fellows like him dangling about down there.'

Mr O'Brien gave a smile so devoid of charm that Edie instantly decided she didn't like him after all and wouldn't offer him a cup of tea. He might resemble a Greek god, but his manners were more like those of a troll.

'Shall we get going?' she suggested.

He gave her a hard-nosed look. 'I don't need you to show me around thanks, Miss,' he said. 'I'd prefer to do it under my own steam.'

Please yourself, Edie wanted to say, but didn't. Instead she said, 'Take all the time you want. If you need me, I'll be in the kitchen.'

'I shan't need you,' he said, and started up the staircase, taking the treads two at a time.

Edie glowered at his retreating back, hoping to see him stumble on a step, but he ascended as if he had wings on his feet, like Mercury on a mission.

Heading back towards the kitchen to resume her

skivvying, she saw that the light streaming in through the open half-door at the end of the corridor resembled a golden pathway, beckoning her outside. Damn it! She wasn't going to get down on her hands and knees and scrub floors for the benefit of a berk like Mr O'Brien. She'd go outside and take her ease in the sun as the original chateleine had done on her first visit to Lissaguirra, and dabble her toes in the stream. Detouring via the library to help herself to another tranche of Eliza's manuscript, and the kitchen to help herself to an apple, she settled down on the smooth, sun-warmed rock, pulled off her plimsolls, and began to read.

⌁ E. D.

A supper of salmon trout with parsley-and-butter and new potatoes was awaiting St Leger upon his arrival. The table was laid with a damask half-cloth, upon which a jug of yellow irises had been set. I had decanted a fine burgundy into an elegant carafe clasped around with beaten silverwork, and dressed myself in the green tabinet gown given to me by Mrs O'Dowd which had, until now, been too big for me. The evening sun bathed the dining room in a roseate glow (the effect enhanced by the wallpaper I had picked out, patterned in hues of plum and apricot), a log fire burned redundantly, and beyond the open window my black-bird sang lustily.

'Well, Bastet,' he said when he had finished (he called me that sometimes, as he had promised he would, after the great Egyptian cat goddess. In return, I called him my flea). 'You have hired yourself an excellent cook. And the maid seems competent.'

She had served us earlier, with rather more efficiency than finesse.

'I did not hire either,' I told him. 'Your steward got them at the hiring fair. If I had had my way, I would have chosen my own staff.'

'Why? Do you think you could have done better than Christy?'

'No. He has chosen well; they are both more than capable. But had I known there were people living in the village beyond the lake who are in desperate need of work, I would have taken them on instead.'

'You have been there?'

'I drove there last week.'

'On your own?'

'Of course. I have scant need of a chaperone, Jamey.'

'I will not have you go there, Eliza. It is no place for a gentlewoman.'

'There are no cut-throats in these parts,' I scoffed. 'The Irish seem to me to be a peculiarly sanguine race, though I wonder at their stoicism, for this is a country ripe for revolution. The people make the sans-culottes look privileged.'

St Leger threw aside his napkin. 'Don't think you can distract me with talk of politics. I say, I will not have you go there in your condition.'

'I have heard that a daily rattle in a bouncing carriage, seven or eight miles along a jumbling road is excellent for both the mother and the child.'

'What madman told you that?'

'It is said to make childbirth easier.'

'I will not hear of it, Eliza! Besides, the houses in Aill na Coill are unsanitary and – '

'You call them houses? They are *hovels*! And why are they unsanitary? Why does Lord Abingdon not take better care of his tenants?'

'That is not my business, Eliza. I purchased this land from him for the fishing. You are well set up here, and I would thank you to keep your mouth shut about things that don't concern you, and allow me to advise you about things that do.' He stood up and moved to the window. 'By going to that pestilent place you are not putting solely yourself at risk, you are endangering our son.'

Our son? It felt oddly gratifying to hear him use the possessive plural: heretofore he had referred to the child only as his. I gave him a fond look. His back was to me, his shoulders braced defensively, and I felt a pang of contrition. He was right: I had no business hectoring him, for it was Lord Abingdon, not he, who was to blame for the squalid conditions in which those poor creatures beyond the lake strove to survive. I resolved instead to confine my disquietude to the pages of my journal, in which I wrote every day, sitting at the rose-wood escritoire I had bragged about to William.

I reached for the decanter, poured wine, and joined St Leger by the window. 'Look at my charming garden,' I said, handing him a glass. 'I have instructed Christy to have the beds planted with roses and lupins, and I want a laburnum, for its golden flowers.'

'You should have a hawthorn for the May blossom. The blossom around Dromamore gladdens my heart at springtime.'

'Dromamore?'

'My Irish seat. My great-grandfather built it.'

'Is it a grand house?'

'Not so grand as Doneraile Court, but I was born there and I have an affection for it.'

'How much land is attached?'

'Ten thousand acres.'

'Ten thousand! And here am I puffed with pride for my two acres of garden.'

'Two acres will keep you busy enough. Tell me more of your plans.'

I linked his arm and intertwined my fingers with his.

'There will be paths along the borders – see where they have been marked out? – and an orchard. Imagine! We shall be able to pick apples and pears and plums straight from the branches. And there'll be an arbour there, where you can sit and watch the sun go down over the lake when you come back after a day's fishing.'

'I'll need to get the boat seen to.'

'I'll ask Christy to attend to it.'

'What did he do with my gear?'

'It's safely stowed in the boathouse below. I've asked him to build on an annexe.'

'To the boathouse?'

'Yes. He's had a word with your ghillie. Between them they'll have something dandy ready before the end of the year, so you'll have your own dedicated hideout down there by the lake, like Bonnie Prince Charlie.'

'Bonnie Prince Charlie was a pederast.'

'Very well – Rob Roy, then.'

'Are you trying to outlaw me?'

'No, no!' I protested, kissing him fondly. 'It's a place for you to go when you have had enough of my company, for you know I will not let you be when you are here. Besides, you will distract me from my novel-writing.'

'Only unattractive women write novels.'

'Pray furnish me with examples.'

'Maria Edgeworth. Jane Austen.'

'Have you read either?'

'No. Sophia has.'

'And what makes you think they are unattractive women?'

'They never married.'

'Perhaps they chose not to. They could certainly afford not to marry, for they earned their own income.' I looked at him with some hauteur. 'Bear in mind, Mr St Leger, that *I* am unmarried.'

'You don't need to earn money, Eliza.'

'Ah, but every gentlewoman needs a hobby, just as you gentlemen do. So when I am scribbling in my silly little notebooks, you can take yourself off to your boat-house and enjoy more manly pursuits.'

He looked uncertain.

'Such as . . . looking through your telescope,' I essayed.

'I don't have a telescope.'

'I shall buy you one. And I shall wave at you from the dining-room window when it is time for dinner, and from my bedroom window when it's time for bed, and we shall both be perfectly happy. Now, come and let me show you what else I've done with your money.'

Together we embarked upon a tour of the house. Directly opposite the dining room a small lobby led to the new kitchen I had had built. A narrow staircase ascended to the servants' quarters above. The rooms were not yet finished, but for the time being it suited me to have no one living there. Until the baby was born I wanted to guard my privacy. I had arranged with the cook to come in from town twice a week with provender, and the maid came daily from the nearby farm where she lived.

'Look at my beautiful floor!' I said to St Leger, as we passed along the downstairs passage, newly paved with quarry tiles. 'See how painstaking the craftsmen were. I shall have no need of rugs here, for the pattern is too lovely to be covered up.' I led him into the double salon, the smaller half of which I used as a morning room. 'Are not my skirting boards handsome? I should not have known that carpentry was such a skilled job until I saw the men at work.'

I showed him the carving I had asked the carpenter to make on the inside of the shutters: the date – 1841 – surmounted by an ace of spades and surrounded by a wreath of oak leaves. The ace symbolized the house, which was the pinnacle of my life's ambition so far (although I told St Leger that the ace stood for him, of course), and the leaves represented the sessile oaks that grew in the forest all around.

'And see here, how smoothly my shutters work!' I drew them to, and apart again, and urged him to try them for himself. 'And how slender the glazing bars on the windows!' I watched as he took in every detail of the room: from the stuccowork on the ceiling to the slate slabs surrounding the hearth. Registering his nod of approval, I smiled and prattled on. 'I thought I might not have ordered enough wallpaper, but the paper man was clever. It fits to within a half-inch.'

The salon was papered in the same pattern as the dining room, but in a restful shade of eau de Nil – although the matching damask chaise upon which I planned to recline had not yet been delivered. Many of the items ordered in Cork had failed to arrive, and most of the rooms were but partly furnished. I had essentials – linen and plate, but no carpets; lamps, but no curtains. I yearned for books to line the library shelves and paintings to hang from the picture rails; I longed to see the garden grow, and for the scent of lilac and honeysuckle to fill my house, but in the meantime I needed to learn patience.

'It will be a pleasure to sit here with you of an evening,' St Leger remarked finally.

'Just think! After a day spent fishing, you can cast off your wet clothes and take your ease in front of a fire, or on the terrace in front of the view. You can sit down to an excellent supper and as much wine as you like. You can choose a book from the library, and we can read together, or play bezique or chess.'

'I should love to listen to you play after dinner,' he said. 'Did you include a pianoforte on your list of necessities?'

'A pianoforte is hardly a necessity, St Leger.'

He frowned. 'It will be quiet in the winter, and when it gets dark early there is no birdsong. You need a piano, Eliza. I will see to it. Show me the rest of the house.'

I showed him the library, where my empty bookcases stood sentinel on either side of the door, and where my escritoire was tucked between the French windows with their low cushioned seats. I showed him the candle sconces by my fireside chair that I had had fixed to the wall at eye level, so I could read easily. I led him through the main entrance hallway where I had insisted on another fireplace: every visitor to this house, I told St Leger, should be greeted by warmth and light.

Upstairs, the bed had been made up with the finest quality linen from an Ulster mill, and draped in shawls from Kashmir. It was the only item of furniture in my bedroom. Earlier, I had asked the maid to light a fire and set a tub by it. The water was still warm. I added some drops of lavender oil, undressed my lover and invited him to step in. I lit a dozen good wax candles and poured more wine.

In the dusk, beyond the open window, the blackbird was singing.

It was a luxury to sit in my library and write. It was a luxury to have my meals prepared and my fires set and my water drawn and my furniture polished and my bed made. It was a luxury to curl up solitaire in the window embrasure with that vista of lake and hills before me, and from time to time to have the company of my lover to admire it with me. But mostly, it was a luxury to have the pleasure of my company to myself.

Every day I took a quire of paper from my escritoire (it was a thing of beauty, of rosewood, with many ingenious compartments and drawers) and laid it on the Morocco leather inlay of the fold-down lid. Every day I wrote hundreds upon hundreds of words. William had said in one of his letters that he had found a character for a story that he was sure would be amusing, but I would challenge him to find one more amusing than the heroine *I* had dreamed up! Ideas came crowding into my head. They congregated there, jostling for position, before escaping from the nib of my pen onto the paper, with each 'i' dotted and each 't' crossed.

Letters in which William and I compared plots and characters sped to and fro across the Irish Sea.

My heroine is a clever woman, highly accomplished, after the French rather than the English mode, I wrote.

Mine is a sweet-tempered, uncomplicated girl; sadly, she will be widowed young, returned William.

I have conjured a demon of a voluptuary! I told him.

And I, a termagant of an aunt! came the rejoinder from William.

Between us, a narrative began to take shape. I made

my heroine first governess to the children of a lecherous old gentleman, then companion to a peevish old gentlewoman. I had her flirt with a squaretoes and make merry at Vauxhall and elope with a dashing – though rather empty-headed – cavalry officer. Sometimes I spent the entire day at my desk, only realizing how much time had gone by when, on hearing the bell ring for dinner, I looked up to see that the sun had gone down behind the hills.

I did not know what either of the women who had been engaged as my servants made of me, nor did I much care. They were good women, strong and reliable, and I knew that St Leger was right to have insisted on taking on staff from the hiring fair. The wretched creatures I had visited in the hamlet across the lake would not have had the strength to work as these women did. I paid them a decent wage, and was rewarded with excellent service. They were both named Bridget, so I called the cook Old Biddy and the maid Young Biddy.

Young Biddy supplied me with fresh eggs daily and sometimes a chicken from her family farm; Old Biddy made sure that the larder was well stocked, and baked bread for me twice a week. The steward, whose name was Christy Cassidy, dug a fine kitchen garden adjoining the stable yard, and planted it with currants and gooseberries and rhubarb and raspberries and all sorts of vegetables. He built beehives. He cleared a section of forest and planted it with fruit trees. Every so often he brought fish or a rabbit for Old Biddy to serve up; sometimes there was venison, and game birds – quail or pheasant – were plentiful.

Each time St Leger visited, his saddlebag was full of presents: chocolates, books, ornaments, sheet music, lace handkerchiefs, items of intimate apparel. On occasion there were cut flowers from his hothouse. He brought me a silver gilt inkstand and a tortoiseshell casket and a mechanical bird in a cage; a pair of Limerick gloves, a morning robe of embroidered Chinese silk, a pearl necklet and a fan painted with peacocks. Sometimes he stayed just one night, sometimes two or three consecutively. Sophia did not question him on his whereabouts, for she knew that he was spending time at my house. Indeed, she often enquired after my health. It was an unorthodox arrangement, but it seemed to suit us all. For several weeks it was as if we were living in Voltaire's Best of All Possible Worlds.

Then one day, because the baby had shifted inside me and I suspected it was about to start its journey, I asked St Leger to send for Maria, who was to be rewarded munificently for her complicity. She arrived in his carriage with items I had not thought to buy: squares of flannel and yards of fine linen, tiny woollen caps, soft little blankets, divers unguents, scissors, a wicker bassinet. Her eldest daughter, who had been charged with the care of her siblings in the house in Cork, had made a patchwork counterpane for the new arrival.

Maria told the Biddies that I was suffering from a sick headache, and that while I was indisposed she would take over the running of the house. I don't imagine either of them was fooled, but because they were handsomely paid and treated well, they entered into the spirit of connivance without comment. Maria oversaw the thorough cleaning of my bedchamber and the stock-piling of linen, made sure there was sufficient food in the larder, fuel for the fires and water drawn, then dismissed both women, saying that she would send for them when I was recovered. She unpacked the layette, uncorked a bottle of St Leger's best wine, and together we waited.

During the intervals between cramps, which were initially quite bearable, she entertained me with stories of Lord Doneraile's liaisons with an actress in Dublin, and of the lady's maid who had been discovered bound to some peculiar contraption in Sir Silas Sillery's cellar, and of an uncle of hers who had left his wife and gone to live in India with a punkah wallah. We agreed that men were peculiar, irrational creatures.

She fed me tiny quails' eggs and morsels of almond cake and slivers of crystallized fruit, and when I could no longer eat or drink she soaked a flannel in honey water so that I could suck on it, and rubbed my belly with peppermint oil.

She made and remade my bed, and pummelled my pillows to make me more comfortable. 'What is this doing under your bolster?' she asked, holding up the knife that I kept there.

'It is for any man who dares to take me against my will,' I told her.

'It will come in useful now,' she said, sliding it under the mattress. 'A knife under the mattress is said to cut the birthing pains by half.'

Some hours later, Maria told me it was time to start work in earnest. She squeezed out the flannel and gave it to me again so that I could tear it with my teeth. She did not give me her hand to hold for she knew I would break the bones, but she supported me when I could no longer endure lying still, and encouraged me to walk up and down the corridor: up and down, and up and down again, and again and again, to bring the baby on.

And finally I squatted in a corner of my bedchamber and forced it out with a howl.

'What is it?' I asked, as the infant slid between my legs.

'A boy. It's a boy!' said Maria. She held the tiny thing up to slap life into it, then, at the first cry, she laid it on my belly, reached for the scissors and cut the cord, knotting it with astonishing dexterity. She sat back on her heels, pushed her hair back from her face, and smiled at me. Then she took the baby over to the basin that was waiting by the fire, poured water and wiped it clean.

Slumped against the wall, I waited for the pain to ease at last. But the spasms kept coming and the bloodstain on my nightgown kept spreading and the baby kept crying.

'Why hasn't it stopped? Maria? Maria!'

Maria glanced over her shoulder as she swathed the child in linen.

'The afterbirth is coming,' she said. 'Wait – I'll help you now – let me settle him.' She laid the infant in the bassinet, where it meowed like a cat. 'It's nearly over,' Maria assured me, hunkering down. 'Once you've passed the placenta, it's done.'

I felt a twisting inside me, like a great snake. I got onto my forearms and knees, tugging at the cuff of my sleeve with my teeth and pushed with all my strength. Something else slid out of me. Completely spent, I fell with my face against the floorboards.

'Is it finished now? Is it over? Is it over now? Please say it's over, Maria.'

She said nothing. I twisted my head around to look.

Maria's hands were clamped to her mouth. Still crouched between my legs, she raised her eyes to mine and stared at me; her brow was furrowed, her hair damp, her face smeared with my blood. Then she reached for the scissors, fumbled and held something aloft. It wasn't the placenta. It was another baby.

For me there had only ever been two possible outcomes to the status quo I had engineered, neither of which involved my direct participation. The birth of a boy would have meant a journey to the wet-nurse who had been engaged by Sophia, whence the child would be borne away to its adoptive parents. Had it been a girl, she would have been spirited off to the foundling hospital in Cork. Either way, I should have been rid of an encumbrance, and free to resume my life as lady novelist and mistress of Lissaguirra. But this! This was a card I had never foreseen as being part of the hand dealt me.

As I lay curled upon the floor of my bedchamber, I watched Maria busy herself. She was efficiency personified. She made up the bed with fresh sheets, stoked the fire and stripped me of my soiled linen. She washed me, put me to bed in a clean gown, fetched me hot negus, and combed my hair. She opened the window to let in fresh air, and then she set the bassinet of sleeping babies beside me on the bed.

'What do you want me to do with them?' I asked.

'You worked hard enough to bring them into the world; it would be churlish not to bid them farewell.' Maria picked up her shawl, and made for the door.

'Where are you going?' I called after her.

'To harness the pony. I shall need to get the boy to the wet-nurse post haste. He's a puny little thing.'

And off she went.

From downstairs I heard the clock chime: four, five or six, I could not tell. How long had I been in labour? How many hours had passed since yesterday evening, when I had been childless and carefree?

Now I found myself shored up in bed with two babies I had never met before. They were hideous little things: like the organ grinder's monkeys I had seen once in Vauxhall. Which was which? It would be easy to find out, but Maria had swaddled the pair so expertly I did not dare touch them. Their skin was the same plum shade as the dining-room wallpaper, and the same texture as the gloves St Leger had given me – the ones so fine they could be packed into the shell of a walnut.

One of the babies yawned, making its aspect even more hideous: like the gargoyle on the corner of Notre-Dame in Paris, which had fascinated me as a child. The other one's face was all puckered, like the toothless old beggar man who had used to importune me for alms in Chiswick. The one who had yawned made a mewling sound, and I peered more closely at it. It started scrabbling around, its tiny fingers like bats' claws, and then it scraped the face of the other one, and woke it up. It blinked, its eyes all squinty, like Sir Silas Sillery's after too much claret.

Now they appeared to be looking at each other. How strange, to be seeing for the very first time someone you'd been cooped up with for nine months! The blinking one started mewling in harmony with its sibling. They must be hearing each other for the first time, too! A funny little song, it was. I supposed they must be hungry. I joined in – a half-hearted la-la-la. Then Blinky's little hand clenched, as if it was shaking its fist, and it landed a thump right on the other one's nose. It made me laugh. It made me laugh so hard I had to wipe tears from my eyes. All in all, the babies were the silliest, ugliest things I had ever seen.

When Maria came back with a dish of raspberry tea, I had unwrapped both of them, and had one at each breast.

'I had thought the one with the flailing fists to be the boy,' I said, conversationally, coaxing a nipple into a tiny mutinous mouth. 'But it turns out she's the girl. I'm glad she has a pugnacious streak. She's going to need it.'

'I'm sure St Leger will see to it that she's well taken care of,' Maria assured me, taking a peek under the shawl draped over my shoulders. 'The orphanage is as susceptible to bribes as any other so-called charitable institution. With a sweetener from her father she'll fare better than most of the poor bastards there. Which one's which?'

'This is St Leger's boy,' I said, indicating the infant on my right breast, 'and this is the girl.'

'Dear God they're ugly, aren't they? You'd think that such handsome parents could have managed to produce a more comely pair of babes.'

'Don't call them ugly!' I said. 'They're the most beautiful babies ever made. Especially you, my little minx,' I told the one nearest my heart. 'My fighting girl, my darling, my sweet little hellion, my pretty pet!'

'Have they taken to the teat?'

'She has,' I said with pride. 'He seems altogether more fussy.'

'It's not good for you to get your milk flowing, Eliza. It will be agony once they're gone.'

Maria reached for St Leger's son and heir and unlatched him from my nipple. He puked in protest.

'Take him and welcome,' I told her, pulling the shawl back over my shoulder. 'He can sup his fill at the wet-nurse's dug.'

I shifted in the bed, resting my left elbow against the pillow so that my daughter's head nestled more comfortably in the crook of my arm, watching the rhythmic pull of her mouth.

'You must stop, Eliza!' said Maria crossly. 'You'll rue it if you get an infection. I came down with a bad fever when my youngest wouldn't take to the nipple and my breasts became engorged.'

'*She's* taken to it! See how she has! My little guzzle-guts.'

'But she'll be gone from you soon,' went on Maria. 'Mark my words – you'll regret then that you allowed her to feed so lustily. Here – give her to me.'

'No, no, Maria,' I said, looking up at her with a smile. 'You may take the boy. I won't renege on my promise to St Leger. But I'm not parting with this little miss.'

'You're not keeping her!'

'Yes, I am.' I looked down at the fierce, tiny face, and my daughter returned my gaze, her slate blue eyes full of ancient, arcane knowledge. 'She's my kismet – my Ananke. Her name's Clara Venus, and she's staying with me.'

19

THE RUSHING SOUND of the river splashing over the rocks meant that Edie wasn't aware of Mr O'Brien until he was almost upon her.

'I'm done now,' he said.

Edie set Eliza's manuscript aside and scrambled to her feet. From where he was pootling about in the shallows, Milo shot Mr O'Brien a belligerent look. He clearly didn't like the cut of his jib, either.

'You've had a good scout around, then,' said Edie. 'What are your thoughts?'

'The place has potential,' he conceded.

She was glad to see that he had at least a modicum of aesthetic sensibility. 'I think so too,' she enthused. 'Simply *masses* of potential. Are you planning on converting it, or might you live here yourself?'

Mr O'Brien looked as if she'd just asked him a question in Ancient Egyptian. 'Live . . . *here*?'

'Well – yes.'

He shook his head. 'I'm interested in getting an industry going.'

'An industry?'

'A fishery.'

Edie had never heard of a fishery being described as an 'industry' before.

'I run one up in Connemara,' continued Mr O'Brien, 'and I'm planning to expand. There's increasing demand for Irish salmon worldwide.'

Edie looked down the garden towards the lake. Beneath the glittering surface swam silvery specimens weighing as much as seventeen pounds, like the one Uncle Jack had landed. She remembered how he had taken her and Hilly on an angling expedition, the summer they turned thirteen. She had caught nothing, but Hilly had hooked a little silver trout that they had immediately disengaged from the fly and sent spinning back into the water, praying it would survive.

'How do you propose catching them?' she asked. 'With lines?'

Mr O'Brien gave a derisive snort. 'With draft nets. There's no money in line-caught fish, dear.'

I am *not* your dear, Edie wanted to say. How dared this man condescend to her just because he was wealthy and handsome! But it behove her to be civil if she was to get Uncle Jack's house sold.

'Won't there be transport costs involved in getting produce to market?' she enquired.

He gave her a blank look.

'All that ice, for instance, for packing.'

'We'll not be transporting fresh stock. We'll do everything here. Hold 'em in ponds, strip the ova, rear the fry in a hatchery.' Looking down at the tumbling river, he made a clicking sound with his tongue against the side of his teeth. 'As an added bonus, looks like we could operate an eel weir. Boil 'em, pack 'em, seal 'em and sell 'em.'

'But . . . what will you do with the house?'

He looked at Edie as if she were half-witted.

'What do you think? Pull it down.'

Edie couldn't countenance this man any more. Casting around for an escape route, her eyes fell upon Milo frolicking in his paddling pool.

'Oh, my little dog!' she cried, rounding upon the startled animal and scooping him into her arms. 'He's drowning!'

'He looks perfectly fine to me,' said Mr O'Brien, reaching out a finger to scruffle Milo under his chin. 'Jolly little chap, isn't he?'

'Fuck off,' said Milo.

Edie was genuinely shocked. 'Milo! Mind your mouth! Don't growl like that at the nice gentleman.'

Mr O'Brien quickly withdrew his hand and stuck it in his pocket. Looking around, he squinted up at the window of the bedroom that overlooked the stream and shook his head, making that clicking sound again. 'What *amadán* thought it would be a good idea to put a window in directly above a river?' he said. 'You wouldn't get a wink of sleep all night.'

Now Edie really was fed up with him.

'Well, good day to you, Mr O'Brien. I must go and dry my dog.'

'Just as well I didn't bring my fella along with me,' said Mr O'Brien. 'German Shepherd, he is. He'd have made mincemeat of your cream puff.'

'Now, there's an idea! Canned minced meat for dogs.'

'I've already thought of that,' smirked Mr O'Brien. 'There are hundreds of ponies running wild in Connemara. Dime a dozen, they are. Boil 'em, pack 'em, seal 'em and sell 'em. That's my motto.'

And Mr O'Brien tipped his hat at Edie and was gone.

She watched his progress as he rounded the corner of the stable yard and set off along the overgrown avenue, swiping at rhododendron bushes with a stick. 'What a B,' she said. 'What a thoroughly unpleasant oik. I hope he doesn't get this place. I shall tell Uncle Jack he's a bounder.'

'A fucking bounder.'

She looked down at the little dog in her arms and gave him an ebullient squeeze. 'There were two babies, Milo!' she crowed. 'There were two! And she's keeping one!'

'Sophia did not quit her chamber for a month when she had our daughter. She did not leave the house until two months clear had gone by.'

'Your daughter was born dead, St Leger. No wonder Sophia did not choose to quit her room.'

'I cannot condone this behaviour, Eliza! You will wear yourself out.'

St Leger had happened upon me as I walked in the garden of Lissaguirra with Clara in my arms. It was washday, and the smell of lye from the scullery pervaded the downstairs rooms; I would have gone mad cooped up inside. Besides, the weather was fine – blue-skied and mild for so late in the autumn – and I wanted the exercise. Having spent so many months carrying a pair of rowdies around inside me, I took great pleasure in having my body all to myself for a change. I yearned to let loose and kick up my heels. I longed to dance. If Sir Silas Sillery had asked me to accompany him in a quadrille, I would have accepted in a transport of ecstasy.

'Oh, tush, you old fogey!' I said, lobbing an apple core at the donkey (who had been acquired as a companion for my pony). 'Babies are portable, and women are the stronger sex. If I were Chinese I would be hard at work in the paddy fields by now.'

'Sophia says that – '

'I care not what Sophia says! I simply could not bear to be indoors in this weather.'

I tramped on down the path, my boots making a satisfying thud against the packed earth. St Leger followed, looking put-out.

'She is not making a public show of herself, at any rate,' he muttered.

'Is she confined still, with our son?'

'Yes.'

'And nobody suspects a thing? Not even the wet-nurse?'

'If she does, she is not likely to put her job in jeopardy. She is paid well for her trouble.'

'How is he?'

'He's thriving.'

'Does he sleep?'

'Very well. The nurse tells me that she is hardly disturbed at night.'

'She doses him with Godfrey's Cordial, I have no doubt.'

I sounded pettish, and I was. I was jealous of anyone who slept through the night. At three weeks old, Clara Venus was the most beautiful and intelligent baby who had ever drawn breath, but Morpheus was her enemy, and she was perpetually hungry. I carried her everywhere with me, slung in a shawl like an Indian papoose, so that I could nurse her on demand to keep her quiet.

I knew little about her brother, for St Leger had managed to pay me but one visit since the babies had been born. The boy was called George, after Sophia's father. By all accounts (well, by St Leger's account, and his was the only one that mattered) George the elder had been so overcome with joy at the birth of his grandson that he had staged a show of fireworks in the grounds of his palatial home, Roesworth House in Buckinghamshire. Thanks to the fecundity of his daughter and her husband, the male bloodline was established, succession was secure, the family fortune was safe in St Leger's hands, and Sir Silas Sillery could go sing for his supper. There was to be a great christening in London in Westminster Cathedral, his godfather was to be Sir Huddlestone Fuddlestone (or some such blue blood), and he was to have his 'manly character' instilled from the age of five, when he would be sent away to be educated first at Mr Pampellone's Academy in Wandsworth, then at Eton. I was mildly surprised that he was not already in line to be married to some Spanish infanta or Austrian princess.

'Are they alike, the twins?' I asked St Leger.

'All babies are alike to me,' he said.

'Look properly!' I said, presenting his daughter's adorable face to him.

'George is uglier.'

'What do you mean, "uglier"?'

'He's – well, he's a boy. He's bound to be uglier.'

I gave him an affronted look. 'From that I infer you think Clara Venus ugly.'

'No. No, Eliza. She's not ugly. She's a bonny wee thing. Or would be if her ears didn't stick out so much.'

'Her ears do not stick out! And if they do, it's your fault, for she inherited them from you.'

He laughed, and caught me by the waist. 'She will be a beauty,' he said, kissing me. 'How could she be anything but, with a stunner like you for a mother?'

I took his arm, and we strolled on towards the lake.

'How long can you stay?' I asked.

'How does tonight and tomorrow night suit you, my lady?'

'I shall have to consult my pocket-book.' Clara Venus squawked, and I began to unbutton my bodice. Uneasily, St Leger looked around. 'Don't be alarmed,' I told him. 'Christy has seen me nurse her, and he didn't bat an eyelid.'

'I wish you would hire a wet-nurse. It is unseemly for a gentlewoman to give suck.'

'If I did not suckle her, you would not be so free and easy with my person. A wise old *accoucheuse* once told me that –'

'A pox on your wise old *accoucheuse*! Has anyone asked about the child?'

'Oh, yes. I've told everyone I found her under the gooseberry bush.'

'No one has been curious?'

'I'm sure there is gossip galore about St Leger's brat. But I have heard none of it. And it is unlikely to be malicious, for both the Biddies are fond of me, and they *love* your daughter.'

'You are cosy then, and happy.'

'Yes. Although I am glad you are come. The Biddies are good women to be sure, but I can't converse with them on any subjects other than the weather or what is on the menu for dinner. It's salmon tonight, by the way. Christy took it straight from the lake this morning.'

'He could be had up for poaching the next time he does that,' said St Leger with a laugh.

I gave him a curious look. 'Why?'

'Lord Abingdon dropped down dead taking a fence with the Red and Blacks last week.'

'What has he to do with anything?'

'He owns the fishing rights hereabouts. They'll pass to his son once the will has been ratified.'

Everything stopped suddenly. The breeze stopped ruffling the lake, the blackbird stopped singing, I stopped walking.

'You mean the lake isn't yours?'

'No. I lease the rights from His Lordship on an

annual basis. He owns the hunting and fishing rights for miles around. Or rather, his son does now.'

'But isn't that why you built the house? So that you could come here to hunt?'

'I built a bothy, Eliza. The house was your idea.'

Clara Venus spluttered at my breast. I looked down at her, trying to think.

'And I don't hunt here,' he continued. 'I hunt with the Red and Blacks. There is no fox hunting hereabouts.'

'But you're always going off shooting!'

'Shooting and hunting are very different. You're such a townie, my sweet! It's rather endearing to know that you can be rattlebrained about some things.'

'So unless you pay the new Lord Abingdon, you can neither hunt nor fish?'

'That's so.'

I had got it wrong. So egregiously wrong. I had just learned that my house, my two acres of land and my little stretch of lakeshore were worth nothing.

'I'll have to decide whether it's worth paying to keep the permit on,' continued St Leger. 'Especially now that Sophia wants to remove to London.'

'Why does she want to do that?'

'Her father has expressed a preference that George be reared in England.'

'He's *your* son!'

'His future is there, Eliza. He'll be heir to the Roesworth estate one day.'

And your daughter will be heir to a poxy so-called hunting lodge in a poxy bog in the poxy county of Cork! I wanted to say, but of course did not. It was imperative to keep my mouth shut and think strategically. But I couldn't think, I couldn't think of anything any more. All I knew was that the house I had gone to such pains to have built had suddenly become as cumbersome as Coleridge's albatross, and that if my cook put trout or salmon or bream on a plate in front of me from this day on, I could be had up for poaching.

'Well, I'm sure George will make a very handsome country gent over there in Buckinghamshire,' I sniped. 'Perhaps his sister could get a job as an under-house-maid at Roesworth House.'

St Leger gave me a sharp look, and I sheathed my claws at once. When in doubt, be winsome.

Clara Venus burped on cue.

'Look at the pretty mite! Do you really think her ears stick out?' I said, dimpling up at him. 'Perhaps I should take to winding a strip of linen about her head. They say that if you bind a baby's ears tightly enough, they will grow fine and regular.'

'I will not hear of you binding our daughter's ears, Eliza! How could you think of doing such a thing?'

'In Japan they bind their daughters' feet to keep them dainty.'

'I'd rather her feet were the size of an elk's! Give me the child.'

He took Clara Venus from me and slid her under the lapel of his coat to keep her warm. A posset of milk had pooled around her mouth. I handed him her bib, and he wiped her clean.

'Come, little jolly,' he said to her, as he descended the grassy bank that sloped to the shore of the lake. 'Dance to your daddy!' He turned back to me, smiling. 'Do you know the rhyme, Eliza?'

'No.' No one had ever thought to sing nursery rhymes to me when I was an infant.

'It goes: Dance to your daddy, my little lassie! Dance to your daddy, my little lamb!'

I pasted a smile to my face.

'You shall have a fishy on a little dishy!' went on St Leger, bouncing the child in his arms. 'You shall have a fishy when the boat comes in!'

Unlikely, I thought. Not from that lake. There'd be no fishy for me or for Clara Venus. No kedgeree, baked pike, smoked eel nor potted salmon. Nor – in spite of all the endeavours I had made to set myself up with a nice little nest egg in the form of Lissaguirra – had my boat come in. Yet.

*

Dear William,

When are you coming? I had thought to have company here occasionally, but no one comes. During the winter it rained and blew and not a creature but a mad peddler selling gewgaws came to the house from November till March. I yearn for someone to amuse me and make me laugh. The only thing that makes me laugh now is the future I had pictured for myself, in the Best of all Possible Worlds. Here it is — the picture I painted of me, in my rosy future:

    Sitting at my desk, in artful déshabille, I dip my pen into my silver-gilt inkwell and the words flow from my nib. Occasionally I lean my cheek on my hand, and gaze at the view beyond my window, seeking fresh inspiration. Once I have covered a ream of paper with my elegant script, I write FINIS. I smile to myself and pen a letter, which I send along with my manuscript to your venerable publishers Messrs Chapman & Hall, in London. Two weeks later I get the response I have been hoping for, and off I go to be feted and lionized. My book is a great success, and I am set up for life.

    Isn't this how it happens?

    Eliza

Dear Eliza,

I am coming in August. Messrs Chapman & Hall want

the Irish book that they paid me to write two years ago. From Dublin I intend to travel south before proceeding through Connaught and Ulster. Perhaps I will include a chapter on an idyllic hunting lodge in County Cork? Might you let me have a bed for a night or two?

Yours in haste,

William

I told St Leger of the famous contributor to the *Times* of London who was visiting Ireland to write a guidebook. 'His name is William Thackeray. He is very clever and erudite, and is much in demand by all the best publications.'

St Leger did not seem impressed by William's credentials. 'He sounds like a bore,' he said. 'Erudite people always are. Look at Silas and his dusty old library full of books that nobody but he wants to read.'

'Mr Thackeray is a great friend of Charles Dickens,' I persisted, 'and very entertaining. He is keen to visit obscure places, so I have invited him to stay here.'

We were lounging, all three of our little family, on my bed. Because I had not believed St Leger when he told me he had a wolfskin, he had presented it to me, with a red ribbon tied around its tail. Both my babies had lain swaddled on it after they were born, looking quite the little wolf-cubs. It now lay on an ottoman at the foot of my bed as insurance against cold weather.

I had lifted Clara Venus from her crib so that she could lie naked and kick her delicious legs in the air. Even at barely nine months old, it was clear that she had inherited the elegant dancer's legs of which my mother had been so proud. The evening sun was streaming through the window onto the counterpane, and she was bathed in a nimbus of golden light, talking in the mellifluous language only she understood.

St Leger had brought me several pairs of clocked stockings in a variety of colours. I was sporting the blue ones – complemented by an exquisite lace-trimmed garter – for his delectation.

'Wouldn't you like to meet Mr Thackeray?' I asked, stretching out a leg to admire the fine embroidery. 'I am sure he would be interested to learn about this country from the point of view of an absentee landlord.'

'Don't call me that, Eliza.'

'Why not? It's what you are.'

'"Absentee" implies that I don't look after my estate. I do.'

'While you are here, you do. Who looks after your tenants when you're away?'

'I have a responsible agent. And I have scarcely any tenants now.'

'What happened to them?'

'I sold the larger part of my land.'

'Why?'

'It's not worth holding on to when I have no household to maintain.'

It took me a moment to catch the inference: he no longer needed the income from rent because his family was safely provided for in Buckinghamshire under the aegis of the Earl of Roesworth.

'But you love Dromamore.'

'I do.'

I tucked my legs under me and gave him a challenging look. 'How do you know that your agent is a responsible man? Have you spoken to your tenants lately?'

'Oh, you are a trying woman! Don't vex me.'

'I vex you because nobody else dares to. When was the last time someone questioned your authority?'

'Cerberos did, until I put manners on him.'

'Who's Cerberos?'

'My new pup.'

'So your puppy dog and your mistress are the only souls in the world who stand up to you?'

'Sometimes it's the other way round.'

'What do you mean?'

'*I* stood up for you twice this afternoon.'

I returned his oblique smile and moved in to kiss him, but a tremolo from Clara Venus distracted me.

'Look at my bonny girl! She loves this time of the

evening – it's when she gets her exercise. Look at her sturdy little legs! *Il n'y a rien de plus beau que la grasse sous la peau.*'

'What does that mean?'

'It's an old French saying. It means, "there is nothing more beautiful than a little fat under the skin". Oh! I could spend a whole lifetime kissing her belly.' I leaned over my daughter and pressed my lips against her tummy, making her squeal with delight.

St Leger untwisted his fingers from my garter, then reached for his shirt and pulled it on. He got up from the bed, strolled to the window and leaned his elbows on the sash.

'Christy has done good work in the garden,' he observed.

'Yes. He has a knack. The kitchen garden is thriving, too, and the orchard. It will be a fine thing, to have our own fruit next year.'

'And you're happy with your staff?'

I nodded, blowing on Clara Venus's belly button and producing another gale of giggles.

'Are you feeding well?'

'Exceptionally well. We even have poached poached salmon from time to time.' The tautology was intentional. I gave him a defiant look.

'You little delinquent.'

'I needed all the sustenance I could get while I was nursing your daughter. She has a prodigious appetite.'

'You've weaned her?'

'She's weaned herself. Once she got a taste of custard and boiled bread and honey she refused my dug for the first time.'

'Doesn't she suckle at all now?'

'Yes – for comfort.'

'We should be taking every precaution we can against another pregnancy happening.'

'I already have.'

'How?'

'Another invaluable secret I learned from that wise old *accoucheuse* in Soho.' I slanted him a smile and loosened my hair.

I had not told him about the sponge soaked in *eau de vie*. It was, in fact, a tip I had had from Maria, who swore by it, claiming that it had worked for her after the birth of her last child. Since her husband had died shortly thereafter it was hardly a proven method of contraception, but having recourse to the trick in conjunction with the fact that I was still producing milk meant that the chances of my conceiving again in the first year were slender – especially since I had given birth to twins. Everyone knew that Nature allowed a woman's body more time to recover after twins.

'George is still latched onto his wet-nurse,' said St Leger. 'Sophia says he'll be walking before he gives up the dug.'

Reaching for my hairbrush, I started on the first of my hundred strokes. 'Hereabouts, I've seen infants of two years and more importuning their mothers for milk.'

'Two? A child should be well weaned by that age, shouldn't it?'

'The children are hungry, Jamie. And so are their parents. Christy tells me that there is real hardship amongst tenants. You know that most of them subsist on a diet of potatoes and buttermilk?'

'They've lived on that for years. It's said to be the healthiest diet in Europe.'

'Christy says if the potato crop fails it could lead to wholesale famine.' I tugged the bristles through a tangled strand of hair. 'Oh! See how you've mussed me, you bad man! I shall need to take a fine comb to it. Imagine if I ever had lice! I should have to crop all my hair off. I would have a pate just like yours, Clara Venus!' I blew her a flurry of kisses, then teased my hair with my fingers. A moment or two passed during which I made inconsequential small talk with my daughter before I deemed it opportune to return to the subject of politics. 'Christy says that Lord Faulkes's tenants live in such unsanitary conditions that they are falling prey to disease.'

'That's because Faulkes is an irresponsible and profligate fool. He is the kind of landlord who gives others among us a bad name.'

304

'But aren't Irish landowners spending more time in London generally? Lord Meresford was in residence only once last year, and beggars are crowding the roads around his demesne.'

At the window St Leger was still contemplating the view with his back to me, his shoulders set in an attitude that clearly said he did not want to be having this conversation. Knowing that no one else would have it with him, I continued, regardless.

'Didn't you see them on your way here? They are stick thin and ragged.'

'It's called the summer hunger,' he said. 'It ends in October, when the lumpers are harvested.'

'Lumpers?'

'A variety of potato. Trust me – things will improve, come autumn.'

'And if they don't?'

'Eliza – my interests in Ireland now lie mainly in seeing that you and my daughter are comfortable and happy.'

'I'm glad we are part of your rubric.'

'You are very dear to me. Both of you. But I would quit the country tomorrow were it not for you.'

I felt the grip of fear. The prospect of being left on my own in this godforsaken place with no sponsor was unthinkable.

'We are comfortable,' I assured him. 'But we miss you. If we were in London you could visit us more often.

Cannot you buy us a little house there? We would not require anything so large as this.'

'Sophia would not tolerate it.'

'She was not averse to your building this house.'

'In Ireland you are out of sight, sweetheart, and that is how Sophia likes it. If you came to London we could not conduct our liaison with the same discretion.'

'We are hardly discreet, St Leger! Everyone in North Cork knows of our affair.'

'Ireland is another country. London is the hub of the universe.'

'And people there are sophisticated enough to know that gentlemen keep mistresses,' I argued.

'Most gentlemen's mistresses have not borne the heir to a fortune. If word got out that George is not Sophia's natural child, the calumny would ruin her.'

'How could word get out?'

'The popular press thrives on speculation. Remember what became of Sarah Lennox.'

'Who's she?'

'The daughter of the Duke of Richmond. Her husband divorced her because she bore him a bastard child, and she died in poverty. It was reported in the most lurid prose in all the scandal sheets. That is what Sophia fears more than anything – public humiliation.'

I gave my hair one last vigorous stroke of the brush and shook it out. 'Imagine being concerned about what people say about you! I should hate to have a good reputation.'

'Why?'

'You can't lose something you never had in the first place.'

I sent him a winning smile, then set my hairbrush down and returned my attention to Clara. She was still kicking her heels in the pool of sunlight, telling herself jokes and gurgling with laughter.

'She's talking already,' I said. 'Listen to her! I've been speaking French to her – haven't I, *mon petit chou*!'

'She will be as fluent *en français* as in English by the time she's old enough to go to school.'

I bit my tongue. School! What school was there hereabouts for my daughter? I had heard that poor Irish children were educated in what were called 'hedge' schools, where they were instructed in Irish grammar and the lives of the saints. What use would that be to Clara? And what would become of her when she wanted companions? She would not lack for company in London. In London she could have access to proper education as well as to society. I longed to say all this to St Leger, and more, but I knew he would not care to hear it. Clara Venus was not his primary concern: George was.

'They're burning gorse somewhere,' he said. 'I can smell it on the wind.'

'The smell is like roasting chestnuts, isn't it? I used to love the smell from the braziers of the vendors in Regent's Park. How I should love to walk there with you! We could go skating on the pond in winter, and take Clara to the zoo.'

'Are you really so eager to be close to me?'

'Yes,' I fibbed.

He smiled at me indulgently, then came back to the bed and bowed his head to kiss my foot. I wriggled my toes prettily, and leaned back on my elbows, looking ruefully at his dear, silken head.

The fact was, it was not his company I craved; it was the society of like-minded people, for I was suffering from chronic ennui. I could not write, for Clara Venus was jealous of any time I spent at my desk; besides, my head was too moony with motherhood to concentrate on my manuscript. I could not pay social calls upon anyone in the neighbourhood, for since news of my affair had got out I had become a pariah in polite circles. I had no inclination or aptitude for pursuits such as embroidery, and felt incapable of reading anything more demanding than frivolous French novels.

I had lived here alone in Lissaguirra for nearly a year, and the winter had been a sore trial. Never in my most far-fetched dreams had I envisaged a future rearing a child in a remote corner of a benighted country with no one but two biddies and a donkey to talk to. It had been short-sighted of me not to have anticipated the possibility of a second baby: I should have known that fraternal twins were a possibility, since my mother had been one. It is, however, easy to be wise in hindsight.

'Who's that?' St Leger had been distracted from his nibbling of my toes by the sound of approaching hooves. 'Are you expecting someone?'

'Oh, yes. It is my knight in shining armour. I had forgotten he was due today.'

He gave me a testy look, and made for the window.

'It's a man on a roan mare,' he observed.

'What does he look like?'

'He's tall. Heavy built.'

'Bespectacled? Wavy hair?'

'Yes.'

'It's William!'

I shrugged into my negligee, scooped up Clara Venus and ran to the window.

'William!' I called down to him. 'William Makepeace Thackeray! Up here!'

'What do you think you're doing, Eliza?' snapped St Leger. 'Waving at a man from your bedroom window!'

'He doesn't know it's my bedroom window. Besides, it's only William. William!'

Thackeray looked up short-sightedly, finally pin-pointing whence I was hailing him.

'Hello there!' I called again. 'Meet Clara Venus!'

I held Clara up so that he could get a good look.

'Clara Venus,' echoed William. 'Good God. Is she yours?'

'Yes!' I said. 'And St Leger's.'

'St Leger? Who the deuce is he?'

St Leger looked testier than ever. 'I am,' he said interposing himself between me and the window frame.

'Come in, come in!' I cried to William over his shoulder. 'You're just in time for tea!'

20

E DIE SET DOWN the manuscript. William Thackeray had been in this house? William Thackeray – who had been lauded as lustily as Dickens, whose *Vanity Fair* appeared routinely in lists of the top ten most beloved novels of all time, whose Becky Sharp was the nineteenth-century prototype of heroine *du jour* Scarlett O'Hara – had actually hacked through a forest on a roan mare to pay homage to the chateleine of Lissaguirra? How devoutly he must have admired her!

The library fire was almost out; the mantel clock struck twelve. Edie threw a handful of sticks into the grate, lobbed on another sod of turf, and reached for the next page as if it were gift-wrapped, and had her name on it.

E. D.

It was the first time ever I had entertained a guest in my salon. The Biddies were overcome with excitement. We had griddle cakes and cinnamon biscuits and rhubarb wine as well as copious amounts of tea, which young Biddy served as decorously as if she had been to the manner born, instead of in the usual slapdash fashion.

William's dear candid face had registered nothing but confusion from the moment he had arrived, and I knew his discomfiture would not be assuaged until I had a chance to explain everything to him. The fact was that I had not acquainted him with either my maternal or my extramarital status. He knew nothing of St Leger or Clara Venus; all he knew from my letters was that I had come into money somehow, and had stayed on in Ireland to embark on a career as a lady novelist.

'You have taken me quite by surprise,' I told him, as I fussed over the tea things, 'so you must excuse our shortcomings. We are mighty quiet and comfortable here – we live in a muddle, and dress in the morning for all day. That is why you find me in déshabille.' I had thrown on a morning robe and a fichu of Alençon lace that St Leger had given me, and my hair was undressed and tied up in a silk scarf. 'Now, have some of these griddle cakes that Biddy has made especially for you,' I said, settling down next to St Leger on the sofa opposite William, 'and tell us all about your journey – whence you have come and where you are going.'

'I travelled by coach from Waterford,' he told us, 'and hired a horse at the posting house in Lismore.'

'So your baggage has gone south, with the coach?' I asked.

'Yes. To Cork. I will catch up with it there.'

'You have had fine weather for travelling,' said St Leger.

'Yes.'

'How did you find Dublin?'

'The leaves on the trees in Fitzwilliam Square are not as sooty as in similar parks in London.'

I wanted to laugh at the pair of them sitting stiff-backed on my eau de Nil brocade upholstery, eyeing each other like a couple of wary dogs. Because they were both big men, the teacups and saucers in their hands looked like dolls' dishes, and I guessed that they would rather be drinking whiskey: however, there would be time for that later.

'You came through Carlow town?' asked St Leger politely, taking a sip from his porcelain cup.

'Yes.'

'So you saw the grand new cathedral.'

'Rather overloaded with ornamentation, to my eye,' said William. 'And some of the spires were out of the perpendicular.'

'How did you find Lismore?' enquired St Leger. 'If the cathedral in Carlow was not to your taste, you must allow that the Duke's seat is an outstanding example of Gothic architecture.'

'It is a magnificent castle to be sure, and worthy of a plutocrat such as His Grace. But it is a pity that with such a noble residence – and with such wondrously scenic country round about it – he should not inhabit it more.'

I folded my hands in my lap and tried not to look smug. This had been my very point earlier, when St Leger and I had been talking politics!

'His Grace travels extensively,' said St Leger, by way of excuse for the Duke of Devonshire, who owned acre upon acre of Ireland's woods, mountains, farms and rivers. 'He has a keen interest in horticulture.'

'Yes. I understand he has had a banana named after him.' William helped himself to another biscuit. 'He certainly benefits from his Hibernian estates – I believe that the salmon fishery on the river beneath the castle is let for a thousand pounds a year.'

A thousand pounds a year! I thought of the lake that lay shimmering a hundred yards from where we were sitting, and how much the fishing rights might have been worth to me. I remembered how I had once joked with William that I could be a good woman if I had a thousand pounds a year . . .

'However, there seemed to be few signs of industry or commerce in the country generally,' continued William. 'I have been taking notes.'

He produced a small notebook, and St Leger threw

him a look of disgust. He was bored with this talk, I could tell, and had given up hope that he might engage our guest in the topics that interested him most – hunting, fishing and gambling.

Luckily, we were rescued by Clara Venus, who chose that moment to waken from the cosy nest of cushions I had piled for her upon the sofa. 'Laaa!' she sang, and I swooped upon her like a turtle dove upon her chick.

'Come and stroll with us before the sun goes down,' I said to William. 'It is a dream of pure pleasure to walk by the lake on an evening like this.'

William tucked his notebook back into his pocket. 'Might you lend me a pencil?' he said. 'I should like to take some notes, but I have taken so many already that mine is but a stub now.'

'Of course.'

St Leger, too, had risen to his feet. 'I'll go and fetch my gun,' he said. 'Head up into the woods and see if I can't bag a pigeon or two for Biddy.'

St Leger loved to walk with me at this hour of the evening, but I could tell that he had had enough of William.

'See if you can't get a fox too,' I told him. 'I'm sure William would love to take a brush home as a souvenir of Ireland.'

We all laughed at my little pleasantry, and St Leger

kissed me on the cheek before quitting the room. I busied myself with Clara Venus, straightening her bonnet and retying her bib. All the time, I could feel William's eyes upon me.

'It is a well appointed house, for all you painted such a modest picture of it in your letters.'

'Did I?'

'You called it a lodge.'

'It is more of a . . . dower house.'

'You're not a widow.'

'I was never a wife. And I'm no angel.'

'He is married?' he said, finally.

'Of course he is,' I said, with a challenging look. 'Pray, don't deliver me any sermons, William, for I shan't listen to them.'

I swung Clara Venus onto my hip, and moved towards the French windows, where I paused, waiting for him to open them for me. He did so, giving me a look in which sorrow was mixed with reproach.

'I do not stand in judgement on you, Eliza,' he began. 'You are my friend, and – '

'Indeed, your judgement should have nothing to do with morality,' I said glibly. 'It should be informed only by humanity.'

William looked rather sheepish, and I smiled to myself, pleased that I had usurped the moral high ground with such effortless flimflam. He stepped back, allowing me to pass through onto the white limestone beyond.

I was pleased with my Italianate terrace. I had planted a pair of stone jardinières with bright geraniums and trailing blue lobelia, but had decided against acquiring a sundial, for I had no need of one. In Lissaguirra the daytime hours (and often the nocturnal ones, too) revolved around Clara Venus, who seized every minute of every day, grabbing and plucking with her chubby little fingers from dawn 'til dusk and beyond. Sometimes I felt so wretched with fatigue that I cursed St Leger for giving me a child I had never asked for.

'This is the most beautiful place I have ever been,' said William.

He was gazing at the vista, quite transfixed. Somewhere a curlew was fluting its low, mournful call, and below us I saw the rippling trail of an otter fanning out across the surface of the lake. It was all unspeakably tranquil, unspeakably lovely.

I sighed, and cast a perfunctory eye over the beauty spread before us. 'Sometimes I feel like Rapunzel here,' I said.

William turned to me with a baffled expression.

'Wasn't Rapunzel the princess who was imprisoned in a tower?' he said.

'Yes.'

He laughed. '*I* felt like a prisoner when I was chained

317

to my little desk in my little room in my little apartment in Paris, where the view from my window was of another little room across the street. You – you have all this loveliness to look at, all this air to breathe, Eliza! You step outside into a landscape every morning! How can you say that you are a prisoner?'

'I have nothing to complain of.'

'I should say not!'

'I'm aware that I have been extraordinarily lucky. All this . . . *harmony* – ' I made a baroque gesture with my hand that took in my surroundings – 'is something another woman might dream of: a house of her own, a healthy child, a protector to care for her and ensure that her needs are met. And yes, it is wonderful to step out into a landscape each morning. But . . .'

'Ma'am?' Young Biddy had come out of the house with my shawl. 'You might be needing this. There'll be a chill in the air once the sun is gone behind the trees.'

'Thank you, Biddy.'

I took it from her, and she bobbed a curtsey before retreating. I had to smile: she would never have bothered with the formality of a curtsey had William not been there. As I had told him, we muddled through the days as best we could, the Biddies and I. Draping the shawl around my shoulders, I resumed our conversation.

'But all this harmony, this praiseworthiness is not what I planned.'

William shrugged. 'We none of us live lives we've planned. I did not plan to lose my inheritance. I did not plan to marry a madwoman. I did not plan to find myself scraping a living writing for magazines. A plan suggests something mapped, something over which one has a degree of control.'

From above in the oak wood came the sound of a gunshot.

William started. 'What the devil's that?'

'It's St Leger,' I reassured him. 'He must have found some living thing to dispatch.'

We strolled a little way along the terrace, and descended the steps to the lawn. William's face had assumed an expression of that rather self-conscious benignity that urban dwellers tend to adopt when in a country setting, as if he was posing for a portrait by Gainsborough.

'How is your novel progressing?' I asked.

'It is not progressing at all. But I have some good epigrams to put in it.'

'That's a start. I don't have epigrams, but I have some good characters.'

'It is a universal ambition when times are bad – according to Cicero – to write a novel.'

In my arms, Clara Venus stirred and squinted as a

dragonfly hovered an inch or two above her nose. 'So far, it would seem that our ambitions have been thwarted. Yours by your marriage – '

'I love my wife,' countered William.

'I know. But as you say, you did not plan to marry a madwoman.' The dragonfly lit upon the tip of Clara's nose, and I laughed at her surprise. 'I did not plan to marry *anyone*.'

'You're not married,' William pointed out.

'No. But I am a mother.' I brushed away the dragonfly, rearranged the folds of my shawl so that Clara's head was covered, and put her to my breast.

Apprehending what business I was engaged in, William fixed his eyes upon a distant cloud.

'Think on it,' I said, as Clara tucked in. 'The greatest writer of this century never married.'

'Mr Dickens is – '

'Jane Austen never married.' I threw him a smile as I started off down the path. 'How typical of a man to assume that I was speaking of Dickens!'

'You look content enough, Eliza, all the same,' he remarked, catching up with me. 'You're clearly devoted to the child.'

'Of course I'm devoted to her. And there's the rub! By loving her, by spending all my days loving her, she is my ball and chain, just as Isabella is yours.'

William kicked at a dandelion clock, sending a cloud

of filaments floating off to settle and seed elsewhere.

'Where is she now?' I asked.

'In Paris, still. In a private asylum at Chaillot.'

'Is she improving?'

'No. But she is not deteriorating. She seems happy, for the most part.'

I privately questioned how anybody could be happy incarcerated in an asylum, however costly. And then I remembered that William had wondered how I could be *un*happy, incarcerated here. Ah! *Vanitas Vanitatum!* Which of us is happy in this world? Which of us has his desire? Or, having it, is satisfied? Under the shawl, Clara Venus farted.

'What a rude noise for such a charming *mignonne*!' remarked William.

'Was it Marcus Aurelius who said that a man's worth is no greater than the worth of his ambitions?'

'Yes.'

'I knew you'd know it! But when you substitute "a woman" for "a man" it sounds vainglorious, doesn't it? Try it.'

William gave me an uncertain look.

'Go on!'

'A – a woman's worth is no greater than the worth of . . . her ambitions.'

'You see!' I crowed. 'You say the words as though you were speaking a foreign language. It goes to show,

321

William, that it's acceptable for a man to be ambitious but not a woman.'

'A man is not held back by the same ties of – um . . .'

He hesitated, and I raised an eyebrow at him, waiting for him to continue.

'A man does not have the same vital bond to a child. Perhaps if you engaged a wet-nurse – '

'I've fed her myself from the day she was born!' I snapped, disengaging Clara Venus from my left breast and transferring her ostentatiously to my right. That shut him up.

'Oh, look!' he said. 'A boat!' And off he trundled, to inspect St Leger's rowing boat, which was rotting down by the little stone-built pier.

I sat down on a hummock and watched him pottering about on the shore while Clara Venus suckled drowsily. The truth was that, now that she was gradually weaning herself, I *had* thought of hiring a nursemaid to take over other aspects of child care. That would mean I would have time to myself to set down my thoughts properly. I had diligently curated my journals and notebooks in the weeks leading up to the birth of the twins, sitting on the floor in my half-finished library surrounded by a reef of paperwork: since then I had not written a word.

However, I knew that St Leger would balk at the cost of a nursemaid, and a staff of four did seem excessive. The Biddies got on well and were comfortable in their quarters above the kitchen; Christy came and went as it suited him; to introduce another servant might upset the equilibrium. Once Clara Venus was fully weaned, I decided, I could prevail upon both Biddies to help with her, for they adored the little girl.

After several minutes, William came back with a bleached skull, a pebble and a shard of clay.

'What do you want with those?'

'I always bring interesting things back from the beach. I've been doing it since I was a child. All small boys do it.'

'Interesting things? Thank goodness I didn't have a boy,' I said, stifling a yawn and forgetting that I *had* had a boy, whom I had elected not to keep. 'What's so interesting about them?'

'Skulls are always interesting – '

'It's a rat's skull, William.'

'And the pebble is a perfect heart shape.'

I examined it cursorily.

'And I wondered what this might be.' He held out the piece of clay.

'It's the stem of a dudeen.'

'A dudeen?'

'A clay pipe. It probably belonged to somebody from the village.'

'What village?'

'The one on the other side of the lake.'

He raised his head and peered at the horizon.

'I don't see anything.'

'That's because there's nothing to see. It's not like one of your picturesque, well-ordered English villages. They call them "clachans" here. There are but a half-dozen cabins, and they are all tumbledown. I wrote to you about it.'

'I should like to visit it.' He took his notebook from his pocket, along with the pencil I had given him. 'What is its name?'

'Aill na Coill.'

'Is that Irish?'

'Yes.' I spelled it for him. 'It means "Cliff of the Woods".'

'Woodcliff,' wrote William, and I curled my lip. 'Rather less poetic,' he added apologetically, 'but do bear in mind that I'm writing for an English readership. Aill na Coill will mean nothing to them. Perhaps we might go there tomorrow?'

'St Leger does not like me to go there,' I said. 'He is fearful that I might catch some disease.'

'The place is unsanitary?'

'Yes.'

'I should like to see it, all the same. I feel it incumbent upon me, as a roving chronicler, to detail all aspects of the country, geographical and political.'

I had not thought of Aill na Coill since I had last been there. I wondered how its inhabitants were faring, and if they too had joined the hordes of beggars that were migrating to the cities now there was a dearth of landlords to oversee their welfare in the provinces.

'Take my pony and trap,' I told him. 'I'm sure your joints are aching from a day spent on horseback.'

'Thank you.'

'How long do you plan to stay here at Lissaguirra?'

'If it suits, I should like to stay until the day after tomorrow. I am to dine with the Marquess of Downshire at McDowell's Hotel on Sunday evening.'

'Fa la!'

At my breast, Clara Venus emitted a tiny snore. She had been lulled into a half-slumber by a glut of milk, her lashes like sable against her peach-bloom skin, her fingers curled into tiny, plump fists. Her eyelids fluttered open briefly as, from the ridge beyond the house, the sound of another gunshot came.

'There, baba, there, there,' I said. 'It's just Daddy, gone a-hunting. He's gone to get a rabbit skin, to wrap his baby bunting in.'

'Strictly speaking, it ought to be "in which to wrap his baby bunting",' remarked William.

'You should be writing nursery rhymes for pedants, William, instead of guidebooks.' I shaded my eyes with a hand, to gauge the time by the sun's altitude. 'We should go back. Old Biddy will have dinner under way, and you will want to change beforehand. She is so pleased to have a guest for once that she's serving *Poulet à la Marengo* in your honour.'

William rubbed his hands together like a gourmand in a Molière farce. 'Excellent!' he said.

As he helped me to my feet I cast a look across the lake and at the encroaching shadows and thought how strange it was that just half a mile away as the crow flies was an invisible village, inhabited by invisible men and invisible women, some – like me – with babies at their breasts, who lived, like ghosts, on nothing.

21

THE NEXT MORNING a woman wearing a knitted hat and a man's greatcoat tapped on the open kitchen window as Edie was clearing up after breakfast.

'Miss Chadwick!' she said. 'I'm Mrs Healy, who wrote to you in London. Mr Quilligan said there was a heap of old junk in the stable that you were wanting to get rid of. He asked Mr Healy to come up and take it away, so I thought I'd come with him to say hello.' She stuck her hand through the window. 'I would have been up to you before now, but we've been fierce busy.'

As Edie shook the proffered hand, she saw over Mrs Healy's shoulder that a cart drawn by a horse had pulled into the yard, and a mountainy man was already hefting boxes onto it.

'Please come in,' said Edie, 'and have a cup of tea.'

'Ah, now, I wouldn't want to disturb you at all,' said Mrs Healy.

'You're not disturbing me,' said Edie. 'There's tea in the pot, and I'd be glad of the company.'

'I can understand that. It must get fierce lonely here.'

'I have my dog for company. Down, Milo!' she added, as the back door creaked open and Mrs Healy came through.

She laughed when she saw Milo standing in her way, bristling. 'A dog, is it? It's a queer little clown of a thing. I'd say he keeps you on your toes, all right, but he'd not be much use to you as a guard dog.'

'He's surprisingly efficient, actually,' said Edie, remembering the nip Milo had given Mr O'Brien's finger.

Mrs Healy stooped down and scratched Milo's ears, which set his tail a-wagging. 'Look at his little lamby tail! A dote, he is,' she said, and Milo proudly demonstrated his dotiness by smiling and holding out a paw.

Reassured that he wasn't going to take a lump out of Mrs Healy, Edie set about fetching tea things.

'Don't be bothering yourself with a milk jug,' said Mrs Healy, when she saw Edie reach for one from the shelf. ''Tis grand from the bottle. I'll have two sugars, if you don't mind.' She sat down at the table that was covered still with pages from the manuscript that Edie had been reading over breakfast. 'How've you been getting on?'

'I've finished, more or less. I would have made more of an effort to spring-clean the place, but Mr Quilligan says it'd be a waste of time.'

'Isn't he right? The first thing people'll do when they move in is get the lump hammers out and start bashing the place to kingdom come.'

'Oh, I hope not,' said Edie. 'It's such a beautiful house. It would be criminal to destroy the plasterwork in the reception rooms.'

'They did more than destroy the plasterwork of some of the Big Houses during the Easter Rising,' said Mrs Healy ominously.

Edie really didn't want to talk about anything contentious. Someone had once warned her that in Ireland there were two subjects that should be steered clear of – politics and religion – and she decided that today she was going to talk about neither.

'I loved your handwriting!' she said, out of the blue.

Mrs Healy looked baffled. 'My handwriting?'

'I happened to notice that the handwriting in your letter was copperplate.' Edie set another cup on the table. 'They don't teach that style now. It's an awful pity.'

'I was never taught any other way. That's the way Mrs Callinan taught all of us childer. If there's one thing we learned, it was how to read and write like gentlefolk.'

'Mrs Callinan . . . Somebody else mentioned her the other day.'

'Mrs Callinan was the head teacher in the school in Doneraile. The best teacher you could ask for.'

'Oh, now I remember! Seán the Post said something – he said that she was alive, still. Would you like a Ginger Nut?'

'Thank you kindly.'

329

Edie shook the last of the biscuits from the packet onto a plate. 'He gave me an address. I'd love to talk to her.'

'Why would you be wanting to talk to Mrs Callinan?'

'Seán the Post said that she would know the history of this house.'

'She would do. She was born here, far as I know.'

'What? I mean, was she really? In this actual house?'

Mrs Healy nodded, and bit into her Ginger Nut. 'So I heard tell. She lived here, anyways, as a child. But she's a fair auld age now. I don't know how much sense you'd get out of her.'

Edie wondered what constituted a fair auld age, but felt it would be rude to ask.

'That's the kind of writing she taught us,' said Mrs Healy, pointing at Eliza's manuscript. 'That very hand.'

'I found those papers here, in the room above the kitchen.'

Mrs Healy raised her eyes to the ceiling. 'That dump. Year after year Mr Frobisher threw anything and everything up there. I warned him the place would end up like a stall in the old English market, but there was no telling him. It's all cleared now, is it?'

'Yes. I left most of it in the stable, but anything I thought might make a bob or two I put in the drawing room for the auctioneer to have a look at.'

'He's a sound man, Mr Quilligan. I was at school with him.'

330

'Of course,' said Edie. 'That's why you have the same handwriting!'

Mrs Healy nodded. 'She taught us well, Mrs Callinan. When were you thinking of calling in to see her?'

'Today or tomorrow. But I thought I ought to put a note through her door first, as a courtesy.'

'I'll let her know you're coming. I drop in on her two or three times a week, and I'll be passing that way this afternoon. She can be difficult betimes, but she likes to remember the old days.'

'That's very kind of you. In that case, I'll leave it until tomorrow. Goodness – that's Thursday, isn't it? I shall be going back to London on Friday. Thank you so much, by the way, for stocking the larder. It was lovely, on my first night here, to have something to eat and the stove going and everything.'

Edie remembered how, when she had arrived at Lissaguirra, she had been cold and hungry and lachrymose still after Hilly's death, and how welcome small things had been: the food in the larder, the hot-water bottle warming the bed, the basket of turf by the fire in the library. It was hard to believe that she had been here for over a week. She got up from the table and fetched her purse from the dresser. 'How much do I owe you?'

'Ten shillings will cover it.'

'The soda bread was delicious, by the way. Did you make it?'

331

'I did of course,' said Mrs Healy, pocketing the ten-bob note. 'I've never bought a loaf of shop bread in my life.' She got to her feet and looked out the window at where Mr Healy was finishing loading the cart. 'If you've more junk to get rid of, Mr Healy would be glad to come back for it.'

'Thank you. I think everything's pretty well sorted, though. The only things I can't make my mind up about are the dresses.'

'Whose dresses might they be?'

'I don't quite know whose they were. I think they might have belonged to a lady called Eliza Drury.'

Mrs Healy considered. 'There are no Druries hereabouts.'

'Mrs Callinan might know of her.'

'I'll mention the name when I see her. Are they any good, the dresses?'

'They're Victorian.'

'Not those old yokes that were in the trunk above?'

'Yes.'

'Arra – get rid of them. Sure they'd be half rotted by now. There'd be mice nests and everything in them. A bonfire is all they'd be fit for.' She nodded towards the window and said, 'That's a grand looking laundry plunger Mr Healy has there. Why would you want to be getting rid of that?'

'Feel free to take it,' said Edie, joining her. 'Help yourself to anything at all.'

'I will, so. Thank you for the tea, and good day to you

now, Miss Chadwick. I'll be sure to tell Mrs Callinan to expect you.'

'Thank you. Goodbye, Mrs Healy – it was good to meet you. I'll leave the key under the stone by the boot scraper when I go.'

Edie watched as Mrs Healy crossed the yard to where her husband was waiting beside a laden cart. Then she sat back down at the table and poured herself another cup of tea.

A bonfire! She could not bear to think of Eliza's dresses and petticoats and dainty kid boots ending up on a bonfire: the ultimate Bonfire of Vanities! If no one wanted them, she would have the trunk delivered to her flat in Onslow Gardens, and damn the expense. She'd find out the name of a haulier when she was next in town . . . which would be tomorrow! Time was running out. If she was going to call in to Mrs Callinan, she'd want to finish Eliza's manuscript first.

E. D.

That night after dinner, I did not withdraw to the salon and leave the gentlemen to their brandy and cigars, for I knew that St Leger would not thank me if I left him alone with William. He had quizzed me about Thackeray earlier in the evening as we were dressing for dinner:

333

what was his background, what was our connection, how we had met. I reassured him that William was happily married (I did not add that he had committed his wife to a lunatic asylum) with two small daughters, and that our connection had been forged through a mutual appreciation of culture.

'Culture?' St Leger sounded mistrustful.

'Yes. He was educated in Cambridge and in Paris.'

He shot me a splenetic look.

'He's passionate about classical civilization, the silly old square-toes,' I improvised hastily, trying to make William sound as dull as ditchwater so as not to arouse St Leger's jealousy.

I had found out long since that St Leger's knowledge of Greek culture was confined to a handful of Homeric heroes, and that the learned reference to Bucephalus which had so impressed me when we first met had been singularly out of character. I confess I found his lack of sophistication rather endearing; besides, he possessed other attributes that compensated for it.

'I found old Thackeray in your library earlier,' he grumbled, 'scribbling in his notebook. He told me himself he's a man who would rather read a book than hunt.'

'Shocking, isn't it? Help me with my necklet, Jamie. The catch is snarled.'

St Leger fastened the clasp of the necklet, a pretty

thing of silver and Venetian glass that he had purchased in the Burlington Arcade (I had had the nous to pocket the receipt), then embarked upon a trail of kisses that ran from the nape of my neck to the tender hollow beneath my collarbone. Since I had not yet donned my dress, I allowed him to tup me unceremoniously before resuming my toilette, and surprised myself by taking as much pleasure from the hasty act as he did.

A soupçon of salve, a dab of scent, a rustle of silk, and I was ready.

'You look beautiful,' St Leger said, adjusting himself and straightening his cravat.

'Thank you. It's agreeable to dress up from time to time. I so seldom have visitors.'

Behind me, in the looking glass, I saw the corners of St Leger's mouth turn down.

'I suppose you will talk about Greek civilization together all evening,' he huffed.

'I don't mean William!' I added smoothly. 'I mean you, of course! I wish you could come more often. I should make myself look pretty for you every night, and then you would have the pleasure of undressing me at the end of each evening. I should be like a present that you could unwrap over and over and over again.'

Up went the corners of his mouth, and I smiled back at him, thinking how absurdly easy it was to mollify a man.

Downstairs, after a dinner that boasted mock-turtle soup and greengage tart as well as *Old Biddy's Poulet à la Marengo*, St Leger opened a bottle of poitín and poured liberally.

'I dare not drink too much of it,' said William apologetically, 'for the first time I drank poitín I could not get out of bed the next day.'

St Leger took this as proof that William was indeed a lily-livered square-toes, and proceeded to boast of the quantities of poitín he had consumed in his career as a hell-raiser, illustrating his prowess by pausing every so often to throw back another hefty measure. Soon he was so paralytic with drink that I was obliged to escort him upstairs with the help of Young Biddy. Together we laid him on the bed and removed his boots. Then I covered him with his wolfskin and kissed him on the forehead, gazing at him fondly before snuffing out the candle.

'Mr Thackeray and I will have some hot negus in the library,' I told Biddy, after I had checked to see that all was well with Clara Venus. 'Is the fire still alight?'

'Yes. 'Tis grand and comfortable in there. I'll clear the table in the dining room, and set it up for the morning. Old Biddy heard the gentleman boasting about the breakfast he had at the Shelbourne in Dublin, so she has near a banquet planned for him of broiled kidneys and poached eggs and rashers and sausages, and a veal-and-ham pie.'

'Something tells me soda water will do for Mr St Leger,' I told her, and she giggled conspiratorially. 'Please tell Old Biddy that Mr Thackeray sends his compliments to the chef, and says he has never tasted a finer chicken Marengo.'

I found William in the library, looking over the gleaming leather bindings of the volumes I had arranged neatly in my bookcase. The collection was still rather spartan, but it afforded me great pride.

'I've been thinking,' he said, taking a map book from a shelf, 'about the question we were discussing earlier.'

'We discussed many things earlier. Motherhood, the parlous state of the Irish peasantry, your predilection for *objets trouvés* . . . Did you keep the rat's skull, incidentally?'

'No. But I kept the pebble, as a souvenir.'

'You sentimental ninny. I expect your baggage will be crammed with such junk by the time you leave the country.'

'No. I only keep souvenirs of places that are special to me. This is one of the most special places I have ever visited in my life.'

'Then we should swap.' I crouched down and held a taper to the fire. 'I could go and live in Paris, and you could come here.'

'But it is your presence that makes this place so very special.'

William was clearly waxing moony. It was time to

change the subject. I lit two or three more candles, then sat down on my fireside chair, arranging the folds of my skirt gracefully around me.

'When do you leave Ireland?' I asked.

'I plan to stay until November.'

'And what places are you visiting?'

'From here I go to Cork.'

'Will you stay at Maria's?'

'Yes. I will remember you to her.'

'I dare say she remembers me quite well.'

The last time we had met – when I had been pushing babies out of me –was certain to be etched ineradicably in Maria's memory.

'Whoever could forget you?' said William.

I was beginning to find his mawkish expression irksome. However, I was spared the necessity of giving voice to my dissatisfaction by the timely arrival of Young Biddy with the negus. William opened the book, and feigned fascination with its contents while Biddy blathered about the weather and riddled about with a poker in the fire. Then she bade us goodnight.

'Where do you go after Cork?' I asked, wrenching the conversation back to the bland topic of travel.

'From Cork, I continue on to Kerry,' said William. Hunkering down beside me, he set the map book upon the small table by my chair and traced a winding road with a forefinger.

In the candlelight, the map – with its provinces marked in different colours, the coast indented with estuaries and dotted with islets, the lines that showed where highways and byways looped and rivers twined – gleamed with magical promise.

'I shall spend August carousing in Killarney, and in September I travel up along the spectacular wild west coast. In October I head north to Belfast and the verdant glens of Antrim. And finally – ' William's finger swooped abruptly down to the dot marked Dublin – 'I return to the capital and a well-earned dinner at the Kildare Street Club, courtesy of Sir Blacker Dosy, Mr Serjeant Bluebag and Counsellor O'Fee!'

He had broken the spell.

'They serve the best wine in Europe at the Kildare Street Club,' he remarked, sitting back on his heels and reaching for his negus.

'Are they real people, Sir Dosy and Mr Bluebag?'

'Not at all. They are names I have dreamed up to be characters in my novel, along with Lady Slowbore, the Earl of Portansherry and Lady Grizzel Macbeth.'

I managed a smile, though I was feeling sick with wanderlust.

'You are here,' said William, indicating a point on the map half an inch away from Cork city, 'between the Blackwater River and the Boggeragh Mountains.'

'Good God,' I said. 'I think I'd rather find myself between the devil and the deep blue sea.'

'Why don't you come with me?'

I looked at him blankly.

'On my tour.'

'What an excellent idea! I shall toss one or two necessaries into a handkerchief like Dick Whittington and jaunt off for a month or two without a care in the world. I am sure that St Leger, my protector and the father of my child, would have nothing to say about that.'

'Come to Dublin, then. At least do that. I shall be there at the end of October.'

It was July now. By the end of October . . . Clara Venus would be nearly a year old, and fully weaned if I wanted her to be.

'I shall be meeting some men of letters there – publishers among them. I could introduce – '

'William, you are a dear person. But my novel is not fit for publication. I deluded myself when I thought I could ever write anything worthwhile.' I rose to my feet. From the room above I could hear the melodic sound of Clara Venus singing for her supper. 'The Irish have the best stories, you know. But they don't go to the trouble of writing them down, and maybe that has its merits. Can you see yourself to bed?'

Taking a candle, I left him to his map book. As I made my way to the staircase, unfastening my bodice with my free hand to ready myself for my starveling child, I narrowly missed bumping into the baby carriage in the hall.

William stayed over the following night. He had returned from his trip to Aill na Coill drenched by a summer shower and in uncharacteristically taciturn form, and at table that evening the conversational onus fell on me. I avoided politics, and discoursed instead on a variety of unrelated topics, working hard to keep my beaux amused. After dinner I played and sang, and read from Maria Edgeworth's *Castle Rackrent*, which St Leger loved for its broad humour, and which I knew William would appreciate for its satire. St Leger suggested a gentle hand of cards but I discouraged William from taking up the offer, for I knew that he would be roundly trounced. Instead, he decided to retire early, for he was to start for Cork the next morning after breakfast.

In my dressing room, as I was folding my new stockings, I noticed on my *table de toilette* a small flat rectangular box. It was of leather embossed with acanthus leaves: the hinges along one side and the tiny catch on the other told me it was a diptych. With a fingernail, I unhooked the clasp that joined the two panels. One of them contained a likeness of St Leger, the other a miniature of Clara Venus. I stood motionless for one, maybe two minutes. I was more affected than I can say. When I heard St Leger come from the bedchamber, I turned with the little case in my hand.

'How did you do it?' I asked. 'How did your artist get the resemblance?'

'I had commissioned a portrait of Sophia with George,' he said, 'and I asked him to make me another as the infant might look as a girl, in miniature, with the features a little softer and the eyes more brilliant. Some whimsy prompted me to do it, but when I saw the portrait finished as I had asked, I thought it astonishingly like Clara.'

'It is like. It is just like both of you.'

'I hope the notion does not strike you as too fantastical, Eliza? I was concerned lest you take umbrage, or scoff at it. That is why I delayed giving it to you.'

'How could I take umbrage at such a tender gesture? It is the loveliest thing anyone has ever given me.' I looked down at the double miniature, then raised the case and pressed it to my lips. 'My best beloveds. I shall treasure it. It is more precious than any formal portrait in a gold-leaf frame.' I set the portrait case upon the table, and then I took St Leger's hand and led him through to the bedchamber.

'Raise the sash,' I said. 'The rain will have brought up the scent of the roses.'

Together we made ourselves comfortable on the cushioned window seat, I leaning against the embrasure with the wolfskin around my shoulders, St Leger with his head upon my breast. We remained like that for a long time, listening to the owls hooting softly in the wood beyond the house and watching the silver path cast by the moonlight on the lake.

It was a moment in my life when I felt truly content.

The next day I walked with William to where his horse was being led from the stable by Christy. As we waited for St Leger to join us in the courtyard, he looked at me sorrowfully, the big lovelorn booby, and pressed something into my hand. It was the pebble he had found on the shore, the one shaped like a heart.

'That is your souvenir of Lissaguirra!' I remonstrated.

'The symbolism of the gesture will not be lost on you.'

On cue, St Leger strode across the yard and adopted a proprietorial stance by my side. I slid the stone into my pocket and together we watched William sling his bag over the saddle and mount the horse that would take him to the next staging post en route for Cork. He cut a comical figure astride the roan mare: the mount was too small for him, and he was clearly uncomfortable in the saddle. His discomfiture was not eased by St Leger's jocularly telling him that he looked as though he had a chronic case of haemorrhoids.

I wandered back into the house, feeling foolishly bereft. St Leger had gone down to the pier with Christy, to see what repairs needed doing to the boat, and Clara Venus was sleeping in her baby carriage under the bough of one of the sessile oaks that bordered the garden. I wheeled her there often because when she woke she loved to lie and watch the leaves move in the breeze, mesmerized by the play of light and shadow.

The baby carriage had been one of the gifts lavished upon his daughter by St Leger: from time to time he brought me such newfangled contraptions because he reasoned that whilst George might be heir to Sophia's fortune, it did not follow that his twin sister should want for material things. In his heart, St Leger loved both babies equally, and in a way I think he loved Clara Venus more because, being a girl, she favoured me.

In the dining room, I heard Young Biddy clearing away the breakfast things; from the kitchen came the smell of baking: Old Biddy was making St Leger's favourite bread-and-butter pudding. In the study I found an unsealed letter propped against the mantel clock. It was from William, formally thanking us for our hospitality, which he hoped to cordially reciprocate before he left Ireland; in Dublin, perhaps, where he would be happy to entertain us to dinner at the Shelbourne Hotel.

I left the letter for St Leger to find and made to leave

the room, but as I crossed to the door I saw on the floor
– half concealed by the rug beneath my chair – a sheet
of paper. I stooped to retrieve it: it was a page from
William's notebook, densely covered with his flowing
script.

> *I am writing this in what is probably one of*
> *the most enchanting corners of the world.*
> *Before me lies a vista of blue hills; before me*
> *a lake bathed in moonlight; beyond the peri-*
> *meters of the domain comes the gentle 'Whoo*
> *whoo' of an owl as he embarks on a night's*
> *hunting, and above me lies the woman I love*
> *above all other.*

What was William thinking? I thanked the Lord that St
Leger had not come across this amorous declaration
before I had, for he would undoubtedly have fallen
straight away upon his pistols, and challenged his rival
to a duel.

On the reverse of the page, William had written his
description of Aill na Coill:

> *Humans & animals – pigs with their farrow,*
> *geese, hens and whatever else – lodge in boggy*
> *dugouts, whose interiors are at most ten feet*
> *long & about half as wide. In one such there*

345

lived a family of no fewer than seven persons. An English or French peasant is a Prince compared to these Irishmen.

It is hard to imagine that only a few miles from this wasteland there lie the castle and the lands that belong to the Duke of Devonshire. Ireland is full of contrasts – here, an opulent demesne with proud avenues, there stony land that only with an effort yields crops. When such miserable creatures as I have described – & of whom there are hundreds of thousands on the island – are hunted from house & home by their landlords, there is nothing left for them to do except take to the road to beg for food & shelter, for I am told they find work only in the sowing & harvesting seasons.

Is what I am saying somewhat exaggerated? Should I withhold the information because it will displease my publishers, who are hoping for something amusing from me? I have no moral alternative, but to speak out what I saw, & feel is my right & my duty to report.

There came the sound of a voice in the hall singing 'Peg in the Low Back'd Car'. Young Biddy came into the library with a basket of logs, a dustpan and a goose wing.

'Excuse me, ma'am,' she said when she saw me. 'I thought you were still beyond in the yard.'

'Come in, Biddy. You're not disturbing me. You might set the fire in my sitting room upstairs if you have not done so already, for we shall have no need of it here tonight.'

'So Mr Thackeray is on his way?' she remarked, hunkering down by the grate. 'Old Biddy took a fair fancy to him, big handsome man that he is.'

I smiled abstractedly.

'What a smoker! I'd wager he puffed his way through an entire box of cigars last night.'

'But he retired early.'

'He must have come down again when we were all abed. I woke at sunrise and came straight to this room, for the smell made me think the house was after catching fire, and there he was, smoking like a dragon and scribbling in his book.'

Hunkering down by the fire, she set about sweeping the hearth with the goose wing.

In the garden, a blackbird sounded a warning note. I turned to the window, picturing William sitting here last night, gazing at the same view St Leger and I had looked upon as we lay in each other's arms upstairs. How strange that such a serene view had produced such different thoughts!

The blackbird's call sounded more urgently, signalling to his mate that there was some danger from fox or feral cat or grey-backed crow. I hastened to retrieve

Clara Venus from her carriage: grey-backs had been known to take lambs, and I had heard stories of cats leaping into bassinets to lick the milky faces of sleeping babies.

She was awake, clutching at shadows with her little fingers, squinting at the dentelled oak leaves overhead, and smiling at the faeries only she could see.

22

THAT AFTERNOON EDIE climbed the captain's stair to the dim box room, and lugged the chest down. It was no easy feat, for it was extremely heavy and she had first to empty it of its contents. It smelt of the Vicks VapoRub that her mother had used to smear on her chest any time she had a cough as a little girl, and when she finally heaved it into the light-filled drawing room she saw that it was made of camphor wood. That would explain the excellent condition of the clothes that had been stored therein. Edie's grandmother had a camphor wood chest that she swore by for keeping silver from tarnishing, and for warding off moths.

At the very bottom of the chest, Edie found a small rectangular leather case embossed with acanthus leaves. Even as her thumbnail sought the catch that held the diptych together, she knew what it contained.

There were the knowing eyes, the sensual mouth, the patrician nose, the prominent cheekbones. It could be none other than Jameson St Leger. And there, opposite, was the portrait of a child whose face bore a structural resemblance to her father, but whose features – tinted in shades of rose and cornsilk – were a thousand times more delicate, a thousand times more captivating. This was Clara Venus, apple of her parents' eyes. And no wonder! She was quite the most delectable baby Edie had ever seen.

Setting the double miniature carefully on a shelf, she went to fetch Eliza's clothes. The taffeta, the moiré and the rose-pink sash with vine appliqué that had belonged to poor Mrs O'Dowd were present and correct; but when, Edie wondered, had Eliza acquired the dinner and evening gowns, the riding habit and walking costume, the day dresses and the luxurious Paisley-patterned shawls?

Edie took off her work clothes and slipped her arms into the sleeves of an Indian robe. It was of fine cashmere, intricately embroidered and lined with silk, and it made her feel as though she was wearing water. Standing amidst the precious things piled in the middle of the salon, she regarded herself in the silvered pier glass. How strange to think that Eliza had stood here once, clad perhaps in this very gown! How strange to think that William had once sat at that desk, writing outpourings of love; that St Leger had leaned against the chimneypiece with a glass in his hand; that little Clara Venus had crawled upon the faded carpet, whose old-rose garlands had, over time, almost merged into the silver-green background.

A sound from the lake made her turn. Rising from the surface with a mighty beating of wings were the two swans. Edie stepped towards the window and settled down to watch as the birds lifted themselves into the air and took off, streamlined and powerful, for the opposite shore.

They said that swans mated for life. She wondered had Eliza taken a mate for life, or if she had lived, as was her intention, solitary and proud? She looked again at the carving on the inside of the shutter, tracing the oak-leaf pattern with the tip of her forefinger, then running it along the elegant moulding of the panel to the very bottom. There, just above the hinges at hip height where dust had gathered were engraved the initials *E. D.* They were conjoined with two others, scratched in a more childish hand – **C. V.** – and contained within a heart.

C. V. – for Clara Venus, of course. Was Clara Venus still alive? It was conceivable, although she would be a very old lady: in her nineties by now. Mrs Healy had said that Mrs Callinan was a fair old age ... Could Clara Venus and Mrs Callinan be one and the same? Mrs Healy had said that Mrs Callinan had been born in this house, she had said that the writing on Eliza's manuscript was the hand she had been taught as a child, the hand that had, presumably, been passed down from mother to daughter, from teacher to pupil? Edie suddenly remembered the daguerreotype that she had found on her first day in the house. Had she consigned it to the rubbish that Mr Healy had carted off that morning?

Heart hammering, she rummaged through the contents of the chest. There! There they were, safe behind glass, the four people who, Edie felt sure, had been the inhabitants of this house. Two women, a man, and a girl in a gingham pinafore. Was that Clara Venus? And which of the women was Eliza? It was evident to Edie that the more *distinguée* of the two was the lady of the house. Her stance was the more graceful, her clothes more elegant by far. She was wearing the walking costume that Edie had found in the trunk, the one lined with quilted coral-coloured satin, and she stood looking directly at the camera with inscrutable eyes. Edie remembered how, when she had first seen the house, she had fancied it wore a similar expression – the merest hint of a Giaconda smile.

As for the man . . . could he be St Leger? Impossible to tell: he had a slouch hat pulled over his face, obscuring his features.

Edie felt a thrill course through her. She peered more closely at the image of the girl in the gingham pinafore. If Clara Venus and Mrs Callinan were one and the same, she would be meeting her tomorrow.

⁓ E. D.

Autumn progressed sedately. Since Lissaguirra was but an hour's journey on horseback from Doneraile, most of

St Leger's time in Ireland was spent at the lodge rather than at Dromamore House. Sophia had questioned the wisdom of keeping up this last tie to Ireland, but he had argued that blood bound him to the country of his birth, and to the house built by his great-grandfather. Even though he had sold the greater portion of his land (to Sir Silas Sillery, whose estate adjoined his and who was driven more by cupidity than common sense), he was fiercely proud of his heritage, and in the complex world of Anglo-Irish politics his stance was resolutely nationalist.

I got letters from William every week during that uneventful autumn, full of entertaining news of his travels around the country: of stag-hunting and the races in Killarney, of the pleasure gardens at Westport and the theatre in Belfast, and each time a letter arrived telling me of goings-on in the world beyond Lissaguirra, I felt more and more like Rapunzel, cut off from the rest of civilization in her inaccessible tower.

In October I received a letter from St Leger saying that he had business in Dublin, and asking if I would join him there.

> *It is a risk,* he wrote, *for you know that Dublin is but a suburb of London, and gossip spreads like wildfire from capital to capital. But I long so to see your sweet face, and I will not be in the country again before next year. Can you*

leave our daughter with your servants and come to me for a week or so? I shall take lodgings instead of putting up at an hotel, and you will be quite comfortable. I am sure you need such necessaries as dresses and baby clothes – and clocked stockings to encase your comely legs, which I should dearly love to see again. Oh! The writing about your stockings and your dear, pretty legs makes me feel what a gentleman ought not to express.

Your most attached,

J. St L.

PS: The nib with which I am writing you all this is so bad it will only write wrong-side up. My brain is a little that way too.

<hr />

Dear Flea,
My heart lifts at the prospect of a week in Dublin with you. I have heard say that Dublin society is racier and less formal than in London – with members of the gentry, the professions and academia all muddling together – so I think we may lark a little without too much fear of censure. Maria tells me the mall is one of the grandest and most beautiful in Europe, and that the pleasure gardens rival Vauxhall. I intend to visit the shops in Sackville Street, for I have my mind set on silk stockings clocked with butterflies, birds

and bees. I look forward to knowing your thoughts on this important matter.

Of course the Biddies have said that they will be delighted to have Clara Venus to themselves to spoil.

Your Bastet

PS: What serendipity! I have heard just this morning from Mr Thackeray, and he is to be in Dublin between the dates you mention.

Of course the PS was a fib. In his letters William had expressed a frequent desire to see me again before he left Dublin for London, and the lure of that city had not been far from my mind since he had first suggested it back in August.

And that is how I found myself in a stagecoach drawn by a four-in-hand, with rain on the wind and two hundred miles between me and my beaux.

Our lodgings were on fashionable Rutland Square, which boasted numerous noble residences, as well as assembly rooms and pleasure gardens. St Leger had reserved a suite on the piano nobile of a town house let by the bankrupt heir of a tea merchant. It was handsomely appointed with white marble chimneypieces, rococo plasterwork and Venetian windows. There were blazing fires and nosegays of hothouse flowers in every room. I found the scent of the lilies overwhelming, but St Leger was so delighted with our *nid d'amour* that I could not bring myself to utter a syllable of complaint.

In nearby Sackville Street and across the river in Grafton Sreet, I went shopping. I had never before shopped for things I did not need, and St Leger encouraged me to spend without reserve. In the drapers' and the silk mercers' I swathed myself in mantillas and shawls of lace and chenille, I ran my hands over bolts of damask and satin, cashmere and brocade, and I calculated how many yards of stuff I should have delivered to the dressmaker in Doneraile.

In the plate-glass windows of the haberdashers, tailors and outfitters, pictures of the latest fashions from *Les Modes Parisiennes* and *Le Bon Ton* were displayed. St Leger told me to choose my favourites: I picked out a riding habit of Brunswick green, a honey-coloured morning dress, a walking dress of serge lined with quilted coral satin, a carriage costume trimmed with chinchilla, an evening dress flounced and edged with Venise lace, and a dinner gown of rich amber and cinnabar-red velvet. As he issued directives to the shopkeeper I protested that these last three were a scandalous waste of money, for when would I find an occasion to wear them? But St Leger insisted upon ratifying the order, observing in a murmured aside that I could wear them for him in private so that he could have the pleasure of taking them off.

I visited the glover and the bootmaker to be fitted (here I pounced upon some little embroidered morocco slippers), and in the milliner's I chose a bonnet trimmed with a cockade of Argus feathers, and another trimmed with purple velvet pansies.

I took coffee among the *flâneurs* in Mitchell's coffee house, and visited the hairdresser. I bought a pigskin writing case and a mother-of-pearl blotting book at the fancy stationer's, and white almond soap at the perfumer's, and a box of Cuban cigars for St Leger at the tobacconist's. All these spoils were bought with his money, and with his blessing. When I discovered I had forgotten my *mouchoirs* he bought me a dozen, lace-trimmed; when I complained that my hands were cold, he bought me a doeskin muff, and when it came on to rain he bought me an umbrella with a carved jade handle.

Finally, I visited a bookshop and helped myself to a dozen novels, among them *Barnaby Rudge* by Charles Dickens and *Catherine*, by William Thackeray.

What an enigma was William, for he had been uncharacteristically circumspect on the subject of this novel! However, upon settling down to read it, I understood why. Compiled from instalments that had appeared in *Fraser's Magazine* two years previously,

Catherine was a rambling and gory tale of a murderous wife. It was based on a true account that had been published by the more sensational pamphlets, and was quite unworthy of William's talent.

And yet, and yet . . . there was something about the eponymous heroine that I found oddly likeable. She was a spirited, impudent minx who, despite being treated ill by a drunk and brutish husband, gads off to become a captain's lady, sporting a red riding coat trimmed with silver lace, and with a blue feather in her cap.

I set William's hodgepodge aside, then reached for *Barnaby Rudge*, whose heroine, the colourless Emma Haredale, soon sent me off to sleep.

I slept often during my time in Dublin, for sleep was my ultimate luxury. When Maria told me that all her babies had slept through the night at six or seven months old, I had thought she was jesting, for Clara Venus seemed to feign sleep, springing to life like a jack-in-the-box the moment she knew I was dropping with fatigue. She had been teething the week before I embarked for Dublin, exacerbating my exhaustion: nor had I slept a wink in the jouncing coach that had taken the best part of a day to reach the capital, so I spent most of my time in the city gorging on sleep as though it was ambrosia and I was a glutton.

One evening, when he was to dine with some cronies at the Kildare Street Club, St Leger delivered me to the house of the writer Mr Lever, with whom William and I were to dine, with the assurance that he would send a chaise for me before midnight.

William had wangled me an invitation to what he assured me was an informal supper party. He had met Mr Lever back in July, and was anxious to be re-acquainted with him, for he was a rising figure in the Irish literary world. He would, he said, have preferred to have invited me to dine with him at the Shelbourne or at Morrison's hotel on Dawson Street, a lively, fashionable place frequented by visiting artists, but I knew that St Leger would not tolerate the notion of William and I dining *à deux*. Unfortunately, when we arrived at Mr Lever's house in Templeogue, we realised to our mutual discomfort that it was a gentlemen-only soirée.

'I regret that my wife is not here,' Mr Lever told me, after his maid had divested me of bonnet and pelisse. 'She has gone to her sister. If I had known that Thackeray was bringing a lady this evening, I would have commanded her to stay, for then you might have spent your time more fruitfully, consulting on bonnets and ball dresses. As it is, you will be obliged to listen to us gentlemen discoursing on subjects that I am sure will be very tedious to you.'

'Oh, pray do not concern yourself on that account,' I told him, with a brilliant smile. 'I am merely here to act as a foil to your erudition and superior intellect.'

'Good, very good. Ha ha. I love a sense of humour in a woman.'

I smiled smoothly and took a seat on the low slipper chair that he drew up for me by the fire.

Beyond the double doors that opened onto the dining room, the maid was touching a taper to the candlesticks. The candlelight enhanced the dewy rosiness of her cheeks, and cast the declivity between her breasts into tantalizing shadow. A gentleman lounging by the fireplace was ogling her through a horn-rimmed quizzing-glass.

'Allow me to introduce my friend, Mr Butler,' Mr Lever said, and then he backed off hastily, leaving Mr Butler to tear his attention away from the embonpoint of the maidservant and take up the conversational baton. He looked so discomfited by my presence that I felt obliged to set him at ease by essaying another little joke.

'I have come this evening to catechize all here upon the vital question of the relation between mind and matter,' I said good-naturedly, 'and to outline the drinking rules as laid down in Plato's *Symposium*.'

'Goodness. *You* have read Plato's *Symposium*?'

'Yes. And his *Apology*, too.'

'Ha ha ha. Joking aside, I am delighted to know that literacy is on the increase amongst women.'

'I am all in favour of an educated woman, you

know,' put in a gentleman wearing a clerical collar, 'as long as she makes some use of that education.'

'How do you propose she does that?' I asked.

'There are boundless opportunities in the field of private philanthropic endeavour.'

'And if a woman cannot afford the luxury of philanthropy?'

'Why, then, she might seek employment as a governess or a schoolteacher,' suggested Mr Butler.

'That is something that only the most desperate or hardy would contemplate,' said the dog-collared dolt. 'I have heard of women who are gainfully employed in the safe environs of their own homes, thus obviating the necessity of having to venture abroad.'

'What kind of gainful employment might keep them at home?' I asked.

'I believe there is a growing demand for the hand colouring of prints, flower paintings, silhouettes, and so forth.'

'Might they not employ themselves in writing?'

The reverend gentleman tittered behind his hand.

'Don't scoff, Hayman,' said Mr Butler. 'My publisher tells me that there is a new category of literature emerging, directed at and written by women. Books of advice on household management, fashion, cookery and such ephemera.'

At last I heard William speak up. 'Fiction is a

department of literature in which women can equal men,' he said. 'One great name in particular stands as evidence that women can pen novels that have a precious speciality of their own.'

I favoured William with a warm look.

'If her career had been longer,' he continued, 'I dare say Miss Austen would have inspired many more women to follow her example.'

Mr Butler curled his lip. 'I would hardly say that she wrote books to confound philosophers.'

'Perhaps because she chose to write books to delight them,' I said, smiling sweetly.

'Where there is one woman who writes elegantly,' opined the reverend gentleman, 'I believe there are dozens who are moved only by the foolish vanity of wishing to appear in print.'

'Yes, yes!' concurred Mr Butler. 'And they are encouraged, don't you know, by the impression that to be able to spell words of more than one syllable is a proof of ability.'

Mr Hayman tittered again.

'Aha!' said Mr Lever, breezing into the conversation. 'And so we have again the old story of La Fontaine's ass, who puts his nose to the flute, and, finding that he elicits some sound, exclaims, "Oh! I can play the flute, too!"'

'Ha ha ha!'

'Any novels I have read that were written by ladies tend to mistake vagueness for depth, bombast for eloquence and affectation for originality.'

'Full of drivelling dialogue and drivelling narrative.'

'Such scribblings are less the result of labour than of busy idleness.'

'I just wish the products of their "busy idleness" did not find their way into print!'

'Confiscate their pens and substitute crochet hooks, say I!'

'Ha ha!'

'Ha ha ha!'

I could bear it no longer.

'That is because a deliberate male conspiracy has contorted women into trivial and worthless beings,' I said loudly.

The men started. I think they had forgotten that I was there.

'Give girls the same educational fare as boys, and provide them with jobs which would allow them to live independently, and they would emerge as rational and as strong as men.'

'Hear hear!' said William robustly.

There was silence as the other gentlemen looked at him. Then they all busied themselves with masculine rituals of stroking their moustaches, examining their fobs, tapping their pipes, etc.

'I hope you are not one of those women who has such a feverish consciousness of her education that you will spoil the taste of my roast beef by harping on polemics,' said Lever, eventually.

'Educated? Alas, my nature is too shallow and feeble a soil to bear much tillage; it is fit for only the very lightest of crops,' I smiled. 'I spent this afternoon on my chaise longue, munching macaroons and reading a wonderfully silly novel by the name of *Catherine*. But bear in mind, Mr Lever, that from most silly novels we can at least extract a laugh.'

The men looked sulky and crestfallen, like small boys who have been caught tormenting kittens.

I might have said more, had not the maidservant chosen that moment to reappear.

'Dinner is served, if it please you, gentlemen,' she said, bobbing a little curtsey, and keeping her eyes respectfully downcast.

'Excellent! Shall we go through to the dining room?'

'*Catherine?*' Mr Butler said, raising the eyebrow that wasn't clamped over his monocle. 'One of Miss Burney's novelettes, was it?'

'I cannot recall who wrote it. It was, as I say, incomparably silly.'

As I laid my hand upon the arm that Mr Lever extended to me, and passed between the dividing doors,

I slid an oblique look at William. He was looking gratifyingly sheepish.

'What a crowd of ill-mannered boors!' I remarked some hours later. William and I were heading to Rutland Square, ensconced in the carriage that St Leger had sent for me.

'Boors or bores?' he asked, removing his eye-glasses and polishing them on the sleeve of his jacket.

'Both. They were the most insufferable men with whom it has ever been my misfortune to dine. As our host led me in to supper I saw him give a wink to his cronies as much as to say, "Now look out for some sport!"'

'He was put out of countenance rather when he realized you were poking fun at him.' William hooked his spectacles back on, and peered at me through them. 'You know you are at your most dangerous, Eliza, when you adopt that demure, ingénue air.'

'It is a weapon favoured amongst the more resourceful of us women,' I said. 'I have had recourse to it on numerous occasions. By the way, I thought your novel *Catherine* not at all bad. I was teasing when I called it silly.'

'It was intended as a parody, but the critics could not see that.'

'I dare say they thought it immoral.'

'That's why I was not keen to admit authorship. Although I confess I developed a sneaking fondness for my heroine as I penned the thing.'

'I could tell. That is just the sort of heroine – or anti-heroine – you want, you know. A character who breeds controversy.'

He gave me a sceptical look. 'One can't have an out-and-out criminal as a heroine, Eliza. If I've learned nothing, I have at least learned that.'

'You're right,' I said, after a moment's contemplation. 'Nothing so low as a murderess will do as a protagonist. But you want a clever woman, one who will appeal to other clever women, like me, who love to read. Such women are legion, despite what Lever and his cronies may believe. Balance your narrative with a virtuous, milk-and-water martyr to please the critics and the clerics, and you have it.'

William smiled. 'What name do you suggest for my heroine?'

'It goes without saying that it should be memorable. A name that will make the reader realize at once that she is a character to contend with; one that conjures a quick wit.'

We were traversing a crossroads, where a ramshackle inn squatted. The proprietor's name on the board read, 'P. Keane, Esq.'

'Keane,' suggested Thackeray.

'Too Irish.'

'Sharp?'

'That's better. Sharp. Rebecca Sharp.'

He gave me a quizzical look. 'Rebecca. Why Rebecca?'

'For Becky. Because she's like a little bird, peck peck pecking away at the social order. And call your milk-and-water heroine Millie.'

'Millie is a mill worker's name!' said William disdainfully.

'Oh, don't be so pernickety! Why shouldn't you have a mill worker for a heroine?'

He looked dubious.

'Oh, make her Millie, for Amelia, then,' I said impatiently. 'Sedate, biddable Amelia Sedley, of the middling merchant class. There!' I sat back against the upholstery, triumphant. 'You have your characters, now go and write your novel. And do stop prevaricating.'

William was looking at me curiously. 'Will you help me?'

'Will I help you what?'

'Will you help me write it?'

'Don't be stupid.'

'I am in earnest, Eliza. You are so clever, and you write so well – your letters are a delight – and you have such excellent ideas!'

'What excellent ideas have I?'

'You've had two there, in the blink of an eye. I have spent a year hemming and hawing over names for my heroines, and you – you have conjured them in no time at all! Becky Sharp and Amelia Sedley!'

'Good God, Thackeray. They're just names.'

'They're more than names! They're perfect! They're – they're onomatopoeic!' He leaned forward, eyes agleam. 'Don't you see what astoundingly good sense it would make for us to collaborate? I don't have the time to embark upon another novel, or the money to finance such an undertaking. My writings for *The Times* and *Fraser's* and any other publication to which I can prostitute myself – I ask your pardon, Eliza – take up all the time I have. And there are my domestic responsibilities. Taking care of the children, and anguish, perpetual anguish over Isabella, uses up any vigour I have. I – I sometimes feel as though I've been broken on a wheel.'

He slumped, and – to my astonishment – began to cry. I resisted the temptation to tell him to stop at once and be a man, and waited for him to finish. But he didn't finish. He went on crying and crying, and finally, unable to help myself, I said, 'Oh do stop at once, William, and be a man.'

He snuffled and looked at me shamefacedly, and I reached into my reticule and produced one of the lace-trimmed *mouchoirs* St Leger had bought me.

'Very well,' I said, handing it to him. 'I'll help you if

I can. But please to remember that I, too, have a baby carriage in the hall to which I am fettered.'

'Of course.'

We sat in silence a while as the conveyance swayed and bumped over the cobblestoned thoroughfares, and then William said, tentatively, like an unrehearsed actor uttering the first line of a play, 'This – erm – this "Rebecca Sharp". Where do you think she originated?'

'That's easy,' I said. 'She was born in France of an opera dancer and a penniless artist.'

'Has she received any formal education?'

'Yes, indeed. A very good one, in England.'

'But if her father was impoverished, how could she afford an education?'

'Providence,' I said. 'She was, of course, an articled pupil in a seminary. A superior one.'

'An articled pupil?' William was picking up his cues smartly, now. 'And what might be the name of the establishment?'

'It was,' I said, 'Miss Pinkerton's academy.'

'In Chiswick?'

'Yes.' I gave him a brilliant smile. 'And I happen to have in my possession the letter of reference that that venerable lady wrote for her star pupil.'

23

EDIE WAS STUPEFIED. Eliza Drury was the template for Becky Sharp! She *had* to be!

Springing up from the fireside chair where she had been reading for the past hour, Edie went straight to the bookshelf where *Vanity Fair* was tucked between *Hard Times* and *Bleak House*. She read the title (*Vanity Fair. A Novel without a Hero*), she read the inscription (*To Eliza, my very dear friend and soulmate*), she scanned the first chapter, and there she found Miss Pinkerton's letter. Except, of course, it extolled not the virtues of Miss Sharp (for she had none) but those of that most colourless character, Amelia Sedley. Becky came into her own when, several pages on, her story proper began.

Edie leafed through the pages with mounting excitement. That Becky Sharp had lived and breathed here in this house, and that she had left a record of her time spent under this very roof, made Edie's head spin. She felt as though a glamorous partygoer at a masked ball had suddenly revealed herself to be her best friend in disguise.

As she reached into the box file like a child scrambling for more pieces of a jigsaw puzzle, she heard voices from outside.

'I don't think there's anybody here, Iseult.'

Edie's ears flattened against her skull in the manner of a cat that hears sudden birdsong.

'Maybe we should just go.'

'Maybe. We can always come back another day.'

'We should have telephoned the auctioneer first. I feel like a trespasser.'

You *are* trespassing! thought Edie. What are you doing, snooping around *my* house?

'There's a phone box a couple of miles back. We passed it at the crossroads.'

'Wait a minute. That window's open.'

Edie rose to her feet as the couple – for it was a young, very handsome couple – stepped into her view.

'Oh!' The girl jumped backwards, pressing her hands to her mouth. 'Oh, my God! It's a ghost!'

'I'm not a ghost,' said Edie. But as she moved towards the window the girl turned and hightailed it, and Edie realized that she was still wearing Eliza's flowing robes. 'I'm not a ghost, I promise you,' she said to the man, who was looking as though he, too, was poised for flight. 'I'm – um – I'm a relation of the owner. I'm here to pack the place up and get it ready for the auction.'

371

A look of relief crossed the young man's face. 'I don't blame Iseult for pegging it. You really do look like a ghost in that get-up, if you don't mind me saying so.' He turned in the direction that Iseult had taken and called, 'Iseult! Come back. It's not a ghost.'

Iseult retraced her steps, looking sheepish. 'Sorry,' she said. 'It's just that someone in the village said that the woods around here are haunted. I don't usually believe in ghosts, but you did give me rather a fright.'

'I suppose ghosts don't have dogs like that,' said the man, looking down at Milo.

'What an adorable little pet!' Iseult hunkered down, and Milo danced out through the French window to say hello. 'Is he a Bichon Frise?'

'No. A Maltese. He's a very silly dog, but he's frightfully good company. Are you here to see the house?'

'We don't have an appointment, I'm afraid.' The young man held out his hand. 'I'm Jeremy Darling, and this is my wife, Iseult.'

'Darling? As in *Peter Pan*?'

'Yes.'

'How do you do? Welcome to Prospect House! You don't need an appointment – I'll be glad to show you around. Come in.' Edie stood back to allow them access. 'How did you hear about the house?' she asked, as they stepped over the threshold.

'From the hotel barman in the Doneraile Arms.'

'Are you staying there?'

'Yes. Well, we stayed last night – we'll be moving on tomorrow.'

'Unless we've found what we're looking for.' Iseult smiled up at her husband. 'We're rather taken with this place.'

'Sweetheart! We haven't seen any of it yet.'

'We saw the outside. We liked that. And it has a good atmosphere.'

'A minute ago you thought it was haunted.'

'If it is haunted, it has a friendly ghost. I can tell these things.' Iseult crinkled her nose like a Bisto kid. 'It smells wonderful.'

'That's camphor. I was unpacking a camphor-wood chest earlier. My grandmother swore by camphor.'

'Mine too! She stored all her old clothes in camphor chests, and they're still as good as new. I've even worn them in productions.'

'Iseult's an actress,' said Jeremy.

'*Was* an actress, Jeremy.' She turned to Edie. 'I've decided to give it up. That's why we're looking at houses. We want to start a B&B. A really lovely one, with fishing.'

'Then you've come to the right place,' said Edie.

'We can't afford to build, so we're hoping to find somewhere that we can do up ourselves. Jeremy's an architect. And he loves to fish, so this place would be perfect. We really need to get cracking right away because . . . Can I tell her, Jeremy?'

Jeremy gave his wife an indulgent smile and said, 'Go on, then.'

'Because I'm expecting a baby!'

'Oh! How lovely to think there'd be a baby living here! When are you due?'

'In the autumn.'

'There's an old pram here that you could have – a beautiful, old-fashioned one. It's in the salon.' The hem of Edie's robe caught on the edge of the window as she started to lead the way. 'Damn. Perhaps you'd give me a minute to change into something rather less outré.'

'No, don't change!' said Iseult. 'You look perfectly lovely in that gown.'

'I'm tempted to keep it. I'm tempted to keep lots of things. Just look at all the antique thingamajigs.' She opened the door to the salon and gestured at the boxes and crates she had spent the past week amassing there.

'Goodness!' cried Iseult. 'What treasure trove!'

'Are you visiting from overseas?'

'No, we're from Dublin. We just don't sound very Irish. I talk posh because I went to RADA, and Jeremy talks posh because he *is* posh.'

'What made you decide to start a B&B?'

'Jeremy's always wanted to live in the country, and I do whatever I'm told, don't I, Darling? That's not an endearment, by the way. I always call him by his surname.'

She gave her husband a fond look. Jeremy had picked

up *Mrs Beeton's Book of Household Management* from a box that Edie had marked Kitchen Odds & Ends.

'Listen to this, Iseult: "Cleanliness, punctuality, order and method are essentials in the character of a good house-keeper." This book should go straight to the top of your reading list.'

Dropping a kiss on the top of her head, he handed her the book before ambling off in the direction of the dining room.

Iseult hefted it. 'Dear God, it weighs a ton – it has over a thousand pages. Look – someone's made notes in the margin. "Mrs Beeton is a . . . an *óinseach*." I wonder what that means.' Iseult dropped the book back into the box and turned to Edie. 'Can we go upstairs? I noticed that one of the bedrooms overlooks the river. I can't imagine a more glorious way of falling asleep at night than listening to the sound of falling water.'

And off they went on their guided tour, Milo leading the way.

By the time Jeremy and Iseult had seen around the house and taken tea and bade Edie and Milo a fond farewell, Edie decided that she really, really wanted them to get the house. The Darlings were the kind of people she'd like to have as friends: they were bright, amusing; artless yet urbane, screwy but grounded, and they had moxie. She decided she would wangle it for them with Uncle Jack. He wouldn't want Lissaguirra to be turned into a fish factory, with salmon cooped up in man-made ponds. He would love the idea of a young couple taking the place on and running it as a B&B for anglers. Maybe he and Aunt Letty could return on a sentimental journey, once the place was up and running! She would go straight away to the crossroads where the telephone box was, and call him.

She put on her wellingtons, fetched Milo's collar and lead and set off. But this time she didn't head down the drive, she went through the forest, where a boreen had led to Lissaguirra long before the new road had been built. What remained of the path was overgrown and muddy and, to judge by the plethora of cowpats, now used exclusively by stray cattle. But it was an afternoon dapply with sunshine and full of the burgeoning promise of spring, and Edie felt she had done some good by coming here and opening up the house and securing a future for it. She looked down at Milo. He was barrelling through a puddle like a miniature paddleboat, his snowy chest caked in mud, his tail toing and froing in the mire.

'Milo! Look at you, you filthy beggar!'

'I like it,' protested Milo, little legs all ascramble as Edie stooped to pick him up. She held him at arm's length until they had traversed the worst of the boggy bit, then she took out her handkerchief and started wiping bits of him.

'Are you feeling better now?' he asked.

'Better than what?'

'Better than when you first came here. You were very glum then.'

'How do you know I was glum?'

'Because I'm a dog. Everybody knows that dogs have extrasensory perception. Humans are so stupid. They are *stupid*.' He blinked as Edie rubbed muck from his muzzle, and then his ears pricked and he started to wriggle about in her arms. 'Woahoroharrrr! A rabbit a rabbit a rabbit a *rabbit* let me *go*!'

And off Milo went, shooting into the brambles after Flopsy, Mopsy, Cottontail, et al.

Edie considered. Milo was right: she was feeling better. And Ian had been right, when he had told her that Hilly would have wanted her to crack on. After all, that was all anybody could do, from day to day. So she and her little dog cracked on all the way to the crossroads, and by the time they got there she looked like the troll that lived under the Billy Goats Gruff's bridge, and Milo looked like a back-combed Tasmanian devil.

When the operator had finally connected her, it took her no time to persuade Uncle Jack that the Darlings were the only people in the world worthy of taking on Lissaguirra.

'Is there anything you'd like me to bring back for you?' she asked. 'As a memento?'

'Not a thing,' Uncle Jack told her. 'Your aunt Letty is spring-cleaning. She'd go crackers if I brought more junk into the house.'

'There are some things I'd like to keep, Uncle Jack. Some old books and scrapbooks and journals I found in the attic. There's a first edition of *Vanity Fair*, signed by William Thackeray.'

'Who's he?'

'He wrote it.'

'Take whatever you like, my dear.'

'Thank you. You're sure there's nothing you want?'

Her uncle sighed down the line. 'One reaches a stage in one's life when there is no room for sentimentality. If we all clung onto bits of the past, we'd be too encumbered by bloody stuff to move forward. Excuse my French.'

That's nothing, Edie wanted to say. You should hear Milo's.

'Goodbye then, Uncle Jack.'

'Goodbye, Edie.'

Edie put the receiver down and turned to see Milo cowering in the hedge, being roundly scolded by an indignant wren. From the aghast expression on her little dog's face she fancied that the wren's language was saltier than any he'd heard before.

As they headed home by the lakeshore road, Edie noticed for the first time that alongside the more recently built bungalows and farmsteads the countryside was mapped with crumbling drystone walls, overgrown potato drills and piles of tumbled rocks. Those boundaries, those drills, those abandoned dwellings – all had been part of

Eliza's geography; the people who had lived here had been her neighbours. It seemed to Edie that an entire community had vanished, leaving their homesteads to subside into the ground: this was a palimpsest of past and present, a place where ghosts resided alongside the living. She wondered what it must be like to live in a country where the very fabric of the landscape was a perpetual reminder of whole-sale famine; where an encounter with the relics of unspeakable calamity was quotidian.

Back at Lissaguirra she gave Milo a bath and a Bonio, made herself cheese on toast, and took the last quires of paper from the box file. There were still hundreds of pages to be read. At this rate, she'd be up half the night. She made sure there was enough oil in the lamp and turf in the basket, and made a start.

~ E. D.

The following morning, St Leger and I breakfasted in the comfort of our apartment. It was the last day we were to spend together in Dublin: he was to return to his family on the other side of the Irish Sea, and I, to our daughter in Lissaguirra.

I had opened the window to escape the suffocating scent of lilies. Clad in a morning robe of embroidered Chinese silk, I was leaning on the wrought-iron balconet that looked out over Rutland Square, drinking my coffee while St Leger perused the *Morning Register*.

'Why are those houses so dilapidated?' I asked him, pointing at the roofs opposite. 'Look – there are weeds sprouting from the chimneys. And why are so many of the windows boarded up?'

'The gentry have departed from the city.'

'For London?'

'Not all of them. Some have moved south of the river. You must have seen the fine houses as you travelled back last night from Templeogue?'

'No. I was too engaged in conversation to notice.' On seeing St Leger's lips purse, I swiftly added, 'William and I were discussing the merits of Aristotle's unities.'

In fact, William and I had spent the entire journey back to Dublin talking about the novel we were planning to write together. Even when the carriage dropped him at his hotel, he stood on the pavement and would not allow the carman to drive on until we had resolved our dispute as to what the name of our book should be. Since we had hit upon the idea of having two female protagonists, we had finally decided to call it 'A Novel without a Hero', until a more engaging title might suggest itself.

I took a sip of coffee, and turned again to look out over the square, to the Rotunda that housed the elegant assembly rooms where we had dined two evenings ago, and the pleasure gardens where I had strolled wearing a new pelisse and matching fur-trimmed bonnet. The place had *seemed* elegant then. Now I saw a troop of shabby dandies lolling by the entrance, grinning and taunting a passing gaggle of girls. Arm-in-arm, the bareheaded colleens sashayed down Cavendish Row, insouciant in tattered brocade and down-at-heel boots. Apple women shrilled their wares, and hucksters, their carts piled with cheap crocks, tinware and assorted junk, trundled towards the quays to set up their stalls. An endless line of carriages waited for fares, the horses as ill-nourished looking as their drivers. And everywhere, I saw now from my vantage point above the streetscape, there were beggars. Toothless, ragged, filthy, sick, old and young, crippled and nimble, and – the ones I found most affecting of all – the gaunt women, many of them girls still, holding babies to their breasts.

I glanced over my shoulder at St Leger. 'This really is a bedevilled country, isn't it?'

He shrugged. 'Why do you think Sophia was so desperate to leave?'

'It was Sophia who persuaded you to sell?'

'It took little persuasion. While I may not honour all my debts, Eliza, I don't expect my son to honour them for me, and the way things stand, a year or two hence even my most productive farmland would be too expensive to maintain, in this obscure corner of Empire.' He drained his cup. 'Shall I ring for more?'

'No, thank you.'

I thought of the boy I had given him, who would inherit a mansion in Buckinghamshire, a town house in London, acres of pasture and arable land, as well as plate and paintings and antiquities of inestimable value. He would have no difficulty in honouring his father's debts. My son would be well provided for. My daughter, on the other hand, had nothing – not even status. There would be no debutante's ball for her, no suitors and no society wedding. She would be obliged to make her own way in the world, as I had. Except that I had made my way in the thriving capitals of Paris and London. How was Clara Venus to do it in Boggetybeyondbackwards?

I took an oblique look at my beau. He was scanning the advertisements page in the *Register*.

'There are estates for sale all over the country,' he said. 'Things are coming to a parlous pass.'

'I wonder how much I would make for my house if I sold it?'

'Who do you think would want to buy it? Nobody wants land in Ireland. That's why the prices are so risible. Besides, why would you want to sell it? You've only just had it built.'

'An idle question, that is all.' I took another sip of my coffee, watching St Leger over the rim of my cup. 'But I may want to sell when Clara Venus is of an age to attend school.'

'I've been thinking about that. Why should she need to go to school?'

'Don't you want our daughter to be educated, St Leger?'

'Who better to educate her than you? She would learn more from you, my sweet, than from any rubbishy schoolteacher in the entire county of Cork.' He gave me a smile of beaming benignity, then turned the page of his newspaper. 'In any case, the only way you could get a decent price for that house would be if you sold it as a fishing lodge, with rights. And you don't have fishing rights.'

'I know that!' I said, more snippily than I intended.

'You're happy there, Eliza, aren't you?' I could not see his expression behind the paper, which meant, fortunately, that he could not see mine. 'You drove a hard bargain, but you got what you wanted in the end.'

'Yes, I did. But when I consulted my crystal ball, I did not see a child living there.'

'That's because you were going to deliver it to the foundling hospital. Remember?'

'I remember,' I said, poking my tongue out at him.

St Leger's pragmatism sometimes vexed me beyond endurance. Reaching for the remains of my breakfast roll, I threw it at a passing seagull. It missed, and to my astonishment, before the bird could swoop to retrieve it from the pavement, an urchin below had fallen upon it and was stuffing it into his mouth.

'What *did* you see in your crystal ball?' St Leger asked, as I fetched a basket of uneaten rolls from the table, and began to split them in two.

I could hardly reply 'I saw an astute investment', so instead I said, 'I saw Lissaguirra as my own rural retreat, where you might come with your hunting friends and we could spend our days enjoying outdoor pursuits and our evenings cosily at home or entertaining on a modest scale from time to time.'

'That is a pretty picture.'

'Yes,' I said. 'But it's hardly likely to happen now that you're spending less and less time there.'

'It's a dilemma,' he agreed. 'Cork is an interminably long way from London. And now I've no tenants to answer for, I've no real reason to visit, except during the hunting season. Happily, the hunting in Buckinghamshire is a good second best.'

Oh! I thought. How damnably clever Sophia had been! Get him to dump his mistress in the back of beyond, then sell up, and scarper with the heir!

'Perhaps I should move to Dublin,' I suggested. 'You often come here for business, don't you?'

'I do. But you mustn't think of moving here, Eliza. This is no place for a gentlewoman on her own.'

Nor, I had discovered, was Lissaguirra.

'But wasn't Dublin once the most prosperous city in Europe?' I persisted. 'My mother's friends used to regale me with stories of their glory days, when they worked the theatres here.'

It was the first time I had ever made reference to my theatrical origins. St Leger jerked his eyes up from his paper, his expression like that of one of the performing dogs that had once competed with my mother for top billing.

'Your mother was an actress?'

'Yes.'

'Where?'

'In the *Théâtre des Variétés* in Paris.'

'I know it well.'

He gave me that long, brazenly appreciative look that men always did when they learned of my theatre background, and I wanted to slap him. Instead I took up a knife and started scraping at a pat of butter.

'Why are you so set against the notion of me coming to live here?' I asked.

'There are a number of reasons. Since the Act of Union, forty years ago . . .'

St Leger started droning on and on about agrarian unrest and Catholic Emancipation and economic depression and I nodded along sagely, not listening to a word he said.

Why shouldn't I remove to Dublin? I thought. I'm

sure if I sold Lissaguirra it would fetch enough to buy myself a little pied-à-terre in Templeogue next door to Mr Lever. I thought how cosily that gentleman was set up from penning his rollicking war novels (which William had told me were populated by such outlandishly named characters as Major Monsoon and Mickey Free). In Templeogue I could invent silly novelettish heroines and call them Penelope Pureheart or Seraphina Swoon. I could concoct preposterous romances in which Miss Pureheart is abducted by pirates and rescued by a dashing sea captain before marrying the curate, and submit them to a publishing house under a nom de plume and –

'So effectively I'm telling you not to waste your money.' St Leger's voice broke into my reverie.

'What? I beg your pardon, dearest heart, I was miles away.'

'Don't waste any money buying a house here.'

'London, then. I could get a little house in Fulham or somewhere.'

'You can't come to London, Eliza. You know you can't.'

I gave him a challenging look. 'Because poor Sophia is afraid of scandal?'

'Yes.'

'That is hardly my concern,' I rejoined.

'It *is* your concern, Eliza. I am prepared to keep you

as my mistress in Ireland, but I cannot do so in London.'

'Why? Because you have a dozen mistresses there already, I suppose.'

'*They* are not the mother of my son.' He spoke with uncharacteristic belligerence, and it took me aback.

I held his gaze for a second or two, then dropped my eyes and made a show of daubing more butter onto rolls.

'La la la,' I sang, while under the silk of my Chinese robe my heart went pitter-pat, as it did any time I came near to overstepping the mark. How lucky I was! How enviable! For a man was unquestionably the best available source of income for most women, even if he was not a husband. And a good man, as St Leger was, was a prize indeed. 'When Venus roams by eventide, la la, la la, la la la la . . .'

'That's a pretty song,' remarked St Leger, shaking out his paper in that way men do when they deem it expedient to move on to other subjects.

'Yes, isn't it? "'Tis Venus who at midnight passes, la, la la la, la la la . . ."' I sent him a charming smile as I reached for a dish of raspberry jam. 'It was a song my mother used to sing. The stage was always ankle-deep in roses afterwards, which the gentlemen had thrown to her.'

'Was she very beautiful?'

'Yes.'

'So now I know where Clara Venus got her looks,' he teased.

I made a little moue. 'Not from me?' I said, in a piteous voice.

'Of course from you, my beauty! She certainly didn't get them from me.'

'That's for sure.' Playfully, I lobbed an apple at him.

'Do you like it here, Eliza?' he asked, catching it adroitly and taking a bite.

'Here, in Rutland Square? Yes, I think I do.'

'So next time business brings me to Dublin, shall I request the pleasure of your company?'

'Kind sir! Now that my baba is weaned and is in the charge of two doting nursemaids, that is hardly an offer I could refuse.' I dropped a mock-curtsey, smiling at him from under my eyelashes. 'How sweet that would be! We'd be like a pair of proper lovebirds, returning to the same cosy nest.'

St Leger set his paper aside. 'Come here, you minx, and let me tousle you.'

'Not until I've finished what I'm doing.'

'What *are* you doing?'

'Watch.'

I dolloped another spoonful of raspberry jam onto one of the rolls I had split, and sandwiched the halves together. 'There! Ring down for some more, will you?'

'More breakfast rolls?'

'Yes.'

Taking up the silver toast rack, I relieved it of its dainty triangles, dropping them into the bread basket alongside the buttered rolls.

'Why do you want more? You can't possibly still be hungry. You guzzled an entire chafing dish of scrambled eggs.'

'You'll see.' I gave St Leger my best mischievous look.

'Good God, Eliza. You're not expecting again, are you? Didn't you have a craving for bread rolls last time?'

'I should hope I'm *not* expecting,' I said, 'after the sacrifices you have made to ensure against that happening.'

We shared another smile. As well as my dandy little *eau de vie* sponge, St Leger and I relied on *coitus interruptus* as a means of contraception. It worked well for us because – aside from possessing enormous powers of self-control – St Leger was an experienced lover, who knew exactly what to do and when to do it.

Scooping the contents of the fruit bowl into a napkin, I carried it and the bread basket over to the window. The opportunistic seagull must have spied my robe fluttering in the wind, for he appeared from out of nowhere, looking for his breakfast.

'Begone!' I told him. 'If you're not careful, I shall dispatch you, as the mariner did the albatross.'

'Eliza,' said St Leger, casting his newspaper aside and rising to his feet, 'what the deuce are you up to?'

'Did you ring for the maid, as I asked?'

'What? No.'

'Well, do,' I said, 'because I shall want more provender than this.'

Raising my fingers to my mouth, I blew, producing a whistle so shrill that the seagull backed off on a downdraught. Below me, two dozen or more corner boys lifted their grubby faces.

'What ails you, Missus?' one of them called up.

'Have you had any breakfast?' I asked.

'Divil a bit.'

'Here, then!' I called back, skimming a slice of toast in his direction.

He snatched it from the air, and saluted me with a grin.

'Hey! Any more where that came from?' shouted one of his pals.

'Yes! I've apples, too.' I fired one down, but misjudged the trajectory. It hit the hat of a passing dandy in a canary yellow waistcoat and sent it spinning into a horse trough.

'Good shot!' said St Leger, applauding.

'My apologies, Monsieur!' The gent shook his fist at me in mock reprimand, then blew me a kiss and sauntered off to retrieve his hat.

'Here! Brat face!' I pitched another bread roll at a snot-nosed tatterdemalion, but an even snottier-nosed one intervened and snatched it. Away they went, one hot on the heels of the other, pell-mell towards Sackville Street.

By now a crowd of street urchins had congregated, harrooing and catcalling and cutting capers to attract my attention. One of them had produced a penny whistle, and another had got up upon the railings of the square and was singing over and over the same verse of a song (presumably because he knew no others):

> *At seven in the mornin' by most of the clocks*
> *We rode to Kilruddery in search of a fox.*

'Here you are, Reynard!' I called. He looked like a Reynard, too, I saw, as he grabbed the bread and crammed it into his mouth: a little starveling red-haired foxy thing, with button-beady eyes, like so many Irish children. 'And here's one for you, whistler! Fresh out of the oven!' The tin whistle went clattering to the ground as the boy lunged for his prize.

'She has buns in the oven!' came a shout, and the crowd whooped with laughter.

'More!'

'More buns, Missus!'

I made to throw another, but St Leger caught me by the wrist.

'You're a feeble shot,' he said, taking the bread basket from me and assessing what was left. 'Anyway, that won't go far. Look – they're coming now from all directions. Word must have got out that a madwoman's started a bunfight on Rutland Square.'

'It's like feeding the multitude,' I said, laughing up at him. 'I warned you we were going to need more.'

St Leger took aim, and lobbed a plum at a pretty girl who was smiling up at him, holding out her apron to receive it.

'They'll have stopped serving breakfast by now,' he said. 'What if they have none left?'

I stepped off the balcony and reached for the velvet bell-pull. 'If there is no bread,' I said, giving him a look of mock hauteur, 'I shall simply ask them for cake.'

24

THEY SAY THAT words come back to haunt you: I wish
it was just words.

Some years after I uttered that facile remark I was
reminded of it, as if some malicious revenant had whis-
pered into my ear. I picture myself, smiling over my
shoulder at St Leger as I pulled on the bell rope; hear
the banter of the corner boys ascending from Rutland
Square; smell the lilies that had started to droop in their
copper and gilt vases.

It was Young Biddy who first brought news, breezing
into the library after a visit to her mother. It was a fine
day in August: my fourth in Lissaguirra. I was at my
desk, responding to a letter from William. Clara Venus
was sitting on the step down to the terrace beyond the
library window, playing with a peg doll that Old Biddy
had fashioned for her. She was singing a song we had
invented as I abstractedly fed her the cues. My daughter
was already proficient in her ABCs, and prattled to her

dollies in a curious mixture of English, French and Irish.

'A?'

'A – apple!'

'B?'

'B – baked it!'

'Yeuch! The smell from Páidi O'Keefe's field!' said Young Biddy, setting the tea tray on the side table. 'You'd think a pack of monster dogs had laid down and died there.'

'Which field is that? C?'

'C – cored it!'

'The one down by the crossroads.'

'D?'

'Dropped it!'

'Páidi O'Keefe? Is he the big man – spiky hair, going grey?'

'That's him. I'd to cover my face with my skirt, the stink was so powerful.'

'The stink! The stink!' sang Clara Venus, skipping forward to the end of the song. 'X! Y! Z! All had a big bite and went off to bed!'

I finished the paragraph to William that read: *Setting the novel at the time of the Napoleonic Wars is a good idea, but you must not include scenes of battle. Too much braggadocio over war and politics will not go down well with your lady reader. Another thing to keep in mind (I know it is difficult for you, dear William, for you feel so passionately): you must restrain your inclination to make overt social commentary. Allow your characters to do it for you. Think of Miss Austen's meticulous satire!*

I set down my pen. 'Did you ask about the smell, Biddy? Was it manure, perhaps?'

'Sure, who can afford manure in these parts? And there was nobody round about to ask. I did not meet another soul on the way between here and the crossroads.'

I shrugged. 'I dare say it'll pass when the weather changes.'

'Please God it'll change soon. Old Biddy says it's been like living in a baker's oven these past weeks.'

Young Biddy rattled the tea things importantly; after four years at Lissaguirra she still loved playing at being a parlourmaid: I would have dispensed with the ritual altogether had it not afforded her so much pleasure. She set the muffin dish on the table and poured milk into the cup with a picture of a robin on it that was Clara Venus's favourite.

I stood up and eased into a stretch. The Biddies were right – the weather had been so hot and humid that for the past week I had scarcely bothered to dress: just reached for something muslin in the morning to throw on over my chemise. In the evening I cooled off by taking Clara Venus down to the lake where I was teaching her to swim, as St Leger had taught me. I thought of the time many years ago when my mother and I had holidayed at some seaside town – Deauville, I think – where the ladies had entered a bathing machine to disport themselves in flannel gowns and oilskin caps, concealed from the public gaze by canvas awnings. Here St Leger and I swam as nature intended, for there was no one to hide from, and Clara Venus too ran in and out of the water, naked as her namesake on the half-shell.

'Goodness! Those look good, Biddy,' I said dutifully, as she removed the lid of the muffin dish. 'Clara – come and have your milk and honey cakes.'

But Clara was too busy dancing her dolly along a crack in the pavement to bother with her milk and her honey cakes. 'S – sliced it! T – tasted it! The stink! The stink! The stink!'

The next day I set off on the two-mile journey to the crossroads on Minerva, the little mare that St Leger had taught me to ride. He had bought me a side-saddle, and – when I pooh-poohed the necessity for decorum, saying that I would be just as happy riding astride – he had pointed out quite rightly that form, not style, was paramount, and that most equestrian etiquette was plain common sense. Riding astride was out of the question, because – as he put it – the 'deliciously tender' skin on the inside of my thighs would get rubbed raw, unless I wore breeches. The notion of breeches appealed to me, but as I was considered more than a little eccentric in the neighbourhood and life was lonely enough already, I had no wish to be ostracized. Besides, St Leger assured me that side-saddle was an infinitely more comfortable way to travel.

We had taken to riding out together when he visited. As we cantered through the fields or along the lakeshore, St Leger on his beautiful bay hunter, his pointer racing beside him, I often laughed out loud with delight, for I felt as though it was as close as a being could ever come to flying without a broomstick. He spoke of buying a mount for Clara – a Connemara pony would suit her admirably, he said. Did George have a pony? I asked. Yes, a chestnut filly that he rode in the parkland at Roesworth and on Rotten Row when in London, accompanied by his groom.

When I pressed St Leger, he admitted that the child had been kitted out with miniature gilt spurs and a gold-headed whip. He would buy Clara a riding habit, to compensate. I told him that a riding habit would be wasted on her here in Boggetybeyondbackwards, and that we would rather have the money to spend on something useful. And then we had a row, which ended in my enraging him further by deliberately jumping a stile.

I took particular pains to provoke him while we were riding, because any rows conducted on horseback always finished amorously. I had found that one of the greatest substantiations of our erotic compatibility was through an out-and-out brawl. We would end up tumbled in a field somewhere, or racing each other home to bed, and once we were surprised in the wood by a poacher, who nonchalantly crossed our path with a brace of quail slung over his shoulder, knowing that in our scantily attired state we were scarcely in a position to accost him.

Nearly five years after we had first met, we were still taken with each other. In return for his support and protection, I worked hard to keep St Leger intrigued. In my formative years I had learned much through listening. The artists' models who had frequented my father's studio in Soho spoke highly of certain *techniques de la chambre*, and I was not afraid to practise them. I never waited upon St Leger, but I made sure he was comfortable. I took care not to carp or nag, but was not chary of engaging in lively debate and – most importantly – I made him laugh. The direction our affair took was unorthodox by any standards, but he seemed to enjoy its singular unpredictability. If I cared to scrutinize our partnership, I would attribute its success to mutual respect – which seemed then as now to be in scarce supply between the sexes.

Our only constraints were geographical. These might have proved insuperable, had not Clara Venus been part of the rubric. She had the power to draw St

Leger to Ireland; she and the prime horseflesh he had kept on at Dromamore. His equine concerns justified the maintenance of his house and grounds, albeit with a much-reduced staff: in those days he employed fewer domestics than stablehands. But because the world knows that an Irishman's bloodstock is his passion, no one questioned his frequent trips to Cork.

The crossroads that Young Biddy had spoken of marked the stage where the coach passed on its way to the city, and where arable land met forest. When I say arable land, I mean the patches that had been scraped out of the ground to grow potatoes.

St Leger had once told me that the Irish had the best staple diet in Europe: potatoes and what the Irish called *bláthach* – the residue left after the cream had been skimmed from the milk. I had thought at the time that he was being facetious, but he was not: I had found out for myself that buttermilk and potatoes were filling and nutritious. That was just as well, for while ships routinely sailed from the country's ports laden with wheat, oats, beef, pork, eggs and butter, all that remained for the Irish poor was potatoes. And because potatoes were easy to grow – even in bogs and on rocky hillsides – *The Times* of London had egregiously described the Irish as indolent drunkards who were perpetually inebriated with poitín distilled from their abundant crops.

Paídi's field by the crossroads was corrugated with

potato drills. Before I reached it, I caught the first trace of the stench that Young Biddy had told me about. So noxious was it that I took off my gauzy scarf and wrapped it tightly around my nose and mouth.

In the field stood two men, shoulders hunched, their backs to me. The foul smell emanated from the crop that not two days ago had been green and blooming with white flowers. It had rotted in the earth; the field was a discoloured blanket of corruption. I went to dismount, then thought better of it. I had seen the face of one of the men as he stooped to dig with his hands in the fetid mulch; I had seen his features contort, seen the wet runnels on his cheeks. Paídi O'Keefe was a proud man; he would not want a woman to see him weep. I turned my little mare, hoping that her hooves would make no sound on the packed earth of the pathway home to Lissaguirra.

The potatoes rotted in Cork and in Waterford and in Galway. They rotted in most of the counties where they were grown, and in all four provinces. They rotted while the ships continued to sail from the western ports crammed with their cargoes, like seaborne cornucopias, and the Irish began to starve.

The London *Times* editorial that derogated the Irish as drunken ne'er-do-wells had been written before the famine struck. But even afterwards, when the people had nothing to eat, nothing at all, the condemnation came spewing forth in pronouncements from politicians, landlords and clergy.

'Rotten potatoes and sea-weed, or even grass, properly mixed,' declared the Duke of Cambridge, 'afford a very wholesome and nutritious food. Everyone knows that Irishmen can live upon anything, and there is plenty grass in the fields though the potato crop should fail.'

I had thought there was no further for the Irish to fall. In Cork city I had seen half-naked women begging for alms, and in Dublin's Liberties I had seen emaciated children, filthy beyond apprehension, offering themselves for sale. I had seen animals sharing cabins with the starving wretches beyond the lake in Aill na Coill. At a tender age I had seen squalor that would have appalled St Leger and his ilk; scenes of Hogarthian depravity in the Haymarket and Soho, and harrowing acts of violence in the *ruelles* of Montmartre. But I had never known what depths of misery humankind could plumb until I saw skeletons walking the roads of County Cork.

I had taken Clara Venus off to the city, where we were to spend a day or two with Maria at Grattan Hill. Maria seldom visited me at Lissaguirra; with no transport of her own the journey was a protracted one, and she was reluctant to leave her daughters unchaperoned.

St Leger did not like me to drive alone, but

sometimes I yearned so desperately for company that I had to cut loose from Lissaguirra. On my trips to Dublin I was escorted everywhere by my beau, and fettered by *comme-il-faut*. In the village of Doneraile I was, unsurprisingly, *persona non grata*: the last time I had ventured there Mrs Grove-White had set the brim of her bonnet firmly against me as I approached.

In Cork I could kick up my heels a little, even if only to promenade Grand Parade or take a stroll through Daunt Square, or gossip over a glass of gin-and-water with the shabby gentry, the half-sirs and male and female dandies who congregated in Maria's lodging house. The stir, the tattle, the general buzz and hum of the place aroused in me a kind of *nostalgie de la boue*; it reminded me of the brouhaha backstage at the *Variétés*, or the more swagger of the Soho dens frequented by my father.

On my way there I drove past straggles of ragged families making their way to the poorhouse in Mallow. The strength had failed many of them; they lay listlessly by the wayside, and I knew from their demeanour that they were unlikely to get up again. As I passed the phalanx of walkers, a boy who was not much older than my Clara wavered, stopped short and stared after the others with eyes dull as stones before dropping to his knees.

I could not stop; I could not. I was afraid of these silent spectres, these fleshless walkers. I remembered the woman I had seen in Dublin's Liberties, so infested with vermin that she had torn the clothes from her back in her frantic attempts to rid herself of them: I could not risk having my daughter exposed to the diseases that these people would be carrying. Old Biddy had told me that her niece had died of the measles after inviting a vagrant into the kitchen for a bowl of soup.

'What's wrong with that boy?' Clara Venus asked, craning her neck.

'He is sick, sweetheart.'

'Like when I had croup?'

'Yes.'

'And Old Biddy made me rice-milk?'

'Yes.'

'You should tell his mama to give him rice-milk.'

I tried to concentrate on my driving.

'They look hungry, Mama.'

'We have some lemonade you could give them,' I said. The carriage was jolting, for the road was full of ruts and puddles; however, I did not slow Minerva's pace, but urged her on. 'That might be just as good as rice-milk. Look in my carpet bag – there are sandwiches there too.'

She rummaged in my bag and produced the bottle of lemonade and the packets of sandwiches that Old Biddy had made for our journey.

'Mama, stop, now,' she commanded.

Panic clutched at me – the walkers were conceivably

desperate enough to dispatch my pony and have her boiled in a pot – but stop I did, some yards ahead of the procession. I took my scarf and covered Clara's mouth and nose with it, drawing it into a knot at the back of her head.

'What are you doing?' she protested, but I had no chance to explain, for within seconds the chaise was surrounded by a throng of supplicants. On every grimy brow the word 'hunger' was imprinted. I could not look. I raised my face to the sky, so that any tears that might form would lodge behind my eyes, and gazed at the cloud formation.

Above us, there was a funeral in the air. It was Christy who had told me about this phenomenon, which was said to happen in the vicinity of an imminent death. As he described it, on the day his mother died he and his brothers witnessed a procession of mourners made up of clouds, moving slowly across the sky. 'First came the dray carrying the coffin,' he said, 'then the horses and horsemen, and then the people on foot: as plain as any funeral I ever saw.'

I saw it now, hanging in the sky over the road to Mallow as my daughter distributed food to those souls who were seeking sanctuary there. I heard her prattle as she delved into the bag. 'Lemonade,' she said. 'And here are cheese sandwiches. If you are sick, rice-milk is good for you, and beef tea. Oh! You must be very hungry.

Wait. I have more.' She rummaged again. 'Apples. And look – hard-boiled eggs, and here is some ginger-bread. I'll give you some, and you and you and – oh! Stop! Wait!'

Turning, I saw thin arms stretching from the rag-gery, hands grabbing, voices calling, 'God bless you, little Miss! May your pretty eyes never see anything that saddens them! God bless you for a kind and generous . . .' A baby was crying, a woman keening, a man retching: a nauseating effluvium rose from the emaci-ated bodies. A toothless man coughed in Clara's face, and a boy tried to snatch the carpet bag from her. I pulled her back, then touched up the mare with the whip. She trotted briskly forward.

'Wait, Mama!' cried Clara.

'No.' Lifting my skirt, I fumbled for the purse that I kept tucked into my garter. I spilled a handful of coins onto my palm, and thrust them at Clara. 'Here – throw them this.'

As Clara sent the coins spinning into the road, I tore my fichu away from my bodice and held it to my face, to block the smell and stanch the hot tears that had sprung. I heard but did not see the scramble that ensued, the cries and the stumbling feet of the pitiful crowd that pursued us pell-mell.

When I finally glanced back, the wretched proces-sion had resumed. Two men had returned for the boy who had fallen: one of them lifted him as he might an empty creel and hefted him onto his shoulders. They continued on their way like sleepwalkers.

Clara turned and looked up at me. 'Was that the stink that Young Biddy was talking about?' she asked. 'Why do those people smell, Mama? And why are they so hungry?'

I could not bear to tell her why. I could not bear to tell her that the world beyond Lissaguirra was a harrowing, hellish place. Instead I pulled her closer with my free arm, and started to sing 'The ABC Song'.

25

IN THE HOUSE on Grattan Hill, an impromptu party had been got up to celebrate a win at the races by a gentleman friend of Maria's. It had clearly been a substantial hit: champagne, wine and whiskey were flowing freely and there was a buffet, of which I was inordinately glad, since all the food that Clara Venus and I had brought with us for the journey had been distributed on the road.

Once Minerva had been installed in the livery yard and I had washed and changed, I felt sparky and animated despite our long journey. Clara Venus was spirited away by Maria's girls and I was reminded of how they had adopted Annie Thackeray as a little sister five years ago, and taught her Corkonian skipping rhymes and hopscotch.

Amid the dandified rag, tag and bobtail, Maria looked resplendent in a gown of silk dupion, which she had refashioned from one of her sister's cast-offs. Since she was not much of a letter-writer, we had plenty to catch up on. Her eldest daughter, Harriet, had finally inherited a substantial sum from her superannuated aunt, and was to be wed to a baronet.

'A baronet!' I said. 'How much is he worth?'

'Ten thousand a year – '

'How comfortable!'

' – with a castle in Scotland.' Maria's expression told me that she could not bear the notion of her beloved girl fetching up in Scotland, even with a castle and a title.

'My condolences, darling. But a castle is good!'

'Not this one. It's in the Highlands somewhere north of Inverness,' she went on. 'A ghastly, gloomy dump, by all accounts, that was built some time in the Middle Ages. He is more than twice her age, with a glass eye.'

'A war injury?'

'No. A shooting accident. So he is not even heroic.' She aimed a kick at a little Griffon dog with a bow in its hair that was snuffling around the buffet table, then reached for a bottle of champagne and refilled our glasses. 'You must be sick and tired of being stuck in Bogland, dearest. Isn't it time you asked St Leger to set you up in London?'

'He won't hear of it. He cannot afford to be anything less than an exemplary spouse to Sophia until her father dies.'

'He'd better die soon. You're not getting any younger.'

A silvery laugh caught my attention. On the other side of the room, a ravishingly pretty girl was preening the whiskers of a drunken dragoon into a fantail and admiring the effect.

'Who is that child?' I asked.

'She's an actress, on tour with *The Maid of Milan* and some rubbishy comedies. That mangy dog belongs to her.'

I remembered my time as the star attraction at Doneraile Court, presiding over after-dinner divertissements with Sooty on my lap, and conducting *conversazioni*.

'I was a fascinating woman once,' I said, mournfully.

Maria smiled sympathetically. 'It will come back. Give it time.'

'Time? How much time have I left? Look at that doxy. She can't be more than sixteen.'

Maria gave me a sideways look. 'She's fifteen.'

There came a chime of merry chattering from beyond the door, as of Indian bells floating up the stairway, and a flurry of satin and Chantilly lace announced the entrance of a gaggle of chorus girls. Their dresses shimmered multihued in the candlelight, their shoulders were white as buttermilk, their coiffures so heavily looped at the napes of their necks that they had perforce to elevate their chins, in a manner both haughty and provocative. They were nymphs clad as sophisticates, little dressing-up dollies: they did not yet belong to their clothes.

'Some of those girls are on the job,' said Maria, elbowing her way across the room. 'I'll have no charges of brothel-keeping levelled at me.'

Straight away the new arrivals fluttered to the supper table. Glasses chinked, silverware clinked, the hubbub and bustle rose tenfold, and across the room laughter rang out as the dragoon started to belch the alphabet.

As the actresses helped themselves to savouries and sweetmeats, I diverted myself with a little eavesdropping. I heard details of a dispute with a leading lady, a *diner à deux* in a private dining room, a scandalous *crime passionnel* – and then someone dropped a name that caused me to freeze mid champagne sip.

'There's a horse race called that, isn't there?' said a girl with blue eyelids and blackened lashes. 'The St Leger Cup.'

I gripped the stem of my champagne coupe, and helped myself randomly to some tasteless tidbit.

'A jockey, no less!' smirked another girl. 'That explains the bruises.'

'He's a gentleman, not a jockey; they're love bites,

not bruises, and they're worth it every one, for the brooch he gave me.'

'Show us!'

'I sold it. For forty pounds.'

'Lydia! You lucky rogue!'

Forty pounds! I stopped pretending to scrutinize the buffet and stared openly at the girl. Lydia was a svelte little thing, exotic and dark. She was not rosy or blond or kittenish like most of the other girls there. There was a shrewdness in her veiled eyes that meant business. She was competition.

'Are we going to meet him?'

'He's coming tonight.'

'Isn't this place too seedy for a toff like him?'

Lydia gave an oblique smile. 'Toffs love to slum it.'

Just then her eyes met mine, and I nearly spilled the contents of my glass. She regarded me as if she knew me, even though we had never met, with an insight that startled me.

Suddenly Maria was at my elbow. 'St Leger's here. I've just seen him at the front door.'

'Stall him, Maria!'

'How?'

'I don't know. Start a row, set fire to something, push someone down the stairs. Just give me five minutes. Please.'

Maria knew better than to quiz me. Abruptly, she

411

scooped the Griffon dog up from the floor and made for the door, holding it ostentatiously aloft, the way she had Lady Charlotte's pug after it had been mauled by the house cat.

'This stinking animal has fouled my premises,' she said loudly. 'I am evicting it.'

The doxy to whom the dog belonged leapt to her feet. 'Leave him be!' she shrieked, as Maria sailed towards the door. 'Somebody stop her! She has my little Pantaloon!'

The drunken dragoon reared up, caught the toe of his boot on a rug, and toppled to the floor. Girls clucked and squawked and scurried in Maria's wake, protesting clamorously, and in the melee I slid unobtrusively from the room, and went to my own chamber.

Clara Venus was there, sleeping soundly through a din that would have awoken Perrault's sleeping princess. Setting down my fan, I reviewed my appearance in the flyblown glass. I bit my lips and pinched my cheeks to add colour, I rearranged my décolletage, I tugged a tendril or two away from my coiffure, so that they ringleted becomingly onto my bare shoulder. Then I smoothed my daughter's hair, gathered her into my arms, and sallied forth.

A crowd had gathered on the landing to watch the eviction of Pantaloon. His ribbon was askew – lending him an incongruously jaunty look – and amongst the battalion of painted ladies lolling against the balustrade, Lydia's laugh sounded the most deliciously flagrant of all. Between her fingers her folded fan looked as deadly as a poniard. As I watched, she laid it against her left breast, just above the heart, and aimed her gaze downward.

In the stairwell below, St Leger was lounging against a pillar, looking up at her. There was something in the impertinence and bland mockery of his smile that made me almost shudder with longing for him. I determined to stake my claim in a manner that would brook no dispute.

'Excuse me,' I murmured to the nearest gallant. 'May I pass?'

Seeing the child slumbering picturesquely on my shoulder, the gent stood back at once. 'Make way! Make way for the lady!' he hollered, and the sea of iridescent satin sighed and parted. I arranged my face in attractive lines, and descended the steps.

'Jameson,' I said, pointedly using his Christian name, 'I am so glad you are come. Clara has been hoping and hoping to see you. I trust you are not too tired after travelling such a distance?'

He shot me a look. I sent one back that I contrived to make warm, alluring, compassionate, soulful, humorous and full of promise. Oh – and Madonna-like, too, because I had our daughter in my arms. In short, I managed the look hankered after by portrait painters since Hans Holbein.

Above me, I heard Lydia's fan snap open, but it was too late. Jameson stepped forward to embrace me, and over his shoulder I saw my opponent's face glaring down at me, taut with suppressed fury.

'Does anyone want this hideous dog?' Maria had dropped Pantaloon to the floor and was wiping her hands fastidiously on her skirt. 'It's slobbered all over my fichu.'

Later, when the burnt-out wicks of the lamps were glowing red within their globes and the merrymakers had dragged themselves home to bed or on to the next party, Clara Venus crawled onto her father's lap and fell asleep. Her sprawled limbs pinioned him to the sofa where we sat, I with my feet tucked beneath my gown, Jameson with an arm slung around my shoulders. The room had that strange, haunted air that seems almost tangible after parties; the grey, otherworldly light that filters through closed curtains just before sunrise makes me think for some reason of the drowned city of Atlantis. The only sound was the cry of gulls, come in from the coast to start their daily scavenge.

Now that the menace posed by Lydia had receded, I felt limp and velvety with relief. It was as though Jameson and Clara Venus and I were the only people left alive in the world; everyone else had receded like shingle with the tide.

'I am glad you are here,' I said. 'Were you surprised to see me?'

'Yes. How did you get here?'

'In my jingle.'

He slapped my arm lightly in reprimand. 'Eliza. You know I don't approve of you going abroad unaccompanied.'

'Who is to accompany me? I should go nowhere if I sought an escort every time I travelled beyond the bounds of Lissaguirra.'

'Driving alone is hazardous. You're exposing yourself to danger at the hands of brigands, and our daughter, too.'

I felt something clog the air. We were not the only ones in the world after all, the three of us cocooned in our auroral bubble.

'There are no brigands,' I told him. 'The people have not the vigour for violence. They are *dying*, Jameson!'

I looked at the pretty face of our daughter with her tumble of golden hair and her perfect peachy skin and rose-petal mouth, and I remembered the boy whose eyes had been dull as stones, the boy who had fallen on the road to Mallow, and as a great fathomless sorrow began to rise within me, tears pooled in my eyes and started to stream down my cheeks.

Jameson's arm around me tensed. 'Don't,' he said. 'I cannot bear to see you unhappy.'

'Then do something to help!'

'I am not a landlord, sweetheart. I am not responsible – '

'We are all responsible.' I shrugged away his arm and sat up straight. 'We *all* have a responsibility to help people in need. It says so in the holy writ.'

'Hush, darling. You'll wake Clara. I will help. I promise that I will do whatever I can.'

'Don't promise. Vow. Vow on your daughter's head.'

He set his hand on Clara Venus's forehead, and gently pushed a strand of hair away from her eyes. 'I vow to do whatever I can to help.'

I dashed away my tears and wiped my nose with the back of my hand, and then he reached in his pocket for a handkerchief and held it to my nose and said, 'Blow.'

I blew my nose, and Jameson said: 'Do it again.'

'I don't need to.'

'I want to hear it. The noise you make is like a little pig.'

I blew my nose again, and because it did sound like a pig, I started to laugh, and Jameson started to laugh with me, and soon I was weeping with laughter rather than distress.

Clara Venus blinked sleepily and said: 'Stop it. I'm having a dream about ducks,' and then her head lolled

416

back against her father's chest and she was fast asleep again, and the cocoon-like feeling was restored. I sighed with a contentment so profound that when the breath expired I scarcely dared inhale again.

'You told me you were a pagan,' said Jameson, wiping away the last of my tears. 'How do you know what it says in the Bible?'

'I read it in Miss Pinkerton's academy. It says: "for the poor will never cease out of the land: therefore I command thee, saying, Thou shalt open thine hand wide unto thy brother, to thy poor, and to thy needy, in thy land".'

Jameson smiled. 'You should be teaching Sunday school,' he said.

26

THE NEXT HARVEST came, and this time the potato blight was even more widespread. In the second year of *an Gorta Mór*, as well as famine, disease began to spread – typhus, dysentery and dropsy. The contagion was not confined to the starving poor: doctors, nurses, hapless do-gooders and members of the clergy succumbed to fever.

We did what we could, Jameson and I. He sent money to finance the building of extra accommodation in the poorhouse in Mallow, and I and some others who lived in the locality volunteered at the soup kitchens that had been set up by the Quakers. It was not much, but when I likened our efforts to bailing out a sinking ship with a sieve, Young Biddy scolded me roundly.

'You're doing all you can, ma'am, and you're doing it with a heart. The Relief Committee is full of ignorant blackguards. My cousin got some of that Indian corn they're after bringing from America, and it made her babby sick to his stomach.'

The Indian corn that had been imported arrived unground, and was largely inedible – even when cooked after hours of soaking. Nor was it distributed freely. It was paid for with money earned by starving people labouring on building projects set up by bureaucrats – senseless schemes designed by insensible people: canals and roads that started nowhere and finished nowhere, thoroughfares that no barges would ever navigate or grain carts traverse.

And the crews of the sailing ships continued to load cargoes of Irish-grown provender – now under armed guard lest they be set upon by starving indigents – and transport them overseas to the country where the land-owners lived.

A rare letter came from Cork, from Maria:

Here is news that breaks my heart to write. The mayor has decreed that anyone suspected of carrying disease be denied entry to the city, and now there are thugs employed to guard the city gates. But still poor wretches come from the country in their thousands. They linger until evening, when they creep in under cover of dark, and when they see there is no help for them, many simply lie down and die. As I write this, there is a child lying dead in the street outside my house. He has lain there several hours by the side of the footway,

*and I dare not go near him for fear of disease. I have heard
hellish reports of dogs eating the flesh of the dead bodies.*

*My sister is repairing to London and has invited me
to join her. I shall shut up the house in Grattan Hill and
depart post haste on the boat to Bristol. I can no longer bear
to stay in this benighted place. Eliza, I beseech you to do the
same. Ireland is no place for you or Clara Venus.*

I, too, had heard the reports of dogs eating the
bodies of the dead. The notion of emigration had
occurred to me, but it seemed that leaving the country
could no longer be done in any orderly or rational
manner. It had become the last refuge of a population so
desperate that they were willing to risk the hazards of
long sea voyages in dangerously overcrowded vessels.

I was at a loss what to do. It was a bitterly cold
winter, the worst in living memory, Old Biddy said. The
prevailing winds blew from the south-west into the
north-east, bringing gales of hail, sleet and snow. I dis-
continued my visits to the soup kitchens and ventured
out only when absolutely necessary. I gave Christy
money to go to Doneraile to stock up on dry goods, for
whilst food was in short supply everywhere, it could be
got there at a price. We had our hens for eggs, a couple
of goats for milk, our vegetable garden, and meat in the
form of whatever game or fowl Christy could shoot or
trap. He ignored the proscription on fishing, and took

what he could from the lake.

I discouraged the Biddies from stirring abroad, for I did not want word getting out that there was food to be had at Lissaguirra. I think they were afraid to, anyway. There were ghosts roaming everywhere.

And then one day when I was stamping through the snowy wood with Clara Venus, gathering pine cones for kindling, and singing her current favourite nursery rhyme (it was 'Who Killed Cock Robin', and though it was a grisly ditty, it afforded me more amusement than our ABC song), I heard a horse approaching. I thought it was Christy with a rabbit he had promised for the pot: he had come earlier that day with a letter – the first I'd had for weeks on account of the weather. The thaw was starting at last, he told me, and we were no longer snowbound.

It was St Leger on the bridle path. I had not seen him for five months.

I let Clara go first.

'Papa!' she shouted, rushing at him as he swung himself out of the saddle. 'Yes, yes! You are come! Look at my boots! Look at the footprints they make in the snow!' She cavorted and jumped for him, like a dinky circus pony. 'We can make a snowman! Lots of snow-mans! And look! Look at all the pine cones we've gathered! They will do for the snowmans' noses. Mama says pine cones are better than carrots. Look how many we have – a hundred, at least. And listen! I can speak Irish even better than you! The Biddies have taught me. *Conas atá tú? Tá mé go han-mhaith . . .'*

He marvelled at her boots and her footprints and her pine cones and her Irish, and agreed that they should build a snowman – three snowmen – as soon as he had changed out of his travelling clothes. And then he took off a glove and trailed a finger along my frozen face.

'I've missed you,' he said.

'And I you.'

We smiled at each other with our eyes until Clara Venus commanded him to look at her gloves. 'They have robins on! Young Biddy knat them for me.'

'Knitted,' I corrected automatically, stooping to pull the matching cap over her ears. 'How did you find us, Jamey?'

'Old Biddy told me which direction you'd gone. I followed your tracks through the wood.'

'Did you hear my song?' demanded Clara.

'Yes.'

'"Who killed Cock Robin!"' she began, and he joined in:

'"I, said the sparrow, with my bow and arrow, I killed Cock Robin!"'

Making a lunge for her, he began tickling her through her layers of clothing, and Clara wriggled and giggled and begged him to stop.

'I have a present for you,' he told her, while she was still breathless from being tickled.

'What is it? What is it? Can I have it now?'

'It's waiting for you at home.'

'Let's go!' Clara looked to left and right. 'Which way? The woods look different in the snow.'

'Follow your footprints,' I told her. 'See if you can make fresh ones all the way home, and we will follow them as if we are tracking a wild beast.'

'What kind of beast?'

'A warthog,' said her father.

'Papa! No!'

'A marmoset,' I said.

'What's a marmoset?'

'A marmoset is the prettiest, cheekiest monkey there is. I saw one once in London. It belonged to an organ grinder, and it danced.'

'Like this? La la la . . .' Clara Venus performed a sweet but graceless arabesque.

'Just like that.'

'Then, come! You must follow me, Mama and Papa.' She set off, kicking her way through the snow.

I picked up the basket of pine cones, and Jameson reached for it. We were standing so close that we might have kissed.

'How have you been?' he asked.

'We have been . . . managing.'

423

We continued to smile at each other. The scrunch of the snow beneath our feet, the effulgence of the surrounding whiteness, the mist from our breath mingling and dissolving in the clear cold air, all combined to make me feel a peculiar, paradoxical . . . *chaleur*. If we had been alone I do not doubt that we would have fallen into each other's arms and onto the ground, but the horse – clearly hungry after the journey from Doneraile – whinnied with impatience to be on his way, and 'La la *la* – ' sang Clara up ahead '– come *on*, slowcoaches!'

So, each holding a handle of the basket, together we started to trudge forward.

'Things are very bad,' he said.

'Yes. The people hereabouts are scarecrows – *épouvantails* – literally. They are nothing more than skin and sinew and bones, with all muscle and tissue gone.'

'They are everywhere around Doneraile.'

Ahead, Clara Venus had hunkered down by the bole of a tree and was digging in the snow for pine cones. Even they were in pitiful supply this year: it seemed that the entire country had withered and shrunk, as if Nature had turned her back on poor, green Erin.

'How much does Clara know of what's happening?' said Jameson.

'She doesn't talk of it; I don't imagine she can make sense of it. It's so long since she has been beyond the boundaries of Lissaguirra that it's a foreign country to her. The bad weather has kept us here perforce. But what child could remain unscathed by the things she has seen? I cannot bear that she has to learn so early in life what atrocities humankind is capable of.'

'I think you must get out of here,' he said.

'Yes.'

'They say things are not so bad in the north of the country. I have friends there who will be glad to take you and Clara in. You can stay with them until this calamity has run its course.'

I did not want to go to the north of the country! I did not want to travel hundreds of miles of highways and byways with Clara, encountering human skeletons at every twist of the road and over the brow of every hill. It was my plan to travel to Cork city under cover of night and board a steamship that would take me to Bristol, and thence to London.

I reached into the pocket of my pelisse and took out the letter that Christy had brought. 'This came today.'

'What is it?'

'It's a letter from William.'

Jameson looked blank.

'Thackeray.'

'You still correspond with that booby?'

'Yes. Although I have not heard from him for some months. He is living in London, now, with his daughters.'

'And with his wife?'

'No. Isabella is still unwell. She is being cared for in Camberwell. He needs someone to look after Annie and Minnie. Listen.' I skimmed through the first few paragraphs, which were given over to William's horror at what was happening in Ireland. 'Here we are. "My house is a substantial dwelling, three storeys, with servants' quarters, study, dining room, drawing room and capital bedrooms. Kensington Gardens is at the gate, and there are omnibuses every two minutes. What can mortal want more? Might you think of coming, for I am need not just of inspiration –"'

'What does he mean by "inspiration"?' asked Jameson sourly.

'Nothing. It's a joke. We came up with an idea for a book, years ago.'

'A book?'

'The night we went to dinner at Templeogue, do you remember? You were at your Club – we talked about collaborating on a novel. I thought it was just an idle piece of nonsense at the time – we called it a novel without a hero – but it appears he may have struck lucky. See, here he says, "*The Novel without a Hero* has been accepted by *Fraser's* for serial publication in monthly instalments. The first was published on New Year's Day. I have two more written, but after that I don't know where Miss Sharp will lead me . . ."'

'Miss Sharp?'

'She's a character in the novel. He goes on: "The fact is I need a very good governess and perfect lady to command my house and children. Miss Hamerton, who is currently residing with us and instructing the girls, is not a lady – "'

'What does he mean by that?'

'How should I know? I shall stop reading, Jameson, if you persist in interrupting.'

'Go on,' he said, sulkily.

'"I know Annie will love you as much as ever she did, and Minnie, too. I will pay you a decent salary, of course. Money is still tight but easing a little, and you will be glad to know that I have made a donation of five pounds to the British Relief Association to help the needy in Ireland."'

'Five pounds!' scoffed Jameson.

'Five pounds is a lot of money for most people. He pays two pounds a week for his wife's welfare –'

'I dare say he is glad to be rid of her.'

'Jameson! What a horrid thing to say! Isabella is a sick woman.'

'You told me she was a lunatic.'

'It is the same thing, in a way.'

A melt of snow dropped from a branch suddenly, onto Jameson's hat. He took it off and shook it, and then he said, 'Anyway, I won't hear of it.'

'Hear of what?'

'You gallivanting off to be "governess" to an ass like William Thackeray.'

The stress he put on the word 'governess' made it sound like 'whore'.

'I am neither "gallivanting", nor am I to be *his* governess. I have been asked to be governess to his children. And who are you to tell me what I may or may not do?'

He was about to retaliate, but at that moment Clara Venus, who had been ploughing ahead, swinging her arms marmoset-style, tripped over a tree root hidden in the snow and went flying face first. She let out a howl in the way that children do who are more shocked than hurt, and immediately Jameson went pelting to her rescue.

'Carry me, Papa!' she entreated him. 'Carry me the rest of the way home.'

So we trailed back to the house, the three of us, Clara Venus on her father's shoulders, me leading the horse and carrying the half-empty basket of pine cones.

Clara Venus was asleep upstairs. She had tried her hardest to stay awake, but finally Jameson had carried her up and tucked her into her own bed, which had been warmed first with a hot brick. His present to her had been a Noah's Ark, beautifully carved and painted, with a menagerie of tiny wooden animals. Clara had spent an hour lining them up, two-by-two, marching them up the gangway to the ark where Noah and his rosy-cheeked wife stood ready to welcome them.

Jameson and I were sitting by the fire in the library, which was the room I used now for living, writing, reading, eating and occasionally sleeping. It made sense to keep just one or two rooms in the house warm when fuel was scarce. We had firewood aplenty, but splitting logs was time-consuming and turf was hard to come by.

I was mending Clara's stockings. Old Biddy had taught me to darn, for I had never learned any needle-work other than the fancy variety. She had laughed at my first rubbishy attempts, but I had become quite adept at it, and enjoyed it more than I ever had picking out rosebuds and daisies in silk, because there was some-thing honest and no-nonsense about darning. We had enjoyed a supper of rabbit stew and rice pudding, and Jameson had consumed a bottle of claret. I could tell that he was spoiling – not for a fight, but to let rip about something – and I guessed that the bone of contention he wanted to pick had to do with William. I was right.

'So this chap Thackeray wants you to write a book with him.'

'What? No.'

'I thought you said you were writing a book together.'

'We had an idea for a book.'

'And now he's stolen it for his own.'

'You can't steal ideas.'

'Of course you can. If you had copyrighted the idea, you could sue.'

I refrained from pointing out that copyrighting ideas was equally unenforceable.

'Jameson,' I said, coolly, 'William has very kindly offered me a post as governess to his daughters. He could have offered it to any one of the hundreds of educated women who advertise their services in the pages of the *Morning Post*, but he didn't, because he knows that I am in desperate need – '

'I find that a gross insult. You cannot say that you are not well set up here in Lissaguirra.'

I ignored him. 'He knows that I need to get out of Ireland. And if you interpret William's proposal as being motivated by anything other than a generous impulse, then shame on you.'

'I told you that I have friends in the north who – '

'A plague on the north! Would you have me and Clara Venus travel through countryside that is rife with pestilence and fraught with danger, to seek shelter in some strange place where we know nobody? I have been offered a *job*, Jameson. A job with accommodation in a family where I am known and cherished. Why do you try to deny me the right to steer my own course?'

430

'Because whatever course you embark on implicates my daughter.'

'And whatever course *you* embark on implicates my son!'

'He is not your . . .'

I gave him a look, and he tailed off lamely. It was an underhand tactic, and I was not proud of it, but I wanted to remind him that I had a metaphorical axe in my hands that could, with a single blow, fell the family tree that he and Sophia had taken such pains to root.

'I did not intend to rear a child, Jameson,' I said. 'But I am doing it. I am doing it well, and I am doing it mostly on my own.' He opened his mouth to say something, but I held up a hand to arrest him. 'I know that you provide for us financially, but you have not bought us, and you cannot keep us in a place where disease and fever and famine are by-products of the cruellest tyranny.'

'The queen is not – '

'The queen does not live in this country! Her henchmen and her lords and ladies do not live here! Do you think the queen knows that there are babies in this country suckling their dead mothers?'

He slumped, turning his face away as though I had physically slapped him.

'It is true. A woman near to putrefaction was found in a cabin not far from here with her infant still trying to draw nourishment from her dead breast. Your worst imaginings are all true, Jameson. And if you died in your feather bed in your grand house in London next week, Clara and I would not be able to keep the roof over our heads. They say a human being is just three weeks away from death by starvation here. I will not wait for you to give me permission to save my life and that of our child. I am going to work for Mr Thackeray.'

I left the room, shaking with emotion. The chamber upstairs was warm from the fire that had been lit earlier, the bed was toasty from the hot brick. But Jameson did not climb the stairs to keep me company that night.

The next day I packed my bags and set off for London with Clara Venus.

27

THE MISSES THACKERAY had painted pictures to welcome me to the house in Kensington. Annie's showed me in fine clothes standing on the prow of a ship with a misshapen green dwarf by my side.

I hazarded a guess. 'Oh! How lovely! Is that a leprechaun I am bringing from Ireland?'

'No. It is Clara Venus,' said Annie, with hauteur. 'She is green because she is seasick.'

Minnie's picture showed me with a horse because, she said, she had just learned to draw horses (it wasn't at all a bad attempt, even though the animal's knees bent in the wrong direction).

After tea, William told the girls to take Clara into the garden, then set off with me on a tour of the house, talking the entire time.

'I have given up scribbling for the *Chronicle* to concentrate on my novel,' he said, lumbering up the stairs ahead of me. 'I am always thinking about the next instalment, Eliza, and worrying lest I cannot meet my deadline. See, how my fingernail is bitten to the quick! I rise in the middle of the night to write, for the characters parade around in my head so, and will not allow me to sleep.' He paused with one foot on the top tread and cocked an ear. 'Listen to that – isn't it splendid? We get the evening bells at this hour.'

A wind-borne carillon resounded from churches all around Kensington. I smiled, and enquired after Isabella.

'I have good accounts of her from Mrs Bakewell – she and her daughter Mrs Gloyne have charge of her. The change in the little woman is remarkable now that she has someone to look after her and keep her clean. She is tolerably sensible, although she does tend to go rambling off into her own little world. She has a preoccupation with the Queen of Spain, for some reason.'

'Does she go abroad much?'

'Oh, yes. I took her on an excursion to Camberwell Fair and to Beulah Spa – it's sadly dilapidated – and to the theatre: a private box. I think she enjoyed herself in her little way.'

'Has she shrunk?' I asked.

'Isabella, shrunk? No.'

'Then why do you talk about her as though she was some kind of midget?'

'Do I? I had not realized.' A grey cat slunk out from

behind a blanket chest, and William let out an oath as he stumbled over it. 'I was going to set an entire chapter of the book at Beulah Spa, but I have changed it to Vauxhall instead – remember you gave me such an amusing account of a brawl there? It is there that the character of Captain Dobbin comes into his own –'

'Dobbin?'

'My male protagonist. He is hopelessly in love with Amelia. And of course he suspects Becky is up to no good.'

I gave him a look of blank incomprehension.

'You must remember our heroine – Rebecca Sharp? She has issued forth from the inauspicious environs of Miss Pinkerton's academy to wreak havoc in the lives of several of our characters. All the men have become quite besotted with her, of course, and she treats them abominably . . .'

And William continued in this vein, upstairs and down, rattling on about the Novel without a Hero that was now called *Vanity Fair*.

I had imagined that the three girls would get on famously, but in fact both Annie and Minnie were suspicious of Clara Venus. The last time Annie had seen me I had been her mother substitute – Isabella having lately tried to drown her on the beach at Margate – and she was jealous now that I had a daughter of my own. Minnie,

435

being just two years older than Clara, imagined herself infinitely superior, and treated Clara accordingly. She spoke French at her very fast, and had two cats – Nicholas Nickleby and Barnaby Rudge – which followed her everywhere like little grey ghosts and stared at Clara with hostile yellow eyes.

The house, presided over by a housekeeper called Mrs Grey, was a haven. It was big and comfortable and cheerful and rambling and handsome and untidy. It was, I suppose, rather like William himself. It had two bowed bays at the front and a courtyard at the back, which was overlooked by William's ground-floor study. Sometimes when I took myself out there to sit with my book under the medlar tree, I would see him at his desk gazing myopically at his small garden with a look of such contentment that I felt a kind of compassion for him, this great hulking man in a house overrun by clever women (there were six of us, including the housemaid, and I suspected the cats were female, despite their names).

William had, he told me, written to his mother to say that he had engaged as his governess a clergyman's daughter – shy, drab and of an unprepossessing mien. I did not waste my breath asking why. That William felt a puerile obligation to dissemble about both my provenance and my appearance was not my concern.

I gave lessons in the schoolroom on the top floor every morning, and took the children to play in

Kensington Gardens every afternoon. In the evening I would sit with William and discuss the three or four thousand words he had diligently written that day of the novel which was to become as famous as any penned by Mr Dickens.

From the beginning of the year, *Vanity Fair* had appeared in monthly instalments of thirty-two bound yellow pages. William's deadline was the 15th of each month, ahead of publication two weeks later, and there were times when the printer's boy sat drumming his heels in the hallway of the house on Young Street, waiting for overdue copy. I have never seen anybody work with such single-minded determination. Every evening William would leave his study exhausted, and dine off a tray in the drawing room while I read over the day's work, commenting, suggesting, praising and critiquing.

I loved the novel. I loved its insouciant cynicism and its playful *lèse-majesté*. I loved the way William cocked a snook at London society, then took a nimble step back: his manipulation of the reader reminded me of a clown I had once seen at Astley's circus who had shared the ring with a moth-eaten tiger. *Vanity Fair* was brave and funny and tender and moving.

I knew he had based the character of Becky on me; or rather, on a caricature of me. My mannerisms were all present and correct, my speech patterns – with the occasional telltale French inflection – were there too. He stole from me shamelessly – aperçus, *bons mots*, chunks of philosophy from the numerous letters I had written him. The avowal I had made, that I could be a good woman with a thousand pounds a year was there (although he upped the ante to five thousand), and my declaration – 'I'm no angel' – became a fashionable catchphrase overnight. But I did not begrudge William this personal plagiarism, for he had been good to me.

As the spring and summer wore on, *Vanity Fair* caused such a stir that I believe William became slightly unnerved. 'If Mr Thackeray should die tomorrow,' wrote a prominent journal, 'his name would be transmitted down to posterity by *Vanity Fair.*'

To his bemusement, he found himself being lionized by *le tout Londres*. New addresses in Belgravia and Mayfair were constantly being added to his day book: Under 'L' for 'Lords' he had listed Ashburton, Cavendish, Chesterfield, Granville, Hogg, Lansdowne, Palmerston and the comte d'Orsay. If the comte counted as a lord, I told William, he only needed two more names to have ten a-leaping.

Every month, on the day that the latest instalment was delivered, we five – Annie, Minnie, Clara Venus, William and I – would make a holiday. We would go for rambles on Hampstead Heath or Richmond Hill, or picnics in Greenwich (where the deer stole Clara's sandwiches), and pay an occasional visit to the theatre. We spent Minnie's seventh birthday at Hampton Court (where Clara got lost in the maze) and were invited to Mr Dickens's house for a children's party (where Clara puked on the conjurer's shoes), and we spent a day at the zoo where William made up a rhyme that went:

'First I saw the white bear, then I saw the black,
Then I saw the camel with the hump upon his back.
Then I saw the grey wolf with mutton in his maw:
Then I saw the wombat waddle in the straw.'

We were taking tea in the gardens of the zoo when William spied someone he knew – a fellow contributor from *Punch* magazine. He excused himself and went to talk to the gentleman, leaving me with the girls. It had been a long day; they were tired and fractious, and had taken to bickering among themselves.

'The wombat was the best,' pronounced Minnie.

'No. The white bear was the best,' said Annie.

'The wolf was the best,' said Clara Venus. 'We have wolves at home in Ireland.'

'Don't be stupid,' said Annie. 'There are no wolves in Britain any more.'

'I don't live in Britain. I live in Ireland.'

'You do so live in Britain. Ireland is part of the British Isles, and it is ruled over by Queen Victoria.'

'I live in *Ireland* and there are wolves in Ireland.'

439

'There are not.'

'There are so! My daddy killed one.'

'Your daddy must be a liar.'

'He is not a liar! My mama has a wolfskin on her bed.'

'Pooh!' said Minnie. 'Fancy having a smelly old wolf lying on top of you at night. You must live in a caveman sort of house.'

'Papa told me the Irish live mostly in holes in the ground,' said Annie. 'And that they eat potatoes and drink whiskey all day. He wrote a book about it.'

'Do you live in a hole in the ground, Clara Venus?' Minnie asked.

'No! I live in a palace.'

Minnie smirked. 'A palace like Hampton Court?'

'It is much nicer! We have a lake and a forest and a donkey and goats – '

'Are there wolves in the forest?' asked Annie, with a snigger.

'Yes! My mama tells me not to go too far in because one might get me.'

'Then your mama is a liar, too.'

Clara Venus jumped to her feet. 'And your mama is mad! She is locked up because she – '

It was time to intervene.

'Stop it, you three!' I said. 'Clara Venus – come with me. Annie, Minnie – stay there.'

I took Clara by the hand and stalked to the other side of the tea garden, where I prepared to scold her roundly. 'I know you are tired,' I said, 'but that is no reason to behave badly, and no excuse for saying what you just said.'

I waited for Clara to square up and come back with some riposte, but she did not look at me. She stood with her shoulders drooping and her face averted, and when I crouched down to her level, I saw that she was crying.

'I hate them!' she said. 'I hate Annie and Minnie. I hate their house and I hate London. I want to go home.'

I was shocked into silence. I had had no idea that Clara Venus was so miserable here.

Behind us a bench faced the orang-utans' cage. I sat down upon it, and took Clara on my lap.

'Tell me why,' I said.

'They are hateful to me. Annie is far too clever, and Minnie speaks French all the time.'

'You are clever,' I said, 'and you know French.'

'I don't want to speak French. I want to speak Irish. Nobody here understands me when I speak Irish. Annie laughs and says it is bogtrotter language. And Mrs Grey does not love me the way the Biddies do. And I miss my donkey and I miss my papa.'

I felt as if I had received a blow to the heart. In my determination to escape from Ireland I had never thought to ask myself how Clara Venus would feel at the disruption to her life. I had summarily uprooted her from the place where she had been born and reared: Lissaguirra was her world. I had barely given her a chance to bid farewell to her father, for we had parted daggers drawn the very day after he had arrived home, and when Old Biddy had asked when I might return, all I had said was, 'I'll write'. I had left Ireland in such a hurry that I had not even thought to bring my daughter's favourite doll with us.

I took my handkerchief and dabbed Clara's eyes and wiped her nose. There was a blister on her mouth, I saw. She had been chewing at her lips, pulling away slivers of skin with her teeth until they bled.

'Can we go home, Mama?'

'Do you mean to Young Street, or to Ireland?'

'To Ireland.'

'Do you miss it so very badly?'

'Yes. I miss it so much it makes me feel hungry. It makes me so hungry I cannot eat. And I always have a pain here, in my tummy.'

She pressed the palm of her hand against her solar plexus, and I noticed that she had taken on that pallor that I always associated with malnourished city children. Why, I wondered, as I reached out to smooth her hair, was the heart said to be the seat of all emotion? They claimed that people were ruled by either their head or their heart, but it was clear that my daughter was ruled by a more visceral instinct.

'It is called homesickness,' I said.

'Homesickness. That is what my wolf has.'

'What wolf?'

She reached into her pocket and took out a tiny carved wooden figure: a wolf, with spiky tail and pointy ears. I recognized it as belonging to the Noah's Ark that St Leger had given her on our last night in Ireland.

'He is called Romulus,' she said, 'like the twin wolves who made Rome. He misses his brother.'

'Why didn't you leave him in the ark?'

'Because I knew that if I took him, we would have to come back. I promised Remus that we would not stay away long. And now he is in the ark all by himself.'

'He has all the other animals for friends,' I said. 'He has the monkeys and the elephants and the sheep and – '

'He is a *wolf*, Mama. He has no friends.'

I looked across at Annie and Minnie. They were sitting, heads together, speaking in that arcane language that only sisters or best friends speak. No wonder my girl felt excluded. I had no friends in London either. I could not visit Maria, who was residing at her sister's house, for I would not be welcome there after my defection from Doneraile Court. William's circle was made up of literary men, and I disliked them and their wives as

443

much as I knew they mistrusted me. Like Becky Sharp, I had made no friends at Miss Pinkerton's academy with whom I could reconnect, and as an unmarried woman with a child I was unlikely to make any new ones. After all, as I had once remarked to William (not realizing that I had furnished him with yet another aperçu for his novel), the greatest tyrants over women are women.

Clara Venus was looking at me with eyes too big for her face, and a furrow drawn across her brow. She looked as sad as the orang-utan listlessly toying with the straw on the floor of his cage.

'I will see, darling. I will see about going home soon.'

I did not want to make any decisions just yet. I wanted to wait until I heard news of the potato harvest. If it failed again, I might think about taking Clara further afield, to Paris.

'Can we go tomorrow?'

'No. There will be a lot to organize.'

'But we came here without organizing anything.'

I remembered the disarray of my bedchamber as I threw garments into the trunk that Christy had trundled to the staging post. I remembered the blessings of God that Old Biddy called down upon my head when I gave her a purse to tide them over until I could send more money from London. I remembered the look on Jameson's face – bewildered, irate, anguished – as I tied the strings on Clara's bonnet.

'This time things are a little more complicated,' I said, 'for we shall have to help William find a new governess.'

28

I SAID NOTHING TO William about this contingency, but as it happened, something arose that made us both question the wisdom of maintaining the status quo. A novel was sent to him by a publisher friend. It purported to be an autobiography, edited by someone who called himself – or herself – Currer Bell. It was, I suspected, a pseudonym; I was proved right when some months later it was revealed to have been written by a woman called Charlotte Brontë.

Jane Eyre told the story of a governess who falls in love with her employer, a gentleman who happened to be married already to a madwoman whom he keeps isolated from society. Within weeks the book had become a great commercial success, and rumour ran rife among the so-called cognoscenti that I was its author.

I was irritated by this for two reasons. I was appalled that anyone might think I would write about poor Isabella's condition in so callous a manner (the hapless wife in the novel was compared to a wild beast); and I was aghast that words such as the following (spoken by the novel's hero, Mr Rochester) should be attributed to me: 'Jane, be still; don't struggle so, like a wild frantic bird that is rending its own plumage in its desperation.' If I were to write a novel, I liked to think that I might pen rather more elegant dialogue.

The raised eyebrows that greeted me when I made an entrance into a public room, the snickers from behind painted fans, the laboriously affected indifference of the people to whom I was introduced persuaded me that to stay on in London would be inviting public opprobrium, and might even damage the sales of William's book. I stood poised for flight, undecided whether to set sail south for France, or west for Ireland.

Then one day a letter arrived for me at the house in Young Street. It was from one of the Quaker soup kitchen ladies to whom I had written, seeking advice. Her letter assured me that the situation was improving.

I went to William, to hand in my notice. He was in his study. A quire of paper on the desk before him was covered in his dense handwriting, a sandwich lay untouched on a plate. One of Minnie's cats was curled up by the fire, and outside the window the rain was dripping steadily from the creeper that clambered the length of the wall.

'How goes the work?' I asked, taking a seat opposite him. 'Has Miss Sharp moved into her grand house in Mayfair yet?'

William took off his spectacles and rubbed his eyes. 'Yes. But all the ladies of her acquaintance have snubbed her. Lady de la Mole has cut her while riding out in Hyde Park, and Lady Bareacres refuses to acknowledge her in the waiting room at the opera. What is poor Becky to do? What would you do in her situation, Eliza?'

I laughed. 'I dare say she will find a way to win them over. As for me, I have neither the inclination nor the stamina to ingratiate myself. *Moi, j'en ai marre.* I have found a new governess for you, William.'

'What?'

'Her name is Miss Alexander.'

'*What?*'

'We both know that I can no longer continue here. I am giving you my notice.'

'Eliza – '

'You must know what people are saying.'

William looked so blank that I deemed it necessary to elaborate.

'The *on dit* is that we met in Cork five years ago.'

'And so we did.'

'And that Clara Venus is the result of an indiscretion that occurred between us.'

William's face went puce. 'But that is preposterous!

We could never – I mean – how? How – I – it is preposterous!'

I spread my hands in a baroque gesture. 'The more preposterous the story, the more people want to believe it. They can heap all the calumny they like upon me – I couldn't care less. But I will not have Clara Venus implicated.'

'You mean, you are leaving me?'

'I am.'

'Don't, Eliza! Don't go – you can't leave me. I am but halfway through the novel!' William's red face had turned quite pale.

'Come, come!' I rebuked him. 'Did you engage me as a proxy amanuensis or as governess to your daughters?'

'I engaged you because – because I wanted you here with me. I am much fonder of you than of anyone. I would do anything to make you easy. Please stay as my – my companion, my tender friend.'

'William, you know that is impossible.' I realized that I was using the tone I often adopted when schooling Annie in her Latin grammar. 'You are a married man.'

'I am a widower with a wife alive! Isabella does not care for me. She cares not tuppence for anything but her dinner and her glass of porter. Please stay, Eliza. Any constraints you perceive can be – '

'No.'

'The constraints can be – '

'*No.*'

I love the word 'no'. It is the most powerful in any person's artillery. I use it sparingly, but to my mind too many people are afraid to use it at all. It had upon William exactly the effect I intended. He crumpled.

'Oh, stop it, William,' I said, exasperatedly. 'You cannot have your cake and eat it too.'

'What cake have I got?' he said sullenly.

'It is there in front of you. That novel is your cake, and since it is but half baked, you had better make sure that it does not come out of the oven unrisen.'

We looked at each other in a kind of flummoxed silence for a moment or two, and then I raised an eyebrow and William raised one back, and then his mouth quirked in a smile and mine did the same, and then we started to laugh and laugh.

'I delight in your aphorisms, Eliza,' he said, finally, wiping tears of mirth from his cheeks, 'but that one is certainly not worthy of inclusion in the book.'

'I'm sorry,' I said. 'It is the worst I have yet come up with.' Leaning my elbows on the desk, I looked at him with affection. 'You must not worry about your book, dear heart. You are perfectly capable of finishing it without me.'

'I shall miss your company here in the evenings. I shall miss reading aloud to you.'

'And I shall miss hearing you tell the story. You must send the instalments to me in Ireland.'

'And you must write to me.'

'On condition, William.'

'Name it.'

'I want my letters back. Every one I have ever sent you.'

'Why?'

'Because they belong to me.'

William gave a smile that made him look ineffably smug. 'In law, Eliza, I think you will find that they belong to *me*.'

'Oh? I did not know that. In that case, I shall not trouble myself to write to you again.'

'Why not?'

'Because you appropriate some of my best *bons mots* without asking my permission. In *law*, William, I think you will find that that is called plagiarism.'

'That's an infernal allegation!'

'You're the one who raised the subject of legality,' I said with a shrug.

Prise de fer! Of course I had no intention of levelling charges of plagiarism at him. I wanted my correspondence back for my own reasons; so that I could refer to it should I ever find time to pen a memoir. William bridled and blustered, but I ignored him and stood firm until he fetched me the letters I had requested.

'Do you promise you will still write to me?' he said, handing over a sizeable bundle which, I noticed, was endearingly tied up in lavender-coloured ribbon.

'Of course. But I will be sure to keep a copy of every letter I send. As insurance.'

He smiled sheepishly.

'Where will you go?' he asked. 'Dublin or Cork?'

'Lissaguirra.'

'You are not going back there!'

'It is Clara's home. She is not yet ready to leave, and until she is, it must be my home too.'

'But is it safe?'

I took from my pocket the letter that I had lately received from Ireland, and scanned the formalities. Then, '"The blight is on a far smaller scale than last year,"' I read aloud. '"The Temporary Relief Act has contributed to a general feeling of well-being within the community. The crime rate has decreased and it seems that a mood of optimism prevails."'

'Who sent you that?'

'One of the Quaker ladies with whom I worked in the soup kitchen. I don't trust many people, but I suppose I must trust a Quaker to tell the truth.'

'What will you do, in Ireland?'

'What I intended to do – before I was forestalled by the birth of my beguiling daughter. I shall write my novel.' I rose to my feet and moved to the window. The sun had come out, and the small garden was agleam with fallen rain. Barnaby Rudge was sitting on the wall, washing herself. 'I shall have to get some pet animal for Clara. She envies Minnie her cats.'

'Will she go to school there?'

'Yes. There was a schoolhouse built just three years ago, not half a mile from the lodge.'

'Will you not miss society?'

'I have no regard for society here. I prefer the camaraderie of the few friends I have in Ireland.'

'But you will accompany me to Devonshire House tomorrow night?'

'What?'

'I thought I had mentioned it. Did I not? Perhaps I forgot . . . Look, here.' William rummaged among the papers on his desk and picked out a vellum card engraved with gilt lettering. 'It is an invitation I received, to a reception Lord Cavendish is giving.'

Lord Cavendish! I had often passed the mansion where the Duke stayed when attending the House of Lords. I had been told of the opulence contained therein; the paintings, the statuary, the countless priceless artefacts. My contempt for the aristocracy was infinite, but still the artist in me yearned to behold those treasures that had for centuries remained hidden to all but the scions of the Cavendish family and their privileged cronies.

I remembered how the gentry used to visit my father's studio in Soho, masquerading as bohemians. I remembered pouring wine for them, laughing at their odious jokes and being pulled onto their laps to be tickled. Now I had an opportunity to climb the gilded echelons and observe them at frolic on their own territory.

'Is not Cavendish the duke who had the banana named after him?'

'The very one.'

I made a little moue, gave a nonchalant shrug. 'Then how could I refuse?' I said.

Edie would have carried on reading, had she not been assailed by a sudden attack of pins and needles. She had been curled up in the fireside chair for so long that her leg had gone to sleep. Unhooking her foot from beneath her, she started to hobble around the room, in an attempt to get the blood flowing again.

On his pouffe, Milo was chasing rabbits in his sleep, his little ears atwitch, his muzzle all atremble. Had Clara Venus ever got her pet? Edie wondered. Had she sat here, curled up with a book on her lap and a kitty snoozing by the hearth? What might she have read? Edie could not recall seeing any children's books on the library shelves.

She flexed her foot, hopped over to the bookcase and

scanned the titles. There was nothing there that would appeal to a small child, but her eyes lit suddenly on a series of Everyman titles, with their beautifully decorated art nouveau spines. Among them was the *Biographical Dictionary of English Literature*. She slid the volume out from between its companions and started to leaf through the pages.

Every one of the thousand or so writers listed was dead, and most of them were men. Jane Austen had been allocated half a page, Charlotte Brontë even less (with scarcely a mention of her sisters), while Fanny Burney did not merit a single line. Charles Dickens had been apportioned two full pages, as had Thackeray, William Makepeace.

'Novelist. *b*. 1811; *m*. Isabella, *dau*. of Colonel Shawe, an Irish officer,' Edie read, then skimmed the rest of the résumé until she reached the final paragraph: 'For some years Thackeray suffered from spasms of the heart. He died suddenly on December 24, 1863, in his 53rd year. He was a man of the tenderest heart, and had an intense enjoyment of domestic happiness; the permanent breakdown of his wife's health was a heavy calamity.'

He died on Christmas eve. How sad for Annie and Minnie! Edie felt a surge of real affection for Thackeray. Here he was, ranked by the *Dictionary of English Literature* as one of the very greatest of English novelists; but in the end, she knew, he was just a man captivated by a woman, hoping that she might return his love.

She shut the book, then, on impulse, opened it again

and leafed through to 'D'. Between William Drummond (of whom Edie had never heard) and the poet John Dryden, there was no entry. If Eliza Drury had ever become a published author, her works had been erased from literary history along with *Wuthering Heights* and *The Tenant of Wildfell Hall*.

Edie slid the dictionary back on the shelf, and as she did so, she dislodged a copy of *Miss Nettie's Girls – Capital Short Stories for Holiday Reading*. Tucked inside was a photograph of her and Hilly, taken down at the little pier. They were standing arm-in-arm, grinning at the camera, and behind them was the boat that they had taken out onto the lake, the day Hilly had caught the trout.

Edie looked at their freckled twelve-year-old faces, at their gangly, pre-adolescent limbs and their sticky-out pigtails, and then she saw the lockets that each of them wore around their necks – cheap nickel-plated things bought in Woolworth's in Cork. They had made a blood pact the day the photograph was taken, Edie remembered, cutting the pads of their thumbs with a penknife and pressing them together so that Edie's blood ran through Hilly's veins, and vice versa. Then they had stanched the blood with two squares cut from a pocket handkerchief, and encased the scraps of linen in the lockets. Where were they now, those lockets? Edie wondered. Long gone. But that summer the gimcrack trinkets had been invested with as much totemic value as the Crown Jewels.

Edie slid the photograph between the pages of her diary. When she got back to London, she would find a frame for it, and reinstate Hilly on top of her bureau.

Beyond the window, beyond the lake and the hills, a silvery grey light was beginning to creep. It was dawn already; there was no point in going to bed now; besides, Edie was as curious as Eliza to know what the legendary Devonshire House was like: it had lain abandoned since the Great War, and had been demolished just twelve years previously. It tickled her to know that the Duke's wine cellar, which had once housed some of the costliest vintages in the world, had been reincarnated as the ticket office of the Green Park tube station.

She headed for the kitchen to fetch the remains of the toffee she had bought a week ago in Doneraile Stores, and to make herself a fresh pot of tea.

~ E. D.

Never had I seen such sumptuousness as lay hidden behind the high, forbidding walls of the Duke of Devonshire's house in Piccadilly. A staircase with a crystal handrail led to the ballroom on the piano nobile where the gilt, the mirrors, the marble, the tapestries wrought in silver and gold thread, the astonishing plasterwork, the paintings, the hothouse flowers and the thousands of candles all reminded me of stories I had read of the excesses of Versailles. I found myself gaping here at a Raphael, there at a Rubens, and when I saw what was indubitably an oil by Rembrandt, I could scarcely refrain from gesticulating as excitedly as a child at a funfair.

However, none of the other guests seemed impressed by the masterpieces lining the walls. I remembered something I had read in a novel by Fanny Burney: 'There's nothing in the world so fashionable as taking no notice of things . . . all the *ton* do so.' How glad I was to be hoi polloi!

I had not danced since the days at Doneraile Court when I had used to step out with superannuated husbands and second sons. After the Agricultural Society Ball in the Imperial Hotel in Cork, St Leger and I had never again danced together. We had not wanted to draw attention to the astonishing synergy that was manifest when we took to the floor. Now I watched the ladies glide onto the glossy parquet, caught tantalizing glimpses of lace underskirts as their crinolines swayed in waltz-time, heard the swish of silk and tarlatan, and smiled at William as he offered me his arm.

He was a poor dancer, and he knew it.

'I will introduce you to some likely fellows,' he said, apologetically. 'I know you will not care to dance with me again this evening.'

'On the contrary, William, I am very comfortable dancing with you.'

I felt his hand press more firmly against the small of my back, saw a flush rise to his cheeks.

'I wish you would not go,' he said, for the dozenth time that day.

'I can't stay, William.'

'Confound the gossipmongers!'

'It is not the gossip that I'm afraid of. I am one of those women society will find fault with no matter what I do. I could wear sackcloth, and renounce my sinful past and devote my life to good works, and people would still find something to carp about. But I will not have aspersions cast upon you, for – quite apart from the fact that such scandal could damage your career – you are an honourable man.'

'People say I am a cynic.'

'You *are* a cynic – and all to the good, for if people are not shown what is wrong in the world, nobody will ever go to the trouble of putting it right. *Vanity Fair* is quite deliciously iconoclastic.'

'It would never have been written without – '

'Me. I know. I am longing to be able to hold the finished volume in my hands and say "Becky Sharp – *c'est moi!*" I hope you will not be too hard on her when the day of reckoning comes.'

'She is going to – '

'No! Don't tell me! Let me find out her fate by instalments, like all your other readers.'

'I have the last sentence. It is something you said, once.'

'I look forward to reading it.'

The tempo of the music accelerated, and he made an ungainly lunge forward, narrowly missing my foot.

'I beg your pardon. I am sure you wish you had a more gallant partner. The minute we step off the floor, your dance card will be full. I had a letter today, incidentally, from a gentleman who was anxious to know where he might meet Miss Sharp.'

'No! People believe she really exists?'

'They do.'

'That must be the highest compliment a writer can receive.'

'I have had others, from fellows who appear to be quite hopelessly in love with her.'

'What do you tell them?'

'I tell them that Miss Sharp has the most adamantine of hearts.'

I smiled. 'If only they knew.'

The waltz came to an end, and as William led me off the floor, my skirts brushed those of a lady who had skimmed to a halt beside me. I heard a hissed intake of breath, glimpsed a scintillation of emeralds, felt an agitation of the air as a fan snapped open. It was Sophia St Leger.

We looked at one another for a moment, frozen in an attitude of bristling hostility, and then William said: 'Mr St Leger. How good to see you again,' and Jameson said, 'Mr Thackeray!' and suddenly the music started up again. Sophia drew the blades of her fan together in one fluid movement, laid a hand upon her husband's arm and, slanting me a glance over her bare shoulder, glided back with him into the tide of dancers.

I turned and, moving in a random direction, found myself in an anteroom beneath a Titian which – since it depicted a riderless horse pursued by a serpent – perfectly reflected my mood. William had followed me. He drew forward a chair for me to sit upon, and stood awkwardly while I toyed with my fan, running a blade over and over again between forefinger and thumb. Taking off his spectacles, he polished them with his pocket handkerchief, then said, quite abruptly, 'I will take a message to him if you like.'

'To St Leger?'

William nodded, and then he produced his little, ubiquitous notebook, tore off a page and handed it to me as though he were proffering contraband.

I took it, and the pencil he held out, and sat staring at the blank sheet for many moments. Then I looked up at William with a helpless expression. 'This must be how you feel every morning when you are confronted by your *tabula rasa*.'

He shook his head and smiled ruefully. 'Not since you've been living with me. I don't know what I shall do without your encouragement.'

'Don't, William. You'll make me cry.'

'Then I had better turn my back. If I were to see my Becky cry, I might be tempted to allow her to live happily ever after.'

He took a few steps away, and was at once accosted by a lady decked in diamonds who flapped at him so aggressively I saw him wince.

'You must not allow Miss Sharp to get her claws into Mr Osborne!' she squawked. 'Does not Amelia know that she is harbouring a serpent in her bosom?'

Returning my attention to the clean sheet, I wrote, '*Dear Jamey, I wish* . . .' And I could think of nothing else to say. Nothing came into my head but the words of a song that Young Biddy used to sing:

I wish . . . I wish . . . I wish in vain / I wish I was a maid again / A maid again I ne'er will be / 'Til cherries grow on an ivy tree . . .

I could see that William was heroically trying to effect an escape from the pterodactyl in diamonds. Sucking in my breath, I wrote in a hand so untidy it was barely recognizable as my own, '*. . . I wish I could see you. I am going back to Ireland. I will be in Lissaguirra* *from next week. Clara Venus misses you. I miss you. Your Eliza.'*

Then I looked up. Beyond the door to the anteroom my true love was standing with a group of people who were whinnying and braying like donkeys on Derby Day. The men had great equine teeth and the women were sporting the kind of plumes that highfalutin carriage horses wear.

He looked wretched with boredom. Casting around, his eyes lit upon me. I remembered how he had looked the first time I laid eyes on him, and knew now that that impression had been right: St Leger was a thoroughbred – a racehorse, a Bucephalus – and when he smiled I could not but smile back. A be-ruffled beldame standing next to him emitted a nickering laugh; he slid a mock-fearful look at her, then cocked an eyebrow at me. I saw his lips form the word 'Help', and suddenly I felt such effervescence of spirit that I wanted to laugh out loud. It was as though he had just taken hold of my ear bob and tweaked it.

I sent him an invitation with my eyes. But Sophia, ever watchful, laid a hand on his arm and drew his attention to a footman passing with a tray. As the assembled company lunged for fresh glasses, Jameson was lost to view, obscured by balloon sleeves and gauzy stoles, and when the footman resumed his course, he was gone, and so was Sophia.

I looked down at the sheet of paper in my lap.

I miss you. Your Eliza, I read. And then I added three words that I had never in my life said to anyone aside from my daughter.

I love you, I wrote. Then I folded the paper across once, twice, three times, and tucked it between the blades of my fan.

'Dear God, that woman was relentless!' William was beside me, incandescent with indignation. 'She had the nerve to tell me that she was at school with the prototypes for both Amelia Sedley and Becky Sharp, and that Amelia had a pockmarked face, and Becky a squint!' He huffed and puffed for a minute or two more, and then he looked at me and said, 'You have something for me?'

I unfurled my fan, and he glanced at the note I had concealed in its pleats.

'Will I take that to him now?' he asked with a brusqueness I knew cost him some effort.

'Yes, please, William,' I said.

29

BEFORE I LEFT London, I paid a visit to Isabella. Camberwell was three or four miles from Kensington, a pretty place with a village green and solid, respectable houses. William had declined to come with me, saying that he thought it best not to see his wife in the company of someone whom she might not recognize.

Astonishingly, she did recognize me, though she did not know my name. Mrs Bakewell showed me into a dim parlour, where heavy moreen curtains obscured most of the light. Her charge was sitting by the fire on a button-backed armchair upholstered in faded green velvet. She was brushing her hair and looking at an album lying open on her lap. She set aside the brush when I was announced, and invited me to take a seat beside her while Mrs Bakewell went off to fetch tea.

'How good to see you again,' said Isabella, as if we had met just a week or two earlier. 'You look very well, despite the tribulations of that odious sea voyage.'

465

I was about to remark that I had travelled thither by coach, but realized almost at once that Isabella was speaking of the journey to Cork on the *Jupiter*, where we had first met.

'How have you been?' I asked.

'I have been hither and yon, you know, in the place where women go. The woods, mostly.' She began to turn the stiff, gilt-edged pages of the album with her slender fingers. The skin on her hands was the whitest I had ever seen, and I noticed that she still wore the locket around her neck that William had said contained a cutting of her dead baby's hair. 'I liked it on the boat. Did you? I liked it when we sat together that night of the stars.'

She was speaking of the time I had found her crouched beneath the companionway clad in nothing but her nightdress. It had often struck me since that had I not come upon her there, she would no doubt have cast herself into the sea again, and this time there would have been no one to haul her out.

Isabella turned another page. The illustration pasted on the reverse side showed the children of Hamelin following the Pied Piper into the cave.

'The Pied Piper,' she said. 'How wicked he was. He lured all the children away, apart from the lame one. You told me stories that night on the boat. Do you remember?'

I recalled that I had related the childhood tales my mother had read to me, fairy tales by the Brothers Grimm – 'Little Red Riding Hood' and 'Hansel and Gretel' and 'The Sleeping Beauty'. How enduring were those stories! I had told them to Clara countless times, and imagined that one day she would tell them to her children, and so on, and so on. If mothers left their children nothing but a legacy of storytelling, I thought, they had passed on something of inestimable value.

'I like those stories, because they all happen in the woods,' continued Sophia. 'I know the woods well; I never get lost. I met the Queen of Spain there once and showed her the way through, but she didn't listen, so I expect she is wandering there still. Her name is Isabella too. Will you tell me a story now?'

'Which would you like to hear?'

'The one about the princess in the tower with the hair.'

'Rapunzel?'

'Yes. There is a picture of her here in this album. Wait – let me find it for you.'

Isabella turned page after cardboard page upon which had been pasted scraps from picture sheets that she had coloured in by hand. There were images of farmyard animals and flowers and fairy-tale characters, lines of verse copied in careful copperplate, woodcuts and miniatures in watercolour. She paused at a page decorated with a bluebird at each corner. In the centre she had pasted an illustration of Rapunzel high in her tower, waiting for a prince to come and rescue her.

'There she is. You can start now,' she said, folding her hands in her lap and looking at me pleasantly.

'Once upon a time,' I began, 'a wicked enchantress stole the baby of a poor couple, and kept it for her own.'

'Did the baby cry? My babies always cried.'

'I suppose it did. But it soon grew out of it.'

'Was it a girl?'

'Yes. Called Rapunzel. And when she reached the age of twelve, the enchantress saw that with her long golden hair and fine white skin Rapunzel was more beautiful by far than she –'

'Did she look like me?' asked Isabella, reaching for her hairbrush.

'Just like you. And so jealous was the witch of Rapunzel's beauty that she imprisoned her in a tower in the middle of a forest with no door, and just one high window.'

'How did she eat?'

'When the witch brought food, she would call, "Rapunzel! Rapunzel! Let down your hair!" and Rapunzel would wind her beautiful golden plait around a hook and let it down like a rope so that the witch could climb up into the tower with a basket of food.'

'Peaches?'

'Yes. And cake.'

Mrs Bakewell had just entered with a tray of tea things on which a pound cake rested, cut into neat slices. She bustled about, pouring tea and milk and clattering spoons and chatting about the weather while Isabella sat stony-faced, staring down at the picture of Rapunzel, and then Mrs Bakewell withdrew, giving me one of those awful complicit smiles that are supposed to convey sorority.

Isabella waited until the door had shut, and then she helped herself to a slice of pound cake and said, 'Go on with the story. Is she still twelve?'

'Well, she's probably a little older than that now. '

'She's eighteen.'

'On Rapunzel's eighteenth birthday,' I resumed, 'a prince riding by overheard her singing, and was overwhelmed by how beautiful she was, so when he heard the call, "Rapunzel, Rapunzel! Let down your hair!" and saw the witch climb into the tower, he resolved to do the same. And that night he too called, "Rapunzel, Rapunzel – let down your hair!" and when she cast her beautiful golden rope of hair over the sill, the prince climbed up the tower and in through the window and he and Rapunzel fell in love.'

'Did they fuck?'

I hesitated. I had never before heard a woman of Isabella's class use the word, and I was uncertain how to respond. But the way she had asked the question seemed so matter-of-fact that I decided she deserved a matter-of-fact answer. 'Yes, they did.'

'Did she like it?'

'I don't know. But she became *enceinte*, and when the witch found out, she was so angry that she cut off Rapunzel's hair and cast her out into the forest. And when the prince came again and called "Rapunzel, Rapunzel! Let down your hair!" the old witch let down the shorn plait, and the prince climbed up into the tower –'

'Oh, oh!' Isabella put her hands up to her face, covering her mouth. Above her splayed fingertips her eyes were wide, as though she had never heard the story before. 'What did he do? What did he do when he saw the witch?'

'When he saw the witch he fell back into a thorn bush below, and the thorns pierced his eyes so that he became blind.'

'Good,' said Isabella, stuffing the last of the cake into her mouth.

'For months afterwards he wandered through the forest –'

'Did he meet the Queen of Spain?'

'No. He met nobody until one day he heard a girl singing –'

'It was Rapunzel!'

'Yes, it was.'

'Had she had her baby?'

'She had had two. Twins – a boy and a girl.'

'It should have been two girls.' Isabella reached for another slice of cake. 'What happened when she saw the prince?'

'She ran and took him into her arms, and the tears of joy she shed fell directly upon the prince's eyes, and his sight was restored.'

'And then he left her?'

'No. He took her with him to his kingdom.'

'And the twins, too?'

'Yes.'

'Did they live happily ever after?'

'That's what the story says.'

With a finger, Isabella delicately transferred a crumb of cake from the plate to the tip of her tongue. 'She was his *beau idéal*,' she said.

'Yes.'

'That is what William used to call me. His *beau idéal*. You are that now, I think.' She looked up from the plate. 'I don't believe that they lived happily ever after, Rapunzel and the prince and the babies.'

'Oh? What do you think happened?'

'I think he took the boy twin to his kingdom, and that he locked Rapunzel and the girl back up in the tower in the wood.'

471

'Why do you think that?'

'The wood is where women go to hide when their babies are taken away from them. I have met the Queen of Spain in the wood. I don't know what she is doing there. She is far too young to have had babies yet. She is the same age as I was when I married. Are you married?'

'No.'

'Don't marry. I didn't want to, but they made me. They made the other Isabella marry too, even though she is just a child . . .'

I went to pour myself another cup of tea, but Isabella snatched the cup away. 'Do not have any more tea!' she said. 'Just *listen*! It's *important*! You need to *know* this!'

I fixed my eyes upon her and listened while Isabella talked and talked about the Queen of Spain, asking me repeatedly if I could get a message to her. When, growing tired of the subject, I tried to talk of our young Queen Victoria instead, she became quite agitated and dropped her plate onto the floor. The crash brought Mrs Bakewell and her daughter running, whereupon Isabella started to scream and shout abuse, and I was ushered from the house with scant ceremony. As the front door shut behind me I heard Isabella's calls of distress. I did not like to think what humiliating ritual she might have been subjected to, to subdue her.

30

I SUPPOSE I MUST trust a Quaker to tell the truth, I had said to William when I told him I was returning to Lissaguirra. But nobody told the truth. Politicians and clergy and pamphleteers alike all told lies, and until pictorial records began appearing in the newspapers, nobody in England knew what was really happening in Ireland.

On our way home, Clara Venus and I stopped in the Imperial hotel in Cork city for breakfast. Clara had boiled eggs with toast soldiers to dip in the yolks, while I had my eggs poached, with ham and muffins. It seemed that there was still no shortage of food for those who had the money to pay for it. We found ourselves sitting at a table next to a pair of gentlemen whose conversation I could not but help overhearing.

One of them, a handsome, dark-haired man in his middle thirties, had placed a sketchbook before him on the table; he was leafing through it, commenting on the drawings as he turned the pages.

'They are coming to the workhouses now,' I heard him say, 'not for food – for they know there is none – but for coffins. They believe that there at least they have a chance of a decent burial.'

'Or the illusion of one,' the other, older, gentleman said. 'Haven't you heard that the coffins have hinges? The bodies are tipped into the grave on top of the ones that went before, and the coffins reused.'

I checked to make sure that Clara Venus was still engrossed in dipping her soldiers in her egg – 'Higgledy-piggledy, my fat hen!' I encouraged her – then angled myself towards the adjacent table.

'I beg your pardon, gentlemen,' I said, 'I have come here from London. I had it from a friend that things were improving. She said that prayers of thanksgiving had been offered up.'

The dark-haired man looked at me as if I was of unsound mind. 'Thanksgiving for what?'

'For the potato harvest, which I understand did not fail this year.'

'Any prayers of thanksgiving were premature, madam,' he said, scathingly.

'Dr Daniel Donovan, at your service,' said the older gentleman, with emphatic courtesy, as if to compensate for his friend's rudeness. 'And this is Mr James Mahoney.

Mr Mahoney is an artist, who has been commissioned by the *Illustrated London News* to supply eyewitness testimony of the hardship.'

'Miss Eliza Drury.'

'You were not altogether misinformed, Miss Drury,' continued Dr Donovan. 'The blight was not as widespread this year, but the harvest was a scant one, for the people were so famished that they ate the seed potatoes before they could be put in the ground.'

'So the suffering continues?'

'The politicians don't call it "suffering",' said Mr Mahoney. 'They are skilled in the use of euphemism. They call it "distress".'

'What brings you here from London, Miss Drury?' Dr Donovan asked.

'I am on my way to my home by Loch Liath – not far from Doneraile.'

Mr Mahoney cocked an eyebrow at me, and gave me a smile in which there was very little humour. 'Doneraile! A darling place! You will not find the spectre of famine hanging over Doneraile.'

My eyes went to the sketchbook on the table. The uppermost drawing showed a woman with a begging bowl in her outstretched left hand. In the crook of her right arm, a baby lay sleeping.

'I made that drawing not far from here, in Clonakilty,' said Mr Mahoney. 'The mother was

475

begging for money to bury her infant. It had died of typhus.'

'It might have been any number of other diseases,' said Dr Donovan lugubriously. 'Cholera, smallpox, tuberculosis, diarrhoea, pellagra. They are all borne of famine.'

Mr Mahoney slid the sketchbook across the table to me. 'Peruse my drawings, if it please you,' he said, adding darkly, 'I rather think it will not.'

And as I turned the pages, and saw images of suffering beyond apprehension, I heard Clara Venus singing in her sweet, light voice:

'Higgledy-piggledy, my black hen! She lays eggs for gentlemen. Sometimes nine and sometimes ten: Higgledy-piggledy, my black hen!'

The coach took us to Doneraile, where I had expected to find some means of conveyance to Lissaguirra. Clara Venus and I were put down at the staging inn, and I finally managed to engage the services of a carter, who agreed to transport us the rest of the way on a dray drawn by a donkey.

The once prosperous town was looking forlorn: many of the shops were shuttered, and the gates to Doneraile Court were chained. As I made my way along the footpath towards Mr Shinnors's emporium to buy a toffee apple for Clara, I met Mrs Grove-White coming in the opposite direction. Once upon a time she would have shunned me, but today she seemed overjoyed by the encounter.

'Miss Drury!' she said, 'Good day to you! I had heard you were beyond in London. What brings you back here?'

'I had heard that the situation had improved, so I –'

'Oh, no no no no no!' said Mrs Grove-White. 'If anything, things have got worse! It would have been better if you had stayed put, for everybody has upped and left. They are too fearful to remain, for although – thanks be to the good God – we have no scarcity of provender here in Doneraile, there is always the threat of – you know – disease. A lady of my acquaintance was afflicted dreadfully, and has had to desist from her charitable works. But Mr Grove-White is stubborn and will not leave. I wish he would, for there is nobody to visit any more! It has made life so dull – look! Mr Shinnors is practically the only shopkeeper left – the others have all been obliged to close for want of trade. But you must not fear that we are likely to die from a shortage of food – oh no! It is only the poor that are distressed. If you need anything, Miss Drury, Mr Shinnors will get it for you. He has just taken delivery of some pretty albums. I have bought two, for I find that assembling an album is a good way of passing the time. Do you have one? No?

You must call upon me, and I will show you mine with pleasure! Perhaps I could get up a little musical evening or some such. You were always such a delight, Miss Drury, at Lady Charlotte's soirées! So vivacious! Such a talented pianist, and so accomplished at charades!'

I made a polite bow, and was about to take farewell of the garrulous old crone when she laid a restraining hand upon my arm.

'While I think of it,' she said, 'do stock up on some James's Powder while you are here, in case of – you know – ' she dropped her voice to a theatrical whisper – 'any maladies of the stomach. You must be careful of the little one – although I am sure that the chances of her coming into close contact with the wrong class of person are much reduced now that the population hereabouts is so depleted.'

'No! So many are dying still? Can it be true?'

'There have been deaths of course – ' Mrs Grove-White made a little moue of regret, '– but most of the peasantry has left. Gone! You will find that much of the countryside is deserted – and a good thing, don't you agree? For it was quite overpopulated with the most filthy, indolent creatures. There is a great scheme afoot to rid the great estates of tenants. Mr Grove-White is more knowledgeable of it than I.'

'But if there are more evictions, where are the tenants to go?'

'The more munificent landlords are offering each family food, clothing and money to leave the country. It is a scheme designed to encourage the investment of capital – for who in their right mind should wish to invest in a country overrun with riff-raff?'

'How much is each family being given to emigrate?'

'Up to five pounds.'

'Five pounds?'

'Yes! Imagine! Just think how the rogues must be laughing up their sleeves at us as they sail merrily off! But Mr Grove-White tells me that a pauper can be shipped out to Canada or America for half of what it costs to keep him in the workhouse for a year. It is said, you know, that the famine is an act of God, for it has accomplished a task beyond the reach of the government.'

'What is that supposed to mean?'

'Well, the government could hardly legislate for the problem of overpopulation, Miss Drury.'

'The government is largely comprised of landlords, Mrs Grove-White. They could have taken better care of their tenants. Indeed, they had a duty to do so, for they have lived off the misery of the peasantry for centuries.'

Mrs Grove-White looked affronted. 'I cannot agree with you, Miss Drury. This divine visitation – calamitous as it is – has rid us, in one fell stroke, of the burden of the drunken, idle Irish. We all know that they are worthless, good-for-nothing liars and layabouts. Indeed, a learned friend of mine has argued that they are a form of human chimpanzee.'

Before I knew it, the palm of my hand had made contact with Mrs Grove-White's plump cheek. She dodged backwards just in time to avoid the full brunt of the blow, and had I not been so incandescent with rage I might have laughed at the dumbfounded expression on her face, or marvelled at her agility. Grabbing Clara's arm, I turned and began striding back up the street to where the carter had finished loading our luggage.

'Mama! Mama?' said Clara, as she pittered along beside me. 'Why did you smack that lady?'

I did not trust myself to speak.

'Mama!' Clara importuned me again. 'Why did you do that?'

'I will tell you when we are on our way.'

Beside me, Clara Venus fell silent. We reached the dray, and I told the driver to make haste as I climbed aboard, pulling Clara up behind me. As we passed Mr Shinnors's shop, I saw through the window that Mrs Grove-White had taken refuge inside.

'Mama, you must stop and say sorry,' said Clara. 'Look at the lady! Her bonnet has come off. She looks like a poor old sheep.'

Clara was genuinely stricken, but there was something else about her demeanour, something that was so redolent of indignation and repulsion at what I, her mother, had done, that I felt it incumbent upon myself to explain my behaviour.

'I hit her because she was stupid and wicked,' I was about to say. And then I realized that what I had just done was in itself stupid and wicked. Mrs Grove-White was unspeakably ignorant and unforgivably prejudiced, but she was not, I think, wicked, nor did she deserve to be violently assaulted. I felt a pang of guilt for having lashed out at her. But I could not bring myself to stop and apologize, despite her affecting resemblance to a poor old sheep (Clara Venus was right: Mrs Grove-White did look as if she were baa-ing her head off in Mr Shinnors's shop). So instead I said, 'I hit her because there was a cleg on her.'

'What's a cleg?'

'One of those nasty, stinging horseflies. And then – then I had to make a run for it, in case the cleg got me.' It sounded so lame that I felt I had to proffer a more nuanced explanation. 'A cleg can spread disease, you see.'

'Does that lady have disease?'

'No. But the cleg could have been on somebody who did have a disease, and then brought some of the disease with it when it landed on Mrs Grove-White.'

'Would the cleg have been on that baby?'

'What baby?'

'That baby I saw a picture of in the hotel. The man said it had died of disease.'

How I had underestimated my daughter's powers of observation! While I had thought she was engrossed in singing 'Higgledy Piggledy' and dipping toast soldiers in her boiled egg, she had been quite cognizant of the conversation going on around her.

'Did you see other pictures, Clara?' I asked cautiously.

'Yes. Why did that man want to draw dead people?'

'It's his job.'

'Why?'

'So that he can show people how important it is to stop disease spreading.'

'Because people die?'

'Yes.'

'How do you stop it?'

'It's difficult. Disease is passed on from one person to another by animals or insects, and sometimes by other people.'

'What people?'

'Sick people.'

'Like the people we saw that time going to the workhouse?'

'Yes.'

482

Oh, name of God! I did not want to have this conversation! Clara Venus was too young, too new in the world to learn of the horrors and the evil that thrived in this imperfect place.

'What animals spread diseases? Are they bad animals?'

'No, sweetheart. They are not bad. They don't know that they are carrying disease.'

'Did the cleg not know when he landed on the lady who looks like a sheep's face?'

'No. The cleg didn't know.'

'So it wouldn't be his fault if the lady died?'

'No.'

'The poor cleg. If he knew, I don't think he would have landed on her.'

Clara Venus drew her brows together in a perplexed frown, and I decided to distract her from the morbidity of the subject by pointing out the lovely things by the side of the road along which we were travelling.

'Look!' I said, pointing randomly at a whitethorn, the leafless branches of which were clawing at the sky. 'A lovely tree! See how lovely is its shape, against the blue! And look at the cloud above! It looks like the wombat we saw in the zoo! And look at . . . look at . . .'

I had been going to say, 'Look at the birds!' But there were no birds. There was nothing to look at, or rather, there was nothing lovely to look at in the surrounding countryside. It was blasted and desolate and bleak, and the cabins that had once housed the poor peasantry, and the drills where potatoes had grown, had been levelled into an expanse of barren earth that stretched as far as the eye could see.

Until we arrived at Lissaguirra. My house and its surrounding purlieus were like a haven in a wilderness. It was late in the year, but the evergreens tinged the landscape here and there with a verdant hue, and though the birds were silent, I knew they were there. We startled a wood pigeon; it flapped up from the forest floor to take refuge in a thicket, and a pheasant broke cover to run across our path on its silly stick-like legs. A robin followed us along the last quarter-mile of our journey, flitting from twig to twig, regarding us curiously. When we emerged from the trees, I saw that a pair of swans were skimming serenely over the surface of the lake towards us.

Clara Venus turned to me and smiled. 'We're home,' she said. 'We're home! Hooray, hooray!' And before the donkey had turned into the courtyard, she had hopped off the cart and gone racing towards the kitchen door.

The carter offloaded our luggage and dumped it by the storm porch, and as he turned the dray around I heard the sound of our own little donkey calling from the stable. Passing the open half-door, I put my head through to say hello, and there found stalled, as well as

Dolly and my little mare Minerva, a glossy chestnut hunter.

I smiled as I heard behind me the tread of a man's boots. I did not need to glance around, for I knew who it was.

'Eliza,' he said, and then he drew the collar of my pelisse aside and kissed the nape of my neck.

I turned to face him as his arms went around my waist.

'You got my note,' I said.

'I did. Your postscript was the sweetest I have ever read.'

'Remind me of it.'

'It was a line of but three words.'

'I remember.'

'Say them.'

I smiled, and stood on tiptoe to kiss his mouth. 'I love you,' I said.

31

LATER, WE SAT by the fire in the kitchen, all six of us: Jameson, Clara Venus, me, the two Biddies and Christy.

We were eating griddle cakes with honey – Christy's beehives had produced a bumper harvest that autumn – and Clara Venus had reunited Romulus with Remus and reinstated the wolves in the ark, which she had set upon the kitchen table. Christy was desperately downcast, but the Biddies shot him warning looks every time he made mention of *an Gorta Mór*, or touched on what had become known as the 'coffin ships' that were transporting their wretched passengers across the Atlantic. I was glad that they had the wit not to speak of such things in front of Clara Venus, for I knew that, preoccupied as she seemed in marching the animals two by two up the gangway of the ark, she listened constantly.

'Little pitchers have big ears,' said Old Biddy, when Christy made some reference to mass graves in Cork.

And between the pair of them, through nuance of word and tone, the Biddies let me know that they had been lucky; that they had survived in this hidden corner of North County Cork, and were well set up for the coming winter. For Clara's benefit, they made the events of the past year seem like a big adventure.

'Most folk hereabout have gone to the cities,' said Old Biddy.

'Why?' Clara Venus asked, arranging the animals in order of size on Noah's gangplank.

'Because they hope to find work in the big, bustling towns.'

'Why?'

'Because then they will have money for food.'

'Where does our food come from in Lissaguirra?'

'Not a year away, and London has made a townie of you, girleen! We have our chickens for eggs and goats for milk and our kitchen garden for vegetables and the little orchard that Christy planted for apples. And if we need anything else, we can fetch it from Doneraile. We are very lucky here.'

'And fishies from the lake,' said Clara, balancing a penguin on the poop deck.

Christy harrumphed and looked shifty.

'Take all the fish you want,' Jameson said, 'for I have bought the rights.'

'The fishing rights?' I asked.

'You got the rights off that poxy –' began Christy, but Old Biddy cut him off with a 'La la la!'

'His Lordship needed little persuasion to sell them to me,' said Jameson.

'That *amadán*. You heard he burned the roofs over the heads of his tenants in Aill na Coill?'

'La la la la la, Clara Venus!' trilled Old Biddy. 'Let's have a song! Did you learn any new ones while you were across the sea in England?'

'London Bridge is falling down!' sang Clara Venus as the penguin toppled off the poop.

Christy leaned back in his chair and gave Jameson a level look. 'It is still against the law for a Catholic to take fish from a lake,' I heard him say in an undertone.

'Anyone can take fish from my lake,' replied Jameson. 'There will be no censure from me. Besides, I don't imagine the law has stopped you before now.'

'Nor would it have stopped the people in Aill na Coill, so desperate were they. But they had no means of catching fish. And they are all dead now.'

'London Bridge is falling down!' I pulled on a smile and clapped my hands as I sang along. 'Falling down! Falling down!'

And so we continued in a merry vein, as if the abominations and the atrocities that lay beyond the enchanted woods surrounding Lissaguirra did not exist.

*

Later still, Jameson accompanied me to the bedchamber, where the bed had been aired and a fire lit.

'What made you decide to come back?' he said, as he divested me of my shawl and started to undo the small buttons that ran from the neckline of my bodice to just below my waist.

'Everyone has asked me that,' I said. 'I came back because Clara Venus was homesick.'

'It's the Irish blood in her. Help me with this, darling.'

I raised my hands to his and freed a button from its eyelet. 'I had thought of going to Paris.'

'Paris is no place for a child. There is political unrest there. Stay here a while. You have a roof over your head here.'

'A roof over my head is not the same as a home.'

'It is,' he said, dropping a kiss on the declivity of my collarbone, 'for you built it.'

He continued to unfasten my bodice with unhurried fingers. He was right. Lissaguirra had been my home from the day the last slate had been nailed down. Intended as a cynical profit-making venture, the house that had risen from St Leger's bothy had become more than stones and mortar; it was my anchorage. I had designed it, I had overseen the building of it, and I had grown to love it. It was, I realized, my most cherished possession.

'Give it time, Eliza,' he said, as I shrugged my shoulders free from my sleeves. 'The situation cannot worsen here. In a year, things will have changed. When Ireland is in the whole of her health, she is the loveliest country in the world. You cannot continue to travel hither and yon searching for a place to call home when you have found it already.'

From beyond the window there came the hoot of an owl, and the ragged soughing of the wind through the trees.

'What if I become one of those women who wander in the wood?' I said.

'What do you mean?'

'It is something my friend Isabella said to me. She feels as if she is lost in a wood, drifting aimlessly in search of . . . she knows not what.'

'Give it a year at least. A year is no time. Then you will know better what to do.' He tugged gently at a silk ribbon on my chemise until it gave way. 'If you settle here, Clara Venus can go to school. I can visit. When this crisis is over, I shall have every reason to come, and Sophia will not begrudge me time spent here.'

'How so?'

'Investment in bloodstock will be one way to get the country on its feet. Dromomore will thrive again.'

'But how am I to live?'

'As you have done. Have I ever kept you short of

money? I am sorry if I have, for I should not like to think that you might feel obliged to earn a living.'

'It's not about –'

Jamey was not listening. He was fingering the broderie anglaise trim of my chemise, the opening of which had parted to reveal my breasts. 'And you will have income from fishing rights – for I have signed them over to you.'

Once this news would have filled me with jubilation. I could have sold the house and sallied forth into the world with my own independent income, a woman of substance. But everything had changed since the day Clara Venus made her unplanned entrance into the world hot on the heels of her brother. My Ananke.

I realized I had spoken the word aloud.

'Ananke?' queried Jamey.

'It means "Destiny". It's from the Greek.'

'She speaks Greek, too, my accomplished lady-love!' He dropped a kiss on the sweet satiny place where the pulse beat, just below my ear. 'What about your writing? That would keep you employed. Didn't you have an idea for a book?'

I laughed. 'William Thackeray has written it. It's called *Vanity Fair*.'

'Then write your own book.' His voice was low, cajoling. Pushing me onto the bed, he reached down and pulled up the hem of my petticoat. 'You are a clever woman, Eliza. You can write a book that will outsell any of Thackeray's feeble scribblings. You are the cleverest woman I have ever met.'

Those were the most seductive words he had uttered yet. I smiled and stretched and sighed with bliss. Jamey always brought me to the brink of *la petite mort* before I even realized I was ready.

The next morning I rose at first light, before anyone else in the house was awake. Wrapping myself in my peignoir, I made my way to the library, where I heaped cushions onto the window seat overlooking the lake and made myself comfortable. It had rained during the night; outside everything was fresh and dewy and silent. The swans were abroad, cruising as if they had no care in the world, as if they had no reason to be there but to admire their own beauty in the aqueous mirror. They mated for life, I had heard.

A year. Give it a year, Jamey had said. There would be no hardship in staying here for a year. I looked around at my beautiful room, at the belongings I had accumulated: my writing desk and accoutrements; the bookcases, with space still on the shelves for more; the wing chair by the fireplace where I curled up on winter evenings – a novel always within arm's reach; the Japanese *cloisonné* vase that I had admired in a shop during one of my visits to Dublin and which Jamey had promptly bought me; the Isfahan rug upon which Clara Venus had learned to crawl; the display case in which I kept my most precious things: a drawing titled 'Mama, Papa and Clara Venus in the Woods' that she had made; a baby shoe; a shell into which she told me I could whisper all my secrets; the double miniature that Jamey had commissioned of himself and his daughter as an infant.

There was no hardship here.

I felt cold, suddenly; I needed a shawl. I hauled my trunk from the storm porch where it had been dumped the previous day by the carter, and dragged it into the centre of the room. Undoing the catches, I opened the lid and rummaged among the contents.

There was my honey-coloured morning dress, and my velvet dinner gown, and the dress I had worn to Lord Cavendish's ball in Devonshire House. There was the day dress that William had encouraged me to buy in Regent Street, printed with tiny heliotrope-purple flowers and boasting gauze undersleeves, and the wool-and-silk dressing gown to which I had taken a fancy in a fine India shop on Ludgate Hill, and an evening dress in dark green silk damask, made for me by a modiste in Oxford Street.

Flush with the success of *Vanity Fair*, William had paid for all three garments, and I had not demurred, for had I not advised him on Becky's wardrobe? Had I not suggested details of her toilette – her *mouchoirs*, caps and satin scuffs; her rouge, curling papers and frizettes; her eau de cologne and pomades and other intimate female gimcracks of which poor William had but scant knowledge? I had earned the clothes.

It made me smile to think of the dividends Becky Sharp had reaped. So desperate was the reading public to keep up to date with the exploits of our godless little governess that they queued outside the bookshops every month, paying one whole shilling to find out where her chicanery and stratagems would take her next. When I had left the house in Young Street, I knew that Becky's next goal was to be presented at court: I had given William a clue as to how she might acquire the diamonds to wear there.

It had struck me more than once that I deserved formal acknowledgement for my contribution to the book, but I shook off such snippety concerns, upbraiding myself for an ingrate. William had provided me with a home and friendship and a job: indeed, he had paid me over the odds for looking after his girls. For a fallen woman who had borne a child out of wedlock, I had done very well.

And yet, and yet ... when I had read *Jane Eyre*, I had been full of envy. Despite my quibbles, I knew that its author had achieved something remarkable. *Jane Eyre* was a story written by a woman for other women, to show them that life could be lived on a divergent path.

The heroine was not the kind of person with whom I could ever be friends – for she took herself too seriously – and it irked me that she ended up with Mr Rochester, for he took himself *far* too seriously, but I understood that it was an important book, and I wished that I had written something like it.

As I drew from the trunk the silk moiré that Mrs O'Dowd had given me when I first came to Ireland (over seven years ago – how long ago that seemed!), I wondered when I might wear such finery again. I would have to ask young Biddy to make wrappers for the gowns and store them in the camphor chest, where the moths would not get at them. In the meantime, while Jamey was here, I would make myself easy on his eye. Today I would don the heliotrope print dress with the open sleeves.

Searching for the fine crocheted pelerine to wear with it, I found a parcel of what appeared to be books. I loosened the string and unwrapped the canvas in which they had been tied. One was an edition of William's *Irish Sketch-Book*, dedicated to me; the other a volume of Shakespeare's sonnets. On the flyleaf was written in William's most careful hand, the following verse:

> *April is in my mistress' face,*
> *And July in her eyes hath place;*
> *Within her bosom is September,*
> *But in her heart a cold December.*

Oh, what a tiresome booby William could be! Waxing maudlin like a lovelorn swain. Still, it was a very pretty edition of the Sonnets, leather-bound with gilt-edged pages and marbled endpapers. I slid it onto the shelf between Keats and Shelley, and then I closed the trunk and went to make myself a cup of tea.

Young Biddy was descending the narrow staircase from her room above the kitchen. Wiping sleep from her eyes, she was tousled and yawning and limp-looking.

'Ma'am!' she said, when she saw me. 'You put the heart across me! Didn't I think you were a ghost?'

'There can be no ghosts in a new house,' I said, moving to the range to warm myself.

I thought – but did not add – that whilst the house itself was unlikely to be haunted, there were bound to be plenty of tormented souls roaming the environs of Aill na Coill and beyond.

'Sit down, ma'am,' she said, all anxious, 'and let me make the tea. You must be fierce tired after coming all that way.'

'I'm not at all tired.'

I felt full of a kind of exuberant impatience; I could not wait for Clara Venus and Jamey to rouse themselves, so we could embark upon the day in earnest. I did not know how long Jameson planned to stay in Lissaguirra, but while he was here I was determined that we should enjoy our time *en famille*. The day was fine – we might

496

take a picnic on the lake if the boat was in good repair, and Jamey could teach Clara to row. I hoped I had remembered her fleece-lined gloves.

'Tell me how things have been, Biddy,' I said.

She took up a poker and started to stoke the fire. 'For us here, things have been grand, ma'am. It is true, what Old Biddy said yesterday – we want for nothing. We are lucky, for we are away from the main thorough-fare. It is to the cities that everyone is headed, in the hope that they might find food. There is nothing for them in the country. I was afeared that someone might take the hens or the goats, but no one has been near us. Apart from the fox, that Christy has been after, that helped itself to a chick the week before last.'

'What of your families?'

'Mine are gone to Liverpool. Old Biddy's daughter and her son are in service in Dublin.'

'And you are in good health?'

She would not meet my eyes. She looked pale, still, after the fright I had given her.

'Yes, ma'am.' She set aside the poker and turned to busy herself with the teapot and the caddy. 'How could we not but be in good health, for Mr St Leger makes sure that we have everything we need.'

I had not known that Jameson sent money. I had sent what I could, fearful always that it would not be enough, but now I saw that young Biddy was spooning tea liberally into the pot, and that the sugar bowl was full and that, under a square of gauze, a bowl of oats was soaking for the breakfast porridge. Outside the kitchen door I heard the cock crow, the clucking of hens in the yard, the bleating of my goats. If I wanted an egg, I could step out and help myself to one, freshly laid; if I needed milk, I could ask Young Biddy to fetch me a pitcher.

I moved to the larder. Inside, it was redolent with the smell of apples. The shelves were lined with bottles and jars of preserves and jam and pickles and frames of honeycomb; a sack of flour, one of rice, and one of legumes were neatly stowed in an alcove; on the cold counter a ham stood alongside a slab of cheese and a tub of butter. A rabbit hung from a hook. It would not have surprised me to see a cornucopia spilling cherries and strawberries, or a hog's head garlanded with a wreath of bay leaves, or a five-tiered cake iced and decorated with candied fruit.

From beyond the small glazed window of the larder, a gunshot rang out. I turned to young Biddy.

'Christy is out already,' she said.

'After rabbits?'

I saw that her pale face had coloured. 'Ma'am,' she said in a rush. 'Christy has asked for to marry me.'

I knew, without her having to volunteer the information, that young Biddy was pregnant. I had noticed last night that she was wearing her apron higher, to try to disguise the bump. I was not surprised that she was with child; when last I had been in Lissaguirra, she had been stepping out with a lad named Phelim Daly, a handsome butcher's boy from Doneraile with whom she had been quite besotted. But I was bemused by the notion that Christy might be the father.

'Phelim is gone to America,' she told me, pre-empting the question. The colour rose higher in her face. 'He left a month ago.'

I had noticed, when I passed through the town, that the butcher's was one of the many shops that had been boarded up. 'And when did Christy propose?' I asked.

'After Phelim left.'

What a good man Christy Cassidy was! I saw at once that he had volunteered himself as a player in a drama that was none of his making. Since the father of young Biddy's child had been forced to emigrate and leave his sweetheart and unborn baby behind, Christy had stepped in as a substitute.

Young Biddy folded her hands across her belly in a dignified manner. 'You might have noticed, ma'am, that I am expecting. I am mindful that you may no longer require my services.'

Oh! It was pitiful, how she felt she had to tell me in words that were so formal and unfamiliar to her! It reminded me of the way Annie Thackeray spoke, when she was pretending to be a grown-up. Young Biddy was little more than a child herself; I had taken her on when she was just thirteen. And now, instead of romping up the aisle with her childhood sweetheart, she was marrying a man she did not love.

'Come here to me, darling,' I said, wrapping my arms around her. 'Come here to me, mavourneen. What makes you think I'd want to be rid of you? I'd be lost without my pair of Biddies – you know I would!'

Young Biddy clung to me, and buried her face in my shoulder.

'You're not going to dismiss me?'

'How could I dismiss family? You've looked after me and my little one for long enough; it's time you had someone to look after you.'

'Oh, thank you, ma'am! I was scared, so scared that you might put me out, and then where would I be? My mam is gone, and my pa, and Phelim, Phelim is gone, and he's the only man I ever loved, ever! And Christy is so good and kind, and you are too, ma'am, but my heart is broke. My heart is broke, for I know I never will see my Phelim again.'

And as young Biddy gave way to tears so copious they soaked the sleeve of my robe, I racked my brain for the comforting words a mother might say in a similar situation; no easy task, since I had never had the benefit of any such words myself.

'Won't a baby be a grand thing!' I there-there'd. 'What fine news, to welcome me home! Shh, shh, Biddy, shh. Just think – a companion for Clara Venus! I must look out all her old baby clothes. And the baby carriage, and the bassinet! I'm delighted that there's to be a new little one at Lissaguirra.'

Especially, I thought wryly, since I did not have to give birth to it.

32

CLARA VENUS SLEPT so late that morning that I began to fret. Might she be ill? Might she have been exposed to one of the diseases Dr Donovan had mentioned? Cholera, smallpox, tuberculosis, pellagra ... Drowsiness was one of the symptoms of tuberculosis, I knew; then remembered with alarm that numerous passengers on the voyage from London had been suffering from colds: one gentleman had sneezed numerous times without recourse to a handkerchief, and I had been obliged to proffer him a handkerchief of my own.

When I expressed my concerns to Old Biddy, she brewed up a vile-smelling concoction of linseed oil, liquorice, preserved lemons and rum, which she swore would ease any symptoms. She was businesslike and reassuring, but I could tell that she was masking her discomfiture, because she put quantities of water on to boil. Jameson told us to stop fussing. Clara was, he insisted, simply worn out after the long journey, and should be allowed to sleep as late as she liked.

I passed the time puttering around the courtyard, saying hello to Dolly and Minerva, poking about in the kitchen garden, then sitting on a bench by the kitchen door with the wan winter sun on my face while Jameson and Christy talked horses and husbandry. Christy was concerned about the fox that had been staking out the chicken coop. He'd seen in the past the havoc that could be wreaked once a fox gained access – an entire flock would be left dead and maimed – and he was determined to get shot of the animal, for it would be nigh impossible to replace our chickens. Dusk was the best time to nab a fox, he said, for they left their lairs then to go hunting.

I listened in that absent way one does when suffering fatigue – for of course, I had had little sleep the night before. I heard the drone of voices rising and falling, the lazy flap of the laundry on the line, the lively bleat of a young goat, the low clucking of the hens. It was wonderfully slumbrous: my limbs felt liquid and heavy as mercury, and behind the closed lids of my eyes I saw the sun dance in patterns that reminded me of a kaleidoscope my mother had shown me as a child and then I was travelling with her along a track between bean rows with the sky big and high and we kissed each other adieu and then there was no one there except a tall, lean fellow, a scarecrow far away who was moving nearer with every step of his long legs clad in tattered trews that flapped around his bony limbs and he stretched out a hand and I realized that he was not supplicating or begging, no he was here to take something from me and when I saw his face under the broad brim of his hat I knew that he was Death.

The crowing of the cock woke me, and I opened my eyes to see Clara Venus standing in front of me in her nightgown. She was backlit by the sun, clutching a thick slice of bread and honey, and regarding me curiously.

'Mama, were you sleeping?' she said.

'Yes.'

'There is drool coming out of your mouth and you were snoring.'

'Oh!' I laughed and dug in my pocket for my handkerchief. 'You mean creature, to tell me so! I must look a fright.' I wiped at my mouth and blew my nose.

'Why do people snore when they're asleep?'

'I don't know.'

'Were you having a dream?'

'I can't remember,' I lied.

'Old Biddy made me porridge. I ate it all. I ate two bowls full.'

'Good girl.' There was clearly nothing wrong with Clara Venus. Jameson had been right when he'd said we were fussing over nothing.

'Did you eat all yours, Mama?'

'Yes.'

Another lie. Fatigue made me nauseous, and I could not have stomached porridge for breakfast. I yawned and stretched, and found that my limbs were aching; unsurprisingly, after three nights sleeping at sea with Clara Venus in a cramped bunk.

'Look,' she said, 'Young Biddy sewed daisies on my slippers.'

I looked down at Clara's feet. Her little slippers were scattered with silk daisies that had once trimmed a summer bonnet of mine.

'You silly child!' I mock-chided her. 'You will catch your death, coming outdoors in nothing but your night-dress and slippers!'

'Don't you think they're pretty?'

'They are very pretty, but they are not made for traipsing over a stable yard.'

Scooping her up, I wrapped her in my shawl, then helped myself to a handful of Brussels sprouts from the trug that I had set beside me on the bench. 'Come,' I said, jouncing her on my hip as I made my way around puddles to where the goats were penned. 'These fellows have been waiting all morning to welcome you back. They've been calling you non-stop. Clar-raaaaa! Clar-raaaaa!!'

She wriggled and giggled as she fed the goats

sprouts, and when they had been devoured and the animals were shrilling for more – *Clar-raaaaa! Clar-raaaaa!* – she gave them her bread and honey, then begged me to pull up some carrots. I set her on the stone pier of the gate, and crouched down by the vegetable patch, feeling a horrible sense of shame as I tugged the tubers from the ground. Old Biddy had told me that earlier in the year she had seen people pulling turnips from the earth and eating them raw.

'You must not think we can feed the goats every day,' I said, wiping earth from the carrots. 'This is a treat. We need to be careful with what food we have.'

'I hate carrots,' announced Clara Venus. 'I think we should let the goats have all our carrots.'

I was just about to embark on a sermon about what a precious resource they were, and how nutritious, when a shriek made me whirl around. 'Look! Mama, Mama – look!' Helpless with laughter, Clara was watching two of the goats play at tug o' war with my shawl. They had each taken a fringed edge between their teeth, and were capering like a pair of Morris dancers, snickering and rolling their devilish yellow eyes.

'Deuce *take* them! Clara, how could you let them! My shawl will be *ruined*!' I dropped the carrots and hastened over. The nanny goat had joined in now, chewing on the woollen cloth as implacably as though she were chewing tobacco, while the kids cavorted around her

506

with scraps of fringe dangling from their mouths. Clara couldn't stop laughing, but I didn't think it was at all funny. The shawl was an old one, but it was one I kept handy on a peg by the kitchen door, that I could sling around my shoulders any time I stepped out, and I was vexed that she had been so careless with it.

'It's just a shawl.' Jameson joined us, and tried to slide a hand about my waist.

'Just a shawl?' I shot him a cross look, took hold of his hand and removed it. 'What does that mean? Is that *just* a hat you're wearing?'

'What do you think, honey sweet?' he asked Clara, with a complicit smile. 'Would you like to see the goats eat my hat?'

'Yes, yes!'

With a cavalier gesture, Jameson doffed the slouch hat he was wearing, then tossed it to the goats. The kids lit upon it with glee, trying to impale it with their baby horns, while their mother looked on approvingly.

Clara Venus laughed so hard that she toppled backwards off the pier, but Jameson caught her just in time, swinging her around so that her nightgown billowed out around her like a white flag, making her crow even louder and sending the hens scuttling in alarm. She had lost a slipper – it had gone spinning into the goats' pen – and as I hurried to retrieve it, one of the kids strutted up and butted me in the derrière.

I would have laughed, another time. Another time I would have joined in with Clara Venus and Jameson as they spluttered and roared with mirth, but something had piqued me, and I could not allow myself to engage. I felt that not only my dignity but my authority had been undermined, and that by taking such a *laisser-aller* stance, Jameson was endorsing – even encouraging – Clara's giddy behaviour. I was not in the mood for this. I felt excluded and school-mistressy and – worst of all – I felt unwelcome.

I shook my head in annoyance. 'What has possessed you?' I snapped, thrusting the slipper at Jameson.

'You're a sourpuss today, aren't you?' he said.

'And you are irresponsible and childish.'

'What? Having fun with my daughter is childish? I should damn well hope so. You should try it some time.'

'Oh, shut up,' I told him, turning on my heel.

'Liza! What's up with you?'

I didn't reply. As I stalked back into the house I knew that I was behaving like a spoilsport, and even when I heard Clara call, 'Mama! Come back!' I refused to turn around. I kept going with my chin in the air, carrying my stupid dignity with me as if it were something valuable.

For the rest of the morning I sulked. I sulked in my bedchamber as I unpacked my clothes and Clara's. I sulked at lunchtime and would not come down, claiming I had a headache brought on by falling asleep with the sun on my face. I sulked as Clara and Jameson played a rowdy game of hide-and-seek upstairs and down, and I sulked when I heard their receding chatter below my window as they headed off along the path that led into the woods, Clara's light, reedy voice in contrapunto to Jameson's velvet drawl. She was saying something about how cruel it was to kill foxes, and he was explaining that foxes were the cruel ones, for they killed the chickens that laid our eggs. They hadn't bothered to bid me farewell, I observed peevishly. But then, why should they, since I had been behaving like a prize sow? Feeling foolish and uncherished, I donned my Chinese robe and descended the stairs to seek sanctuary with the Biddies in the kitchen.

It was warm there, redolent of comforting stockpot smells, and the sound of the ticking clock was curiously pacifying. Old Biddy was rolling out pastry and singing one of the Irish airs that she had used to sing to Clara when she was colicky as a baby. I had a sudden intense yearning to be mollycoddled, to have someone put me to bed between smooth, freshly laundered sheets, to pull a soft quilt over me, to stroke my hair and sing me lullabies until I fell asleep.

'Sit down, ma'am, and I'll make you a cup of tea,' said Old Biddy, drawing out a chair for me at the kitchen table. 'With cinnamon. I swear by cinnamon for a headache. Are you feeling any better?'

'A little better, thank you.'

In fact, I was feeling dreadful. The headache that I had invented as an excuse for my ill humour had, ironically, become a reality.

''Twas exhaustion from all the travelling that brought it on. And you were up at the crack of dawn this morning, by all accounts.'

We exchanged an eloquent look. Clearly young Biddy had told her of our early-morning tête-à-tête.

'I understand there is to be a wedding,' I remarked.

'Something to celebrate at last.' Old Biddy took down a canister from the shelf by the stove and extracted a cinnamon stick. 'It will need to be done soon. She cannot afford to leave it much later, in her condition.'

'Indeed.'

In her condition . . . Old Biddy had, in that laconic phrase, neatly précis'd the lot of thousands of girls: unmarried, poor, abandoned, pregnant, comfortless and – in the eyes of many – fallen, sinful magdalens.

'She's a very lucky girl,' continued Old Biddy. 'Christy will be good to her, and she is well set up here, with such a beautiful mistress as yourself, ma'am.'

I looked towards the window. Outside, Young Biddy was carrying the laundry basket across the yard. She looked ruddy and robust, and I thought of what might have become of her had not Christy come to her rescue, had she not been 'well set up' with a 'beautiful mistress'.

There would have been no future for her, and no future for her unborn child. Mother and child would be dead, or destitute at the very least. What, I wondered, might have become of me, and of Clara Venus, if our circumstances had been different? If I had become pregnant by some man other than Jameson St Leger, if the father of my child had been heartless or dissolute or penniless, or all three? I had gambled wildly, but I, too, had been very lucky. I had had more than my fair share of cake, and I was still tucking into it with an appetite. I managed a smile. 'When is the baby due?'

'In the late spring.' Old Biddy poured water from the kettle into the teapot, then set it aside to allow the cinnamon to infuse. 'She has said that she wants a girl.'

'A girl?' No reasonable woman wanted a girl child! Girls were a vexation: they cost money to feed and rear, and were doubly burdensome if they were not comely, for at least a pretty face meant they could more easily be got rid of once they were marriageable. All mothers-to-be prayed for boy babies, because boys would grow up to be sturdy, dependable men who would provide and care for their mammies in their old age. 'Why should she want a girl?'

'She sees how much you and Mr St Leger dote upon Clara Venus. She wants her little girl to grow up to be as special as yours. And isn't she right? There will be a future for clever girls like your Clara: it will be a special kind of child who will pull through these benighted times undamaged. But there is no future for boys here. They are all dead or emigrated, like Phelim Daly. This is no country for young men.'

From the yard I heard a laugh. Christy had set his rifle and a brace of pheasants on the low wall by the gate and had joined young Biddy by the washing line, to help her unpeg the clothes.

'I wish he'd got that fox,' went on old Biddy. 'I won't rest easy 'til it's gone.' She poured me a cup of tea, and set an oatcake on a plate in front of me.

I pushed it aside. 'No thank you, Biddy.'

'But you've had nothing all day! Young Biddy told me you didn't touch your porridge this morning.'

'I'm not hungry.'

'Try it with a little honey,' she coaxed.

I shook my head. Then something seemed to snap behind my eyes, and I heard myself say, 'Oh, dear God,' and then, for some peculiar reason, I started to cry.

'What ails you, ma'am?' Old Biddy leaned her hands on the table and peered into my face. I saw her eyes narrow, heard a sharp intake of breath.

'I don't know.' I fumbled in my pocket and produced the handkerchief that I had been using all morning to blow my nose.

'No, no,' scolded Biddy. 'It's a clean one you'll be needing.' She went to the door, opened it, and called out

512

to Young Biddy. 'Come here, you – young one! Bring the handkerchiefs you're after taking off the line!'

Through the window I saw Young Biddy turn, alarmed at the urgency in Old Biddy's voice. I saw her grab the laundry basket and cross the yard at a lick, heard her come into the kitchen, and then a muttered confab went on behind my back. I felt a handkerchief being pressed into my hand, and cool fingers against my forehead, heard Young Biddy say, 'She's very flushed.'

Old Biddy uncorked a bottle and poured a measure of the vile-smelling liquid she had prepared earlier for Clara Venus. 'Take this,' she said, holding the medicine glass to my lips.

I forced back the liquid and gagged, holding the handkerchief to my mouth. Why was Old Biddy making me drink this stuff? It was Clara Venus she had made it for. Where was Clara Venus?

'Here, ma'am. Have your tea now. It'll do you good.'

Old Biddy handed me the teacup, and I sipped obediently as, behind me, I heard the sound of logs being lobbed into the stove.

'Fetch more, Christy,' Young Biddy said. 'And take a load upstairs. We'll need a basket-full in the bedroom. Warm a brick for the bed, and bring up the tin bath.'

What was all the fuss about? A flare caught my eyes as a candle was lit. I looked at the kitchen clock. It was getting late in the afternoon. Where was Clara Venus?

'Where is Clara Venus?' I heard a voice say.

'She's with her father,' said Old Biddy. 'They went off for a walk in the woods.'

'No,' said Christy, 'he sent her back. She was distressed, so she was, by the notion of him killing the fox, so he sent her back. Sure you'd have seen her come by the yard, or in through the kitchen.'

'I never saw her,' said Old Biddy. 'Did you see her, young one?'

Young Biddy had lit another candle. The light played on her face, casting strange shadows on the planes and hollows. 'No,' she said.

'She must have slipped by me, so. Likely she's in the library; her play animals are there. Go and see.'

I heard the scuff of the kitchen door against the tiled floor, and footsteps receding down the passageway, and a voice calling, 'Clara! Clara?' And then again, further away, 'Clara! *Clar-raaa!*'

Old Biddy poured more tea and forced the cup between my hands. I had started to shiver, and could barely hold it. There was further muttering, and then I heard Christy go back outside, heard the sound of his boots cross the yard. Above my head came the thud of more footsteps, running now, running along the upstairs corridor, and again a voice was calling, 'Clara! *Clar-raaa!*'

'She'll be here somewhere,' said Old Biddy. 'Hiding,

I've no doubt. She had a grand game of hide-and-seek with her daddy earlier in the day.'

I heard a voice say, 'But I heard them – heard them go off somewhere . . .' And I realized it was my voice, and that I had forced it from somewhere deep and painful in my throat.

Old Biddy gave me an anxious look, and set about folding the laundry that had come in from the line. 'They went to the woods, so they did; they went off for a dander. She was in fine fettle. She'd had a bowl of soup, and she ate it nearly all but the carrots. Isn't it funny the way she never will eat a carrot? I made sure she was all wrapped up in her muffler and that she had her gloves on, and her cap and her new little boots that you got for her in London. She was excited; she was hoping to see some of the animals she might have in her ark, like the fox or a wolf even, or a giraffe, God bless her soul! Isn't she the funniest little creature, with her notions and her . . . her little ways. It's good to have her back again. It's good to have the two of you back, so it is. And Mr St Leger, too. It's a pleasure to – always a pleasure to . . .'

Young Biddy came into the room, and we looked at each other, the three of us, in silence, Old Biddy with a little chemise between her hands. The clock ticked on and on and then the gunshot came and I rose to my feet and dropped the cup. It broke so slowly that I could have

515

counted the smithereens as they skimmed the floor. My skirt was stained with cinnamon; the liquid spread over the tiles like a dark tide, like mercury.

Through the window I saw an agitation of wings as a clamour of rooks rose from the forest beyond the stables. Young Biddy wrenched open the back door, and then she was racing across the yard, skirts gathered up above her knees. Old Biddy turned to me and gripped my hand and said, 'Settle yourself, ma'am. 'Tis naught. Mr St Leger'll have dispatched that fox at last.'

But her hands were trembling, and I knew. I knew as surely as if my heart had cracked the same moment I had heard the shot.

I disengaged my hand and went out into the wood. I searched and searched, calling her name. I pushed through tangles of briars and brambles that caught my hair and tore my robe and scored my face, calling all the time, and finally, at the far end of a tunnel of trees, I saw them.

St Leger was carrying Clara Venus in his arms. Christy and Young Biddy stumbled behind, arms outstretched towards her. Falling aslant through the branches, the evening sun gilded the curve of my daughter's cheek, the crush of her new dimity pinafore, the fall of her bloodied hair.

*

There was an envelope pinned to the last page. Edie opened it with clumsy fingers and found a yellowed newspaper cutting.

DEATH BY MISADVENTURE

An inquest was held some days since at a sitting of the Special Commission at Doneraile before the Chief Coroner of the county and a jury, on the body of Clara Venus, illegitimate daughter of Miss Eliza Drury, who came by her death in consequence of a gun-shot wound inflicted by Jameson St Leger on the 24th day of November, 1847. It appeared from the evidence of reliable witnesses that the deceased, a girl of some six years old, was walking in the wood by Lissaguirra Lodge when Mr St Leger, who believed himself to be alone, accidentally discharged his gun, which he had neglected to break. The jury retired, and returned in about ten minutes with a unanimous verdict of death by misadventure, which was unhesitatingly endorsed by the coroner.

The clock was near midnight as the court was cleared and the whole of the proceedings was solemn and impressive in the extreme.

It may be right to observe that throughout the investigation Mr St Leger's demeanour was decorous and sombre, and on being asked whether he had any observations to offer, he simply enquired after the well-being of the mother of the deceased.

33

THE FIRE HAD gone out, and it was light outside. Edie put the manuscript down and went into the kitchen. She poured herself a tumbler of water and drank it. She took an apple from the fruit bowl, and a heel of bread from the bread bin. She put on her polo coat and her boots and walked out into the grey dawn, Milo at her heels.

She walked through the yard, past the shed where Eliza's horse and donkey had been stabled, past the vegetable garden where nothing now grew but wild rhubarb, past the gnarled trees of the little orchard, past the dilapidated hutch where the hens had laid fresh eggs every day. She walked a short way into the forest, along the track that had once been the main approach road to the lodge. In her mind's eye she saw Clara Venus running ahead, saw St Leger's horse come down the trail, saw Eliza in her walking costume with the satin lining, coming together all three beneath the boughs.

She walked down to the lake and waited for the swans

to come to her, watched their elegant necks curve as they retrieved the crusts she tossed to them. She looked across the water to where Hilly had caught the small fish, and beyond to the far shore, where wraiths had once scraped a living from the earth around Aill na Coill, and where no one lived now. And when the swans had eaten their fill and sailed slowly back to their nest in the reed beds, she turned and looked at the house and started to climb towards it up the grassy slope. And as she walked, a poem came into her head that she had learned years ago at school:

> *I went out to the hazel wood,*
> *Because a fire was in my head,*
> *And cut and peeled a hazel wand,*
> *And hooked a berry to a thread;*
> *And when white moths were on the wing,*
> *And moth-like stars were flickering out,*
> *I dropped the berry in a stream*
> *And caught a little silver trout.*
>
> *When I had laid it on the floor*
> *I went to blow the fire aflame,*
> *But something rustled on the floor,*
> *And some one called me by my name:*
> *It had become a glimmering girl*
> *With apple blossom in her hair*
> *Who called me by my name and ran*
> *And faded through the brightening air.*

Though I am old with wandering
Through hollow lands and hilly lands,
I will find out where she has gone,
And kiss her lips and take her hands;
And walk among long dappled grass,
And pluck till time and times are done
The silver apples of the moon,
The golden apples of the sun.

Then Edie went back into the house, sheafed together the pages of Eliza Drury's manuscript, secured them with a stout elastic band, and laid them carefully at the bottom of her suitcase.

Mrs Callinan lived in a neat cottage in a row of other neat cottages on the Mallow road. In front of the house was a tiny square garden with a flagstoned path and a circular flower bed in which a straggly fuchsia bush grew.

Edie knocked on the front door and a voice called, 'Come in. I'm expecting you.'

She pushed open the door into a small porch where outdoor paraphernalia was tidily arranged, then stepped into a room that was dim and chill, for though the sun was bright outside it struggled to infiltrate the putty-coloured lace curtains.

Mrs Callinan was sitting very upright in a chintz arm-chair by the fireplace with a shawl over her lap and her hands resting on the arms of the chair. A small table had been set for tea, and a kettle stood on a brass trivet on the hearth, even though there was no fire. A paper fan had been set in the grate, as a background to a sickly-looking plant of indeterminate species; both were specked with soot.

'You see?' said Mrs Callinan. 'I have everything ready. I didn't want to waste time foostering about because I tire easily and I know you want to quiz me about Lissaguirra. Prospect House, as it's called now. Your name is Edie Chadwick; I shall call you Edie if you don't mind. I'm used to calling my pupils by their Christian names. I won't stand up.'

'How do you do, Mrs Callinan? Thank you so much for agreeing to see me.'

Mrs Callinan inclined her head and indicated an armchair opposite. 'You may take a seat there. Please pour us both tea, and help yourself to tea brack. I won't have anything to eat. A drop of milk, no sugar.'

'I brought you some chocolates.'

'Thank you. You may leave them on the sideboard.'

Edie had bought a box of Milk Tray in the posher of the grocers' shops. She had brought Mrs Callinan another gift – a memento of the house where she had been born – but the chocolates had been received with such indifference that Edie felt apprehensive about presenting the old lady with something that might prove even less welcome. She set the box on a crocheted runner, then poured tea into

521

porcelain cups and cut a thin slice of brack. She hated tea brack, but she said, 'Goodness! This looks delicious.'

'We have dispensed with the formalities. You may ask your questions. And please hurry up about it.'

Edie felt terribly nervous, suddenly, and then realized that it was because Mrs Callinan reminded her of the maths teacher at her prep school who hadn't liked her. She supposed that to a lady in her nineties she, Edie, must appear a mere youngster. If that were the case, she decided, she'd do exactly as she was instructed.

'As you wish, Mrs Callinan.' She cleared her throat. 'Why was the name of the lodge changed from Lissaguirra to Prospect House?'

'The Frobishers decided that the house should have an English name.'

'Who did they buy it from?'

'Some English nobleman. I never met him. He sold the place because he had no use for it. He lived in England: it was no longer the thing to keep a residence in Ireland. It was the time of the Nationalists and Charles Stewart Parnell, and unrest was fomenting.'

Edie felt as though she were back in her loathsome history class. She didn't want a lecture on politics, she wanted a personal account of the house and the people who had lived there. She had pictured herself and Mrs Callinan sitting down and having a cosy natter together in front of a turf fire, with Mrs Callinan calling her 'lovie' while she reminisced about the old days, and then Mrs Callinan might have come out with the great revelation that she was Eliza Drury's daughter, and the whole story would have been resolved and maybe wound up with a happy ending, with news of grandchildren and even great-grandchildren. But Clara Venus was dead, and so were Eliza and St Leger and William Thackeray, and really, what was the point in Edie having come here at all?

'So who lived there before the Frobishers?'

'My mother, Bridget Cassidy, and a lady named Eliza Drury.'

'You're Young Biddy's daughter!'

'I beg your pardon?'

'I mean – I have a picture of you with your mother and father, and another lady, standing outside the house.'

Edie delved into her bag and produced the framed daguerreotype that she had wrapped in pretty floral paper and tied with a ribbon.

'Unwrap it for me, if you would be so kind. I have difficulty untying knots.'

Edie noticed for the first time that Mrs Callinan's hands were gnarled and claw-like, like the hands of an Egyptian mummy. She felt a rush of sympathy. The former schoolmistress had clearly gone to some trouble to have tea ready and laid out in advance of Edie's arrival so that she did not betray telltale signs of arthritis. She unwrapped the daguerreotype and laid it on Mrs Callinan's lap.

'My mother,' said the old lady, leaning forward and peering at the photograph. Edie saw her smile for the first time, a smile so minuscule it was as though a tiny pin-tuck had lifted the corners of her mouth. 'And my father. He died shortly after that picture was taken. Eliza – Miss Drury – was the last to go. She and my mother died within weeks of each other. They had become quite dependent upon each other in their old age, but I was married then, you understand, with responsibilities, and could not take them in. I was schoolmistress here in Doneraile for many years.' She looked up from the photograph and regarded Edie with a kind of challenge, as though defying her to doubt that an old lady such as she should ever have held a position of authority.

'I have met some of your old pupils,' said Edie. 'They speak of you with great affection.'

'I doubt *that*!' said Mrs Callinan, with a rusty laugh. 'Respect, perhaps, but hardly affection.'

'You taught them well. I have never seen such beautiful handwriting.'

'Of whom do you speak?'

'Seán the Post and Mrs Healy. They write in the same hand.'

'It was Miss Drury who taught me copperplate. She taught me to read and write when I was very small, and to appreciate art and philosophy. I was reading Voltaire when I was ten. We studied all the classics together. And of course, she taught me to speak French. *Parlez-vous français, mademoiselle?'*

'*Un peu.*'

'I spoke French continually with Eliza. She always made me call her Eliza, never Miss Drury. *J'étais une babillarde formidable!*' Mrs Callinan laughed again, and this time her laugh was that of a much younger woman, bell-like and rather flirtatious. She looked down at the photograph, and Edie saw her expression change. Suddenly she was grave again. 'You came for something, Miss . . . Miss Drury?'

'Chadwick. My name is Edie Chadwick.'

'Of course it is. And I am tired now. It is time for you to go. I have answered all your questions, I think. You came to find out about the history of the house, didn't you?'

'Yes.'

'Yes. Yes. There it is. I have it ready for you.' She nodded toward a large manila envelope that lay on the stool beside her. 'There it is,' she said again. 'Take it. Take that . . . thing. It has papers in it. Take it!'

Edie reached for the envelope. 'What is it?'

'I told you! It contains some writing of – of the woman of whom we were speaking. It was in the strongbox in which she kept her will. Have you had your tea?'

'Yes.'

'Then go.'

'May I do anything for you, Mrs Callinan? May I fetch you something before –'

'No! Go. Just go.'

Edie took a step towards the door. She felt dreadful, leaving the old lady all on her own. She owed it to her to be at least of some small service. She turned back to reiterate her offer of help, but Mrs Callinan had forgotten she was there. She was sitting hunched over the photograph, gazing at it.

Edie stepped out onto the front step and closed the door behind her. Mrs Healy was hovering by the garden gate.

'I guessed you wouldn't be long,' she said. 'Did you have any luck?'

'I don't know.'

'She was looking forward to a visit.'

'She was?' Edie sounded dubious.

'She always does. But then she gets confused and isn't able for it, and covers by being cantankerous.'

'She was very dignified,' said Edie.

'I'm glad. That would be the end for Martha, if she thought she was losing her dignity. That's the worst thing for us women – when the dignity goes. It's the only thing we have to cling onto, to remind us that we were once somebody.'

'I'd say Mrs Callinan was . . . formidable, in her time,' said Edie.

'She was. She can be, still. I'll go in to her now, and give her a hand.'

'That's neighbourly of you.'

'We mind each other hereabouts. Always have done, and – please God – always will. Good day to you, Miss Chadwick.'

'Good day, Mrs Healy.'

'Have a good trip back to London.'

'Thank you.'

Edie walked back to where she'd left her bicycle, on the main street of the village. When she reached it, she laid the manila envelope carefully in the wicker basket. Eliza's writings, Mrs Callinan had said. She thought she had read all of Eliza's story. Maybe this was the last chapter.

Sending a smile to Seán the Post who was cycling down Buttevant Road, Edie stepped down on the pedal of her bike and started off for Lissaguirra.

34

⟋ E. D. 1884

I AM LOOKING THROUGH the library window at the lake. The swans are there: they are not, of course, the same pair that glided across the water to greet us when Clara Venus and I arrived that November day decades ago, on a dray drawn by a donkey. There have been generations of swans at Lissaguirra since, and they have all mated for life – but for one pair whose union ended when the chicks were killed by a fox.

I remember very little about that time. From the moment I woke on the morning of the day Death came lurching into our lives, memory and nightmare are merged in one grotesque chimera. It was as if that day, and the days and weeks that followed, happened to someone else. I liken it to the parlour game called Consequences, where neither the beginning, middle nor end of the narrative makes sense. '*Eliza Drury* met *Jameson St Leger* in *a wood*. She said to him, *Where is my child?* He said to her, *I was after the fox.* And the consequence of the story was: *chaos, horror, madness.*'

They say I tried to dispatch St Leger with a knife, as Rochester's mad wife had done in Miss Brontë's novel: I used on him the knife I had never thought to use on one so dear. They say I tried to kill myself by walking into the lake. They say I nearly died of the fever I contracted – and of course I wished I had, because after Death took Clara Venus there was nothing to live for.

How fortunate was the poet Wordsworth, that the images that flashed upon his inward eye happened to be a field of beauteous daffodils! I wonder what he might have made of the images that ambush *my* inward eye, leaving me stunned and sick with shock. Sometimes I relive snatches of that evening: the frantic stumbling through the wood, the brambles that tugged at my hair and sleeves, the taste of blood from the lacerations on my face, the howls of anguish that tore my throat. St Leger slumped at the kitchen table, head upon his arms, the expanse of his broad shoulders, the grip of Young Biddy's fingers as she wrested the knife from me. The shingle beneath my bare feet, the heavy silk of the water, the weight of the stones in my pockets, the frigid, welcome embrace of the lake, Christy's strong arms as he carried me back to the house.

They bathed her and dressed her in a white

nightgown, and laid her on the dining-room table, with her face shrouded. It was cold, and her feet were bare. I asked where were the slippers with the daisies that she had worn that morning, but they had gone missing. They covered her with my cashmere shawl, under which I slipped the pair of little carved wolves that she had doted upon, the ones that she had called Romulus and Remus. I asked that they be put in the coffin with her.

I remembered her as I had last seen her, laughing, hair flying as St Leger spun her round. I will not forget that the last words I spoke to her were spoken in anger. I will not forget that her last words to me were, *Mama! Come back!*

If I had gone back, I would have taken her from her father's arms and carried her into the house. I would have dressed her in the clothes that William had given me before we left London, hand-me-downs from Annie and Minnie, but pretty garments nonetheless: a pinafore over a red wool dress and cream kid pumps, or half-boots and the hooded cape if we had designs on going out. We might have sat together by the fire in the library, where she had left her animals filing two-by-two into the ark. I might have given her paper to draw on while I wrote to William to thank him for his kindness. I might have read her a story from Grimm's Fairy Tales: 'Little Red Riding Hood' or 'Hansel and Gretel' or 'The Sleeping Beauty'. Whatever we had wound up doing, she would not have wandered into the woods alone.

In the six short years of my daughter's life she might have died a dozen ways: she might have been poisoned by the laburnum tree that I was foolish enough to have planted; she might have drowned in that part of the lake where treacherous weeds grew; she might have succumbed to starvation, or to one of the numerous diseases that raged rampant in Ireland during the years of the potato famine; she might have suffered any of the fates doled out by Mr Dickens to his juveniles, for a huge percentage of children in those days did not reach the age of five. So, yes, it surprises me still when I find myself writing the words: Clara Venus died at the hand of her father.

St Leger did not know that she had gone back into the wood. He had been careless, she had surprised him, the gun had gone off. Clara Venus had died instantly, shot through that sweet place where the pulse beat, just below the left ear.

She was buried in the graveyard of the little church in Doneraile. Only three people attended the funeral: St Leger, Christy and Young Biddy. Old Biddy stayed at home to mind me and to negotiate with Death. I begged him to take me. I promised that if he let me join Clara Venus I would be his worshipful and devoted handmaiden for ever. But Old Biddy thwarted me. I saw the pair of them muttering together hugger-mugger at the foot of the bed: the parley went on for weeks, I am told, until Death finally found Old Biddy's haranguing so wearisome that he stalked off and went elsewhere. God knows, he had plenty of people to call upon in Ireland at that time, and as I write this, I realize that most of the dramatis personae who played a part in this tale are dead.

I never met William again. He wrote to me, of course, but as his reputation as a literary colossus grew, so his letters became less frequent. He arranged for money to be sent to me on a regular basis, in recognition of my contribution to the book that had made him famous. We could not decide whether this payment – which I was not inclined to refuse and which I invested prudently – should be designated an 'honorarium' or a 'stipend'. I favoured the word 'emolument', for Johnson's *Dictionary* told me the word came from the Latin *'emolere*: to grind out' – an emolument being originally a fee paid to a miller. This, of course, put me in mind of *Rumpelstiltskin*, the tale of the miller's daughter who spun corn into gold, and I wrote to William to tell him so. William declared that my aperçu made him laugh heartily, for *Vanity Fair* made him a fortune. I don't think he quite got the joke.

He sent me a copy of the novel when it finally appeared in a bound edition, but I did not open it until after his death, and by then it was too late to voice my reservations. I did not like what became of Becky Sharp (stuck in Bath, doing charity work!), and I thought the character of Dobbin (whom William had clearly modelled on an ideal version of himself) insufferably smug.

Who else has died? Old Biddy – unsurprisingly – died of old age. Christy died of septicaemia. Both the O'Dowds died of drink (I heard it from Mrs Grove-White who forgave me for slapping her across the face, because she was a Christian). Maria died after a fall from a balcony in Venice; her sister died in a coach accident. Sir Silas Sillery died of syphilis.

Young Biddy (who is no longer so very young) and I are the only survivors of this dirgeful tale; apart from Isabella Thackeray, who, I understand, is still immured with her gaolers. Since poor Isabella had invested so much time and energy in doing away with herself, the notion that she is likely to outlive us all is a *beau idéal* of irony.

But there is one major player left alive withal. It was his unlooked-for return to Lissaguirra that inspired me to resurrect this manuscript, and to write an epilogue to it.

People seldom come here. Lissaguirra has always remained off the beaten track, and Young Biddy and I prefer it that way. Those few who have sought out these heavenly hunting grounds with any view to a sojourn have been sent unceremoniously packing.

I was taking my constitutional one afternoon as usual, in the woods. I walked there most days even though I had never acquired a dog: Young Biddy's daughter, Martha, had begged me to get one, but I did not care to become too emotionally attached to any creature.

The sound of hooves on the bridle path made me stop dead. Between the trees I discerned that the approaching animal was a chestnut hunter, ridden by a gentleman whom I can only describe as . . . equally thoroughbred. His appearance was sleek, yet he had about him an untamed air. The symmetry of the bones beneath the wind-burnt face recalled to me a painting my father had made of the Greek hero Achilles. He sat astride with that easy grace peculiar to men who have practised those arts essential to true manliness – boxing, riding and dancing.

As he drew nearer I felt as though he had just taken hold of my heart and tugged it. After thirty-five years I knew him, even though we were barely on nodding acquaintance. I may have dropped a cursory farewell kiss on his fuzzy head the night I gave birth to him, as he lay on my wolfskin wrapped up like a parcel and ready to be delivered to Sophia St Leger, but we had not exchanged so much as a pleasantry before he had been spirited away.

As my son approached, I stepped forward and said, 'Good afternoon, sir.'

'What the *deuce*!' Reining in his horse, George St Leger recovered with an effort. Then he dismounted, doffed his hat and said, 'Madam, I beg your pardon. You startled me.'

I am sure I did startle him. For a moment as he had approached, I had thought myself a girl again, and had, accordingly, adopted the demeanour of a much younger woman. Poor George! I have to laugh now, when I think of it. I was wearing the walking costume that Jameson had bought for me in Dublin and carrying a switch of stripped hazel. The costume fitted me still, but was distinctly outmoded with its bell-shaped skirts and open sleeves, and because I wore it to tramp out in all weathers, it was dark around the hem with dried mud. I rarely bothered with a bonnet or a parasol, so my face was brown and weathered from the sun, I wore my hair (which had grown quite silver) loose about my shoulders, and when it blew about too much I simply made a rope of it and looped it through my belt. Altogether I resembled some old woman of the roads. And yet I advanced towards the unfortunate fellow as though I expected him to kiss my hand and lead me onto a dance floor!

'You are St Leger, are you not?' I said, deciding there and then to dispense with formalities.

'Yes, madam. I am pleased to make your acquaintance. I – '

'You must come home with me at once and have

tea. My house is not half a mile down the track.'

'That is indeed where I was heading, madam. I – '

'My name is Miss Drury, but if it does not make you uncomfortable, I should prefer if you called me Eliza.'

He actually did look rather uncomfortable, but since he had clearly deduced that I was a deranged crone, he sportingly acceded with a 'Very well,' and took the hand I proffered.

I was glad to see that he had a good, firm grasp. It was an honest handshake, and now that I looked more closely at him, I saw that he had candid eyes. Honesty and candour! I wondered from whom he had inherited *those* attributes.

'You are a lord now, I suppose?' I said, as we started off along the path.

'Yes, I am.'

'What is your full title?'

'Duke of Roesworth and Marquess of Cholyngham.'

I laughed. 'La-di-da! And what Christian names have you?' Jamey had listed them for me once, but I had forgotten them.

'George Frederick James Richard Patrick Charles.'

'Goodness! What a mouthful. Which do you prefer?'

'Patrick, because my father was Irish. But I'm stuck with George, after my maternal grandfather.'

I wondered what he would have thought of his real grandfather's name, which was Ignatius Drury. I tucked the corners of my mouth into a smile and slashed idly with the hazel switch at a clump of nettles growing by the side of the path.

'I knew your father, a long time ago.' This was where I should have to tread carefully.

'He spoke very fondly of this part of the world. That is why I've come here. I had hoped to visit the house, but it's in such a state of disrepair that there is nothing left to see.'

'Dromomore? It was a fine house once.'

'Were you ever there?'

'No. But I knew of it. Many splendid houses fell into dereliction in the first half of the century, when the aristocracy abandoned them.'

Out of the corner of my eye, I saw George stiffen.

'I know your father had no choice but to leave,' I hastened to add. 'Since he was posted overseas. To the Punjab, wasn't it?'

'Yes.'

'Did you and your mother join him there?'

'No. He died at the Battle of Gujrat in '49.'

'I'm sorry.'

Of course, I knew that St Leger had died. But he had not died in an obscure war waged on behalf of the East India Company. That was a story put about by custodians of Roesworth family history. I had heard from Maria that he had been killed in a brawl in Lahore. I glanced up at George's face, stamped with his father's heroic Greek profile, and thought again how ignoble a demise it had been. It would perhaps have been more fitting if he had died by my hand, when I had tried to kill him the night our daughter lay stretched out in the dining room, her face covered with a damask napkin.

'Are you unwell?'

George's voice brought me back from the image of St Leger weeping at the kitchen table, the pitiful hunch of his broad shoulders, the grip of Young Biddy's fingers as she wrested the knife from me . . .

'No. I beg your pardon. I am a mad old woman, so I tend to wander off in my mind from time to time. Now, tell me all about you. What brings you here?'

George looked at me cautiously, as though gauging how much a madwoman might remember of what he had already told me. 'Well, my father was born not far from –'

'No, no! I mean, what brought you *here*, to Lissaguirra.'

'I have heard that there is excellent fishing to be had.'

'And who might have told you that? A poacher?'

He smiled apologetically. 'Yes. I heard it at the inn in Doneraile.'

'I am glad to know it. Poachers I tolerate. Those chaps who come with a view to mounting their swag in a glass case I do not. I have the lease of these fishings, and I will gladly allow you to fish here if you swear to me that you will never have your catch stuffed and hung on your wall as a trophy.'

'That's an easy oath to make.'

'Good man. Here we are. This is my house.'

I looked at him as he led his horse out of the wood onto the greensward.

'This is a fine place,' he said, gazing as stout Cortez might have done on viewing the Pacific. 'This is splendid!'

'Isn't it? I designed it myself. Once upon a time it was a ramshackle bothy, but I knew it had potential.'

The French windows to the library lay open. I knew that Young Biddy would have been anticipating my arrival, and would have set out the tea things. After all these years, she still clung to the shreds of refinement that the ritual conjured.

'I shall ask my housekeeper to lay another place. Tether your horse there, outside the window. That way you can feed him sugar lumps.'

George looped the bridle over the handle of one of the stone jardinières that I had bought decades ago when I was fitting out my house. No geraniums grew there now. Ox-eye daisies had seeded themselves, and I encouraged them to grow in profusion.

I stepped from the terrace into the library, and for

the first time in years I allowed myself to see the room through the eyes of a stranger. There was clutter every-where – books and manuscripts and memoranda, newspaper clippings and diaries and heaps of corres-pondence. It was not unlike an illustration from Dickens's *Old Curiosity Shop*. But there was method in my madness, and the library made sense to me, for it had been arranged with the precision of an ordnance surveyor, to accommodate my own idiosyncratic filing system.

'Forgive the disorder,' I said. 'I do not allow Young Biddy to disturb my things.' I had come across her one day, surreptitiously trying to cull my papers, and I knew she occasionally helped herself to them when we were short of kindling to light the fire. She was also on a per-petual mission to get rid of things belonging to me that were not to her taste, or things that she hated having to dust. She had always had an aversion to the wolfskin rug Jamey had given me, she loathed the climbing monkey that he had won for me at a funfair in Dublin, and she had thrown out the heart-shaped pebble that William had presented to me on his last day at Lissaguirra, because it was 'just a stone'. And wasn't she right? Some say the heart is just like a stone.

But George seemed unperturbed by the clutter. 'I should love a room like this,' he remarked, allowing his eyes to travel over the accumulation of *objets trouvés*. 'A room of my own in which to seed my own private chaos.'

'Don't you have any number of rooms of your own at Roesworth House?'

'Not with a view like this.'

'Make yourself comfortable,' I said, hefting the manuscript of one of my novels off the seat of a rush-bottomed chair. 'I shall tell Young Biddy that we have a guest for tea. She will be overjoyed.'

Young Biddy was not overjoyed when I told her that George, Duke of Roesworth and Marquess of Cholyngham was in the library. She went into a flap and hurried into the pantry to dust down the best china, bemoaning the fact that she had had no time to bake.

'Do griddle cakes,' I said.

'Griddle cakes!' she said with scorn. 'Griddle cakes are so passé.'

Biddy had been given a present of *Mrs Beeton's Book of Household Management* by her daughter, and spent hours poring over it, making corrections. The pages were covered in marginalia written in her neat, girlish handwriting, such as *1/2 lb of suet = far too much!* or *Isabella Beeton is a fool!*

I hung my shawl on the hook by the kitchen door and went back to the library, leaving Biddy to her conniptions. George was standing with his back to me, looking out over the lake where the swans sailed serenely, followed by a trail of cygnets.

'They will chase their babies away in a few weeks,'

I told him. 'They like to have the lake to themselves.'

'How lucky you are to live here.'

I made a noncommittal hmm-ing sound. Since I had only just met the man, it would be churlish to dispute the remark.

'It is a perfect place for a writer,' he continued.

'How do you know I am a writer?'

'I guessed.' He gestured at my desk, where a half-finished manuscript sat alongside my pens, the silver-gilt inkwell I had bragged to William about, and the mother-of-pearl blotting book that Jameson had bought me many years previously in a swanky stationery shop in Dublin.

'What are you writing?'

'Rubbish. I have had manuscripts rejected by every publisher in London.'

'Oh. I am sorry to hear it.'

'Not as sorry as I am to say it. My head is full of stories, but I don't seem able to express them in the way Messrs Chapman and Hall would like me to.'

'Who are Chapman and Hall?'

'The men who publish Dickens and Thackeray. And that simpering sap Elizabeth Barrett Browning. Have you read *Aurora Leigh*?'

'No.'

'Well, don't. And don't bother with *The Pickwick Papers* either. It is not Mr Dickens's best effort.'

'I am a great admirer of Mr Thackeray.'

I laughed shortly. 'Pah! William was a frightful plagiarist. Oh, here is Young Biddy.'

Young Biddy stumped into the room and dropped a curtsey, which must have been painful on her poor old knees.

'Begging your pardon, ma'am,' she said (she *never* called me 'ma'am' nor 'begged my pardon' these days). 'We are out of whiskey. Will you have rum in your tea instead?'

'Oh, rum will do nicely, thank you, Bridget,' I said with exaggerated *politesse*.

'And I'm sorry to say that there has been a run on Bermuda arrowroot in Mr Shinnors's shop, so I have not been able to bake your favourite Snow Cake. Will griddle cakes do you?'

'Griddle cakes! I love 'em!' said George.

She shot him a grateful look, and stumped out again.

'Young Biddy has been with me since I first came to live here,' I said. 'For many years her daughter, Martha, lived with us, too. But she is married now, and headmistress now of the school in Doneraile. She is a bright and beautiful creature of whom we are both inordinately proud. Here she is, as a girl.'

I showed him a daguerreotype that I had had framed and hung on the wall. It had been made two decades ago by a journeying photographer, who had put us standing stiffly on the terrace beyond the French windows: Christy and Young Biddy and Martha in a gingham pinafore, and me. George looked at it with an expression of polite interest. Manners precluded him from asking questions about the domestic set-up, and me from boring him with answers – even though I could have sung songs of praise to kingdom come and back about the people grouped around me in the photograph, for they had saved my life.

In the years since Old Biddy and Christy had died, a retinue of housemaids and manservants had succeeded them, but not one had matched those two in loyalty or affection, and when a kitchen maid from Carrigtwohill had scarpered with the few trinkets I owned (most had been presents from St Leger), Young Biddy and I had decided that we would manage very well without live-in staff. Families were putting down roots again in the vicinity, and I was glad to be able to provide the newcomers with ad hoc work.

I saw George's eyes go to the display case, saw his brow furrow as he contemplated the treasures contained therein: the drawing titled 'Mama, Papa and Clara Venus in the Woods'; the baby shoe; the double miniature that Jamey had commissioned of himself and Clara as an infant, that had been modelled on a portrait of her baby brother.

'Family mementos,' I said airily. 'What a sentimental old fool I am to keep them!'

He looked at me curiously. 'Who is Clara Venus?'

For a heady moment I longed to be audacious, and tell him the truth: that Clara Venus was his twin sister, and I, his natural mother. Instead I said, 'Clara Venus is a ghost. A glimmer child.'

George looked nonplussed by this non-sequitur. How liberating it felt to be a dotty old lady! I could say whatever I wished without anyone challenging the veracity of my pronouncements.

'Do you have any children?' I asked.

'Yes. I have three girls. Georgiana, Beatrice and Florence.'

'And your wife's name is . . .?' I had heard he had married some *contessa* whom he had met on his Grand Tour.

'Consolata. She is Italian.'

'Is she beautiful?'

'I think so.'

'Three children is perfect. Mrs Dickens had to endure ten.'

I wondered if poor Consolata would be obliged to endure more pregnancies in order to produce a male heir. I wondered if the title and the estate would revert, in the absence of a boy, to some male cousin, as once it would have reverted to that syphilitic halfwit, Silas

Sillery. And for the first time, I wondered what would happen to Lissaguirra when I died. I had not made a will, and it was about time I did. I had thought of leaving the house to Martha, but she would not care to live here, and the place would end up being sold to the kind of person who would have their fish stuffed and mounted in glass cases instead of eating them.

'Where are you staying?' I asked George abruptly.

'I have taken a room at the inn in Doneraile.'

'You surprise me. I should have thought a coaching inn rather déclassé for a duke.'

'I am not particular.'

'Then come and stay with me,' I said.

He looked so startled that I almost laughed.

'Why look so flabbergasted? It makes sense. You want to fish in my lake, why shouldn't you stay in my house?'

'It is most generous of you, Miss – '

'Eliza.'

'Eliza, but – '

'Listen to me, George St Leger. If you will not do me the honour of staying here as my guest, I shall not grant you permission to take my fish. *C'est la règle du jeu.*'

He went to protest again, but I made a baroque gesture of indifference and said, 'Fa la la! Do what you like. It makes no odds to me.'

He must have seen the yearning behind my affected nonchalance, because he smiled and said, 'The honour will be all mine.'

'In that case, I shall ask Young Biddy to prepare a room for you. Ah, here she is with the tea.'

The tray had been set with the Chinese porcelain I had not laid eyes on for over thirty years. How pretty it was! I had forgotten all about it, and I resolved there and then that we should use it every day from then on, for what was the point of it gathering dust in a cupboard?

I turned to George. 'Do I refer to you as his His Grace?'

'Please don't.'

'Lord Roesworth will be staying for a few days, Bridget.'

Young Biddy looked both alarmed and animated at the news.

'You might want to consult the fish department of Mrs Beeton,' I continued. 'We shall be having salmon for dinner tomorrow.'

Setting down the tea tray, Young Biddy gave me an inscrutable look. 'Salmon à la Genevese. Without the essence of anchovies. Mrs Beeton does tend to be over-zealous with the anchovies.' She moved to the door, turned, and 'bobbed' a curtsey. 'I'll make up the Blue Room, so,' she said.

*

George stayed for three days and three nights. Every morning young Biddy wrapped bread and cheese in oiled paper for him before he set out, and every evening he came back with the pick of the day's catch for her.

I spent the mornings sorting through my papers, trying to make some sense of this chronicle, the most recent instalment of which – if it has not been destroyed – you are holding in your hands. The whole was put together with the help of sundry journals I kept while I was an articled pupil at Miss Pinkerton's academy, and thereafter right up until the death of Clara Venus. When she died, I no longer had any inclination to keep a journal. It was not until the demise of poor William that I re-embarked upon my inchoate career as a lady novelist. By then St Leger was dead, too, of course, and it seemed a fitting time to tell our story at last. That's an imperative, I think, one of the most pressing imperatives in life: to want a story for oneself, even though life alone should be enough. But it never is, is it? We feel compelled to record it in word or in image, to leave behind some tangible evidence that we were here once, that we lived and breathed and laughed and cried and suffered and celebrated and mattered, in some small way.

I knew that no reputable publishing house would touch the manuscript on account of the scandal it would generate, and I did not wish to falsify the story, or present it in a sugar coating, because that would be to compromise its worth. So I did not send it to Messrs Chapman and Hall. I sent them other, invented stories. But somehow those fictions seemed pallid in comparison to my story, no matter how I tried to embellish them. No glimmer child that I conjured could move me in the way that Clara Venus had moved me, no anti-hero rouse me to such passions as St Leger, no archimime inspire me as William had inspired me, no soubrette make me laugh as Maria had.

As I write this, I remember an evening spent in her apartment in the house on Grattan Hill, when we had sat together at her out-of-tune piano and made up songs about the snobs who paraded the Mall in Cork. I remember how we laughed and laughed until the tears rolled down our cheeks as we composed verses such as the following:

> *Among those whom we love to pillory*
> *Is sibilant Sir Silas Sillery.*
> *When holding forth with unstopped throttle*
> *His spit's enough to fill a bottle.*
> *A gag on him! Go let him dribble*
> *On the phlegmatic Lady Sybil.*

So it is with proprietorial fondness that I look upon the reams of paper upon which I have penned the tens of thousands of words that constitute my story. For me this memoir is a treasure chest as precious as the album of keepsakes to which Isabella Thackeray was so attached, the one in which she pasted picture-sheet characters from fairy tales.

The story will be over soon. But before I let it go, let me tell you of the pleasure that three days in the company of my son afforded me. Every evening he would come home and change for dinner into the clothes that his valet had packed for him (the valet remained in the inn in Doneraile – I wanted no liveried servants in my house). I too dressed for dinner. Young Biddy redeemed from the camphor-wood chest the finery that had been acquired for me by the two men whom I had loved: the dress edged in Venise lace, the cinnabar-red velvet, the dark green silk damask.

Ah! *Vanitas Vanitatum!* But it made me feel happy to do it, and – as I have already said (and William, more famously, after me) – which of us is happy in this world? Which of us has his desire? Or, having it, is satisfied?

During those three days Young Biddy was as animated as I have ever seen her. She spent the best part of an hour each morning bragging to George, as she stirred his porridge, about Martha the prodigy, singing the praises of her beautiful daughter – who had, for the most part, been schooled at home. You will remember that St Leger once said that Clara Venus would learn more from me than from any schoolteacher in the entire county of Cork? Well, I had not been given the chance to educate my daughter. But I had been given Martha Callinan, née Cassidy.

As well as regaling George with tales of her daughter's brains and beauty, Young Biddy was delighted to have the opportunity to put upon the dining table not only Salmon à la Genevese, but Trout with Caper Sauce and Stuffed Baked Bream. I came upon her the day after George departed, happily scribbling contumely beside a picture of a cod's head on page 174 of Mrs Beeton.

If George thought it peculiar to dine with an elderly lady dressed like something out of *Pippa Passes*, he did not show it by his behaviour. He was courteous, witty, thoughtful and engaging, and I felt very proud that he was my son. Huzzah for Sophia St Leger! She deserved to enjoy every hour of her gilded widowhood in the Dower House of the Roesworth estate, for she had raised a perfect gentleman; I am not so deluded as to imagine that George would have flourished half so well under my aegis.

On the morning of the fourth day, he left. I was sorry that I had nothing to give him; no Pautrot bronze or engraved silver penknife or other manly gewgaw to remember me by. I searched the house to see if I might perhaps find something that had once belonged to his father – a snuffbox or a half-hunter or other such trinket – but there was no trace left of St Leger's paraphernalia.

From my dressing-room window, I watched as he harnessed his horse. Young Biddy was standing by with several packets of oiled paper, one of which doubtless contained half the Pavini cake that she had baked last night especially for him. I could not let him go without some memento!

As I turned away from the window, my eyes fell upon the pelt that St Leger had given me, taken from the wolf that he had claimed to have dispatched himself even though the animals were long extinct. I dragged it off the ottoman at the foot of the bed, and hurried downstairs and out into the courtyard.

George had mounted his horse. 'Here!' I said, thrusting it at him. 'Here is a present for you!'

Dust motes went spinning into the air as he took it and looked at it uncertainly.

'Is it a wolfskin?' he said.

'Yes. It's to take home, and wrap your Baby Buntings in.'

'Thank you very much,' he said in the diplomatic tones of a man humouring a *zanni*.

'Wrap them carefully.'

'I will.'

He rolled the pelt up, and stuffed it into his saddlebag. He would never know it, but it was probably the most apropos hand-me-down he had ever been given.

That night, I wrote my will. I left all dividends from my investments to Young Biddy. If she should predecease me, they will go to Martha.

As for my personal things – my papers, notebooks, my unpublished novels – I imagine they will end up where they deserve to: on a bonfire of the vanities. How strange to think that once I was arrogant enough to believe that I could make a living as a lady novelist; how, when I failed, it was so convenient to blame the baby carriage in the hall.

'Great geniuses now in petticoats . . . shall write novels for the beloved reader's children,' William wrote in *Vanity Fair*. 'Twas a fond fancy; still, it gives me comfort to conjecture that one hundred years from now geniuses in petticoats will outnumber those in breeches.

But just because *my* play is played out, don't think that by putting the cap on my pen I am shutting the lid on the cardboard theatre. I will end this chronicle with a flourish – by telling you that I left the house and its happy hunting grounds to George, Duke of Roesworth and Marquess of Cholyngham. Bravo!

I don't know what will become of Lissaguirra. But I would like to think that as long as these walls stand, there will be no trophy hunters living here. As I sit looking out over the lake, I think of the houses I've heard tell of over the course of my life that have been crammed *cap à pie* with accumulated treasures: old masters, statuary, gold plate, antiquities. Great houses in great cities, all intended as display cases for the accumulated wealth of their owners. I never could understand how anybody could be happy living in such places. I never could understand what it all meant. Because as long as Clara Venus was alive she was all the treasure I could ever hope for.

The swans have re-emerged from the rushes. Perhaps, in years to come, somebody will sit upon this window seat and watch another pair glide past on the water. I like to think that some day someone will be happy here. I like to think that some day, there will be another heartbeat in this house.

35

EDIE HAD NO choice but to take Milo with her. Every time she shut the kitchen door behind her, he set up a wailing so plaintive and sustained that she thought his tiny lungs would burst.

'This is the second time you've gone out today without me!' he sobbed. So, by shortening his lead and securing it to the wicker carrier on the bicycle, she strapped him in as one might strap a baby into a pram. Milo looked surprised and not a little resentful, but he soon settled down and seemed to enjoy the ride, his small ears buffeting in the breeze as they set off down the hill.

As she pedalled along between hedgerows with her little dog in the basket and the wind in her hair, Edie wondered if she might come back some day and spend more time exploring these environs; perhaps she could persuade Ian to come with her?

Once Jeremy and Iseult Darling were ensconced in Lissaguirra with their baby – their darling baby! – she and

Ian could come here on a fishing holiday. Or – if Ian wasn't taken with the idea of fishing – they could hire a car and follow the route taken by Thackeray up to the north or along the western coast, of which he had written, *'It forms an event in one's life to have seen that place, so beautiful is it, and so unlike all other beauties that I know of . . .'*

Down towards the crossroads Edie bowled: past fields that were full of gambolling lambs and their stoic, ruminant mothers; past neat homesteads with washing dancing on the lines and bold-eyed, snotty-nosed children at play, and past cows being herded off to the milking parlour across a landscape that had once been a blasted wasteland. It had all the appearance of an idyll, a scene Wordsworth might have penned paeans to, or Constable immortalized in oil on canvas. But Edie knew that if you took hold of a corner of this arcadian backdrop and pulled, the layers beneath would tell a very different story. She wondered how these people had come through, how they had struggled out of the graves that had been dug for them not a century before, the voices of their ancestors urging them on, exhorting, hectoring, imploring them to push forward towards a new, independent future.

She finally came to a stop outside the telephone box, which stood incongruously between a fairy thorn and a well dedicated to Saint Brigid. Unstrapping Milo from his basket, she let him off the lead and warned him not to go adventuring without her.

'A sheep might get you,' she said.

'I don't care!' said Milo, chasing his tail. 'I will charm any sheep.'

Inside the phone box the paintwork was scratched with graffiti. It was mild, inoffensive stuff compared to the hieroglyphics that Edie perused at Gloucester Road tube station most mornings. *Ciarán loves Kitty*, read one manifesto; *Up the Republic!* another.

Because she did not have enough change to make a trunk call, Edie asked the operator if the other party would accept the charges. A minute or two later, she was put through to Mr Byard at Heinemann Publishers. She imagined him sitting at his desk in the office in Covent Garden, surrounded by manuscripts and in a fug of cigar smoke, red pencil behind his ear, galley proofs spread in front of him.

'Edie! What a surprise. I infer from the operator's accent that you're still in Ireland?'

'Yes.'

'Have you had a good break?'

'Yes, thank you. But I'm coming home tomorrow. And I'm afraid I didn't get around to doing any copy-editing whatsoever.'

'Never mind. You needed the time off.'

'But I'll be back in work on Monday.'

'Splendid! We're rather snowed under with manuscripts, I'm afraid.'

'I have another one for you.'

Mr Byard gave a tiny sigh. 'Unsolicited?'

'Yes. Well, no, in a way.'

'Either you asked to see this manuscript or you didn't, Edie.'

'I didn't ask to see it – it presented itself to me. But it was almost as if it was meant to come my way, as if it had been waiting for me to find it.'

Mr Byard's next sigh was rather more world-weary.

'Did you write it yourself?'

'No!'

'Very well. I'll have a look. Is it fiction?'

'No.'

'In that case, is it libellous?'

Edie thought of the individuals who had played the more nefarious roles in Eliza's narrative; the family secrets that had been unearthed; the political misdeeds that had been connived at, or edited out of an entire generation of history books.

'Not any more,' she said. 'You can't libel the dead. It was written nearly a hundred years ago.'

'Does it have a title?'

'No.'

Mr Byard's sigh was lugubrious this time.

'I could make one up for you,' Edie suggested. 'It's a first-person narrative . . . How about *Eliza Drury*?'

'No. I'm going to be giving eponymous heroines a wide

berth. Daphne du Maurier's new novel will generate a devil's spawn of copycat titles next year.'

'What's it called?'

'*Rebecca*.'

'What's it about?'

'An old house haunted by a dead woman, and a young woman who finds –'

The pips went, and the operator enquired whether they wished to extend the call.

'No, thank you,' Edie told her, feeling rather relieved not to have to hear any more about Daphne du Maurier's new novel. She didn't want any charges of plagiarism being levelled at *her*. 'I'll see you on Monday, Mr Byard.'

'I look forward to it. Goodbye, Edie.'

'Goodbye.'

Rebecca. The name would lend itself to a striking jacket design: it was wrong what they said about not judging a book by its cover – the cover of a book was important. She wondered if Hilly had known about this new novel of Miss du Maurier's; if she had perhaps seen an outline, or even a first draft.

If Hilly were still alive, Edie knew, they would be comrades withal. They would sit together over tea and cakes in Valerie's Patisserie and swap stories about their forthcoming projects; Edie pleased as punch for her friend's success, Hilly listening eagerly as Edie related the story of the remarkable manuscript she had uncovered. She could hear

Hilly now – her delighted laugh, and her voice saying, *It looks as though you might have found your bestseller, Edie!*

Edie stood deep in thought for a moment. Then she took from her satchel the clover-bowed house key of Lissaguirra Lodge and – locating a patch of pristine paint beneath the telephone – she scratched on it the following: *Edie & Hilly For Ever*. It might not be as artistic as the wreath of oak leaves and the ace of spades that Eliza had had carved on the shutter in her house, but it had totemic significance all the same. Maybe a hundred years hence someone making a phone call would spot it, and wonder who Edie and Hilly might have been.

She opened the door of the telephone box to find Milo doing his wees up against the stone that marked the holy well.

'Milo! That's very disrespectful,' she chided.

'I'm no angel,' said Milo.

'That's for sure.'

Edie waited for him to finish, then dumped him back in the basket, and fastened his baby harness.

'Imagine Mr Byard asking me for a title,' she said sniffily as she pulled on her beret. 'A title's the last thing he should be concerned with. You'd have thought he might have shown rather more interest in the author.'

She wheeled the bike away from the verge and pushed off, wobbling between the potholes that pockmarked the road.

'You are a dunce, Edie,' said Milo. 'The book already has a title.'

'Oh, really Mr Clever Clogs? What is it, prithee?'

'La la la,' sang Milo.

'Oh, come on! Tell me.'

Milo turned to Edie and smiled in such an insufferably superior way that Edie wanted to hit him a dig.

'Haven't you guessed?' the little dog said. 'It's called *Another Heartbeat in the House*.'

THE END

ANOTHER HEARTBEAT
IN THE HOUSE

The Story Behind The Story

Home is a name, a word, it is a strong one; stronger than magician ever spoke, or spirit ever answered to, in the strongest conjuration. *Charles Dickens*

HAVE YOU EVER seen a house and thought: *this is the one?* I don't mean a house you might aspire to buy, or one you wish you had bought, or one you could never, ever afford and can only fantasize about. I mean one that takes you by surprise, that fills you with powerful, complex feelings: a sense of loss, a sense of belonging – even a sense of déjà vu. One that seems to reverberate with an echo of memories you never knew you had: the walls, the window-panes, even the silence speaks.

Such houses are generally empty, waiting for someone to inhabit them; like rescue dogs, they have been loved once and yearn to be loved again. Ireland is full of them, from mansions to the meanest cottages: erstwhile homes that retain some essence of the people who lived there, and have been abandoned for reasons – financial, geographical, political or personal – about which we can only speculate.

The heartbeat of this book is such a place: a house that lives and breathes, as many of the characters who populate the pages once did. I came upon it by accident one day whilst driving in a remote and outstandingly beautiful tract of countryside. On rounding a bend in the road I saw first a lake, then a stone-built pier, then the house. The style was Georgian, I guessed, or early Victorian: two-storeyed, six-bayed, it reclined at the top of a grassy slope, gazing over the water at the blue hills beyond. It was unoccupied, and it was for sale. It was love at first sight.

I asked an historian friend to do some sleuthing, but there was scant information available. All census and Land Registry documentation had been destroyed in the National Archive when the Four Courts in Dublin was set alight during the Irish Civil War. The Ordnance Survey records of 1838 showed that a dwelling had been extant: it had been restructured shortly thereafter into a sizeable house, which was known to have been let as a hunting lodge from the late 1800s.

My friend came up with two significant results. One was a valuation report dating back to 1891, on which the following observation had been written in a clerk's neat hand: 'House vacated furnished. Value reduced one half for extreme remoteness of situation: dwelling is approached by a bridle path 1/2 mile away from a very bad road.'

The second was a personal narrative written in 1927 by a Dr Crowley, a Dublin surgeon who had taken a long lease on the property, then owned by an absentee English landlord. Dr Crowley was clearly a keen fisherman, remarking: *The fishing was superb (perhaps too easy)! We had over three hundred trout – white and brown – in the larder, and had difficulty in giving them away*. But what interested me more was his chronicle of the lodge, which read as follows:

> In the first half of the 19th century the region was the haunt of sportsmen who enjoyed the excellent shooting and fishing that were to be had thereabouts. However, the necessity of travelling thither from their estates morning and evening over bad roads, either on horseback or by pony and trap, curtailed their hours of sport in summer and ruled it out altogether in winter.
>
> One day, one of the gentlemen suggested that they would glean more enjoyment from the hunting if they had a cabin where they could stable their horses, kennel their dogs, and eat and sleep without the effort of the tiresome daily journey. All readily agreed that it was a good idea and should be adopted – but where to site the cabin was hotly disputed. Eventually one of the ghillies suggested that they leave the site to chance – 'where the next hare got up.' This was agreed to, and the next hare got up where the lodge now stands.

The original building was a long narrow cabin that ran diagonally to the river. The construction had a flagged floor, stone and mortar walls and thatched roof, which suited the requirements of young men who needed no more than a dry bed and a hot meal. Over the ensuing years it was extended: a second storey was added and a series of six bay windows put in. The result was a hunting lodge in the French style, of pleasingly simple proportions, planted in an Arcadian idyll.

When I happened upon the lodge, it had been converted into a youth hostel. But since the adjacent river had burst its banks – causing landslides and flooding – it had fallen into a sorry state, and had lain for some years disused and derelict. Inside, the once spacious rooms had been converted into dormitories and partitioned by plasterboard walls. Many of the floorboards were rotting; the smooth marble of the mantelshelves was chipped and broken; windows were boarded up, there was damp everywhere. Along the hallway, the great hooks were still in place that had once supported heavy fishing rods; beyond the French windows there was evidence of the limestone slabs that had formed the parterre, and on one of the shutters in the former drawing room the initials '*E. D.*' had been carved.

I longed to buy it. I dreamed of rehabilitating it, of transforming it into a writers' retreat or an auberge for hillwalkers; but even if I could raise enough for a deposit, it would cost a small fortune to replace the roof, the windows, the floors, the heating and the plumbing. There was no way I could afford to resuscitate the faltering heartbeat of the house.

I felt sorry for it: its history had been obscured for over half a century, the valuer had disparaged and underrated it, an online review by hostelz.com had described it as 'shabby chic at best' and bemoaned the fact that there was 'no television, no internet, no nothing . . .'

But its isolation was integral to its beauty. After visiting it on half a dozen occasions and falling ever more deeply in love, I decided that if I couldn't breathe new life into the house, I could at least give it a story. What, I wondered, might have happened in the half-century between the Ordnance Survey report of 1838 and the bargain-basement valuation of 1891?

I set to work. I knew that William Thackeray had travelled extensively in the region when he was writing his *Irish Sketch-Book* in the early 1840s. I knew that he had visited Ireland two years previously in an attempt to reunite his poor deranged wife with her mother and sister. I also knew that in 1847 – the year *Vanity Fair* was published – Thackeray had engaged for his daughters a governess who had lived with them in their home in Kensington for several months. Her name was Eliza Drury. *E. D.*!

A narrative started to take shape. In my imagination, E.D. was clever, audacious and beguiling. She was an adventuress, a prototype feminist. She recalled to me Becky Sharp, the heroine of Thackeray's most famous novel. And when she and her modern-day counterpart Edie Chadwick – accompanied by a little dog – danced into my head, when Jameson St Leger strolled in with a roguish smile, and when two women – both called Biddy – were enlisted to house-keep, some sixth sense, some providential sprite, told me that the house had a story to tell, and that its heart had started to beat again.

You can find images of the house and some of Eliza and Edie's friends by visiting
www.pinterest.com/heartbeathouse/

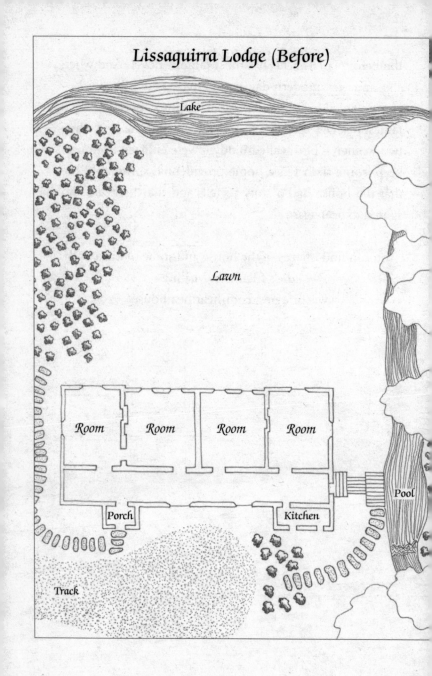

Lissaguirra Lodge (Before)

Lake

Lawn

Room

Room

Room

Room

Porch

Kitchen

Pool

Track

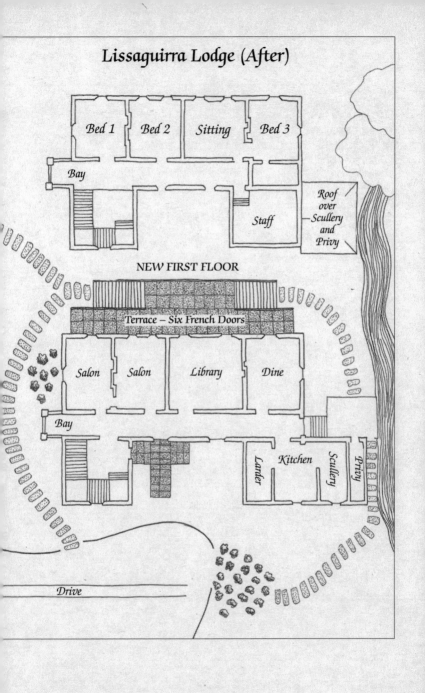

Lissaguirra Lodge (After)

Bed 1

Bed 2

Sitting

Bed 3

Bay

Staff

Roof over Scullery and Privy

NEW FIRST FLOOR

Terrace – Six French Doors

Salon

Salon

Library

Dine

Bay

Larder

Kitchen

Scullery

Privy

Drive